STACKING THE DECK

Anne Marie Becker

COPYRIGHT

DEDICATION

For my readers.

And for Kim and June—thanks for helping me chase down and round up those plot bunnies!

ACKNOWLEDGMENTS

A wealth of gratitude to my fabulous editors Deborah Nemeth and Emme Adams for their expertise in shaping this story.

To beta readers Andrea Edwards, Kim Law, and June Love, thank you for your encouraging comments and assistance with filling those pesky plot holes. Also, my appreciation to my local RWA chapter mates who loved the Redemption Club concept years ago. Their curiosity and support pushed me to keep working on this series, and this story, in particular.

Thank you to Brian Edwards for the torturous hours of mixing and serving cocktails so I could come up with the "Redemption" cocktail. And Daniel Warniment, I'm thankful for your assistance with translating Latin phrases.

As always, my love and gratitude to my husband Tim and our three children, for understanding why I need to get lost in my head sometimes. I'll always come back to you.

Other Books by Anne Marie Becker

MINDHUNTERS SERIES

CHAPTER ONE

One woman's rooftop sun deck was another woman's sniper roost. Skye Hamilton's index finger hovered near her rifle's trigger as she perched on the flat roof. Slightly higher in elevation to the neighboring estate, her location allowed a convenient overlook to the party going on fifty yards away.

Through the scope, cross hairs were tattooed across her target's chest, which was covered in a cobalt blue shirt and dark-gray suit jacket. Around him, the Malibu home's tiled poolside patio was like the red carpet on awards night, populated with Hollywood's rich and powerful. The trees glowed with fairy lights, and the tall cocktail tables set up for this event twinkled with tea lights in crystal-cut holders that winked in the darkness like stars. The stars that shined the brightest were actors and actresses, directors and producers—many of whom Skye recognized, though she didn't get to the movies much.

A hair had escaped the tight bun under her black skullcap and now tickled her cheek in the cool April breeze, but she resisted the urge to swipe it away. Making a quick mental note to buy more bobby pins, she forced the distraction from her mind and focused on her other senses. Her vocal cords tightened, her pulse kicking up past the normal adrenaline-induced high.

She shifted the cross hairs higher. Robert Stone had thrown his head back in laughter, exposing the tan column of his throat, at something said by one of the party guests surrounding him. Laugh lines bracketed his mouth and eyes, evidence of the fifty-seven years that had shaped his body, carving rivulets across his forehead and painting a few gray hairs among the ebony at the temples. With manicured fingers and soft hands, he tipped his champagne flute to his lips. As her research had indicated, he was the epitome of a wealthy and powerful individual, pampered and confident in his place in the world.

And someone wanted to do bad things to him. More specifically, someone wanted to pay *her* to do bad things to him. But Skye only used extreme force when it was justified, when the law had failed and there was clear evidence the bounty was worth the cost. Mark Sheldon hadn't come through with the burden of proof—yet. She was only staking this spot out for later, for when that proof came in and showed Stone was as ruthless as the rumors about him suggested.

The cool night breeze drifting over the surrounding mountains carried the heavy scent of jasmine and prompted the loose hair to resume its dance against her jaw. A light dusting of tangy salt from the nearby Pacific clung to her lips. Skye absorbed this sensory information but centered on the source that mattered most in this particular hunt—her sight. Unfortunately, she had yet to see Loretta Sheldon, the young woman she'd been sent to retrieve, or proof that Stone was involved in her disappearance.

Kill Stone. Bring Loretta home.

That's what Mark was paying her for.

Because, by all accounts, including the good-bye note Loretta had left behind, Robert Stone appeared to have lured the seventeen-year-old from the safety of her family and friends. And that was an unforgivable breach where Skye came from. One defended one's self, property and family, at any cost.

Skye's finger caressed the trigger, but she didn't apply pressure. *There's no evidence.* The reports of people she'd talked to said Stone was only nice on the surface, that he'd been known to use violence to settle scores. *Rumors. There's no proof.* She'd resume her investigation tomorrow, confident that persistence would lead to Loretta and evidence that this man had taken her.

Her attention shifted again, sliding down Stone's black silk tie and to the right, to the magenta square of silk sticking out of his breast pocket. Silver initials stood out against the colors, declaring his conceit. The colors echoed those in the logos of his film production company, hotel chain, cruise line and other businesses sheltered beneath the Stone Corporation umbrella. Despite the passing thought that his attire was more suited to a peacock than a mogul, the ornamentation seemed to emphasize, rather than contradict, Stone's masculinity. It was all about confidence, and how one wore it. Stone wore it like a second skin.

A diamond signet ring flashed as Stone's hand tipped the champagne flute to his lips. She tracked the movement as he placed an arm around a smiling blonde who wore a magenta evening dress that coordinated with his attire. The woman must be his latest arm candy. She damn sure wasn't Loretta.

Her research into Stone's past revealed two failed marriages and a string of heartbreaks. Either the man fell in love hard and often or enjoyed the chase, particularly when young, beautiful women were the prize. Skye was betting on the latter, especially since Loretta had been lured with some very enticing bait—an offer of a part in Stone's next movie.

Skye wondered if the blonde was aware of her sugar daddy's reputation. Likely not. If so, the woman wouldn't smile in that wide, vacant way. Or maybe she would. For the past ten days, the Hollywood lifestyle Skye'd been observing was so far from her world and everything she understood about the way one should live life, and what was normal, that it seemed she was in some kind of warped dream. Or nightmare.

The blonde's red lips parted on a laugh and Stone drew her in closer to his side. Protected and cherished.

Skye hadn't been held that way since she was a child. Actually, she'd never been held that way. Only in her dreams.

In an instant, her focus shattered as memories of the past and a sharp pang of longing intruded. She sucked in a shaky breath and set down the rifle. She might as well call it a night. Loretta wasn't here. She'd continue searching for the proof she needed and return another day—because she didn't know the word failure, and she sure as hell knew about patience.

She sat back on her haunches and began methodically packing her equipment into her duffel bag. Taking a quick inventory, her fingertips moved swiftly across her rifle, handgun, hunting knife—

The soft sound of a footfall, lost immediately in the breeze among the gentle rattle of leaves in the surrounding treetops, alerted her to someone else's presence. She palmed the throwing knife from her black boot, pushed to her feet and spun to face the threat. She shifted her weight to the balls of her feet. Adrenaline pumped hard and fast into her system, and the need to run rolled over her limbs—but she froze as she realized there was nowhere *to* run.

A tall, broad-shouldered man effectively blocked her main escape route. Dressed in a simple, but elegant, suit that somehow made him seem more dangerous, he stood between her and the spiral staircase that twisted down to the patio below. It was the only access to the sun deck. *Damn.*

She recognized him as one of the three bodyguards working Stone's party. Fifteen minutes earlier, he'd slipped out of her field of vision when one of the young, drunk starlets at the party had almost fallen into the pool and he'd escorted her into the house.

A slice of moonlight painted a streak of silver in his hair, but she guessed he was around thirty years old, just a few years older than her. But several inches taller—about six foot three, if he was an inch. And shoulders so broad he could pass as the great Atlas himself. His size was misleading. She'd watched him weave with predator-like stealth and grace among the throng of guests. She wouldn't underestimate him.

"I'm glad you chose not to shoot Mr. Stone." His gaze moved to the bag at her feet before shifting back to examine her face. She fought the urge to squirm as he seemed to memorize every feature.

He stopped several feet away, out of arm's reach but close enough for her to see his hair was a dark blond. The ends curled against his neck, and the breeze lifted the top briefly, like a caress. Everything about him was hard, including his eyes. His hands stayed loose at his sides, as if he might draw on her, though there was no telltale bulge of a concealed weapon. There were quieter ways to deal with her, anyway. Those hands—strong fingers with a couple of flecks of old scars, thin white lines glowing in the moonlight, decorating the surface. Like a bruised apple. One hard knock wasn't going to keep her from tasting it.

She rather liked a couple of scars on a man. They were evidence of a survivor, a hard worker, a warrior—and likely, this man knew his craft well. Unfortunately, his skills probably included killing. Ex-military? He didn't look like your average Army Joe, but she could see him as a Special Forces guy. His erect posture hinted at the hard edge of a soldier, and the casual way he took in every part of their surroundings without seeming to indicated his experience. That didn't bode well for her. Still, she'd trained with men like him, and he seemed more curious than dangerous at the moment. Besides, based on her reconnaissance, he was trespassing just as much as she was.

Her fingers tightened around the small knife tucked against her side, between her palm and her hip. "I wasn't going to shoot anyone." *Not yet.*

She calculated the distance to the edge of the roof and the jump it would require to land in the pool below. According to the very chatty gardener she'd encountered when she'd posed as a local out for a morning jog, the owners of this lush spread were in Europe for several months but had kept up the grounds and the pool. The deep end was just below her side of the roof.

"It's a twenty-foot drop." Her rooftop soldier's voice was cool as he guessed her thoughts.

Better than being six feet under. But climbing out of the pool, running while sopping wet, and making it back to the truck before this man could catch her, didn't boast encouraging odds. Worse, she'd have to leave her equipment behind. She'd done it before—in her training, the ranch's own version of a *mud run* during the Arizona summer's monsoons—but she'd rather choose an option with a better chance for success.

"I'm not going to hurt you." His arms went out to his sides in a gesture of trust and he grinned, all boy-next-door charisma. Oh yes, this soldier was dangerous. Good thing she was immune to the man's charm.

She stifled a snort. "That's good, considering I didn't do anything except observe a party. From private property, I might add." At her condescending tone, his eyebrows lifted.

"This isn't your property," he said. Hell, what if the groundskeeper had been wrong? What if this was the soldier's home? Maybe he wasn't security after all and the starlet was his girlfriend, and he'd escorted her into this very house, right beneath Skye's nose.

But that didn't ring true. *Trust your instincts.* Her uncle's voice rang in her head. Besides, she'd already begun the lie. Better to stick with it.

"It isn't yours either." She hoped her guess was correct. When he didn't deny it, she continued with the story she'd concocted. "I'm housesitting for a friend while he's in Europe. I just got here today."

"And you thought you'd hang out in the dark?"

"Just came up here for some fresh air." She took a deep breath as if to confirm her lie. His gaze flicked to her breasts as her lungs filled. *Interesting.* Apparently, he wasn't immune to her charms. She filed that information away as a possible weapon.

"I wanted to catch the view of moonlight on the ocean. I've never seen the ocean." That part, at least, was true. Earlier that week, she'd taken a couple of hours to just sit on the beach and listen to the waves, to watch their seductive power.

His gaze took a leisurely stroll down her body and his lips quirked ever-so-slightly. "Kind of strange attire if you're just looking for some fresh air. Or maybe, where you come from, they like to wear skintight black for late-night strolls."

Camouflage was more the order of the day at the ranch. "Huh. I didn't peg you for a fashion icon."

His laugh startled her. She bit back a curse, irked that he was taking pleasure in pinning her like a dead bug—and that he'd gotten the drop on her at all. What would Viper say about her listening skills? She'd let those precious moments of lost focus override her training. And she continued to let her concentration be derailed by the spark of amusement in the stranger's eyes.

So she went on the attack—verbally, at least. Pricking a man's pride could be a valuable weapon. "And maybe where you come from, it's typical to dress in suits and ties and dance for your boss like a puppet?" The brief lightness between them faded and she instantly regretted reminding him he was here on a mission.

"My *client* pays me well to do all kinds of things, including identifying threats." He eyed the duffel bag at her feet. "If you were just up here to observe the ocean, you over packed. I suggest you start talking—the truth this time."

Jared Bennigan wondered how far she would take this charade. Given his mystery woman's attire, and the rifle, and who knows what else peeking out from inside the bulging duffel, there was no excuse she could offer that would make sense—other than she'd come to do harm.

And yet, behind eyes the color of the deep blue Pacific, he could see the wheels turning, sensed her mentally cataloguing the escape routes and calculating the odds of success. And damn if he wasn't enjoying this unscheduled detour in his bland evening. He hadn't been this intrigued on the job—or by a woman— in months, so it couldn't hurt to draw things out a bit. After all, he had her trapped, though he wouldn't even have known she was lurking here if he hadn't had to escort an inebriated young woman from Stone's party to a taxi at the end of the long driveway. He'd seen an old pickup truck that clearly didn't belong among the guests' luxury cars, parked in the shadows just down the street. And he might not even have seen that if it hadn't been white and the moon hadn't chosen that moment to come out from behind a cloud.

Yeah, that lapse in focus jabbed at his pride. He was a man who made sure to do his job well, and ensured that the rest of his team did, too, and yet he'd failed to see the old, dirty truck or the attractive, potentially dangerous, woman lurking near Stone's property.

When Jared had tapped on the truck window, the man behind the wheel had jumped so high he'd nearly bumped his head. In jeans and an old T-shirt, the man hadn't been dressed for a party. Drawing on his experience as an ex-military police officer, Jared had demanded to see identification and the man had produced a driver's license that pronounced him Mark Sheldon, forty-three, from Kingman, Arizona. Realizing Jared wasn't actually a cop, Sheldon had refused to answer questions. Jared had insisted Sheldon leave the premises and alerted the other two guys on his team to be extra cautious. An additional security sweep of the area had led him here, and he wondered exactly what this woman and Mark Sheldon were hunting for so far from home.

A tingle of the old excitement had obliterated, at least for a few moments, the heaviness he carried around. He wanted the feeling to last, so, like a wolf playing with his rabbit, he toyed with her instead of taking her immediately to Stone. Besides, he had no doubt she'd fight tooth and nail when cornered. And if this woman had weapons training, as her equipment would suggest, he'd do well to remember that sometimes rabbits had distinct advantages over wolves.

Then again, she bore no resemblance to a quiet, timid rabbit. She had wide, expressive eyes of multiple shades of blue, and a mouth built for sin—at least of the lie-telling variety, though his imagination quickly came up with several other suggested uses. He couldn't make out her hair color beneath the cap she wore, but the strand that flicked about her face was a rich mahogany when it danced into the moonlight.

Her gaze again went to the roof's edge. Hell, was she thinking to make a running jump for it? She'd break her beautiful neck.

He lifted his hands, palms toward her in a sign of submission. "I'm not here to fight you. Unless you give me a reason." The image of their limbs tangling brought an altogether different type of scenario to mind—one in which she eventually willingly submitted to him in every way. Her gaze slid over his body with the same detailed consideration he'd given her earlier. Parts of him leapt to life, but he ignored them.

"Moon bathing, then?" she asked, lifting one sleek, dark eyebrow.

"Not tonight." A smile tugged at his mouth as his blood thrummed with the excitement of a potential chase. God, he'd missed this. At least the life of a military policeman on an army base had variety, especially while he'd been in Afghanistan. Since leaving the military a year ago, the formation of his company, Global Security Solutions, with his best friend Devlin Grimm, had provided regular doses of adrenaline. But his current contract—working security for Robert Stone these past three weeks—usually meant babysitting a bunch of rich, drunk people and evading the advances of pretty, entitled heiresses and actresses.

It was a necessary evil if he wanted to make headway on his true goal—finding his missing sister, Chelsea, whose last known whereabouts had been connected to Stone. The police were reluctant to believe she'd been taken against her will, since there'd been no signs of foul play, or maybe because Stone was a generous donor to police fundraisers. So Jared had taken the investigation into his own hands. He had the resources, after all.

"Odd place for a midnight stroll, sir." The woman winced as if regretting using the designation, and the delicate point of her chin went up a couple degrees. She had experience with men in authority, then. And she seemed to resent it, at least on some level. The fingers of her right hand clenched, probably around a weapon.

"It's not midnight yet. And I think we both know you're not some Cinderella gazing longingly at the ball." He jerked his head toward the party down the hill, keeping part of his attention on her hand.

She snorted. "Stone's no Prince Charming." She pressed her lips together, as if regretting the muttered words.

That was an understatement. Secretly, he despised the pompous ass, but circumstances required he tolerate the man. Unexpected anger and frustration struck him in the gut but he pressed it down. Working for Stone was temporary—until he could find the answers he sought. Answers he feared only Stone had. But what did this woman want with his client? "So, you *do* know Stone."

She didn't reply, not that he expected her to.

Jared cocked his head, studying his mystery woman. She didn't look like a blackmailer, killer, or kidnapper, or any of the other recent threats that had prompted Stone to hire security, but Jared wasn't about to underestimate her, especially with the distrust and anger shimmering in her eyes. Besides, money could lure even the least desperate of men—or women—to commit unusual acts, and Stone had some very wealthy enemies.

"That doesn't mean he deserves to be shot," he said. She bit her bottom lip, drawing his attention there for a split second. His gaze lifted to her eyes, where he caught a flash of triumph. Clever girl.

"I was only observing the party. The guy's a big-time movie producer and I wanted to catch a glimpse of the glamorous life." She shrugged. "Nothing illegal about that."

He eyed the bag again. Suddenly, he'd had enough of the lies. She stiffened as he took a couple of quick, long strides forward and grabbed the hand that he suspected held a weapon. He twisted her wrist until, with a soft gasp, she released the knife and it clattered to the sun deck. Her muscles bunched in preparation to fight and he sent her a warning glance. "Don't even think about it, or losing your knife will be the least of your worries." He loosened his grip on her slender wrist but didn't let go.

She didn't do anything to stop him as he reached into the duffel with his other hand. She probably sensed it would be a losing battle. Or maybe she was biding her time, waiting for him to expose a weakness she could take advantage of. *Not likely, sweetheart.* Inside the duffel, he spied another knife—this one larger—a rifle, a handgun and several boxes of ammunition.

He straightened. "Why didn't you take the shot?"

She shrugged as if it were no big deal, but didn't answer.

"This may be your lucky day. Mr. Stone is offering a reward to find whoever's trying to pay someone to harm him."

Surprise flickered across her face. "I don't know what you're talking about."

He ignored her denial. A contract had to be the reason she was here, armed to the teeth. "Maybe he'd pay you to tell him who hired you." And Jared could entice her to share with him what she knew about Stone. Maybe it would lead to his missing sister.

Her soft lips pressed into a defiant line. "He can't afford me. Some things are worth more than money."

He nearly laughed but choked it back as he caught the seriousness in her tone. All evidence implied she was a gun for hire, yet she appeared to have her own code of ethics. His mystery woman became more intriguing by the minute. "Either way, I'll be taking you with me to see Stone. You two can sort this out."

He was twisting her arm behind her back to force her to march in front of him toward the stairs, when a gunshot sounded, and shards of broken brick flew from the edge of the rooftop, only a few inches from his other hand. Reflexively, he dropped into a crouch, but in the same moment she twisted, breaking his hold and flattening her body against the deck.

The knife he'd knocked from her hand glinted in the moonlight, out of her reach. He planted a boot on her duffel bag, which lay at his feet, figuring this would keep her from attacking him from behind as he dealt with the more pressing threat—the unseen gunman.

Turning his gaze to the external problem somewhere out there in the dark trees, he remained behind the low ledge that rimmed the sun deck and reached for the mic at his collar. He switched it on, hoping he wasn't too far away from Stone's home to communicate with the rest of the security team. "Shots fired. I'm on the roof of the Montegena property north of Stone's." He switched off the communication. "Is the shooter one of yours?" he asked the woman. When he didn't receive a reply, he swiveled to face her, only to find her gone. Her duffel bag was still in a heap at his feet, deserted in her haste to escape. She'd apparently fled down the spiral staircase, quick and quiet as a... rabbit.

Remaining in a crouch, he skirted the perimeter of the rooftop, glancing out into the darkness but seeing no sign of movement, either from his mystery woman or the shooter. She'd disappeared into the night.

"Shit." He turned on the mic again. "In addition to an unidentified shooter, be on the lookout for a woman dressed all in black. Five-seven, blue eyes, dark brown hair. Armed and..." Dangerous? She might have been unarmed when she left the rooftop, but she could have another weapon stashed somewhere, and her accomplice sure as hell had one. "Approach with caution. Bring her to me." He couldn't wait to get his hands on her.

His grin of anticipation faded as a motor roared to life and the sound of rubber on asphalt squealed from the direction of the road. *Shit.*

He snatched up her duffel bag, noting that the rifle was still there, as well as a handgun, a couple of knives and a rope. He might be able to trace the registration on the rifle or gun—if they weren't stolen. Then he remembered the truck. Had Mark Sheldon been her accomplice? Had he come back for her? It was the most likely scenario.

He made the choice to risk another bullet by scurrying across the roof to the stairs, assuming the shooter—very possibly Mark Sheldon—had fled with his mystery woman. As he descended, two voices replied through his earpiece, indicating that his message had gotten through to the other men monitoring Stone's party. He repeated the truck's license plate information, make and model as he slung the duffel bag over his shoulder and took off running for the place where the vehicle had been parked.

Maybe he could catch his rabbit yet.

CHAPTER TWO

When Jared reached the road, there was no beat-up pickup truck in sight. His lovely rabbit was long gone. Still, he was vigilant in checking between every parked car and behind every bush as he made his way back. Meyer, one of the other two GSS bodyguards assigned to Stone, jogged up when Jared reached the edge of Stone's driveway.

"The hills are clear," Meyer said. "Duffy's inside watching the guests, but the natives are growing restless."

Jared's gaze swept the property, but his instinct, and his eyes, told him the threat was over—for now. At least he had the truck's info, Mark Sheldon's name, and the duffel bag full of weapons. He'd tap his resources at GSS and local authorities in Arizona and hope it led to his mystery woman. "Is the client safe?"

"Duffy personally escorted him inside after the first shot was fired. Stone grumbled a bit, but he complied."

"I think it's safe to let the guests outside again, but we'll need to question each of them individually." If the shooter wasn't Sheldon, he or she could have slipped in among the partygoers. Or maybe a guest had seen something out of the ordinary.

Inside the house, Jared eyed the crowd. No sign of his mystery woman, but there had to be at least a hundred guests. Stone's Malibu home wasn't as expansive as his Las Vegas estate, but it was luxuriously appointed. Food, alcohol, and music would keep most of the guests satisfied, but with this many bodies, they would get cranky and start leaving if Jared's team didn't act fast.

As Duffy joined him and Meyer, Jared gave orders. "Split the crowd into groups and start recording names and asking questions. I need to talk to Stone and then I'll join you." He made his way through the crowd in the living room to Stone's side.

Stone maintained his calm smile for anyone who was watching, but his words vibrated with fury. "What the hell is going on? Did you catch whoever scared my guests?"

"I think we'd better move this discussion somewhere more private," Jared suggested, then parted the crowd as they moved to Stone's private den.

As Stone entered behind him, the man's entire demeanor changed, switching from affable party host to no·nonsense businessman the instant the door closed behind him. Beyond the barrier, Meyer and Duffy called for everyone's attention and began dividing up the crowd.

"Was I the target?" Stone shot his question at Jared the moment they were alone. He could turn his charm on and off so quickly it made Jared's head spin, and validated the rumors that Stone was a self·involved narcissist who used charm only to get his way. Then again, Stone had to be in schmooze mode most of the time for business. Sometimes that business was building and developing his hotel chain and cruise line, sometimes it was making movies, and a lot of the time it was partying with the rich elite.

Had Jared's sister been at one of those parties before she disappeared? If so, where was she now?

Jared ruthlessly ignored the clenching of his gut and shoved thoughts of Chelsea aside. "You weren't the target."

"Explain."

"The shot was fired at the Montegena property, where I was questioning a trespasser." *Interrogating* seemed too strong a word when he'd been toying with her.

"A trespasser? What, like a vagrant?"

"No, sir. The woman on the rooftop was armed." The duffel he'd locked in his vehicle before entering Stone's house contained a portable arsenal. "She'd been watching the party, but she didn't fire the shot. Someone fired at us as a distraction."

"There were two?"

"I believe the other was a man who was hanging around the area earlier. His name is Mark Sheldon."

Stone's eyes narrowed. "Doesn't ring a bell. Who was the woman?"

"I don't know, but she had the most unique eyes I've ever seen. A vivid blue." Arrestingly beautiful, her irises were the sky at twilight, with deeper blues and hints of violet. He shook away the romantic image. "She was in her midtwenties. Sound familiar? Maybe an actress you turned down for a part?" *Or a woman you slept with and tossed aside like the others?*

Jared had observed Stone's relationship patterns over the past three weeks. He'd shower a woman with the finest luxuries money could buy—more as a testament to his wealth than to win her over—tire of her within a few days, and move on to the next in line. Chelsea was Stone's type—blonde, beautiful, curvy in the right places. And desperate for attention. Twin stabs of guilt and regret hit Jared in the solar plexus.

Stone seemed to consider the mystery woman's description for a long moment, but didn't answer Jared's question. "Do you think she's involved in the threats against me?"

He recalled the flash of surprise in her eyes when he'd mentioned accepting a contract on Stone. "I'm not sure."

"I want to talk to her immediately. Didn't you mention the reward?"

"I told her."

"Well, find her and convince her to talk." Stone

fisted his hands at his sides, visibly reining in his frustration. "I'll offer more."

"I don't believe that's necessary." Not everyone was motivated by greed. Jared got the impression this wasn't about money, which meant it was personal for her, just as it was for him.

"Do whatever *is* necessary. It's what I pay you for."

Jared bit his tongue as Stone walked out. He'd take a page from the man's playbook. Gaining the woman's compliance was a matter of figuring out what she wanted. But he had to find her first.

"You shouldn't have fired that shot." Skye's gaze continually shifted from the rearview mirror to the dark road ahead as she resisted the urge to press down hard on the accelerator. California Highway 1 led them away from the mountains of Malibu and toward their motel. Nobody was following, but the sense of someone breathing down her neck wouldn't subside. The soldier had gotten too close, and her nerves were still jangling from their encounter.

Beside her in the passenger seat, Mark rapped his fingertips against the truck's bench seat. "The guy tried to chase me off, but I couldn't leave you there. I had a feeling he'd go after you next." His dark hair ruffled in the breeze coming through the open window as, like her, his attention alternated anxiously between the side-view mirror and the traffic ahead of them. "I hated that I put you in danger. And then I saw you both on that rooftop, saw him grab your wrist."

"You weren't supposed to be anywhere near there for another hour. You were to pick me up at the rendezvous at our scheduled time." All of this could have been avoided if he'd just stuck to the plan. Damn, she should never have agreed to let him come to California with her. She worked so much better when she didn't have to worry about anyone else.

"I couldn't leave you to do this alone, not when

you're doing it for me."

"I'm used to working solo." Besides, he was paying her handsomely to find Loretta and make the man who lured her away pay.

"Except when it comes to proving guilt."

"Which you haven't accomplished yet," she reminded him.

"Stone took my daughter." Mark cursed the man's name. "But I probably should have handled this myself. Your uncle would skin me alive if he knew I'd encouraged you to go out of state, and then to risk your own neck." He shook his head vigorously. "No, I did the right thing by getting you out of there. And we're safe, so it worked."

"Except now Stone knows we were lurking around his property, he may have called the police and we're no closer to finding Loretta." Skye instantly regretted her harsh words, but she was certain the rooftop soldier had already reported to Stone what he'd seen that evening. They were probably reinforcing any weak spots at this very moment. She wouldn't be able to get that close to her target again. "I'm sorry. It's not your fault. I appreciate you coming to my rescue. And now we'll never have to see that guy again." Though it meant leaving behind her favorite rifle and a few other weapons, and that hurt. Mark went quiet—the guilty kind of silence—and she swung her gaze from the road to him. "What? What aren't you telling me?"

"He has my information."

"What? Who?"

"The guy... He asked me for my license."

Skye bit back an expletive. "And you just gave it to him?"

"I'm sorry. I haven't been thinking straight since... *Fuck.*" Mark shoved both hands through his hair and released a shaky breath. Seeing the guy on the verge of a breakdown blunted the sharp edges of her anger.

They'd been sure they'd find Loretta within a couple of days of arrival in Hollywood, following her credit card trail—or, rather, *Mark's* credit card trail, from the card Loretta had taken when she'd disappeared. The last transaction had been made in a convenience store in Hollywood nearly eleven days ago, just a few days after she'd left the ranch. There hadn't been another charge since.

They'd spent the past ten days scouring Hollywood for any sign of the seventeen-year-old, certain a young beauty like Loretta would have caught someone's attention. But Los Angeles was neck-deep in young blonde bombshells. All they'd found were dead ends. The convenience store clerks where Mark's card had been charged hadn't recognized Loretta's picture. Questioning talent scouts, agents, and everyone she could find connected to Stone Studios, had led nowhere. It was as if Loretta had never existed. Nobody had seen her. Stone's party had been Skye's last-ditch effort to spot the girl who'd apparently been swallowed up by the city.

"I know I'm not the only one who's frustrated," Mark said into the silence. "She was your friend, and given what I'd heard about you..." At her sharp glance, his words trailed off.

Nobody was supposed to say anything about the jobs she'd fulfilled unless she gave the go-ahead. Unfortunately, word was getting around her corner of Arizona about her talent as a vigilante. The police couldn't always be trusted to help people like her and Mark—people who lived off the grid and wanted to retain their anonymity. She'd been raised to handle herself, but she'd also been warned to fly under the radar. "You didn't mention this to Tom, did you?"

"Hell, no. The guy would have my hide, especially after sheltering Loretta and me at Three Fortunes. But we've been gone so long your uncle has to suspect something, right?"

"He thinks I do private investigator-type work." What she actually did was completely off the books due to the sometimes sketchy nature of the jobs. He didn't know the lengths to which she'd gone—lengths that had only involved illegal or violent acts a few times, in self-defense or to protect someone caught in the crossfire. She didn't accept dangerous missions without careful thought. Only the worst of the worst candidates passed her stringent checklist. The target had to have seriously harmed an innocent, had to have done so without compunction or regret, and had to have escaped punishment—which was why she hadn't pulled the trigger tonight. Stone might have encouraged Loretta to run away from home, but unless she'd been harmed, Skye wouldn't go after him.

Some called her a hit woman. Some had professed she was an angel of justice. Skye preferred to think of what she did as advocating for those who'd been denied justice. Speaking out for those who were voiceless, because she knew exactly what it was like to suffer at someone else's hands and have no recourse. She'd vowed never again to let evil run roughshod over her or anyone else.

Finn Tucker paced his best friend's room at the Stone estate. "You're the goddamn prince of the castle and you're telling me security won't tell you what happened tonight?"

"Pump your brakes, man," Ryan Stone said. "You're acting like someone shot at *you*." As the privileged, only son of Robert Stone, Ryan lounged lazily like royalty on his bed, his arm around his date, who was snuggled up to his side, passed out and half naked. Ryan exuded entitlement, which stirred Finn's anger, bringing it roaring to the surface. It didn't matter that Finn was more handsome, an up-and-coming actor and soon-to-be-acclaimed director, a prime physical specimen at age thirty, or that they'd been best friends since boarding school. Ryan still got everything and left Finn with jack shit.

Seeing the direction of his gaze, Ryan slid his

palm from the woman's bare shoulder down to her silk-clad hip and squeezed. She let out a soft sigh but didn't awaken. "You're just cranky because that bodyguard muscled Erica out of here. I'm going to get some tonight and you're not." That Ryan was right only made things worse.

"Looks like you started early." The woman's dress was pushed to her waist, her plump, artificial double D's pressed to the side of Ryan's bare chest. Ryan liked his women perfected and enhanced by a plastic surgeon's knife, probably because he'd grown up among people who valued physical beauty and extravagance at any cost. So had Finn, but he liked all types of females. He viewed them more as works of art than something to warm his bed. He prided himself on seeing the humanity, for better or worse, in every living creature.

It was the humanity that made things interesting.

"Had time for a little fun," Ryan said with a grin. "The party was boring, anyway."

"But you didn't fire a gun, just to make things interesting?" It was the kind of thing Ryan would do, especially since disrupting the event would rile up his father, who valued his public image.

"Not this time. I thought it could have been you."

"No, not me, though you're right. Tonight could have used some livening up." Especially after his date had gotten fall-down drunk. Finn gestured to the sleeping woman. "At least I'm not the only one ending the night with a limp dick. Doesn't look like your date is good for much more."

"She will be. I've heard rumors she's into some kinky stuff. Forget shades of gray, she's into every color, if you know what I mean." With his free hand, he saluted Finn with a tumbler of scotch before taking a deep swallow. His eyes glittered with power as they met Finn's over the rim of the glass. "I could pass her on to you when I'm done."

Finn's anger at the insult simmered. No way did he want somebody's seconds, let alone Ryan's. He'd had enough secondhand shit from Ryan during high school, throughout four years of college, and for the years since graduation.

It was Finn's turn, damn it. He deserved a taste of glory. And once he had it, he wouldn't waste it like Ryan did. He'd give the trappings of his success the respect they deserved.

Everything was a fucking game to the son of one of the most powerful men in Los Angeles, Las Vegas, and New York. Hell, Robert Stone probably reigned over the entire goddamn world—at least in the entertainment sector. His films had won every award out there. His hotels, casinos, and themed cruises were world-renowned for their luxury and extravagance, and his son reaped all the benefits without a moment of hard work or stress.

Life wasn't fucking fair.

Still, Finn would rather be part of it all than an outsider looking in, so he'd bide his time. Patience was key, as was hard work. Soon, he would have his own day—no, a fucking *lifetime*—in the sun.

Ignoring Ryan's smirk, Finn shook his head. "I'm covered, thanks. Got enough wannabe actresses in my stable." There was always room for more, but not one of Ryan's. He'd pick and choose his own girls.

Ryan's eyes lit with interest. "The project is going well, then?"

"It is. We'll be ready for a new hunt in a few days. Just one more girl should do it."

"Not just anyone," Ryan reminded him.

Irritation shot through Finn like a jolt of electricity, but he hid it behind a casual grin. "Of course not. I have discriminating tastes." His gaze flicked over the woman at Ryan's side in a silent dig at Ryan's lack of selectiveness.

"Good, because that's what'll bring the big bucks. As long as you're more careful than the last girl."

"Nobody will miss her."

"Someone's already been asking questions about

Loretta at the studio."

Finn hid his surprise. "Only because she stole that damn credit card. I thought using it in Hollywood would throw her dad off the scent—if he came looking for her at all." Loretta had made it seem like nobody would miss her. "She won't use it again. They'll never find her."

Ryan grunted as if withholding judgment. "Who's the new girl you're after?"

"You don't need to know." Another ripple of irritation had Finn turning toward the door. Erica was to have been his next recruit, before Stone's bodyguard ruined it. If only she'd held her liquor and stopped bugging Stone about the movie part Finn had hinted at. Instead, she'd been a nuisance and gotten herself thrown out. Maybe he could still salvage the evening, though. "I'll leave you to your private party. Have fun."

Ryan snorted. "Don't I always? *Intrepidus vive ferociter ludeque.*"

Finn returned the Latin salutation. They'd come up with it when they'd had to study the dead language in boarding school. The *live fearlessly, play ferociously* mentality had become their credo.

In the living room he skirted the crowd, his thoughts on finding Erica. As he reached the front door, he was stopped by one of Stone's bodyguards, who was acting as gatekeeper of the party. The guy, who identified himself as Meyer, wouldn't let him leave until he had Finn's name, rank, and serial number—or at least his name and how he was connected to Stone.

"You guys any closer to catching the shooter?" Finn feigned a concern he didn't feel. After all, he made his own fate by living fearlessly. Some loser who couldn't handle a gun didn't worry him—unless he happened to be connected to Loretta.

"We'll be working on it, don't worry," Meyer said, apparently swallowing Finn's act.

He gestured to the thinning crowd. "Hard to believe one of my friends or colleagues would just open fire."

"I'm sure you have nothing to worry about. We think the shooter is from Arizona." With that, the guard turned to the person waiting in line behind Finn.

Arizona? It had to be a coincidence—because admitting Ryan was right, that Finn shouldn't have hunted so close to home base, was unacceptable.

Finn clamped down on a sudden wave of anxiety as he strode out the front door, got into his car, and pulled out his phone to scroll through the contacts. Under a folder marked *Redemption Club,* he found what he needed.

When the person on the other end mumbled a sleepy greeting, Finn laid out his plan. "Use the credit card I sent you. Tonight. It has to be clear that Loretta Sheldon is far from Malibu."

CHAPTER THREE

Early the next morning, Jared turned in a slow circle, taking in the entirety of the dingy motel room with its double beds that sagged in the middle. In honor of its proximity to the ocean—and apparently as an homage to the 1980s, when the place had last been updated—the décor was a blend of whitewashed furnishings, gold accents, and pastel bedding. But there was no sign of the woman he'd hoped to find here, or the man to whom the room had been rented.

Jared had greased palms along Highway 1 until he'd hit upon this motel. The manager of the rent-by-the-hour, no-tell motel confirmed that Mark Sheldon and an attractive woman with vivid blue eyes had checked into Room 112 a few days ago, but the woman hadn't given a name. Jared could only hope his connections with the Arizona DMV and the ATF would lead to a name as he traced the registrations on the truck and rifle.

In the meantime, he carefully searched the motel room for clues. In the end, he only came away impressed with his mystery woman's attention to detail. She'd wiped all prints, disposed of the contents of the trash can elsewhere, and hadn't left a hair in the drain or lost a receipt behind the dresser. No trace. If he hadn't seen her big blue eyes for himself, he might think she'd never existed. Someone had trained her well in the art of disappearing—or not existing at all. But he had the duffel bag as confirmation his encounter with her had been real.

Jared phoned his team to check on protection for Stone, wondering if she'd return to do harm or retrieve her weapons.

"We're at Stone Studios," Meyer said. "He's been in meetings all morning, but otherwise all is quiet. Duffy's screening people in the lobby before they even get upstairs."

"I'm heading your way now. Don't let him leave." Jared wanted to talk to the studio's employees before reporting to Stone and questioning the man further. Upon reflection, Jared thought maybe Stone was holding something back regarding the blackmail demands he'd received. On the drive, his connection at the DMV called.

"It's a ranch work truck, registered to Three Fortunes Ranch," the guy said through the speaker.

Jared kept his eyes on the road as he scribbled down the northern Arizona address. "Stolen?"

"Hasn't been reported as such."

"Thanks, man. I owe you one."

He parked at Stone Studios before bringing up the maps app on his phone and locating the property ten minutes north of Interstate 40, near the town of Williams and about an hour from the Grand Canyon. But was that where his mystery woman had fled? She seemed the tenacious sort, so she might still be in the Los Angeles area, plotting to go after Stone.

As Jared progressed through the building toward Stone's office, he talked to employees along the way. The receptionist at the sleek, curved cobalt-and-magenta front counter smiled and greeted him. And confirmed that a woman with memorable blue eyes had been in about a week ago, flashing a picture of a pretty blonde teen and asking if anyone had seen her. It had taken the receptionist a moment to recall the details, but she thought the girl she'd been looking for was named Lorraine. Or Linda. Something with an L.

It had been the same story as he progressed down the hall, popping into the various departments to ask questions.

Apparently, though, his mystery woman hadn't been allowed near the back offices, near Stone. Or she'd been ordered off the property for making herself an annoyance. Which was likely why she'd resorted to roosting on the rooftop, observing Stone from afar. Through a rifle scope.

While waiting in the lobby for Stone to emerge from a meeting, Jared researched Sheldon on a computer, as Duffy continued to search a seemingly endless stream of actresses who were arriving for a casting call. Duffy looked to be enjoying the task.

Jared focused on his cell phone screen as he brought up a news article about a Mark Sheldon in Phoenix who, along with his teenage daughter, had survived a violent home invasion three years ago. His wife, tragically, had not. After the trial ended with a shockingly light sentence for the two men who'd perpetrated the crimes, Mark had declared he'd had enough of city life. He fit the description of the man Jared had encountered. Did that mean Mark had relocated to Three Fortunes?

A text popped up from his contact at the ATF. His heart beat with excitement as the next piece of the puzzle fell into place. The rifle had led to a name.

Skye Hamilton.

But no picture to confirm. Still, he felt he was on the right track. And part of his adrenaline came from Skye's apparent agenda. Had it been Mark's daughter Skye was looking for? If she was looking for a missing young woman, and he was looking for a missing young woman...

"He'll see you now." Stone's secretary interrupted his thoughts.

He headed into Stone's office, wondering if the man was somehow luring young women away—and what he was doing with them afterward. While searching for Chelsea, he'd had little to go on. Just that the last job before her disappearance had been working a private party at Legacy, Stone's Las Vegas hotel and casino. But two missing women? Perhaps Skye Hamilton was privy to more information. But it also chilled his soul that Chelsea might not just be missing, that she might have met with foul play.

With a nod to Meyer, who stood posted outside Stone's office, Jared entered and shut the door.

Stone was just getting off the phone. "Did you find her?"

"No, but I have a name. Skye Hamilton. I believe she's connected to a ranch in Arizona named Three Fortunes." He expected to learn she was an actress who'd been looking for a part, or that she'd contacted him, asking about a missing woman, but the shock on Stone's face indicated something more. "Does that sound familiar?"

Stone cleared his throat. "These are names I haven't heard in years."

"How about Chelsea Wright? Have you heard that name?" His sister had opted to use her father's name once she'd turned eighteen, though they could count on one hand the number of times she'd seen or heard from the guy. But that was more contact than Jared's father had initiated.

Stone thought for a moment. "No. Should I have?"

Jared took a deep breath, uncertain whether Stone was lying. But he'd been honest about Skye... "How do you know Skye?"

"I don't. Not really. Her uncle and I were... friends."

"From what I've learned, she was looking for a missing teenager."

Stone's stunned gaze met Jared's. "This isn't about me?"

The man had a healthy ego. Jared tamped down his anger. "Would she have a reason to blackmail you, or try to harm you?"

Stone stood abruptly and walked to the door. "I'll handle this. You can see yourself out." He held the door open.

Surprised by the sudden turn in conversation, Jared rose. "I can help. If she's a threat—"

"I'll handle it," he said again. "This is more delicate than I originally thought. You're dismissed."

Skye was exhausted, having packed up and cleaned the motel room quickly last night before seeking another cheap place, well away from Malibu, where they could hide the truck around back and crash for what was left of the night. She'd slept restlessly, dreaming of caramel eyes that found her wherever she hid.

They'd woken to the sound of an alert on Mark's phone. His credit card had been used—in Las Vegas. Only a few hours' drive away.

Relief at having a reason to put some distance between her and Malibu—and the man from the rooftop—quickly turned to annoyance that she was turning tail and running. During the drive to Vegas, she soothed her pride by reminding herself there'd been no sign of Loretta in California, despite nearly two weeks of looking for her.

Still, if Loretta were seeking a job as an actress, what was she doing in Vegas? Perhaps she'd decided to become a show girl. It could make sense, especially when one considered that Legacy Lounge, the bar attached to Legacy Hotel and Casino where the credit card had been used, was owned by Robert Stone.

"I told you Stone was behind this," Mark grumbled.

"You know my policy."

"We'll get your evidence and you'll make this right—or I will." The bloodlust in Mark's tone had grown over the past couple days. He'd run out of patience. But if Loretta was free to spend money and be seen about town, Stone wasn't holding her against her will. "We should have kidnapped the guy and demanded he take us to Loretta."

"That's not how I work."

Mark glared at her. "I was told you knew how to get justice. Maybe they were wrong." It had to be the exhaustion and fear in his eyes that made him so damn ornery today, so she choked down her anger for the rest of the drive.

Around noon, they entered Legacy through sleek sliding glass doors into what appeared to be the hub of activity. Skye tilted her head back to gape up at the ornate ceiling fifty feet above them. It was early afternoon and the dome—a clear glass center with silvery constellations etched on it and concentric stained glass panels in dark blue, magenta and purple—sparkled like jewels. The kaleidoscope effect scattered rainbows of light and shadows of constellations across the white marble-tiled rotunda. Stone pillars were placed at regular intervals around the circumference of the rotunda, like numbers on a clock face.

Straight ahead, beyond a fountain, was a check-in desk and, like spokes on a wheel, hallways that led into the hotel portion of the complex. To her right was a cavernous casino where row after row of gamblers sat on stools, feeding bills into slot machines. Beyond, tables of card games and roulette offered alternate entertainment. To her left was a restaurant with a separate lounge area. Posters indicated the bar offered live entertainment nightly. Everything from live bands to comedians to exotic dancers was featured over the next week.

"You look in the casino," she ordered Mark. "I'll take the lounge." She needed a few minutes apart from him, anyway. The silence after his suggestion that they should have kidnapped Stone had grown heavier and darker as they'd neared Vegas.

Without a word, Mark moved toward the casino, and she crossed the marble floor and entered Legacy Lounge. A smiling hostess perched behind a podium offered to find her a table for the lunch buffet through the archway behind her. Though delicious aromas wafted from the award-winning restaurant and made her mouth water, Skye declined. She was more likely to find the information she sought in Legacy Lounge, where Loretta had used the card.

The restaurant and lounge were furnished in the same dark wood and richly appointed with combinations of dark blue upholstery and pristine white linen tablecloths. Rings of ivy surrounded the tea light candles at each table. She skirted the clusters of chairs and tables, heading to the long bar that extended the length of the back wall. From there, she could see the entire room, the stage where the band was doing a sound check for the evening show, and even some of the rotunda.

A couple dozen people were seated at the bar and tables, enjoying lunchtime appetizer and drink specials or viewing various sports events—baseball, horse racing, drag racing, golf—on the multiple televisions high on the wall above the racks of alcohol. Small platinum tiles surrounded a long mirror and formed a backdrop. The Legacy name was scrawled in cobalt on a white marble rectangle below the mirror. The entire place bespoke elegance.

And a megalomaniac, protected by several intense bodyguards, owned it all. Her rooftop soldier was likely back among those sentinels, unless her avoidance behaviors yesterday had cost him his job. A small smile tugged at her lips at the thought. It would serve him right for making her leave her duffel behind. She still had a handgun and a hunting knife that she'd left in the truck, but her stores were sorely depleted until she returned to the ranch.

Skye waited for the bartender to finish serving a group of women who appeared to comprise a bridal shower. The woman at the center of it all wore a white veil and, in anticipation of the three shots lined up in front of her, her eyes widened.

"What can I get you?" The bartender asked, reaching Skye's end of the bar. Her short, choppy blonde hair, cheekbones that could cut glass, and a tank top that showed off defined biceps and a couple of tasteful tattoos, created a tough-girl exterior. Her name tag read Emily.

Emily plucked a cocktail menu from behind the bar, the Celtic band tattooed around one wrist flexing with the movement as she laid the laminated list in front of Skye. "The house special is called a Redemption."

"Just a beer, in the bottle—unopened, please."

Emily arched a sleek brow but didn't comment. She brought a bottle and set the beer on a coaster that displayed Legacy's logo, a white Greek marble pillar with a celestial background. She laid a bottle opener next to it on the bar. "Anything else? The live music will be starting in a bit. You might want to place an order before it gets busy."

Skye contemplated how to proceed. What would garner her the most information? Direct questions that seemed to attack Emily's employer could result in a total shutout, if Stone inspired loyalty. But his employees might be disenchanted with him if he was the egotistical, overbearing type. From Skye's brief observation of the man, he had the ability to charm some people, alienate others. Which type was Emily?

"Thanks," Skye said. "I was just thinking what a beautiful place this is, and the employees have been so friendly." Her social skills might be a little rusty from living with a bunch of guys at the ranch, but she knew enough to flatter people if she wanted something from them.

Emily's lips curved. "We work for a great boss."

"The famous film producer Robert Stone owns this place, right?"

Emily's smile faltered. "No, actually. I mean, yes, he owns this place, and a dozen others, but his daughter manages this location. Her name is Ivy."

Skye glanced around. "She seems to do a fabulous job. I'd like to compliment her in person." *And ask if I can view the video surveillance from last night.* She let her enthusiasm trail off as she opened her beer, hoping Emily would fill in the blanks.

"It'll have to wait a couple days, I'm afraid. She's hosting a party for her father Tuesday night. Last-minute thing, so she's swamped."

A thrill of anticipation ran through Skye. She hadn't realized until that moment how much she wanted to see Stone again—this time, up close and in person instead of through her scope. "Mr. Stone's in town?" When Emily's eyes narrowed at the question, Skye shrugged. "If I owned a chain of hotels, I don't think I'd stay in one place for long."

Emily seemed to accept this and relaxed. "He travels a lot, but he has a house nearby. One of those big-ass, flashy estates out in Henderson." Her eyes widened like a doe in the headlights. "Shit, forget I said that."

Skye grinned. "No worries. I'm not from around here, anyway." And she wouldn't be here for long, just long enough to figure out where Loretta was. Did Stone have her stashed away at his Henderson house? "I'd bet a powerful man like Stone flies in guests from all over the world for his parties."

"That, he does. Even the last-minute ones. Must be nice not to have to worry about cancelling plans at the last minute." Emily hefted a bottle of top shelf tequila as a man at the other end of the bar lifted his glass to signal he wanted a refill. Before she obliged him, Emily turned back to Skye and dropped her voice. "Ignore me. I'm a little ticked I have to work the party. I had plans, you know. Instead, I get to play bartender to the rich and famous at the mansion. Lucky me."

Working parties for Stone probably gave Emily a unique insight into the man's life. "Before you go, would you take a look at something?" Skye reached into her purse and withdrew her phone, scrolling to the picture of Loretta she'd been showing around Hollywood and Malibu. "Do you recognize this young woman? Her name is Loretta Sheldon, and I think she was here last night. I've been trying to locate her for nearly two weeks."

"No, I'm sorry." Emily's gaze softened. "I hope you find your friend, but not everyone who comes to Vegas wants to be found."

CHAPTER FOUR

Just before dawn, Skye had fallen into her own bed, safe within the boundaries of Three Fortunes Ranch in northern Arizona, hundreds of miles away from Malibu or Vegas.

Some people might call the large spread a cattle ranch, which is how it appeared on paper. Others might call it a compound for nutcases and extremists who hated the government, which is what most of the residents of the closest towns of Kingman, Seligman, Ash Fork, Williams and Flagstaff thought. Or a training ground for anti-government guys who wanted to be ready for anything, which is what the guys who lived here—guys like Mark—thought.

Skye called it home. And when she woke later that morning, she felt rejuvenated just being among familiar surroundings. Until she remembered the frustration of the day before. And the nightmares, reminders of past and current failures, that had woken her during the night.

Yesterday, Skye had felt like she'd walked the entire Vegas Strip, the highest congestion of traffic and casinos in town. The enormous complexes appeared deceptively close in proximity, but stretched on over four miles. It was more like ten times that if one counted weaving through the labyrinth of gaming areas within the casinos. She and Mark had followed a trail of credit card purchases that, beginning just after Skye's chat with Emily, had set Mark's phone off like a slot machine hitting a jackpot. Unfortunately for them, there'd been no payout. Nobody at the string of restaurants, casinos, and stores recognized the picture of Loretta, despite evidence the girl had gone on a serious spending spree. Of course, they were always a few hours behind the credit card transactions, since they weren't reported real time.

By midnight, shortly after Mark asked the credit card company to have the next vendor call them before authorizing a purchase, they received a call that she'd attempted to use the credit card at a gas station in Kingman, Arizona, only an hour west of their ranch. Maybe Loretta had grown tired of the glamorous life and was going home. But by the time they arrived at the Kingman truck stop and convenience store, the attendant said he didn't recognize Loretta's picture. And there was no Loretta.

It was as if Loretta had become invisible. And how the hell was the girl using Mark's credit card so often without difficulty? Perhaps nobody paid attention to the name. Or maybe she'd tried other places, and it hadn't worked. Or maybe Loretta had a man with her. She kept this last theory from Mark, sensing he was only hanging on to his sanity by a frazzled thread.

They'd agreed to regroup at the ranch, hoping to find Loretta home, sleeping in her own bed. The last hour of the drive had been quiet, and Mark had said little about their failed attempt to find further information about his daughter or what he wanted to do next to find her. She'd sensed the quiet hope, however, that he'd find Loretta in her bed in the tiny cabin they inhabited on the ranch.

But arriving home hadn't made things any better. There were too many memories of Loretta here—and no actual Loretta.

They decided that, after some rest, they'd return to Vegas and follow the credit card trail again. Perhaps a different staff member would recognize Loretta's photo. A blonde bombshell, she wasn't exactly forgettable, nor did she want to be. The complete opposite of Skye. And what the hell had Mark thought, bringing a girl like Loretta to the ranch?

Beyond Skye's bedroom window, there were several outbuildings to the left, including a greenhouse and an irrigated, fenced-in field where they grew as much of their food as they could. Past that lay a couple of overgrown pastures that had once housed cattle and horses, but the ranching aspect of Three Fortunes had dwindled years ago. Now, most of their income came from training and cultivating soldiers, not animals. The entire compound, an island within the bigger ranch property, was enclosed by an electrified security fence.

Other buildings included a large barn and the bunkhouse where most of the survivalists and trainees slept. There were a couple of small, private cabins, reserved for the rare occasions when a family or a female was in residence. Not many women opted to tough it out here. The men usually treated Skye with respect, almost as though she were an honorary daughter. It helped, of course, that her uncle, Tom Hamilton, owned the property.

Loretta had been one of the few females on the ranch in recent months, but she hadn't enjoyed the lifestyle. At seventeen, she'd become like a little sister to Skye, who had no family other than Uncle Tom. But taking Loretta under her wing hadn't been enough to help the younger woman accept life here as her new normal. Loretta had big dreams, which included stardom—the complete opposite of the low-profile life the ranch's inhabitants craved.

Skye hoped Loretta was okay, and was pursuing her dream, but her gut told her something was wrong. She'd give herself a day to regroup, and then return to the Kingman truck stop and the various stops in Vegas where the card was used. She'd ask again about observing surveillance footage. They'd probably decline, or say she had to go through the police, whom Mark wanted to avoid for private reasons, but she could hint that an *underage* girl might have been using the *stolen* card.

She trudged downstairs and into the kitchen of the two-story house she shared with her uncle. She sank into one of the two ladder-back chairs as Tom navigated the stove like someone who'd been cooking for an army all his life, which, as far as she knew, he had.

"The creature emerges from its cave." Tom grinned over his shoulder at her. "I thought the smell of bacon frying might do the trick." With a paper towel, he blotted the grease from a couple strips of heavenly meat and put them on a plate, then moved to the other skillet to scoop some scrambled eggs. In his midfifties, his burly build came from hard work on the ranch and training with the men.

Skye's head pounded, but not from a hangover. Her mind was still spinning from her hasty retreat on the rooftop, clearing out the motel room, and then trudging all over Vegas in the heat yesterday.

She traced a divot on the wooden tabletop. The surface was scarred from use, but she knew how it had come by every cut and watermark. It was home. It was familiar. It was where she belonged—not in California. Not staking out a wealthy man who may or may not have anything to do with the missing Loretta. Not fleeing from the man's minion, into the night, like a coward. That part still grated on her, especially having to leave behind her weapons. She'd paid good money for that rifle.

"It's after ten o'clock, girl." Tom laid a heaping plate of food in front of her. His forehead creased as he studied her face. "Saw the truck out front, but I figured you came in pretty late. Didn't expect you to be away so long. Where'd you go?"

"Business trip." Reluctant to talk about her trip to California, she ducked her head toward her plate and dug in.

Grunting, he turned back to the stove to dish himself up a plate before taking a seat at the table.

"Didn't see your duffel in the hall closet."

"It's in the truck," she lied. "Like you said, I got home pretty late."

Blue eyes, much grayer than hers, narrowed. "You look exhausted. Or defeated."

"The job was a little trickier than I'd been led to believe." And the soldier could be tracing her gun or the truck registration right now. At least Mark's driver's license hadn't listed a current address.

"Yeah, I figured. You've been gone longer than any of your other jobs." Ten days was about twice as long as any of her previous trips, but those had rarely taken her across the state line.

She got up to grab some hot sauce from the cupboard. On her return, as she passed by him, she caught a whiff of the cigarettes he indulged in on occasion—usually when he was feeling stressed and needed to relax. He didn't like it when she left the ranch, but she'd been taking these secret jobs for a couple of years now, and he had little say in it.

Before she could scoot back to her chair, he surprised her by grabbing her hand. "I'm glad you're back, and that you're choosy about your missions. Smart girl." When he released her a second later, his face was red with embarrassment at the unusually affectionate display. Skye's own nerves were a little jittery with emotion. Maybe she needed more sleep. Or a good workout.

Sitting again and shoveling food into her mouth as if she hadn't eaten in ages—mostly because she hadn't—she assessed the events of the past ten days and her uncle's praise. Had she been smart? The mission had been... not a success. But not a failure, either. She had options. She had the credit card trail to go back over. Maybe she'd get a look at video footage this next time. She could confront Stone. She could even trade information, if Stone was amenable. Apparently she wasn't the only person interested in getting to him. She gathered from her soldier's questions that someone had taken out a contract on the man, and she could help him find out who, in exchange for Loretta's whereabouts. Hell, maybe she'd get to see her soldier again.

Get to?

She'd explore her choices after a day at home. Some normalcy would help her reset and regain her objectivity. Looking forward to seeing her soldier was a mistake. He'd backed her into a corner on that roof and made her heart beat double-time. Maybe what was bothering her was that she suspected the elevated rate had not been simply from adrenaline. She'd felt an attraction, a connection.

"Skye? Was it dangerous?" Tom had frozen with a forkful of scrambled eggs hovering near his mouth as her silence stretched on. "Did someone hurt you?"

"Just lost in my thoughts. I haven't had time to process what I learned." Or rebuild her defenses, apparently. As if all the time she'd spent driving, and hiking through casinos, wasn't enough.

"What was it this time—lost dog or lost husband?" His chuckle boomed through the first floor of the old house that had been piecemealed back together like a patchwork blanket as things peeled away, broke off, or began to leak. Tom tried to live off the grid, off the government radar, vowing they had everything they needed to survive right here. But not everyone who came here found what they needed. Loretta certainly hadn't.

Lost girl.

But Mark had insisted Skye not tell anyone, especially the cops. He was embarrassed enough about his daughter's behavior and had his reasons for avoiding the police. The man had come to the ranch with his only child, seeking a way to protect them both. From what, nobody asked. Here, they never asked. But people came for all kinds of reasons, like fearing that a government conspiracy would take over their lives if they weren't armed. Or a personal desire to be stronger, better. They'd even had a potential reality TV contestant who wanted to learn how to survive the wilderness.

But Mark and Loretta Sheldon... something had happened to them. Skye had recognized the soul-shattered look in their eyes when they'd first arrived at the ranch. It was no wonder Loretta had dreamed of something grander and gone for it. Dreaming healed her.

The note Loretta had left for her father was emblazoned on Skye's brain. *I've met someone. Stone's going to make me a star, and I have to follow my dream. I'll be in touch soon. Intrepidus vive ferociter ludeque.*

When the hell had Loretta learned Latin? Mark had confirmed he'd never heard her use the phrase, and was unfamiliar with it. And where had she met someone? She barely left the ranch, and had been taking online courses rather than enrolling in high school, since Mark had led a nomadic life for the couple of years before landing at the ranch. Maybe Loretta had connected with someone online. That kind of thing happened all the time. With her ambition and yearning for excitement, Loretta would have been easy prey. But Mark had kept her isolated, not even allowing her a cell phone. Still, Loretta had accompanied Skye to the library in Flagstaff a couple times.

Skye stood to go to the refrigerator, deciding she deserved something decadent. She spied the ice cream. Could she have that after breakfast? *What the hell?* Her entire body was off schedule, anyway. Snagging it, and a spoon from the drawer nearby, she settled in with the carton. Moose Tracks. The caramel ripples made her think of her soldier's eyes. She obviously needed more sleep. She stabbed at the frozen treat with her spoon.

"It doesn't matter, anyway," she said. "I don't think I'll be taking the job. This was more of a research trip, but the risk probably isn't worth the payoff."

There had to be a safer way to track down Loretta than going through Stone and the soldier. The memory of his intense gaze had her body humming. Disgusted with herself, she put the lid on the ice cream and its delectable caramel ribbons and walked it back to the freezer before returning to the table.

Tom's smile disappeared, his features turning serious. "I'm glad you're being careful. Every time you leave, I worry it might stir things up—" He broke off as he always did whenever the past, or anything connected with it, threatened to arise.

"Maybe if you told me more, I could find a way around whatever the problem is."

"No." As usual, he shut that suggestion down fast. "I need you to be careful not to draw attention to yourself. Promise me, Skye."

"I promise I'm always careful." But she hadn't even heard the soldier climb to the rooftop. Then again, if he was ex-military, it would soothe her ruffled pride. Only someone skilled should be able to get the drop on her.

Actually, he'd reminded her of a younger version of Viper, the camp's martial arts sensei and head of training programs. Viper was bald and fiftysomething, but he was tough. Decades ago, his work as an Army Ranger had turned him off to being a pawn in government agendas. As soon as he'd left the Army, he'd headed for wide-open spaces and helped Tom set up this ranch, turning it into a more organized compound. Now, Viper trained others who wanted to be prepared for the day they might have to defend their own turfs, or their families, from whatever threat should arrive.

But Viper was on her side. The soldier was on Stone's.

Uncle Tom had warned her again and again over the years that she had to lay low, that being noticed by the wrong people could have horrible consequences. Why this was an issue, and who those *wrong people* were, she had no idea, but she'd do anything to please her only family. She figured Tom was a little farther to the "conspiracy theorist" end of the spectrum. Why else would he start a ranch like this?

One day, maybe she'd ask for an explanation. For now, the flash of pain in his eyes if she dared broach the subject of the past was enough to keep her questions to herself. She had a good life. So what if she was, essentially, a nonperson? A ghost.

A ghost who took the risks other people didn't want to take.

Appeased for the moment, Tom pushed away from the table and went to set the skillets in the sink and run hot water over them.

"I'll do the dishes." She rose and took the towel that hung at his shoulder. "You cooked."

Besides, she owed Tom for much more than breakfast. He'd given her a home, a safe and stable life. Tom, Viper and the others had kept the big bad world away and their attention and their love—expressed through their intense training, preparing her to face some unseen enemy— was all she'd needed. *Wasn't it?*

She scrubbed at a pan harder than was required. Maybe she'd go back to Hollywood, after all. Ask more questions. Meet more people. Someone had to have seen Loretta. She'd talk to Mark. Maybe Loretta had tried to use the card again.

She laid the second skillet on the drying rack and drained the sink. "I'm going out."

"Where?"

"Out." She relented when he scowled. "Just to the Pit."

She gave her uncle a quick smile to show him she wasn't holding on to her anger, and practically jogged to the front door. She needed the wide blue sky, the seemingly limitless boundaries of the ranch, and the four sides of the boxing ring they lovingly called Viper's Pit, part of the gym Tom and Viper had created in the old barn after they sold off the remaining animals. It was during training sessions in the Pit that she did her best thinking. Detoxing from the anxiety and emotions she'd rather not deal with would be an added bonus. Pushing herself to the point of exhaustion, beyond coherent thoughts, would be ideal.

"Tell Viper I'll see him later," Tom called after her.

Outside, she turned her face up to the warm sun, enjoying the contrast with the chill in the spring morning air. Only about an hour's drive from the Grand Canyon, this area of Arizona boasted pine trees and a high enough elevation to host the occasional spring snowstorm. It was her refuge, and a damn good place to train, or recuperate between jobs. Maybe she should take on a new job rather than pursue Loretta's connection to Stone. After all, Loretta was probably having the time of her life somewhere. She'd talk to Mark about what he wanted to do next.

But Mark didn't answer her knock. His cabin appeared to be empty. Perhaps he was out for a run, or had gone off on his own to pursue a lead. She shook her head at the frustration she experienced at that thought. If he'd chosen to go it alone, it was his prerogative.

She pulled out her phone as she crossed the open field toward the barn. No messages from Mark. But she stopped in her tracks as her email inbox popped up.

Hope you survived the chaos on the rooftop, though I have a feeling you're just fine. I, however, regret that our conversation was interrupted. My boss wants to talk to you. He'll sweeten the pot. A million dollars. Contact me ASAP.

It was signed Jared Bennigan and had a phone number.

So, her soldier had a name. And some effective resources if he'd found a way to trace her gun and the ranch truck so quickly. But how had he found her email address?

"You getting a workout today or not?" Viper's voice echoed across the distance and she tucked her phone away.

She stomped down her concerns and sucked in a deep breath. Jared Bennigan could wait while she thought things through. The guy was too cocky for his own good. And insulting, assuming money could buy her loyalty and trust.

She jogged the rest of the way to Viper's side. "Ready and willing, sir."

"That's what I like to hear." Viper winked and draped an arm across her shoulders, pulling her into the old barn. The building was now a fully equipped training facility. At Three Fortunes, there were plenty of outdoor training programs, too, such as hiking or running on the trails that ran like veins across the several-thousand-acre spread, practicing survivalist skills, or fine-tuning archery or shooting proficiencies. They also arranged to submerse themselves in nature a few times a year, at least once each season, to hone their camping and outdoor survival techniques.

For now, a dozen men worked out inside the old barn on a variety of weight machines and treadmills, or pumped iron in the free weights area. One man punched at a hanging bag in the corner. The fighting ring, Viper's Pit, sat in the middle of it all.

Skye greeted the men she passed, noting that Mark was absent. For the next hour, she lost herself in throwing punches at whoever dared to step into the ring with her. When her arms tired, she switched to kickboxing at the hanging bag in the corner and imagined it was an unknown enemy, someone she always felt was out there, waiting, spurring her to be better and stronger, but had never been able to put a face to. Was it her soldier, Jared? Or Robert Stone? Or someone else entirely?

When she still had angst to spare, she dared Viper to test her. Soaked with sweat and muscles quivering with fatigue, she wanted more. The Pit beckoned with its ability to both cause the physical, and numb the mental, pain. Viper soon became a nameless, faceless being that embodied everything she was battling against. Her fears, her failures. The battle made her forget, just for a bit, that she hadn't found Loretta, or that Jared had cornered her.

She was still losing herself when one of the newer recruits, a man named Tristan, approached the ring. "Message, sir." Tristan held out the note, catching Skye's eye. That moment of distraction allowed Viper the winning jab, ending their match. At least she'd winded him. Tristan hurried away the moment Viper took the note.

He scanned it and grunted, then handed it to Skye. "It's for you. If I'm going to be your secretary, maybe I should put on a skirt and heels."

"That's a scary image. And, may I point out, sexist. Women don't have to wear skirts and heels and men can be secretaries—or personal assistants."

He gave her a look that said *no shit* and gestured to the note. "I believe I just proved that. Looks like you've got yourself a hot date tonight?"

She squinted at the paper until she could decipher Tristan's scrawl. All the tension she'd just worked out of her body came flooding back, coiling in the pit of her stomach.

Meet Jared at the Roadhouse tonight, 7:00. Wants to return your rifle and discuss your partnership—on neutral ground, since you're scared. (His words, not mine.) Tristan had added the last part.

Had Jared just called her a chicken? Damned if that didn't make her lips twitch with the urge to smile, and her muscles clench again with the need to pummel. And she hadn't agreed to any damn partnership. It just confirmed her opinion that Jared Bennigan was far too cocky and confident—especially for a guy she'd gotten the better of.

Viper was watching the expressions fly across her face. "You okay?"

"Yeah. Gotta go out tonight."

"So, it is a date?" His bushy gray eyebrows rose.

His disbelief was warranted, considering she rarely dated. And if she did, Viper and Tom didn't hear about it—usually because there was nothing to hear about. She had yet to meet a man who'd been more important to her than her training or her duties at the ranch, and she doubted she ever would. Men were a means to an end, to gain information for a job she was working or to briefly satisfy a physical hunger.

Jared... She had a feeling he could fall into either category.

Or both.

"Not a date. More like a lead on a job." Apparently, she hadn't responded quickly enough to Jared's email. How had he figured out where she lived, and found the compound's unlisted phone number? Then she remembered the truck must have been registered to the ranch. It wouldn't have required too many bribes to trace the license plate.

Her heart thumped harder as she realized Jared was already in Arizona. And that he wasn't going to give up. Why was he pursuing her? Was he working under Stone's orders?

"I like him already," Viper said.

She crossed her arms. "Why? You don't even know him." Neither did she, but there was something about him that had intrigued her. At the very least, she grudgingly respected his stalking skills.

"He's basically daring you to meet him, which means he's smart."

"I don't follow."

"You're skilled, darlin', but you also like to win. He's throwing down the gauntlet. Might do you some good to have someone shake you up, test those defenses."

There was a lot of truth to what Viper said. Pride had always been one of her weaknesses, and it was one of the deadly sins. But how could Jared have discovered that about her in their brief few minutes together? Either he was psychic or she had done a piss-poor job of disguising her reactions to him.

Viper tipped his head. "I'm guessing you like this guy, too, or he wouldn't have your rifle. You don't loan your *precious* to anyone."

"Yeah, well, he won't have it long." She scowled. *I'll get it back.* Of course, she'd have to meet him and he'd expect something in return. But why mention a *partnership*? Perhaps he'd discovered she'd been asking questions around town about Loretta. Maybe he'd seen Loretta and Stone together, especially since he was one of Stone's bodyguards. The thought had her suddenly eager to see him again. So she could grill him for answers.

"Hey, do you know what *intrepidus vive ferociter ludeque* means?" she asked Viper. On the back of the scrap of paper that held Jared's message, she wrote the words down as she'd memorized them from Loretta's good-bye note.

Without his reading glasses, he had to lean forward and squint to read the foreign words. "I'm a little rusty. I'd guess it means something about living life and playing hard? No, live fearlessly and play ferociously. That's the more accurate translation, I think."

"No shit?"

He raised his eyebrows at her, objecting to her language. An ex-Ranger who didn't like curse words. Or maybe he just didn't like hearing them from her. Though she'd done her best to disabuse him of the notion she was a dainty flower, she was still blessed with a set of ovaries instead of balls, and was therefore held to a slightly different standard—when she wasn't in the ring.

"No shit," he echoed.

"You speak Latin?" She'd already looked the phrase up online, but hadn't been certain of the correct translation.

"Nobody speaks it, sweetheart. It's a dead language."

"But they spoke it when you were a kid?" She smirked.

He tried to scowl, but the twitch of his lips gave him away. "I learned some back in high school. You know, back when I studied by torchlight. The military loves Latin phrases. That stuff's everywhere. A lot of units have their own mottos. Is your guy military?" Viper perked up at the thought of a comrade in arms.

She thought about her soldier. Jared had a military bearing, but this phrase didn't originate with him. It was something Loretta had learned, but from whom?

Live fearlessly and play ferociously. A mantra or a threat? She rolled the words around in her head, along with what little she'd learned about Stone. Seemingly intent on living the high life, he could have adopted the phrase as his personal credo. Is that where Loretta had heard it? But how the hell had a man of Stone's stature met a girl from the ranch? She supposed he could be shooting a movie in the area. Or maybe Loretta had initiated contact with Stone in pursuit of an acting career and he'd told her to come out to Los Angeles.

She patted Viper's rock-hard pecs. "You're a man of infinite skills, Viper."

He snorted. "Get moving. Don't you have other things to do today, like get ready for a date? That typically takes women hours."

"See, you *are* a great secretary, toots. Thanks for keeping me on schedule."

He glared and, grinning, she trotted out of the barn and back to the house to shower and decide how to get her duffel bag back and ask her questions while keeping Jared Bennigan at a distance. This time, she'd have the home field advantage. And she'd get her rifle back.

CHAPTER FIVE

"It's about time you returned my call." Finn didn't bother to temper his frustration with a polite hello. He hated being out of the loop, especially when that loop might tighten around his neck and strangle him. If that bitch Loretta had said anything to her father about meeting him...

"You were right," his source on the inside said. Tristan was uniquely qualified for the task. He was the loner, tough-guy type that fit in perfectly at Three Fortunes without anyone asking questions, but he and Finn also had similar ideas when it came to pleasurable pursuits. Finn had chosen him from among the Redemption Club members months ago, when first learning Stone owned a stake in Three Fortunes. Together, Finn and Tristan had laid the foundation for the special project on a distant, isolated portion of the ranch. That parcel had become the Hunting Grounds. Tristan kept an eye on the occupied portion of the ranch, to be sure nobody was the wiser about their activities.

"Right about what, specifically?" Finn's patience was near the breaking point.

"The Malibu incident is related to Loretta. Mark Sheldon is her father. He must have hired Skye Hamilton to find her."

"Skye Hamilton? Was she gunning for someone?" Had she been aiming for him? No. She would have been after Stone, since Finn had made sure all roads led to the other man, and away from Finn Tucker. Unless

Loretta had described Finn to Skye.

"I got him skunked when he got back last night. He's probably still passed out cold. He told me he was the one who fired that shot, to save Skye from the bodyguard. She's a friend of Loretta's."

"She's going to an awful lot of trouble to find her friend." Despite Tristan's using Mark's credit card at several hot spots around Vegas where no one would remember a face in the crowd, Skye had persisted. That kind of determined hunter deserved respect, and excited Finn in a new way, as he recalled Ryan's demand for a high-quality target in the next hunt. Perhaps he had a use for Skye after all. "Tell me more about her."

"She's unlike any woman I've ever known," Tristan said. "Her accuracy with both guns and knives is amazing."

"Knives?"

"Throwing them. I've seen her practice with a crossbow, too. Don't get on her bad side."

"She sounds fascinating. Where did she come from?"

"Grew up here, on Three Fortunes. Her uncle runs the place. Otherwise, she mostly keeps to herself."

"Except for befriending Loretta, apparently." Finn had told Loretta not to say a word or the deal was off. It was his own damn fault for trusting a sheltered, desperate seventeen-year-old girl to keep a secret. But damn, she was hot. He'd make sure she paid for this slipup. His lips curved as he contemplated the ways she could redeem herself. After all, the Redemption Club was all about payback, which was, often, a bitch. Loretta would learn that lesson well.

"Is Skye planning to resume the search?"

"Don't know. I think using Mark's credit card drew them away from Stone, and she and Mark are at the ranch now, but I don't think they'll give up."

"One problem at a time."

"Unfortunately, the problems are piling up."

Tristan's attitude was grim. "I took a phone message for Skye from a man named Jared Bennigan. He intends to meet with her tonight."

Bennigan. One of Stone's bodyguards—the one who'd thrown Erica out of the party. "Stone's probably looking for the woman who was lurking near his property, and the man who fired a weapon that created chaos. He's nervous because he's being blackmailed." Which was Ryan's fault, damn him. He wanted his father's money now, instead of waiting for the guy to die, so they'd hatched the Hunting Grounds plan using Stone's stake in the ranch, as well as a blackmail scheme. Both were lucrative but risked Stone's wrath if he found out. "If Jared Bennigan connects with Skye, he'll be on our asses next." Finn thought up a few more ways to pay Loretta back, just to restrain his temper.

"Lucky for you, I intercepted the call and have the details." Tristan listed the place and time. "It's not far from the ranch."

"Describe Skye."

"She's a knockout. Athletic build. Long brown hair, blue eyes. And a great shot. She can best most of the men around here in competition. Then again, she's been training her whole life."

Finn felt himself grew hard at the thought of a woman like that in his stable. She'd bring in the big bucks, like Ryan wanted. Hunters would pay handsomely for the privilege to hunt a huntress. If he didn't keep her for himself. "Text me a picture if you can get one, and any other details you can think of. I'll have someone at the Roadhouse to keep Bennigan from getting his hooks into her or learning anything important." They had to protect themselves at any cost. "But, there's another loose end to snip. We can't have Mark Sheldon looking for his daughter anymore. There are too many people poking around our turf as it is. Do you understand what I'm saying?"

"Absolutely."

Finn relaxed. He'd picked the right man for the

job. "If you do your part, I think it's worthy of an extra turn at the Hunting Grounds."

"Sounds good to me." There was a grin in Tristan's voice. "Especially if Skye's the target."

"I'll see what I can arrange."

The ex-warehouse squatted on one corner of the junction between old Route 66 and the railroad. Like many stretches of the iconic road, this particular extension of the railroad had long since disappeared beneath dirt, gravel, and overgrown weeds, though the tracks just to the south still hosted regular rail traffic. On the opposite corner of the intersection was the shell of an old, abandoned gas station.

Inside the bar, Jared sat in a dim corner, admiring the Route 66 memorabilia and neon beer signs as he waited for his mystery woman to appear.

No, not a mystery any longer. He grinned with the satisfaction of one mystery solved. Her name was Skye, a name that immediately brought to mind her stunning blue eyes.

Stone's declaration that he'd handle Skye hadn't sat well with Jared. He didn't know what the man planned, but he hadn't seemed to recognize Chelsea's name and he sure as hell seemed troubled by Skye's.

Jared had put Duffy and Meyer in charge of Stone's protection and taken a couple days off, driving straight to Arizona. He'd spent the day asking around the area about Skye, and learned about Three Fortunes' reputation as well. Apparently Skye was a woman who knew how to get things done, in a wink-wink, nudge-nudge kind of way. It reinforced the impression he'd initially had of a hit woman.

But was someone paying Skye to find a missing girl or to go after Stone? And why hadn't she followed through? If Stone knew why she'd come after him, and what it had to do with Loretta Sheldon, he wasn't sharing.

There was little else in public records about his mystery woman. He'd found an old record of a Skye Hamilton in Flagstaff, Arizona. She'd applied for a library card, of all things, over a dozen years ago. Given that there were no school records, Jared guessed that she was homeschooled, or possibly even self-taught.

According to the people he'd talked to around town, Three Fortunes was reputed to shelter an anti-government group known to train individuals in everything from how to react to a government takeover or act of terrorism to surviving the next apocalypse. Had his little rabbit grown up there? Remembering the mix of toughness and vulnerability in Skye's gaze, he could see how she might have.

Which made luring Skye away from the compound his main objective. It would have been suicide to go into unfamiliar territory, where an unknown number of men were, most assuredly, armed with an unspecified amount of ammunition and guns—he was certain, from the compound's reputation, it was a large number—and attempt to sit her down for a talk.

The Roadhouse, though surprisingly crowded for a Monday night, was neutral turf. He needed her to come to him of her own free will. He only hoped the bait was enough to seduce her away from her comfort zone. Then again, Skye Hamilton didn't strike him as a woman who needed, or wanted, comfort. It was a refreshing change, given how his mother had needed constant reassurance, mostly about vain things. He and his sisters had learned independence at an early age.

Their mother—an exotic dancer—had been murdered by an abusive boyfriend when Haley was seven, Chelsea twelve, and Jared twenty. Phoebe Bennigan had never had good taste in men, flitting from one relationship to another, producing three children with three different fathers. Still, she'd tried to raise the siblings together.

Jared had already joined the military and was stationed overseas at the time of Phoebe's murder, but

Haley's Aunt Jane had taken in the two girls. Unfortunately, Jane could barely keep the girls reined in as they got older and more rebellious. She'd threatened on more than one occasion to turn them over to the state.

There'd been a pattern of sweet-talking her down from the ledge, usually over the phone, from far away when he'd been stationed elsewhere. He'd happily taken on the role of their protector when he could get back to Vegas, but sometimes it was exhausting. And sometimes he failed.

Like with Chelsea.

Jared reread the text he'd received from his youngest sister, Haley. *My birthday's next weekend. You'd better be home by then.* At seventeen, she was usually the one checking up on him.

He typed the delayed response. *Wouldn't miss it. Make sure you're getting your homework done. You haven't graduated yet.* He added a smiley emoticon because it would please her to know he'd learned it from her.

Bossy pants, she replied almost immediately.

He grinned. She'd tossed his nickname for her back at him.

His cell phone rang and his business partner's *The Good, the Bad, and the Ugly* theme song played until Jared answered. "Yeah."

"Where the hell are you?" Devlin snapped. Of the triad, he was definitely *the ugly* tonight. "You can't go that long without checking in, and you never leave your post without approval."

"I'm a co-owner, for Christ's sake."

"But you're currently acting as a field agent."

"To find Chelsea."

"You know the rules." Dev was controlling in that way, but his rules came from a deep need to keep everyone safe.

"Duffy and Meyer can handle babysitting Stone."

"Doesn't answer my question."

"I'm in Arizona, but I'm guessing you already know that."

"Chasing after Skye Hamilton?"

Jared snorted. At least their GSS agents were still topnotch. "If you know where I am and who I'm after, why the heck are you bugging me? Slow day at the office?" There was no such thing, and they both knew it. Which meant Dev was genuinely concerned.

"You're without backup, in unfamiliar, possibly hostile, territory."

"I doubt she'd meet me if I wasn't alone, on neutral ground."

There was a long silence. "You still think Stone is tied to Chelsea's disappearance?"

Jared blew out a breath. "I'm not sure yet. That's what I'm hoping to find out from Skye. She's looking for a missing girl and I'm wondering if it's all somehow connected."

"I hope she shows up."

Me, too. "I'm expecting her any minute," Jared said, hoping it was true. Hell, for all he knew, Skye could be planning to ambush him when he left. "I was planning to check in when I had more."

"Well, next time, check in at least once a day, even if it's to say you're fucking sleeping."

A woman walked through the front door at seven sharp and his entire body went on alert. *Skye.* Even from across the bar, he'd recognize those eyes anywhere. But the rest of her... The entire package had the power of a stun gun. Skye Hamilton didn't have to be armed to be dangerous. She was a weapon unto herself.

Jared cleared his throat. "My target just showed up."

"Keep me posted. Don't make me track you down next time." Thankfully, Dev let it go and hung up.

Jared remained in the shadows at the far end of the bar, watching Skye as she covertly cased the joint. Every inch of her body had been imprinted on his brain

the evening they met, but now he had more information
with which to fill out and color in the image. On the
Malibu rooftop, she'd been wearing a dark cap that
covered her hair, so he'd only gotten a glimpse of one
long, teasing strand. Now, mahogany waves cascaded
past her shoulders. Instead of the black cat-burglar
suit, tonight she wore a faded denim jacket over a black
camisole and jeans that clung to her hips and thighs
like a lover's hands. She scanned the crowd, the neon
signs that covered the walls reflecting a rainbow of
colors in her eyes and glossy hair.

She'd come.

Skye glanced around the Roadhouse, one of the
few entertainment venues within a short drive, seeking
her target. She didn't come here often, having been
urged for her entire life to keep a low profile, and
having noticed that when people knew she was from
Three Fortunes, they treated her differently—as if she
were peculiar. Normally, she preferred to drive the half
hour to Flagstaff, where she could get lost in a more
populated town. But she had wandered into the
Roadhouse to enjoy herself on occasion, especially after
completing a job. The place was off the beaten path, but
it was packed tonight, probably because a local band
would be providing live entertainment.

Within seconds of entering, she felt eyes on her.
With the awareness of a hunter who was being hunted,
she met his gaze. He lifted his beer in salute, then
tilted his head to indicate the empty barstool beside
him.

Hell, no. She didn't take orders from anyone, let
alone him. If he wanted her, he'd have to come to her.

Ignoring him, as well as the smell of stale beer
and the crunch of peanut shells beneath her feet, she
took a seat along the main part of the bar, several
yards away.

"What can I get you?" the bartender asked.

"Beer. In the bottle, cap on."

"What, don't you trust me, honey?" The guy arched a brow.

"Nothing personal. I don't trust anyone." She'd learned that the hard way, practically in the womb, but she winked to soften the blow to his ego.

With a grunt, he grabbed a bottle from the cooler and set it in front of her.

After he moved on, Skye twisted off the cap. Purposefully turning away from Jared, she leaned back against the polished wood bar and pretended to watch the couples on the dance floor as she enjoyed a few quiet sips. The lively two-step beat had most people out of their seats, but her thoughts were on Jared, what Stone would require of her for a million-dollar payoff, and how she could use both of them to find Loretta. She also wondered how long it would take Jared to approach her, because she damn well wasn't going to kowtow to him.

"Come here often?" The male voice at her ear wasn't Jared's, and she was surprised by a sudden pang of disappointment.

Wincing at the tired pickup line, she swiveled to meet the cowboy's brown eyes—not caramel, just plain brown like his shitkicker boots. This man's gaze didn't suck her in and hold her. There was no twitch of dark humor in his grin. Involuntarily, her gaze sought Jared over the man's shoulder, but he was no longer sitting at the end of the bar. Angry with herself for making comparisons, and for the stab of annoyance that Jared had retreated before even trying to approach her, she focused on the newcomer's pickup line.

"Every night," she said. "I love to drink until I cry, think about all the men who've left me until I get a good mad on, and then castrate the cowboys who try to pick me up. Good thing you caught me early in the evening." She raised her beer bottle to toast him before taking a long swallow. Maybe if he thought she was a high-maintenance bitch, he'd back off.

Instead, he sat down next to her. Crap. Apparently, waiting for Jared to make a move had been a big mistake.

The cowboy didn't pick up on her frosty demeanor. He thrust a hand toward her in greeting. "Darren." There were calluses, as most cowboys had. Hell, most of the people in this area worked hard with their hands. Physical labor was a part of living on a ranch. And the guy had the muscular, wiry build of a ranch hand, but something about the spotlessness and fresh creases of his clothing, and the fact that his boots were shiny, the leather not broken in, made her suspicious. Darren—or whatever his name was—wasn't from here, and he wasn't a cowboy. But that didn't mean he was the cutthroat type, either. There wasn't enough cunning behind his eyes. She'd seen enough evil in her lifetime to know the glint of it. Perhaps he was traveling between Vegas and Texas, and wanted to look the part—or what he thought the part of a cowboy should look like.

So she accepted his hand and shook it. Might as well keep potential enemies close. "Skye."

He held onto her a moment too long, indicating his interest, but was it sexual or an entirely different predatory motive? Or was he linked to a different job? Contrary to rumors, she wasn't a murderer for hire. She preferred to think of herself as a hired gun, but was most like a private investigator. She'd only killed twice—once in self-defense, and once while taking a missing child back from a sexual predator who was about to kill his victim to keep the child from talking. And while the killings had brought justice, they hadn't brought her peace. Nightmares had plagued her afterward. But the acts had given the victims closure.

She mentally indexed the jobs she'd completed recently. A couple of surveillance gigs where she'd caught a cheating wife and an embezzling partner. The return of a child taken by an ex-wife who didn't have custody. Camping out on someone's ranch, flushing out squatters who were planting pot crops. Helping to regain a prize-winning mare for the original owner.

No Darrens popped up in the rundown of her clients and anyone connected with those jobs, but he could be using an alias. *Or maybe he's simply a random guy.*

She chatted with him for a minute, letting him do most of the talking while her eyes roved the crowd. Where had Jared gone? She wasn't so distracted that she didn't notice Darren studiously avoided discussing anything personal. A couple minutes later, tired of the game, she refused an invitation to dance and excused herself to use the restroom. When she emerged, she avoided returning to the same barstool, choosing to stand in the corner as she surveyed the crowd, which had grown in anticipation of the live music. She was surrounded by warm bodies taking drags from cool longnecks as they watched the action on the dance floor.

The hair on her neck stood up as she sensed someone moving up behind her, as if he had a heat signature made for her senses alone.

"Glad you came." Jared's voice took her right back to that moonlit Malibu rooftop.

She turned to face him, drinking in the features that had been partially shadowed two nights before. The strong jaw, now scruffy with a day's growth of beard, and warm caramel eyes were just as she'd fantasized about for the past forty-some hours, but other things, like the crinkle of tiny lines around his eyes and the myriad shades of brown in his dark blond hair completed the picture. He hadn't even attempted to dress like a cowboy, but his blue jeans and untucked button-down shirt, rolled up to his elbows to reveal strong forearms, were enough to let him blend in.

She took a beat to steady her suddenly jangling nerves. "Took you long enough."

He frowned. "Looked like you were busy. Do you know him?" His eyes didn't leave hers as his head tipped toward the bar where Darren still sat, now observing them from the corner of his eye while pretending to watch the band.

"I do now. Amazing how many new friends are popping up. Didn't expect to find you in my neck of the woods."

"I'm sure."

She frowned. "That wasn't a compliment."

"I'm sure of that, as well." Amusement twinkled in his gaze. "But I never could resist a challenge. I'm glad you came. We need to talk." He scanned the tables surrounding the dance floor and snagged her hand.

She let him, but only because she wanted to hear what he had to say. At least, that's what she told herself. If he were any other man, and certainly if he were Darren, she'd have twisted his arm until he cried *uncle*. Her fingers warmed in his as he pulled her to an empty table in the farthest, darkest corner, out of Darren's line of sight.

Little bolts of electricity were traveling from her fingertips to her brain, and then coursing throughout her body. God, when had she last let a man touch her, and had any of them simply held her hand? Usually, she didn't like to be touched in such an intimate fashion. She'd satisfied her curiosity and her sexual needs by fooling around a couple of times, each experiment with a man she'd gotten to know when he'd come to train at the ranch—but only when she'd known they'd soon be moving on, so the affairs had been brief and uncomplicated. It was understood that people who came to the ranch weren't permanent, so she hadn't been setting herself up for disappointment. She knew the score, as did they.

But *this?* This kind of immediate spark, with a man she didn't know, let alone fully trust, was new and uncomfortable. The tingling, pleasurable reaction to holding his hand was a red flag that she had to get a grip on herself, fast. Especially since the man worked for Stone. And if her sexual needs were kicking into high gear, why couldn't it have been with an uncomplicated, clichéd cowboy like Darren, who would have been easy pickings? There was nothing easy about Jared Bennigan.

She willed her pulse to return to a steady, sane rhythm. Thankfully, Jared let go of her as they slid onto the stools around the small, high table.

"Who hired you?" he asked without preamble.

"Nice."

"What?"

"The direct approach. I approve, though I wish you'd bought me a drink first." She could use something to cool her suddenly warm skin.

That seemed to take him aback. "A drink?" His gaze slid to her mouth, and more electricity shot through her.

"On the other hand, I could buy a hell of a lot of drinks with a million dollars."

He sighed and looked away as if she wouldn't like what he had to say next. "I was hoping you weren't counting on Stone's money."

She stiffened. "There's no money?" She wasn't disturbed by the lack of reward so much as the fact that he'd used a lie to lure her here tonight. For some stupid reason, she'd pegged her soldier as an honorable man. She counted to ten to rein in her temper.

"There's so much more at stake than money," he said before she'd reached five.

"You're right. My professional reputation is at risk. If I told you who hired me and why, others could get hurt." What she did wasn't legal, but it was justice. Like the Old West, some people went outside the law to meet their needs, and Skye had found a niche she could fill. It made her feel needed and valued for the first time in her life. She couldn't lose that.

"I can help, if you'll just tell me why you were in Malibu, watching Stone—"

"You've got to be crazy if you think I'm going to tell you anything. I'm not going to let you screw me over and sell me out to your boss." She stood, but he was faster. His hand snaked out to grab her wrist.

"Wait. Let me explain." His hold wasn't as gentle this time, and the urgency conveyed by his grip had her pausing, against her better judgment.

"No, let *me* explain, because you clearly don't understand. I'm not a sellout, and I don't come cheap, especially not for a sleaze like Robert Stone. I only work for people who can be trusted, people who need my kind of help."

"As long as they can pay." For some reason, the accusation in his tone stung.

She twisted to try to get away, but he tugged her back against him where he sat. Suddenly she was nestled between his thighs, her back to his front and her bottom snug against his crotch. One arm was crossed over her chest, his grip on her wrist trapping it against her opposite shoulder. His other hand slid across her stomach to pin her other arm and anchor her against him. Every nerve ending in her abdomen heated as if he were branding her. In a way, he was. She suspected anybody who looked their way would believe them to be a couple engaged in a loving embrace.

The bristles of his five o'clock shadow lightly scraped her jaw as his mouth moved to her ear so he could be heard over the music. "I don't want you to sell out, and I don't want you working for Stone. It's me who needs your help. And I'm the type who can be trusted."

"Yeah, like following me to Arizona fosters trust. Is this some kind of game?" she hissed over her shoulder, but that put his mouth entirely too close to hers so she jerked her head around again to face the dance floor, ignoring the tingle of desire that skipped along her spine. His warm male scent—not cologne, but honest, hardworking man—along with the hint of a beer he'd sipped earlier, filled her nostrils. "I thought you worked for Stone. Shouldn't he have your loyalty?"

"I'm Stone's bodyguard, but he doesn't own me. I only work indirectly for him. He contracted security with my private firm, Global Security Solutions. I'm not here to hurt you. In fact, I'm not supposed to be here at all. Stone doesn't know I came. A few minutes of your time is all I ask, but somewhere private, where we can talk." As he flexed his fingers, fanning them against her stomach, his thumb brushed the underside of her breast, setting off a cascade of shivers throughout her body. That, combined with his warm breath against the most sensitive part of her neck and the feel of his erection against her lower back, had her knees wobbling. She locked them, and her needs, down tight. At least she wasn't the only one affected by this strange chemistry. But it was time to put on the brakes.

"It'll cost you a million dollars." She glared at him over her shoulder. "My time is valuable." As was her trust. She had to get out of here and regroup. She'd never been held this way by a man who took complete command of her body and, damn it, she couldn't think. He'd gotten past her mental defenses and that was inexcusable. She started to step away and his fingers tightened on her wrist and waist.

"What would five minutes cost me?"

She glanced at his face and saw the frustration and need in his eyes, but she didn't know him. Despite whatever spell he'd cast over her body, he was a virtual stranger, and she couldn't let his needs override her own safety.

She envisioned various ways of disengaging herself from the situation. She wasn't scared of him. She had options. Like throwing her head back into his nose and breaking it. Which would be a shame. He had a great profile. Or slamming the heel of her boot into his foot, which was clad in a tennis shoe. Or shoving her elbow into his ribs. The hard washboard abs she felt beneath his chambray shirt wouldn't protect him from a move like that.

Oh, yes, she definitely had options.

Or you could give him five minutes, for free. But after the past twenty-four hours of craziness, and her uncle's repeated warnings to be careful, to lay low, trust was at a premium.

"This guy bothering you?" Her cowboy, Darren, approached, stopping close to her. Apparently, he was going to make himself an option, as well. His aftershave tickled her nose like an annoying gnat. He might not be from the area, and he might not be who he pretended to be, but she wouldn't refuse his help at the moment.

"Yeah." She took a step forward and Jared's hands fell away, leaving a sudden sensation of cold where there had been intense heat. "Thanks, Darren."

"How about that drink?" Darren draped an arm across her shoulders, preventing her from going more than a couple of steps.

"I've got a pounding headache. I think I'll head home, but I appreciate the offer." She glanced back at Jared, who had risen to his feet but made no move to follow her. His hands, which had been so firm on her body just a moment ago, hung loosely at his sides. Smart man. If he reached for her now, she'd land him on his ass. His mouth was set in a hard line and his eyes held questions and no small amount of irritation. For one crazy moment, she was tempted to go back and comfort him, to give him his five minutes.

But he'd stalked her, followed her hundreds of miles, and had even tracked down the unlisted phone number for the compound where she lived and her personal email address. And even if he wasn't here on Stone's behalf—which she wasn't sure she believed—he was contracted with the man.

She needed time to regain the upper hand. If she chose, she could email him later and set up a meeting on *her* terms.

In a smooth move that looked like she was doing a playful dance twirl, she twisted out from beneath

Darren's arm and spun out of his reach, adding a playful laugh to soften the rejection. "Thank you for being my hero tonight, Darren, but I really do have to go."

Darren scowled but didn't reach for her, and certainly didn't volunteer who he really was. Maybe he was a newcomer, intent on trying on the role of cowboy, and that explained the crispness of his clothes. Hell, maybe he was who he pretended to be and it was payday and he'd simply gone shopping in town. Her mind was seriously fucked up sometimes, seeing threats where there were none. But Tom, Viper, and the other survivalists she'd grown up with, as well as her experiences as a young child before her parents had died, had ingrained in her an innate sense of distrust and self-protectiveness that she couldn't shake. And it had saved her enough times that she erred on the side of caution.

Still, like an invisible thread connecting them, she felt Jared's gaze on her back as she left. They were both too proud to bend, so it was better to make a break for it.

CHAPTER SIX

Skye gulped in a breath of cool, pine-scented air as she crossed the parking lot to her truck. Her duffel bag very likely sat in one of these cars. Which one would a man like Jared drive? Probably the big, dark SUV parked near the door, facing front out so he could make a quick getaway after he'd gotten what he wanted from her. The reminder that he could come out at any moment had her deciding she'd have to retrieve her rifle and other weapons another time. *Precious* would have to wait. Besides, she had other weapons at the ranch.

She slid behind the wheel of her pickup before sending a quick text to her uncle. *Home in ten.*

His reply was immediate. *Will be watching for you.*

Her finger hovered over the screen as she debated sending a warning that someone might be following her. Her gaze lifted to the bar's front door, but neither Darren nor Jared exited. Maybe they'd respect her wishes and let her leave peacefully. Maybe all the devious plots really were in her head. And if Jared wanted to find whoever was trying to hire someone to harm his employer, there had to be other people he could pester or bribe—probably for a lot less money and effort.

She started the truck and swung onto the main road. A few minutes later, just as she turned onto the narrower gravel road that belonged to the ranch, she spied a pair of headlights behind her. She kept her gaze on the rearview mirror, peering through the wake of dust she left as she drove, and breathing a sigh of relief as the car continued past her turnoff.

It was another minute before the house came into view, twin arms of warm light spilling through the front windows and slanting across the yard as if reaching out to embrace her. She parked in the circular drive and rushed up the four steps to the porch, forcing herself to slow her strides so she didn't look as flustered as she felt. She hung her jacket on the coatrack just inside the door. The wooden floorboards creaked as she crossed the living room toward the back of the house.

She stopped short in the kitchen doorway and frowned at her uncle's bowl of Honey Nut Cheerios. "That's what you're having for dinner?"

He shot her an unrepentant grin. "And dessert."

"Let me cook you something." She moved to the fridge and started poking through its contents, then remembered she hadn't done the grocery shopping yet. And she'd likely be leaving again in the morning. She'd track down Mark, who she hadn't run into all day, and see if he had any new credit card transactions. Perhaps Loretta had turned west toward LA again, after hitting Kingman. Or maybe she'd bypassed the ranch on her way east and gone through Flagstaff, or south to Phoenix. Either way, Skye would find some trail to follow to keep her busy for a few days. Maybe a few weeks. Let things quiet down again around here.

And let Jared Bennigan return to California.

"I'm okay, really," Tom said, seeing her staring blankly into the open refrigerator.

"It's not healthy." She pulled out some greens for a salad, but they looked wilted. She'd check the greenhouse and garden in the morning before hitting the road, see if she could scrounge up something healthy for Tom before she left.

"Stop." The command in his voice had her turning to him. "Sit down."

She closed the refrigerator and sank onto the chair beside him. "What's wrong?"

"You've been digging into the past, even after I expressly asked you not to and you promised to listen."

"What? No."

"Don't bullshit a bullshitter."

She froze. "I'm not lying."

He scowled. "I got a visit tonight from Robert Stone. Sound familiar?"

Shocked, her hand went to her boot, finding comfort in the bone handle of her blade.

Tom saw the movement. "Relax. He's gone now. I explained you weren't coming after him."

"Is that what he wanted? A guarantee? Because I sure as hell won't promise that. Not after what he's done." She stood so suddenly that her chair fell over backward.

Tom winced at the noise but didn't reassure her. Rather, he looked like the one who might need comfort. His hands started crumpling and smoothing his paper napkin in a nervous gesture that had her gut churning. She watched the mechanical movements of his hands, dotted with nicks and scars that were evidence of a tough, stubborn existence, and leathered with age and sun. Still, those hands had lifted her up into the saddle on her first horse and taught her how to grip a gun. They might not have expressed love as often as she once would have wished, but they'd taught her how to survive, which was more important, and an indication that he cared. A lot of people had a lot less in this world. *She* had once had a lot less.

Tom looked as if he were preparing to say something important but couldn't find the words. And he was avoiding eye contact. The knot in her stomach tightened.

"This is about more than me working outside of the ranch, isn't it?" When she yanked the mutilated napkin out from under his fingers, he toyed with the kissing boy-and-girl pair of salt-and-pepper shakers bought from Goodwill long ago.

"I'm worried about you."

She quirked a brow. *He* was worried about *her*? "I'm fine. What does Stone have to do with digging up the past?"

"I don't know why you wouldn't listen to me, after all I've done. Our priority has always been safety. You shouldn't have taken unnecessary risks."

If she didn't, who would? Who would help those who couldn't get help through the legal channels? "We're also, innately, lone wolves. We have a pack, if we need it, but this kind of work is what you and Viper trained me for." Without a college education, with only a GED she'd studied for herself, they were the only skills she had that could help earn her keep.

He wouldn't meet her gaze. "You've crossed the line, going up against Robert Stone. I want you to leave." It was said so quietly she wasn't sure she'd heard him correctly, at first. As she realized she'd actually heard those words from her only family, the knot in her stomach climbed into her throat.

She croaked out a humorless laugh, determined not to take him seriously. "Leave? I just got back. Do you need something from town? I could make a run for supplies later."

"No, I mean leave for good."

Panic fluttered throughout her body, beating against her nerve endings and numbing her limbs. "Don't say that." Her voice was small, raspy with emotion.

"I couldn't force you." He had forced others out when they hadn't lived by the code of the compound or they'd endangered it in some way. It was a necessary evil when one had to think of the good of the group above that of the individual.

She glared at him, willing him to take back his words. He'd given her this life, a new beginning after the abuse she'd suffered at her parents' hands—and now he was threatening to take it all away. "What did

Stone threaten you with? Is he holding something over you?"

He dragged his hands down his face. For a moment, she read misery in his eyes, but then they turned harder than she'd ever seen. "You need to go. We'll all be safer."

Her temper snapped like a thread stretched too taut. "You're letting Stone dictate your decisions? I thought I meant something to you." She would not beg for validation. She'd grown used to tough love, but ostracizing her from the only community she'd ever known was beyond cruel.

Shouts of alarm from outside interrupted her, just seconds before an explosion from somewhere beyond the house rattled the walls and echoed in her ears.

"What the hell?" Tom stood so fast he knocked his bowl over and milk poured across the table. Skye ran toward the living room window, where she could survey the front yard and the other buildings. Tom joined her.

Flames licked the sky from the rooftop of the bunkhouse a football field's length away. Memories of another fire, which had engulfed her entire life, threatened to draw her inward. She quickly shut that pathway down.

"He's attacking us."

"Stone?" But why? He was getting what he wanted, hurting her. "And how did he get past the electric fence?"

"He has ways." Tom kicked into soldier mode and began barking orders. "Keep low. Get away from the window. Get your gear and head for your truck."

Skye's gaze went to her vehicle, sitting right out front. "It won't provide much protection." As a shield against their enemy's firepower, it was nearly useless. "I've got guns and ammo in my room and there's more in the shed out back—"

"You have your keys?"

Realizing his intent, she froze in a crouched position. "I'm *not* leaving."

"You've got to. Get out of here. Now." His gaze shifted to the kitchen and she knew he was thinking of the back door. "It could just be one guy, but if there's enough of them, they'll be coming here next. These aren't nice men, and they'll be after you. I'm trying to protect you from him."

"So you do think it's Stone?"

He looked uncomfortable for a moment. "Could be a few different groups out to get us, but I don't know who exactly, no."

"For all we know, it could have been an accidental explosion." But as she spoke, a volley of gunfire sounded near the bunkhouse. In the black night, she could vaguely make out dark shapes moving in the shadows, like ants scattering, except these ants had firepower. Was that their guys or someone else's? Oh, God, had she led the enemy to their doorstep?

An image of bright orange flames, flickering upward into a dark night sky—but not these flames, and not this sky—filled her vision. She'd been six, huddled into herself, peeking through the branches in shock as her home, with her parents inside, exploded and was engulfed in flames.

Tom gripped her shoulders tightly, bringing her back to the present. "Skye, *go*. You're all I have. I need to know you're safely away from here, laying low somewhere." He'd been the one to save her all those years ago. He'd found her hiding in the massive tree she'd climbed daily as a kid. He alone had held the power to coax her down. That night, he'd taken her away from the horror that had destroyed her home, and he'd never allowed her to look back. Not that she'd wanted to.

"No. I don't care what Stone threatened you with. You're all I have." The realization snapped her into action. "Go to the men. Get them organized." They would protect him, too. Scooting away from the window, she continued until her back hit the corner, then rose to her feet.

Tom hadn't moved. "Skye—"

"I'm going out the back. I'll flank them if they've left an opening." Their group had run through hundreds of scenarios in their heads. She could almost see the white board in the corner of the big barn where they trained, could smell the marker as Viper scribbled diagrams with arrows and Xs as if from a playbook. She blinked and forced herself to move.

"Be safe," her uncle said, apparently realizing he couldn't convince her to simply run for her life.

"Be safe," she returned with a nod. It was as close as they came to saying they loved each other. In their world, that depth of feeling was something you showed, not something you spoke aloud.

She might never see him again. That was the way they'd trained. If something serious threatened the compound, each went his or her separate way. They had plans and alternate identities in place, and nobody knew about anybody else's because it was safer that way.

She and Tom left through the back door but split up when their feet hit the grass. She didn't look back, couldn't afford to indulge in the emotion that was lodged behind her breastbone like a heavy stone, pressing against her ribcage.

Your fault. You led them here. There was no such thing as coincidence. Stone had to have followed Jared. Or Jared had volunteered her location. She'd brought this evil to her haven and now she'd pay the price.

As the thought that she'd been played by Jared took root and grew in her mind, rage filled her vision and tightened her throat. She struggled to swallow it down. Tom had been right. She couldn't trust anyone. She'd endangered the compound.

She shoved everything but survival instincts to the back of her mind as her gaze searched the darkness. Clinging to the shadows, she headed for the toolshed. There would be more ammo and at least one shotgun stored there. Whoever was coming for her would get the fight of his life.

But before she could reach the shed, a figure came racing toward her from around the side of the house. The large size and broad build indicated a male, and he was armed. One of the outbuildings exploded behind him and the flash of light illuminated his features right before the concussive wave of air knocked them both on their asses. Her head snapped back and hit the hard ground. Some part of her was surprised there was no steam coming off her as the heat of her anger met the cold spring night. She blinked to regain her focus, and a primitive drive urged her to get to her feet, to face the threat that lay only yards away. She'd seen the face of her enemy in that single moment, had recognized him.

It was Darren, the counterfeit cowboy.

Jared coughed into his sleeve and blinked back tears as a waft of smoke hit him in the face. He'd reached the inner perimeter and just gotten out of his car when an explosion rocked the night. Someone had cut the power supply to the electric fence, relieving him of at least one barrier. His gun at the ready, he stuck to the edge of the pine forest and scrubby juniper bushes as he skirted the outer building that was engulfed in flames.

Skye was here, somewhere. On his phone, he brought up the Three Fortunes property map with the parcel boundaries. He'd even found a satellite photo or two that detailed the structures. There was a main house, probably the original homestead. A shed to the rear of the house, next to a greenhouse and plot of farmland, butting up against the tree line. A couple of small rustic cabins. An old barn. And a boxlike rectangular building that could have been a garage for large farm or ranch equipment, but was probably more, given the rumored function of this ranch—and given it had been the building targeted by that first blast and was now going up in flames.

About a dozen men had gone running into the night after that blast. Then the gunfire had erupted. It was too dark and smoky to see who was targeting whom, but things were now eerily quiet.

If Jared hadn't decided to follow Darren when he'd left the Roadhouse a few minutes after Skye, if he hadn't seen Darren talking to another man in the parking lot before they drove off together in the direction of the ranch, if his gut hadn't urged him to get moving and take a chance that Skye would see him again, he wouldn't have heard the explosion or seen the chaos and been here to help. If he could help, that is. He knew only one thing... he had to find Skye.

There was a truck that looked like the one he'd seen in Malibu, but many of the ranch vehicles looked the same. It was parked in the yard, just outside the main house. Was that where Skye lived? On instinct, he headed toward it.

Gasping more from the shock when she was knocked to the ground than from the smoke that was blowing from the burning bunkhouse, Skye ignored her protesting muscles and crawled on top of Darren's prone body before he could react with so much as a moan. His weapon was gone, probably flying out of reach after the impact of the blast. His eyes flicked open and he began to fight her, trying to dislodge her from his chest. Hanging on like a bronco rider, Skye refused to give him an inch.

"Be still," she said in a harsh, commanding tone. "You're bleeding, and flailing about is just going to make it worse." Blood trickled from a wound near his temple and she spied a dark shadow in the grass that could be a rock. It must have stunned him when he hit the ground.

"Get off me, bitch," he said, but his words lacked heat. In fact, fear flickered across his face. It made her pause for a split-second—until she remembered what this man was doing to her family's ranch.

"Who do you work for?" Her thighs clamped, pinning his arms against his ribcage and keeping him from grabbing her. She wrapped her hands around his neck, until his struggles quieted and she relaxed her grip. "Why are you hurting the people I love?" When he didn't answer her question, she thumped his head into the hard ground again, though she avoided the rock. She had a four-inch knife tucked into her right boot if she needed it, but Darren didn't seem to be putting up a fair fight. Besides, at the moment, he was unarmed.

He moaned and blinked his eyes open again. "You don't want to know."

"Is Jared here? What are you after?"

The fear written on Darren's face, illuminated by the light spilling from the house and the flames from the now-engulfed garage, stilled her. A gun for hire shouldn't give in so easily, or be so inept at fighting back. "I had to find you," he said. "You're my redemption."

"Redemption?" That made no sense. Maybe he'd hit his head harder than she'd thought.

Another round of gunfire sounded from the distance. Shit. She had to find cover. The backyard was wide open. The trees had been removed years ago so they could see anyone approaching the house from any direction. The exposure was double with the flames lighting things up as if it was noon. She scrambled to her feet. "Get up."

"I'm supposed to bring you to him—"

"Get. Up. Now." When he was too slow to respond, she reached out and took his hand to help him, keeping her muscles bunched in preparation to react if he tried something, but he was as resigned as a boy facing a whipping for misbehavior.

"I didn't have a choice." His eyes darkened with some unnamed emotion. Was it regret or something darker? He reached into his front jeans pocket. "I need you—"

"Stop right there," she shouted, her fingers inching down her leg toward the knife in her boot. Did he have a weapon in there? Adrenaline rushed to her limbs, fueling her for a fight if he pulled something on her.

"I just want to show you—"

"Don't move!" Jared's voice rang out from the trees off to the side. Was he yelling at her or Darren? She put her hands in the air as she saw Jared approaching, a gun in his hand.

Unfortunately, Darren didn't stop his motions. The light in his eyes turned almost maniacal and he took a step toward her as he pulled his fingers from his pocket.

A shot rent the night air. Darren crumpled to his knees as his hand fully withdrew from his pocket. A scrap of something fell from his limp fingers.

It took Skye a split-second to react, for her brain to process the shock. Darren had been shot. And not by her.

As Jared shifted closer, she spied Darren's gun in the grass a few feet away and lunged for it, then scooped up the paper that had fallen from his hands. Needing some space to reassess the situation—and Jared—she backed away.

"Skye?" Jared swung his aim toward the tree line behind them as he spoke to her. "I didn't fire that shot." His words turned into fog in the chilly night air as his head swiveled to take in the surroundings. Sweat had mingled with smoke from the fires and smeared along his face and neck like war paint, indicating he'd been at the bunkhouse. He reached out to touch her arm and she jerked away. "We have to get to safety."

She wasn't sure she believed him, but being in the house was safer than being out in the open. And if he tried anything, she had a gun. She hurried to the cover of the house while Jared covered their six. Only seconds after she entered, he bolted the kitchen door and joined her on the floor, below the level of the windows. She kept the gun pointed at him, though his look was filled with concern. "Are you okay?" he asked.

"Hell, no, I'm not okay. People are attacking my home and you might be one of them." She scooted away from him.

"Skye, I didn't shoot that guy. There's someone else out there."

"A friend of yours?"

He scowled. "I'm alone. I'm certainly not with them. I saw that guy from the Roadhouse—"

"Darren. His name was Darren." Or at least, she thought it was.

"Friend of yours?" He shot her own words back at her.

"No, he's part of the attack." Which made her feel ridiculous about how she was treating Jared. Even if he shot the guy, he'd probably done it to protect her—or to keep Darren quiet about whatever he'd been about to say to her.

"I saw him call someone right after you left, then he left the Roadhouse a minute later. I followed him. Another guy was waiting in the parking lot, and they took off like bats out of hell. I was still a ways down your driveway when the first explosion went off and I hurried to help."

"*Help?*" She couldn't hide the doubt in her voice.

"Yes." He didn't try to follow her as she backed up farther, toward the doorway that led to the living room.

"Where's this other guy that Darren came here with?"

Jared shoved a hand through his hair, streaking it with soot. "I don't know." He tucked his gun in the back of the waistband of his jeans and crawled forward, stopping next to her and cupping her face in his hands so that she had to meet his gaze. "I know you have no reason to trust me, but I'm not going to hurt you. I need you too much."

Shock at his words had her rooted in place, gripping Darren's gun. He surprised her by releasing her to reach out and brush a long strand of hair from her cheek. The tender gesture socked her in the solar plexus, even as it lit a fire that burned a trail straight to her belly, but she couldn't let her guard down. "Darren said the same thing."

"What?"

"That he needed me. I was his *redemption*, whatever the fuck that means. He was going to turn me over to someone. Was that someone you?"

"No, of course not."

"Was it Stone? He paid my uncle a visit tonight, while I was at the Roadhouse. Basically told him to disown me."

"What? How could Stone control your uncle like that?" Anger glinted in his eyes, outrage on her behalf.

But was it real?

"Great question," she said. "Further evidence that I can't trust anyone." She jerked her face from his hands and sent him her fiercest glare. "I'm going to leave now, and you're not going to follow."

He raised his hands at his sides. "Reach into my jeans pocket."

Alarm shot through her at the prospect of getting any closer to him. "Why?"

"My business card is in there. I was going to give it to you at the bar so you could contact me when you changed your mind—"

"*When?*" She croaked out a laugh. "Not likely." There was too much craziness attached to Stone and anyone connected with him—including, apparently, her uncle.

"When you've had time to think about it, I think you'll realize we need to work together if either of us is going to get what we want." He tipped his head to indicate his right pocket. "Go on. It has information on the company I own with Devlin Grimm. Call him. He'll vouch for me. I also wrote my home address and phone number on the back."

Tentatively, she leaned toward him. He didn't move, didn't even flex a muscle. With two fingers, she reached into his pocket and withdrew the card.

"Go ahead and leave," he said. "Get to your truck. I'll cover you. Call me tomorrow. I can help you find Loretta Sheldon." He dropped into a crouched position and crept to the front window, gesturing that she should make a break for it.

Her breath had caught in her throat. He knew how to find Loretta? And he was letting her leave? This had to be a trick. But she didn't see another option. Her brain screamed at her to get out while she could.

A few seconds later, she was in her truck, which thankfully hadn't become a target for the attackers' explosives, though the barn was ablaze and the bunkhouse was a lost cause. She didn't see anyone, friend or foe—or Jared, and she wasn't sure which camp he fell into—as she sped away from the ranch until the orange glow became a small flicker in her rearview mirror.

Only then did she remember the scrap of paper that had fallen from Darren's lifeless fingers. A few minutes later, when it was clear she wasn't being followed, she pulled to the side of the road and retrieved Darren's paper from the pocket where she'd stuffed it. She frowned at the half of a playing card. An eight of diamonds. She flipped it over and held it to the dashboard light to try to see it better. Her breath froze in her lungs. On the back of the playing card was the logo from Legacy Hotel and Casino. The bottom half of the card was missing. The jagged edges where the card had been torn were worn and soft as if Darren had been carrying it around for months.

From her other pocket, she withdrew Jared's business card. Her thumb brushed over his embossed name as she read his contact information below it. Global Security Solutions. Didn't mean he was trustworthy. He'd said he wouldn't stop her from leaving, wouldn't follow her, and he hadn't. He was leaving the decision to work together in her hands. But trusting him went against everything Tom and Viper had taught her. It went against her most basic instincts. Then again, Tom's behavior had done a sudden one-eighty. Tom had told her to leave and not come back. She hoped he'd gotten to safety, along with the other ranch residents.

She glanced in the rearview, but there was nothing but a black void behind her. No Jared, and no answers, either.

Finn paced his Las Vegas condo. It wasn't posh or extravagant by any means, except for the movie memorabilia that decorated every wall. His insomnia kept him from falling into bed. Or maybe it was waiting for news that had him wound up. It was like anticipating a callback for a primo part. There was always too much time to run the performance through his mind, replaying how it went down, what he could have done differently. Too often, he'd been passed over.

But he was in control here. He got to do the casting, using the resources at the disposal of the Redemption Club. Had he chosen the wrong men for the job?

Finally, as he poured his third mojito, his phone rang. "Is it done?" he asked.

"Darren's dead." Tristan's voice was like cold steel. "Had to off him before he told Skye everything. Jesus. Where'd you find him? The guy was a chickenshit. Even used his real name."

"Fuck." Finn should have gone himself, but he had to have an alibi or a shitstorm of epic proportions could rain down on him, and it wouldn't come from the cops. "What'd you do with his body?"

"Left it there." Disgust filled Tristan's words, as if he would spit on the ground if he could. "Bennigan and Skye were there. Darren was about to tell them everything. I could tell, man. What else was I supposed to do?"

"And Loretta's dad?"

"Dead. I made sure of it."

At least one thing had gone right. Mark Sheldon wouldn't be looking for Finn anymore. "How?"

"Created a bit of chaos and took advantage of it. Shot him and burned down the building he was in."

"You're sure he's dead?"

"I stayed to make sure he didn't come out with the others."

"Good. And Skye? Will she come looking for Loretta?" Finn would never have chosen to lure Loretta, the young woman Tristan had brought to a Vegas party over a month ago, if he'd known this would happen. But she'd been too easy to resist. He'd employed his usual pickup lines, and the girl had been flattered, desperate to become an actress, by whatever means.

"I didn't get Skye."

"Fuck."

"Unfortunately, she won't be your only problem."

Finn slammed back the rest of his drink. "Hit me."

"Stone was here."

Finn froze. "What?"

"He came to the ranch tonight." Stone was part owner, but from what Ryan had said, Stone had never even mentioned Three Fortunes. It was only because the property was in the Redemption Club ledger that they'd discovered it. His current interest could only mean he'd learned Skye had come looking for Loretta, who was from the ranch. Finn's bowels threatened to fail him as he realized Stone was close to discovering what Ryan and Finn had been up to.

"What did he do there?" Finn asked.

"Met with the guy who runs the place, Tom Hamilton. Left about twenty minutes later."

"That's a long conversation." Shit, what could they have been talking about? "Did he visit any other parts of the ranch?"

"I don't think so. But I had to get out of there to back up Darren at the Roadhouse. I'm at the Hunting

Grounds now and the girls are secure. That's all I know, man. Except..."

"Fuck, what now?"

"You may have to deal with the cops. Loretta wasn't even eighteen."

He cursed again. He'd known she was young and naïve, but *that* young?

"Yeah. I'm sorry, man. I never would have brought her to a Club party if I'd known she was underage." Kidnapping charges wouldn't be the worst of their legal problems if they were caught. "At least Mark Sheldon didn't go to the police, and now he can't. There's only Skye to handle now."

She sounded like enough of a problem. Finn bit back his anger. "Let's hope the cops won't come looking for Loretta since her father's gone. Maybe nobody will care." Except for Skye, if she was Loretta's friend. And Stone, if he'd learned anything from his visit to the ranch. "Is Bennigan with Skye now?"

"I don't know. I got the hell out of there while I could."

"So you just gave up?" Finn cursed and pinched the bridge of his nose as he gathered the tattered threads of his composure. "You failed."

"So, my redemption...?"

"Has not been achieved. You still owe me." Finn used some centering techniques from acting class to calm himself and adopt the persona required to deal with complete morons. He reminded himself that Tristan was a friend, and loyal to the Club, and to Finn, in particular. "See if you can pick up Skye's trail. I need her." Maybe sweetening the pot would push Tristan to pull out all the stops. "If you find her, and eliminate any other complications, I'll let you in on the hunt, when she's ready."

"She'll be ours."

He hung up and shot to his feet. He had his own damage control to manage. If Stone was suspicious, he might ask Ryan questions. Ryan would have Finn's hide for letting Tristan into a big hunt for free, but without Tristan's work, there would be no big hunt. Ryan would have to agree that the outcome would be so much more satisfying when they had a true hunter as prey.

Skye Hamilton. She would be his, and he'd make her a star.

CHAPTER SEVEN

The next morning, Skye woke at dawn to unfamiliar surroundings. It took her a few seconds to remember how she'd ended up in the log home in the middle of the much smaller Pinebrook Ranch. Then the memories came crashing down.

The destruction and chaos at the ranch.

The devastation of Tom telling her to get out.

The confusion over whether to trust Jared.

Her gut clenched at the thought of facing the day, but instead of dwelling on things she couldn't control, she pushed herself out of bed and contemplated her next move. Forward movement was the only option, especially if someone—Stone?—was after her.

In accordance with the individual escape plan she'd developed years ago, Skye had driven to their neighbor's ranch. She'd slept restlessly in the home of Diane and Phil Barton. It was quiet, empty. The Bartons lived five minutes from Three Fortunes. Growing up, Skye had worked with their horses and become friends with the couple. They'd long since caught the travel bug and liked to leave for weeks at a time, and had sometimes hired Skye to do some things around the house while they were gone. They'd given her a key and invited her to help herself. They wouldn't be back for a month, after their son's wedding in San Diego and the long post-wedding cruise they'd booked for afterwards to relax. She could hide here for that month until the confusion and pain passed.

But danger and bad fortune would find her. Better

to confront it, head on.

Darren had said his objective was to obtain *her*, for somebody, and that she was his redemption. Was he acting on Stone's behalf, or someone else's? Either way, others might come for her. Now she had to figure out what the hell Darren had meant by redemption, and who wanted her—besides Jared.

And she had to figure it out fast. Standing still was a sure way to get caught, especially since the attackers had to have seen her truck at the ranch and would be on the lookout for it. And Jared obviously knew about her vehicle.

Seeing him at the ranch in the middle of the firefight had been a shock. He denied being part of the attack, denied shooting Darren, but he was always there, always in the thick of things. For all she knew, the attack was his version of *live fearlessly and play ferociously* or some bullshit like that.

But there had also been genuine intensity in his eyes when he'd nearly begged her for a few minutes of her time, when he'd told her to call him. He'd said he needed her, and she believed that. But for what? What would he expect in exchange for helping her find Loretta?

And then she had to consider that the attack had possibly given her a clean slate. Skye Hamilton could now move on, start a new life with a new identity. Again. She'd been banished from the ranch, anyway. Why should she care?

Because it had been home.

She showered and dressed in one of the changes of clothing she kept in the truck. She'd have to be out in public for this stage of her plan, but didn't want to draw attention to herself, so she was thankful the jeans and a white button-down shirt that nipped in at her waist gave her a bit of feminine flare but were nondescript. She kept the top two buttons undone, not to the point of immodesty, but interesting enough to shift attention away from her memorable eyes.

In the tiny kitchen, she scavenged through the cupboards, silently vowing to pay the Bartons back for the beef jerky and granola bars she took. Leaning against the counter, she consumed one of the bars without tasting it.

You never know what—or who—you might have to use to survive. She heard Viper's voice in her head, imparting one of his lessons. This morning's tools of survival? Granola bars and jerky. The work truck the Bartons left in their detached garage. And the angry fire that burned in her gut.

The insensitive morning sky had lightened to a blend of rosy orange and soft blue that was supposed to be beautiful as she made her way to the garage. Skye only saw flames against the backdrop of a dark night. Mr. Barton's truck was cleaned and fueled, the keys behind the visor. Skye wondered what it was like to trust so confidently and completely. She added borrowing the vehicle to her debt.

She avoided driving by the ranch, not certain what, or who, she might run into if she went back. Heading east on Interstate 40 toward Flagstaff, she merged onto old Route 66 to take her into the quaint downtown area just north of the train tracks, parked the Barton truck on a quiet residential side street, and walked the few quick blocks into the business district. The bank was her first stop. From her safe deposit box, she retrieved her envelope containing identification documents, a burner phone and charger, and a couple thousand dollars in cash. Viper's friend had created new papers for everyone in the compound a couple years ago. Though she wasn't ready to give up her identity, the new cards could be useful as she put her plan into play. Once she charged the phone, she hoped to find a voicemail from Tom, who was the only one who had her number, saying that he'd reached safety— if he wanted to talk to her anymore.

Your own fault, her conscience nagged. Her chest ached. Surely, he'd had time to reconsider evicting her from his life. Either way, she wanted to know what, exactly, Stone had told Tom to make him turn her out.

With the cash, she purchased a used vehicle at the car lot a few streets over. The tiny coupe had apparently circumnavigated the globe, based on its odometer reading, but the price was right, and wouldn't deplete all of her cash.

She drove to the recreation center where she kept a gym locker, and retrieved her backup stash. Inside the backpack, there was a spare handgun, some additional cash and ammunition and several changes of clothes. She put it on the floor of the passenger seat and thought about her next move. There were only two paths open to her, it seemed—to pursue her pursuers or to move on and let the attack go. And give up on finding Loretta.

In the end, she couldn't let the asshole who'd torn apart her family and lured Loretta from her home get away with it. Besides, there might be others coming for her, if Darren's message could be believed.

At the downtown library, she used her new identity and the public computers to search the Internet for news of the incident at the ranch. One paragraph summed up the devastation that had changed her life forever. According to the report, several buildings had suffered various degrees of damage. There were two casualties but the names were yet to be released. Skye's pulse accelerated as she searched for more information, finding none. One of the bodies had to be Darren, but who else had died?

Trying to stifle her frustration at the lack of information, she accessed Mark's credit card account, but there had been no further charge activity on it since the Kingman convenience store.

She searched for more information about Robert Stone—in particular, his relationship to Legacy. Darren's card was tied to it all. The Legacy website pronounced the location was a posh hotel-casino complex in Las Vegas, not far from the Strip. The reviews indicated it catered to the wealthy and promised elegance as well as a good time. From what she'd seen during her brief visit a couple of days ago, she couldn't argue otherwise. And Stone would be there. According to Emily, Stone was hosting another party tonight.

It looked like Skye was heading back to Vegas for a good time.

Skye hadn't contacted him. The afternoon after Jared had seen her at the firefight and made the decision to let her go, hoping it would forge the trust he needed from her before moving forward, he still hadn't heard from her.

He'd stayed in a nearby motel overnight, doing his best to rid his hair and clothes of the smell of smoke and hoping Skye would contact him if she needed help. Not that he expected her to. God, the pain and vulnerability he'd read in her eyes, beneath the layers of distrust and anger, haunted him. Had her uncle truly turned his back on her because of something Stone said? Had Stone really been to the ranch? When Jared called Meyer and Duffy to check in, they said Stone had ordered them to take the day off yesterday, but they were back to guarding him today. If Stone had come to Arizona, he hadn't stayed long. Just long enough to wreak havoc in Skye's family.

Even when Jared's family drove him nuts, they'd known he'd be there for them.

Except you weren't.

Fuck.

He hadn't been there when his mother had been murdered by her latest boyfriend. So he'd tried to make up for it when he was discharged. But Chelsea had found him overbearing and pushed him away.

He apparently sucked at knowing what to do with the women in his life. But he'd be damned if he screwed up again.

Using his GSS credentials and a contact at the Las Vegas Police Department, he went into the Coconino County Sheriff's office to ask for an update on the chaos at the ranch.

"Two dead bodies," the deputy sheriff reported.

Jared's gut clenched. Skye had made it out, hadn't she? "Who?"

"Darren Boscoe." Apparently, Skye's cowboy had given his true first name. "And Mark Sheldon. Each shot in the chest."

Mark Sheldon. The man Jared had questioned briefly in Malibu. The man who'd accompanied Skye to California. Was she grieving for Mark? Did she even know he was dead?

"Everyone else scattered," the deputy reported. "The place is like a ghost town. Of course, that's what we'd expect from an anti-government group. It's not like they'd come to us if they needed help. Hamilton and his crew don't trust anyone."

He tried thinking like Skye. If he were alone, looking for whoever was after him, where would he go next?

He'd go to the source, Robert Stone.

So he drove to Vegas. Maybe there was one female on the planet he could please. He drove straight to Haley's high school to pick her up. He'd take her out for a little Tuesday surprise, maybe grab one of those blended frozen coffee drinks she was into. He could use a little pick-me-up, too, mostly from his little sister's company.

As Jared pulled up to the school, he caught Haley's eye. A few seconds later, she'd extracted herself from her circle of friends and launched into Jared, wrapping him in a warm hug. She'd been especially affectionate in the past few months, since Chelsea had withdrawn. It didn't take a family counselor to tell him that Haley was anxious, upset, and needy. Not a good combination in an already spirited seventeen-year-old girl.

"You're back!" she exclaimed.

"I'm back." He gave her an extra squeeze. She looked so much like a younger version of their mother, with her blonde hair flowing loose around her shoulders and her wide smile transforming her face. His heart clenched. "What's new, kiddo?"

She pulled away and wrinkled her nose. "Why do you smell like a chimney?"

Though he'd showered at the motel, maybe he should have taken the time to stop by his house to put on clothes that hadn't been in the same room as the ones he'd worn last night. And to shave, he added as she reached up to scrape a palm against his stubble.

"You should take better care of yourself."

"I missed you, Bossy Pants," he teased.

Some of the concern in her eyes lifted. "Please tell me you're here to take me home." At least one of his sisters was excited about staying at his house.

"Still working on that. I may have to leave town again soon." She frowned and he hastened to reassure her. "It's only for a few more days, I hope. Once I find Chelsea, I'm staying put." The other kids releasing from school were spilling over the sidewalk where they stood. "How about we move this discussion to the coffee shop down the street?"

"But I have to go to Aunt Jane's after?"

"Afraid so. Not for much longer, though." In a few days, she'd be eighteen, and in six weeks, she'd graduate. Still, she'd mentioned sticking around for college, and he could give her a stable foundation to call home. "Besides, at least you have a safe place to live, right?"

"Aunt Jane's on a bender."

"A *what?*" He stopped in the middle of the sidewalk and some poor kid smacked into him from behind.

"Watch it," the boy said, then paled as he looked up from his cell phone to see Jared's glare. The boy hurried away with a mumbled apology.

Jared barely noticed. "Did you say a *bender?*"

Haley tugged him along to his car and slapped the back of her hand against his shoulder. "Not that kind of bender. She just won't stop yelling at me, all because I had Griffin over and forgot to leave my bedroom door open."

It was a good thing Griffin wasn't here right now, or he'd plow a fist into the boy's face. He got in the car and took several calming breaths before pulling out into traffic. "You forgot?"

"Okay, so maybe I did it on purpose. But it's only because we were listening to music, and Aunt Jane hates my music. I didn't want to bug her, or have her embarrass me in front of him, you know?"

He did know. He wasn't so far out of his teens that he could forget that kind of teen angst, or the grip of teen love. Or what seemed like love. He'd had a few crushes in his time, but having an exotic dancer for a mother had a way of making one face the facts of life early on. And watching their mother go through men like tissues didn't inspire a romantic notion of love. Jared wondered if he'd ever find a partner he could trust to love him—and not to leave when life became monotonous.

Being away in the military when Phoebe Bennigan had been murdered had taught him even more life lessons, like the burden of guilt was an unshakeable one. There were lessons he wished he could protect his sister from, but she had to learn some things for herself.

Lessons like, some people don't stay forever, but the ones who matter will choose you over anything else. Or so he'd heard. Also important was surviving until you found the people who *would* stay. The ones who loved you deep enough, hard enough, would withstand the hard knocks life would throw your way.

"Haley, you have to obey your Aunt Jane's house rules. At least for a little longer." He parked and followed her into the coffee shop.

"Don't worry. I won't mess things up for us. I know I need Aunt Jane, but I'd rather it be you."

The knife twisted in Jared's heart as they placed their orders. "How are the birthday party plans coming along?"

Instead of boosting her mood as he'd intended, Haley's frown deepened. "Not sure there's going to be one. She won't let me have it at her house."

"I'll talk to her. We'll figure something out."

"Whatever." She sounded like she didn't believe him.

"You only turn eighteen once. Email me the details of what you want and we'll make it happen."

She sent him a tentative smile. "Only if you have time. I know you're busy looking for Chelsea. That's more important." Before she turned away, there were tears in her eyes. Lately, her emotions tended to swing back and forth like a wrecking ball slamming against his heart.

"Any news from Chelsea?" she asked.

"No, sweetheart. I haven't heard from her."

"Me, either." She frowned down at her drink. "I thought, maybe with my birthday coming up, I might hear something."

He hadn't told Haley he suspected something, or someone, was keeping Chelsea from contacting them. He made a mental note to check in again with the LVPD detective he'd contacted when he'd realized Chelsea wasn't coming back on her own. Despite the information Jared had sent him, the detective's current theory was that Chelsea had indeed left town for the fresh start she'd threatened, but he'd promised to keep his eyes and ears open for any new information. Jared had interpreted that to mean he had to go out on his own to find Chelsea.

Despite the argument he'd had with Chelsea a couple weeks ago, he couldn't believe she would just disappear. First of all, she wouldn't leave Haley. But she'd also written faithfully to Jared, every week, during all the years he'd been stationed away from home. After all their family unit—messed up as it was—had been through, he had trouble believing she would simply abandon them over a ridiculous argument, in the need to display her independence. They'd been too close—if not geographically, emotionally. And if that wasn't enough evidence Chelsea hadn't intended to disappear, there'd been no activity from her credit cards. The detective had pointed out her accounts had been maxed out, so she could be living on cash. But dancing had been her main source of income, so leaving her client address book and costumes behind didn't make sense.

He visited with Haley a bit longer, encouraged her to keep her grades up, even with graduation only a few weeks away, and drove her to Aunt Jane's. He headed toward his own home, where he'd have just enough time to get ready to provide security for Stone's party tonight, but as he was pulling into the garage, his phone rang. His pulse stuttered, hoping the call was from Skye finally reaching out, but he soon recognized Dev's ring tone.

"I'm in Vegas," Jared reported before Dev could give him heck.

Dev snorted. "I know. That's not why I called. I just got done with a very interesting conversation."

Skye. "Yeah?"

"With Skye Hamilton, but I'm guessing by the shit-eating grin I hear in your voice that you already knew that part. You might have given me a heads-up."

"Your responses needed to be genuine. Skye would have scented bullshit from several miles away."

"I'm not sure what I said was enough, unfortunately, to convince her you're a good guy. She's one skittish woman. Demanded to know facts and figures. What kinds of cases you'd been working lately, etc. Hell, for a moment, I thought you were interviewing for another job."

"You trace the call?"

"You know I trace all calls," he said, which was one of the reasons why Jared didn't mind Skye checking up on him. "Came from a payphone here in Vegas, inside Excalibur."

"That's good news." She was here. He glanced out the window as if he'd see her standing in his yard or parked across the street. "How did it end?"

"No clue. She hung up after I expounded on your virtues for a while. I told her to ask you about Chelsea."

Jared was silent a long moment, focusing on relaxing the squeeze that tightened his throat every time he thought about his missing sister.

"Was that okay?" Dev asked, sounding uncharacteristically uncertain.

"She'd have heard about her soon, anyway, if she decides to work with me, instead of against me." He hadn't wanted to tell her the details about Chelsea until he was certain which side she was working for. He wanted to trust she wouldn't go to Stone—for the money or for other reasons—and tell the man what Jared was up to. "She needs to understand she can trust me." And he had to know he could trust her. He just hoped she chose to come to him instead of Stone.

CHAPTER EIGHT

A couple hours later, Jared tried to hide his frustration as he waited in the living room of Stone's luxurious Henderson, Nevada mansion, just twenty minutes from the Vegas Strip. Everything about the estate, from the separate one-third-acre conservatory lined with Greek pillars and overflowing with lush green plants—they were in a desert, for Christ's sake— to the private tennis court, large pool with cascading waterfall and six-car garage filled with classic cars, screamed entitlement and wealth. Power.

If Chelsea had fallen into this trap, Jared wasn't surprised. She'd always been drawn to the glamorous life, wanting the finer things, hoping a man would rescue her. Just like their mother had hoped. But that kind of lifestyle didn't come cheap.

It had cost their mother everything.

Another damn party. Stone was the very definition of a social butterfly, except Jared suspected the parties were a way to stroke the man's ego. Still, like the professional he was, Jared had donned his tux and was ready to serve. He was doing this for Chelsea, still hopeful he'd run across someone at one of the parties who had seen her, or heard about her. And for Skye, who was apparently looking for another missing woman.

"Ivy, people will be arriving soon," Stone said to his daughter as he knotted his tuxedo tie in front of the living room mirror. "Shouldn't you be getting ready?"

Slender and gracefully beautiful like the marble pillars filling Stone's conservatory, Ivy's composure also replicated their hardness. Jared had only encountered her once before, when, as manager of her father's Legacy Hotel and Casino, she'd hosted Stone's birthday party there a couple weeks ago. She hadn't spoken to Jared once. He didn't take it personally. She'd barely given anyone a cursory glance, as if they were all beneath her. Her bearing was as regal as an ice princess. Then again, if Jared had a father like Robert Stone, he'd probably have grown up withdrawn, too.

Stone's son, Ryan, was leaning against the bar that had been set up for the event, already on his second drink. He watched quietly, almost morosely, as the action unfolded around him. As near as Jared could figure, the young man traveled and partied as much as his father. Ryan was thirty, older than his successful half-sister by about a year, but apparently had yet to find his calling.

"I was just about to leave," Ivy replied, her tone cool. She'd been here most of the day, overseeing the setup and instructing the string quartet and catering staff on choice of music and decor. Her personality might be chilly, but she'd created a sense of warmth and elegance in a short time. "I'll return in time for the party but I can't stay long. I'm catching the red-eye tonight."

"Damn it, you don't need to go on this trip," Stone roared. Behind him, Ryan stopped swirling the ice in his glass and straightened, but didn't jump to his sister's rescue.

Ivy didn't back away at the sudden outburst, but Jared caught a quick flinch, a crack in the stone facade. Obviously used to dealing with her father's mercurial moods, she quickly recovered. "You're the boss."

"Damn right, I am." Stone stepped up close to her and gripped her chin. Jared stiffened, not liking how the man was handling her. Though he was still contracted to protect Stone, Jared was ready to step in if Ivy indicated distress. A shield came down over her bottle-green eyes, hard, yet fragile like glass. "I expect my employees to look professional and be respectful. I expect even more from my own flesh and blood. You're a reflection of me. Always remember that."

"I understand." She took a couple steps back to retrieve her purse from the couch, putting distance between her and her father. Jared took a calming breath, admiring how she'd smoothly diffused the tension. Her head tipped upward, the delicate point of her chin and the porcelain of her skin reminding Jared of the columns again. Or an ice sculpture. "May I go?"

"Be back in an hour. I want you here in plenty of time to serve as hostess." With a quick glance at the rest of the room's occupants, Ivy pivoted on her three-inch heels and left. Stone's gaze cut to Jared. "Let your team know that all attendees should have one of these." He scooped a black-and-silver-embossed invitation off his desk and handed it to Jared. "Or at least a printed copy of an email from Ivy, since the invites went out at the last minute and not all of them could be hand-delivered. The man at the gate should keep everyone else out."

Jared nodded. "If I'm to continue as your bodyguard, I need to get some things straight."

"Such as?"

"You can't go off on your own, especially to seek out people you think might harm you, and expect us to protect you. You need to be honest about where you're going. At all times." He was fishing to see if Stone would admit he'd gone to Three Fortunes.

A caterer bustled by with a tray of glasses for the bar.

Stone glared, then barked an order. "Everyone out except for Jared." The caterer left. Ryan took his time finishing his drink, set it on the bar, and sauntered out with a smirk.

"I didn't want to speak of this with an audience," Stone said when they were alone.

"Speak of what, sir? You mentioned you were going to handle the blackmailer personally, and then you disappeared."

Stone sank into a chair and fiddled with his monogrammed cufflinks. "What's important is that I received another blackmail demand. I thought I'd handled the issue." Was he talking about how he'd had Tom Hamilton banish Skye and terrorized her ranch?

"Meyer and Duffy didn't inform me of a new threat."

Stone smiled without humor. "I didn't tell them. I didn't know who I could trust. Still don't, sometimes." His gaze narrowed on Jared. "People lie to me all the time, to get on my good side or get what they want. It doesn't matter, as long as they don't try to use the lies against me. Or use *me*."

Did Stone know about Jared's connection to Chelsea, or why he was really working for him? Jared forced his expression to remain neutral, despite the tension rippling beneath his skin. "I always do my best to ensure the safety and security of those who are entrusted to me. I'm a careful man, as are you."

Stone seemed to weigh Jared's words for a long moment, then nodded. "I am. But I also know when to keep my business, or my travel plans, to myself." He stood, signaling the end of the conversation. "Keep your eyes open for anything out of the ordinary tonight, but the key is that the guests enjoy themselves. I have some important clients coming. I want them to have a great time. No surprises. And no more questions."

Around nine o'clock that night, like Alice falling down the rabbit hole, Skye slid into another world. Actually, she willingly jumped.

She parked a quarter mile down the road, which was lined with the other guests' vehicles, and walked to Stone's gated estate, hauling her box of goodies— goodies she was hoping would earn her passage into the party. She wasn't so much crashing the party as breaking in. At the small guardhouse she pretended to stumble in her heels. The guard rushed forward to grab the box from her before it tipped. She recognized him as one of the guards she'd seen through her scope at the Malibu party.

"Heavy," he observed, then peeked inside. He arched a brow at her. His gaze warmed appreciatively as it slid down her body, no longer obscured by the box. Her weapons of choice this evening were top shelf liquor and a killer dress. And, if necessary, she'd scrounge up some tears. "This isn't BYOB." The guard smiled. Good, he was the flirty type. And he had a sense of humor. "There's free liquor inside."

"Only if I get this in there." She winked. "Emily—she's the bartender tonight—called in a panic. Apparently, not all of the liquor was delivered today."

The man's smile fell away and her gut clenched. Had she laid it on too thick? "I'm sorry, ma'am, but nobody gets in without an invitation. Those are my orders."

She bit the inside of her cheek to make her eyes water. "Please. This is my first week at this job. If I don't come through, Emily said there would be hell to pay for both of us. You know how Stone is." She shifted, making sure the length of her leg, bare from mid-thigh down to her strappy high heels, was evident. The guard's gaze went straight to it. Steam would probably come out of Jared's ears if he knew his elite security team could be manipulated so easily.

"Okay, but I'll expect to see you behind the bar with Emily when I go inside at shift change."

She smiled and took the box of liquor from him. "I look forward to it."

"Service entrance is around the side. I'll radio Meyer that you're on your way."

A burly man with no sense of humor let her in as promised and then disappeared through a swinging door. The noise of the party grew louder before it shut behind him. Inside the immense gourmet kitchen, she set the box on the counter and went through the door as well. She skirted the bar, where Emily might recognize her. Thankfully, the woman was busy fulfilling drink orders and loading servers' trays with champagne flutes and water glasses.

Despite the cloak of confidence Skye had attempted to pull around her, panic crawled up her throat. Even in the sleek, black halter dress and rhinestone earrings she'd found at the secondhand store a couple miles off the Strip, and with her hair scooped up into a pile of curls that cascaded down her back, she felt naked, in more ways than one. Usually, she wore more clothing to hide her feminine curves, not wanting to attract attention among the men at the testosterone-laden ranch, but to blend in with this crowd, she'd worn less. Much less. She wished that included going barefoot, as her toes experienced a painful squeeze within her heels. She channeled the pain, using it to ground herself. Stone currently had home court advantage. She couldn't let her nerves distract her, so she pulled on her tough-girl image and acted as if she belonged among the rich and famous.

But she didn't belong at the lush estate tucked into the base of desert hills, surrounded by the chitter-chatter of conversation and big, overly bright smiles of a party in full swing.

Feeling like a fake made her skin crawl. Life on the ranch was at the opposite end of the noise-and-crowds spectrum. There, the wind through the pines, the birdsong, and the chorus of insects had been her companions, most days.

Choking down a sudden bout of homesickness, she focused on who she was, rather than what she pretended to be. Skye Hamilton fought for the underdog. The forgotten. She'd translate Latin phrases, be her own damn redemption, and fight until the ranch was restored and Loretta was found. And she'd start by searching the sacred ground of the man who seemed to link all of the above.

Stone was currently holding court on the other

side of the enormous living room, wielding his charm like a weapon. Around him, a gaggle of beautiful people hung on every word. *This* was the kind of life Loretta craved? Skye didn't understand it, but she supposed everyone needed a place to belong.

She glanced about, wondering if Jared was here or if he'd finally lost his job when he'd failed to hand her over to Stone. But her body wasn't tingling, as it normally did when he was near, so maybe she was safe from that distraction tonight. Or maybe she'd rebuilt her defenses against him during their time apart.

Jared was who he said he was, but that didn't mean she had to trust him. Devlin Grimm had vouched for his partner's trustworthiness and urged her to call Jared, or to meet in the GSS offices, on semi-neutral ground. Given the way her last three encounters with Jared had gone, she'd passed on the offer. Dev had insisted she ask Jared about someone named Chelsea. Maybe she would. Then again, maybe it would be better to steer clear of the man.

Skye kept her smile in place as she wound her way through the clusters of people that filled the living room. Laughter and conversation danced around her and spilled out through a pair of French doors onto a large flagstone patio that overlooked a vibrant lawn and a swimming pool with a waterfall. The water bill here must be ginormous.

Beyond the grass, the windowpanes of a large conservatory glinted, reflecting the moonlight and the flickering lanterns that surrounded the patio area.

Wanting to cling to the anonymity of the crowd, she stepped back inside and stopped near a table that held a four-foot ice sculpture of a Greek pillar, the same symbol of Legacy Hotel and Casino. How self-indulgent.

"Isn't it gorgeous?" a woman gushed beside her. "Robert throws the classiest parties."

Skye smiled and chatted with the woman and her male companion for a few moments, encouraging them to do most of the talking. But her mind was on her primary objective, counting the seconds until she could slip away. They had Texan accents and an oil-money bank account, and the woman appeared to have no problems with public displays of affection. Skye, on the other hand, squirmed uncomfortably.

She hadn't grown up around touchy-feely people. She'd always been given the impression that outward demonstrations of love were unwelcome.

This man's arm was locked around his woman's shoulder as if it belonged there. His gaze continually strayed to his wife's bosom, which was only fair since she had obviously gone to great trouble to put it on exhibit, even enhancing it with glittery lotion. Actually, her chest formed a nice framework for the diamonds dripping around her neck.

Between socially required responses, Skye's gaze subtly wandered the room, searching for the opening she needed. She couldn't fail. She'd come so far. Hell, she owed it to Tom, Viper and the others. She'd destroyed their family unit. So she kept the interested smile pasted on her face and pretended she belonged here.

Jared had known the moment Skye walked into the party, and it wasn't because Meyer had told him she'd sweet-talked her way through the gate just ten minutes ago. It was the prickle of hair rising along the back of his neck, as if the woman had her own energy source and it was directly connected to his nervous system. A flood of relief that she was safe was quickly followed by a sharp anger that she'd endanger herself by walking directly into the minefield.

But he couldn't fault her. Hadn't he done something similar, hoping it would lead to Chelsea?

He'd had a gut feeling she'd come tonight. Remembering how she'd scoped out Stone from the Malibu rooftop, and walked right into the Roadhouse to meet Jared, he'd anticipated her arrival and instructed

Meyer and Duffy to let her in without an invite. He wanted to see what she was up to, and prove to her that she could trust him.

Discreetly, he shifted to get a better look at the room and spotted her fifty feet away. She was beautiful. His gaze traced the curve of her profile, sliding down her cheek to her bare shoulder. The cut of her halter top dress and the way she'd pulled her hair up and back accentuated the slender line of her throat, the soft slope of her shoulders and her toned biceps. He sucked in a sharp breath as he caught sight of her long legs. He'd only seen her in pants or jeans, so when her dress ended at mid-thigh, her bare, sculpted thighs and calves were like a jolt to his system. The sudden image of those legs wrapped around his waist nearly made him shake with desire. He had to look away for a moment to collect his wits.

When he looked back, she was excusing herself from the older couple she'd been chatting with near the appetizer table. His eyes tracked her—right up until the moment she disappeared down a hallway that led to Stone's private rooms.

His gaze sought Stone at the opposite end of the living room. The man hadn't noticed Skye. Ivy was keeping up her role as hostess, overseeing the catering staff between talking with guests. Ryan and his friends were, as usual, taking up space near the bar.

Skye had selected the perfect moment, slipping away unnoticed by everyone but him. After a word to Meyer to take over the security duties, he casually trailed his rabbit.

In the hallway the sudden abundance of fresh air cooled Skye's lungs and sharpened her focus. She wished she'd asked a waiter for a bottle of water to wet her dry mouth. But that would have risked someone noticing. She still held the champagne flute she'd taken from a nearby tray to fit in at the party, but she had yet to take a sip. She dumped it into a potted plant as she walked farther down the hall and set the empty glass on a side table. She kept the cocktail napkin she'd been using to keep her prints off of everything.

She didn't have long if the guards were thorough about keeping security tight, so she sped her pace, nearly jogging as she tried several doors along the hallway and found them unlocked, but also uninteresting. A couple of bedrooms, a bathroom, a sitting area with a bay window.

She tried the last door, behind her, and found it locked. She pulled out the lock picks she'd hidden as pins in her hair, releasing a soft tendril that curled against her cheek. Making quick work of the lock, she stepped inside the room and shut the door behind her, more relaxed at having one more barrier between herself and that foreign world.

It was Stone's den, complete with an entire wall of ceiling-to-floor bookcases. Skye let only her gaze skim along the spines of several first-edition classics and beautiful sculptures. Again using a cocktail napkin to cover her fingers, she began her search in earnest. Surprisingly, the drawers of the desk were unlocked— probably because he had little to hide in there. Pencils, pens, the usual office supplies.

The second drawer, however, had her sucking in a breath. There were two torn half-cards inside, but they didn't fit together. There was writing along the edge of each, a name and a date scrawled in ink. Darren Boscoe was written on one. She remembered the card that had spilled from Darren's dead hand. Same suit and number—eight of diamonds. This one was a match to the half she had in her things back at the motel. At least now she knew for sure that Darren was connected to Stone.

The other card had another name. Tristan Floyd. Her breath caught. Tristan was one of the men at the ranch, the one who'd delivered Jared's phone message. He'd known she and Jared were meeting at the

Roadhouse. Had Tristan been working for Stone?

She noted the dates on the cards. Darren's was from eighteen months ago. Tristan's was from five years ago, and it was a face card. Did that mean anything? There had to be more answers somewhere. But she found nothing else of note in the drawers.

Her gaze swept the room, looking for something that led to Loretta. Or something she could confront Stone with, and exchange for information on Loretta. The cards, while incriminating, could easily be explained away.

Her attention was drawn to the framed art on the wall across from the desk. The oil painting was massive, but what captured her interest was its subject. Zeus on Mount Olympus. Did Stone think he deserved to be among the gods, or that he *was* some kind of god? From what she'd heard about the man, and observed through her rifle's scope, it was entirely possible.

On a hunch, she felt around the edges of the frame and found a hidden button. Her fingers released it with a touch, and the painting swung out toward her from a side hinge. A safe lay behind it, tucked into the wall. Skye wasn't a safecracker. Her street skills only extended so far.

Footsteps sounded on the marble flooring in the hall, then stopped on the other side of the door. With shaking hands, Skye quickly swung the painting back in place and stepped away, gauging the distance to the nearest exits. She shifted toward the French doors that led outside, but before she could get closer to freedom, the den's door opened and she altered her plan. Running in heels and scaling the six-foot stone wall in her dress wasn't her preferred escape strategy. She'd have to talk her way out of this one.

Her gaze collided with familiar caramel eyes and her thoughts scattered. *Jared.* Had her telltale heart been beating loud enough that he could hear it from across the house? *Impostor. Lub-dub. Impostor.* The *lub-dubs* sped up and became more erratic as his expression hardened.

She straightened, preparing for battle, but her heart continued to hammer out its staccato rhythm.

"What are you doing here?" Jared forced his glance around the den before he allowed himself to look directly at Skye again.

Skye. In the flesh. Safe.

Relief coursed through him, as did a sudden hunger. He'd been totally unprepared for the impact of her lithe body dressed to the nines, her hair swept back except for a piece that had fallen to frame her face and accentuate eyes so deep blue a man could drown in them. They shimmered as emotions—guilt, acknowledgment, calculation—flashed in rapid succession, like sunlight dancing on waves.

She lifted one shoulder as if it were no consequence to get caught inside the host's private study. Not just any host, but the wealthy, powerful Robert Stone.

Her top teeth sank into her plump lower lip. She released it to send him a sheepish smile. "Needed some air."

"Most people go outside for that."

"I was looking for a bottle of water."

His brows went up. "There's a fully stocked, open bar out there. You could have anything you want."

"Except a goddamn *sealed* bottle of water." She pressed her lips together.

"Sealed?"

"It's safer that way." She stopped, as if that was all the explanation required. He recalled how, at the Roadhouse, she'd ordered an unopened bottle of beer. Was she paranoid that someone would drug her?

He shook his head, baffled by the sidetracked conversation. "I didn't mean why are you here, in Robert Stone's private, *locked* den—though that's dangerous in itself. I meant why are you in Stone's home at all. You should have come to me first." Her lack of faith irritated him. "What have you been up to the past twenty-four hours?"

Her chin tipped upward. "This and that. A call to your partner, retracing the credit card trail Loretta left, finding evidence against your boss." She pulled off the cocky, confident attitude, but her eyes occasionally flicked about the room, as if looking for escape.

"I told you, Stone's not my boss. What did you find?" He took a couple steps closer.

She squared her shoulders. "Nothing I'm ready to share with you. Look, I needed a place to breathe. I figured I'd confront Stone, but I couldn't think in there, so I wandered back here." She was back to lying to him, then. *One step forward, two steps back.* She was leading him in a merry dance.

"There were plenty of doors off the living room that would have taken you onto the patio or into the garden." She'd been standing not five feet from one of those exits when he'd first seen her. "Better yet, walk out the front door and don't look back. I'll meet you somewhere and we'll finally talk."

She ignored his suggestion and slipped off her three-inch black stilettos. "Wriggling my toes in the carpet helps. Not sure how women wear these on a regular basis." She dangled the shoes in his face. He wouldn't be surprised if she planned to use them as a weapon, yet he didn't sense she was a direct threat. Not at the moment, anyway.

Her comment had his gaze sliding down her body to the delicate arches of her feet. He just as slowly slid his gaze back up. "I doubt you had much opportunity to dress up at the ranch."

Hurt crested on those waves in her eyes but quickly drifted away. She attempted another casual, one-shouldered shrug but it came off jerky. "Guess that won't be a problem anymore."

Fuck. Was that why she hadn't come to him? She

still thought that he'd had something to do with blowing up her ranch, even after talking to Dev. "I had nothing to do with that. *Nothing*," he repeated when she snorted. He sucked in a deep breath. "Okay, maybe something."

She arched an elegant eyebrow. "Go on."

"Stone or somebody else must have followed me from California. Darren Boscoe, or the guy he met up with. They had to be Stone's men."

A line knit her brow. "I thought *you* were one of Stone's men. You don't seem like the type to be left out of the loop. And you know Darren's full name."

"Because it was on the coroner's report. I was looking into it for you."

"And Tristan Floyd? What do you know about him?"

"I don't know that name." The power of her distrusting gaze—it gave *lost at sea* a new meaning—had him blowing out a breath to steady himself. Her gaze slid to the door behind him and he sensed her desire to bolt, so he stepped closer, putting her within arm's reach. "Are you ready to sit down and talk yet?"

"Maybe." She looked up at him from under a thick curtain of dark lashes. "Maybe I was hoping you'd follow me." Her tone was like a satin-gloved hand sliding down his torso to his groin, even though they hadn't touched.

"Stop with the games." He didn't recognize his own voice, husky with desire.

Her pink tongue darted out to lick her bottom lip. "Maybe I'm starting to trust you." She jerked her head toward the direction of the party and her hair slid across her bare shoulder. He shivered as if it had touched him. "Out there, you didn't raise the alarm when I showed up, did you?"

He took a step closer. "Of course not. I'm the one who told Meyer and Duffy to let you in if you showed up." A flash of confusion crossed her expression. "Cut the bullshit. If you trusted me, you could have called

me or gone straight to my house. You have the address.
Why Stone's study?" What did she think she'd find
here? And would she tell him? It was important to him
that she trust him. In turn, he had to trust that
whatever she'd tell him was the truth. For Chelsea's
sake.

"I was looking for something."

"And did you find it?" He took another step toward
her and she stepped back, bumping against the desk
behind her.

"No." Her blue eyes flared in an intriguing mix of
invitation and warning, strength and vulnerability. Or
maybe he was just seeing what he wanted to see.
"What are you going to do now that you have me
cornered?"

He suspected his rabbit was never cornered, never
completely defenseless. "We're going to talk."

But his body was at odds with his brain as he
lifted a hand to her neck, then trailed his palm over the
silk of her dress to the skin of her shoulder, which was
just as sleek as the material barely covering her. He
wanted more than conversation. He wanted to touch
her. Her expression was wary, ethereal as she watched
him inch closer. His skin hummed with the contact
beneath his palm, and she quivered beneath his
fingertips. Her gaze slid to his lips and she bit down on
her bottom lip. He was tempted to dip his head down
and taste her for himself.

Her teeth released her lip. "This isn't talking.
Touching wasn't part of the bargain."

"We haven't struck a bargain yet."

"Who's Chelsea?" The question was like a bucket
of ice water over his head. "Is she your girlfriend?"

He dropped his hand and stepped back. He sucked
a shallow breath into his squeezed lungs. But before he
could answer, the door swung open.

"Well, what have we here?" Ryan Stone asked.

Jared turned to face the man, cursing his timing.
"I'm handling this. Go back to the party."

"Should we call security?" his friend asked. Finn something.

Ryan snorted. "This guy *is* security, but I'm pretty sure this area is off-limits, even to him. Maybe we should take this to my father." His eyes lit with challenge and a predatory type of glee. The little shit was probably angry Jared had kicked his friend's girl out of the previous party.

Taking advantage of the interruption and Jared's momentary distraction, Skye took off through the French doors.

Fuck, not again.

He was about to chase after her when Finn stepped between him and her escape route. "Guess she didn't want you, man." He grinned.

Jared moved around him and outside. He ran across the grass, but the grounds were pitch black and quiet except for the occasional lights along the footpath, the lanterns on the patio, and the chirp of crickets and soft spray of sprinklers on the lawn. After eyeing the tall stucco wall that bordered the property, he opted to head for the conservatory instead, supposing she could hide in there. Plants of every type filled the space like an overgrown jungle and he kept to the crushed stone footpath, but there was no sign of Skye.

He went back to Stone's study, where the air still crackled with the electric connection between him and Skye. Ryan and his friend were gone. Shit. They were probably talking to Stone right now, telling the man what they'd seen.

"I want all eyes watching for Skye Hamilton and her vehicle," he said into the mic that connected him to Meyer and Duffy. He rattled off the make and model of the truck again, though he doubted that's what she'd been driving. She was too smart for that. He looked around the study, trying to see it through her eyes. What had she hoped to find here? Jared had already looked through everything he could get his hands on, hoping to find a link to Chelsea. Had Skye found anything? She would have had a difficult time concealing any papers or objects within her curve-hugging dress.

"What the hell," Stone snapped as he stalked into his study. His cheeks were ruddy with anger and alcohol. "Ryan told me he saw you in here with a stranger, a woman."

"Skye Hamilton."

"Was she armed?"

"No."

"I thought I'd done enough to keep her away." Stone's gaze moved about his study, not landing on anything in particular. What was Stone concerned she'd find?

"She seems the persistent sort."

"What did she say?" *Say?* That seemed an odd thing for Stone to worry about.

"Your son interrupted before I could talk to her and she took off." He looked toward the open French doors.

"She got away again?" Stone's face reddened further. "I'm ending my contract with GSS. You and the other guards can leave now. I'll find someone who can keep one troublesome girl from breaking into my home." He pivoted and walked out.

Damn it. Skye owed him, big-time, for costing him his only lead on Chelsea. In fact, she owed him a new lead.

His gaze fell on the objects Skye had left behind. Her shoes still lay side-by-side on the floor near the desk where she'd left them, almost as if she'd known from the moment he'd cornered her in the office that she would be making a break for it. She'd jettisoned dead weight and used her escape hatch—again. First her duffel full of weapons, and now these.

He picked up the shoes by their straps. Sexy, simple black, but the heels were deadly, and highly impractical. The scent of jasmine wafted to him. How could someone's feet smell like a goddamn flower?

CHAPTER NINE

"You planted these in my father's study?" Ryan tossed the two half-cards into Finn's face. "That's why you wanted to swipe his key earlier? You're a fucking idiot. What if he'd found them there?"

"He didn't," Finn said. "And now Skye has even more reason to believe your father's the one she should focus on, not us."

"How'd you know she'd be here tonight?"

Finn grinned. "She's a hunter."

Ryan paced his bedroom while the noise from the party continued down the hall. The room was actually a suite, with a king-size bed, a sitting area with a red rock fireplace, and the latest state-of-the-art entertainment system. All this luxury for the prince of sloth while Finn worked his ass off to create something meaningful.

The usual jealousy was there, but it was nothing compared to the high Finn was on. The jolt of awareness and lust he'd experienced in Stone's study still hummed beneath his skin. He'd finally laid eyes on Skye Hamilton. It wouldn't be the last time, he vowed. The picture Tristan had managed to text him hadn't done her justice. The woman was as gorgeous as she was talented in the art of survival. And ballsy, too. She'd waltzed right into the lion's den—and waltzed right out again. The thrill of hunting her would be far superior to any other expedition they'd hosted at the Hunting Grounds.

But what had she and Jared Bennigan been talking about when Finn and Ryan had interrupted? Their expressions had been intense. Maybe Bennigan had been about to take her to Stone for judgment. It didn't matter anymore. Bennigan would soon be out of the way, after failing to do his job so many times. And if that wasn't enough to keep the man away, Finn had other means. But maybe Stone would do the dirty work for him. Stone had no patience for ineptness—which was why Ryan didn't have a job in the family company. The reminder made Finn smile.

"This isn't fucking funny." Ryan stopped his pacing and walked back to him, jabbing a finger in his face. "Nobody is supposed to know about the Redemption Club."

"Relax. They don't know anything about the Club. To an outsider, these are just a couple of torn cards." He bent over to scoop up the symbols of Darren's and Tristan's debts. "When Tristan told me Darren brought his card to the ranch, and he saw Skye pick it up off the ground, I knew she'd come looking for answers. She already thinks your father's responsible for screwing her over. Now, the woman will definitely be gunning for him, instead of us."

"Which will bring my dad breathing down our necks."

"I didn't think you'd mind, considering you initiated the blackmail scheme. You didn't think that'd bring his wrath down on you?"

"Not if he doesn't find out. This is getting out of hand. There are too many curious people involved."

"Skye will be taken to the Grounds before she can find anything. Besides, those cards give her a reason to stick around, looking for answers, and it'll be easier to nab her."

"And if you don't succeed? If word gets back to my father about what we're doing..."

"Nobody can tell him anything, other than Skye found Darren's card. It won't mean anything to him. He doesn't know we rebooted his Redemption Club. He has no clue what you've been up to the past several years, or he would have stopped it long before now."

"And it needs to stay that way." Ryan threw himself into an armchair and slammed his fist into the cushion. "Why did you have to take a girl from so close to the Grounds? It's your poor judgment that brought this down on us." He kicked at the side table next to him, knocking it over.

Finn frowned. "I thought you outgrew tantrums around age twenty-five."

"Fuck you." The heat left Ryan, burning up quickly as it normally did. He expelled a breath. "You were right about one thing. She's a magnificent specimen."

"I told you."

Based only on the photo Tristan had texted, which had shown Skye from a distance as she'd worked out in a boxing ring, Finn had fantasized about the things he could do to her while he had her. But he'd learned over the years that ninety-nine percent of the excitement was in the anticipation, and in the hunt itself, not in the sacrificing of the animal. Patience could be pleasurable in its own way, allowing him to stalk and learn his game's weaknesses. Except, now that he'd seen Skye's eyes, and her fierceness, up close and personal, waiting would be damned difficult.

He murmured their Latin credo, then turned to Ryan. "She embodies our belief, doesn't she?"

"Live fearlessly and play ferociously." Ryan grinned. "From what you told me, and what I saw tonight, I believe she'll fit the bill." His expression turned calculating. "She'll go for a lot of money at the Grounds." The Redemption Club men and women who had unique tastes, who were always looking for a challenge, would pay big money for the privilege of taking down such wild, intelligent game.

Finn's grin dissipated. "I don't want to share."

Ryan smirked. "I just bet you don't, but you owe

me big-time, so you don't really get a say in it, do you?"

"Or I could reveal your blackmail scheme to your father. He has no clue how you like to fuck up his life."

Ryan paled, then shot to his feet and got in Finn's face, his fickle temper reigniting like a flash fire. "You do that, and you'd lose your fun, too—and your stream of income. Besides, if you want that part in the next blockbuster film Stone Studios is making, you'd better play nice."

Finn pushed away from Ryan and stalked to the door. He'd had enough bullshit for the evening. Tristan had reported one of the women was refusing to eat. That wouldn't do. He had to get there and deal with it in person, as well as make room for Skye. Trapping and keeping her would be a special kind of challenge.

"She's mine to do with what I want," Ryan called after him, rubbing the raw wound. "That's not your family's land and the Redemption Club isn't yours." It had once been theirs, together, but Finn didn't point that out. Lately, Ryan's head had swelled with their success and his ego was taking over.

Finn paused with his hand on the knob. "You'd be nowhere without me."

"And you'd have nothing without me."

Angry at the accuracy of that statement, Finn slammed the door. Instead of returning to the party, he went out a back door and headed for the conservatory. Stone had so many things growing there that he wouldn't miss a few items.

Years ago, Finn had discovered the man's stock of plants that could induce psychotropic effects like hallucinations and mimic anything from smoking weed to taking acid. He pulled out the little bags he'd stashed in his pocket and collected seeds, plants and herbs to take to the Grounds. Sometimes the Club members who paid to participate in a hunt partook of substances such as peyote, mescal beans and poppies to enhance the experience. Other times, they enjoyed watching their prey act more wild and animalistic, so

Finn always kept some on hand. The Redemption Club aimed to please its members; after all, they'd worked hard for the privilege of membership.

His phone rang and he nearly dropped the herbs he'd been stashing in a bag in his haste to answer it before anybody heard. Though most of Stone's security guards knew him by sight, and wouldn't think twice about seeing him, Stone had to be in a rage after his private study had been invaded. He might look more closely at anyone, even Finn, found in areas that were supposed to be off-limits.

Then again, the danger heightened the thrill.

"You have an update?" he asked in a hushed voice. He made his way down the crushed stone path to a side exit, so he wouldn't emerge near the more populated patio where someone from the party might see him.

"The ranch is like a graveyard," Tristan said. "And I haven't heard or seen any sign of Skye."

"I have. She was here, tonight."

Tristan whistled. "Did you get her?"

"Not yet, but I will." She'd be back. He'd piqued her interest with those torn cards. "I just have to get her alone."

"I may have something that will help. I was able to follow the trail of one of the injured men at the ranch."

"Who?"

"I know him as Viper."

"Sounds like a tough guy."

"Once upon a time, maybe. He's an asshole who pushes everyone else to their limits, and degrades them when they fail. I may have banged him up a bit more than necessary just for the things he's said to me." There was no apology in Tristan's words, not that Finn expected one. There were no surprise agendas or hidden motives when dealing with Tristan. It was refreshing.

Finn's mind spun through a variety of options until he selected his next move. "Where is he now?"

"I have him in a shed outside my trailer, away

from civilization. Thought we might need him as insurance."

"Can he identify you as the person who attacked him?" Not that it mattered. Tristan Floyd's full name had been on the cards he'd left for Skye to find, and he was betting at least Skye, and maybe Bennigan, had seen it. He felt a twinge of regret and guilt that he'd had to do that to his friend, but Tristan could take care of himself, and he was currently flying under the radar. Once they took care of Skye and Bennigan, there'd be no threat. And Finn would make it up to him. If the guy ever found out, that is.

"I don't think so. I keep the mask on when I'm around him, and the guy's been in and out of consciousness, running a fever. He'd bled out quite a bit before I found him. It was just like following the trail of a wounded animal." Excitement, pride and pleasure laced Tristan's words.

"You wore your hunting mask?" A stupid move, but Finn supposed it was better than if Tristan had revealed his true identity to a man who knew him.

"He probably thought he was hallucinating. He was already wounded and dehydrated when I tracked him. Still, he's a tough old bird and tried to fight me off. A few well-placed cuts with my knife put him over the edge." Satisfaction filled Tristan's voice.

"Remind me never to make you angry."

Tristan chuckled. "Never make me angry."

"Yeah, thanks." Finn found a small box and dumped the baggies he'd filled into it, wondering what it would be like to be under the influence while hunted by Tristan. "For your next move, you're going to get Viper to the hospital."

"The hospital?"

"You don't have to go in with him. Dump the guy there. Word will get out soon enough." Viper would be the perfect bait.

Skye had scraped her bare knees as she'd fled, practically flinging herself at the wall that bordered the estate to haul herself over the stucco surface before Jared could catch up to her. The abrasions stung as her legs pumped, carrying her through the night to her clunker. At least she could move faster in bare feet than in heels, and she had a pair of athletic shoes in the car.

She hated running away, but it was better to be safe than sorry, and Stone's party wasn't the place to linger when she was uncertain. She'd almost succumbed to the plea—and the heat—in Jared's eyes. And she still didn't know who Chelsea was. But she was alone and had to be extra cautious as she decided whom to trust.

Uncle Tom hadn't replied to the voicemail she'd left for him that afternoon, after arriving in Vegas and charging the phone at a motel. Maybe he was still angry she'd brought hell down on the ranch. Or maybe he didn't want to hear from her. Perhaps it was best he kept his distance. Stone would likely come at her harder after learning she'd been in his study. Let him come. She had no other family or friends for Stone to attack. She liked it better this way, defending only herself. At least, that's what she told herself.

But she'd sure like to know that the other dead body found at the ranch wasn't Tom.

As she stuck her key in the ignition, she saw movement down the street. A dark shadow that could be a person. Otherwise, it was a blessedly dark and quiet neighborhood, and the houses were on expansive private lots that kept their owners from seeing the street. She started the engine and did a U-turn away from the dark form. Likely, it was Jared or one of his security team. Would Jared lead the hungry pack once Stone set his guards after her?

She drove without direction, simply eager to put distance between her and Stone. Still, she'd gained something from this evening. Finding out Tristan Floyd worked for Stone had been a shock. If she knew how to reach them, she'd confront Tristan and warn her fellow ranch residents. She left Uncle Tom another quick message, telling him to beware of Tristan Floyd, just in case he ran into the man.

After several minutes of driving, she realized her subconscious had steered her toward the past and what had once been home. Not home, a house. The place where she'd spent her early formative years had never been a home. A home was made with love.

Ten minutes later she pulled off the freeway and down a street with houses on either side. At one time it had been dirt road through an open field. Now it was subdivided into lots, with trailers or manufactured homes indicating life had gone on here after the night that had changed her life forever.

She slowed to a stop in front of one of the lots. Flashes of memory haunted her as she spied the tree she'd hidden in when the house exploded. It, too, had gone on with life, stretching taller and wider than Skye remembered. The blast had nearly knocked her off the ten-foot-high branch where she'd been clinging. The branch was still there, thicker and longer than ever. A mobile home squatted farther back on the lot. The red dirt that tried to swallow up everything in these parts coated the bottom third of its metal sides. A sagging porch was a deterrent to visitors, not that Skye was tempted to stay.

She drove a quarter mile farther, to what had been one of her favorite parts of the property, and breathed a sigh of relief when she realized nobody had taken over or stripped down her favorite grouping of red-and-gold striated rocks. She left her car at the side of the road and, ignoring the scrape of rock against her already-raw palms and knees, scaled the rocks as if she were still six years old and looking for an adventure. Thirty feet above the ground, she sat in her ridiculous party dress, her hair now loose from its confines and tangling in the wind, the lights of Vegas beyond and the darkness of the desert at her back, and contemplated her next move.

She could continue retracing Loretta's credit card trail. But the time she'd spent today doing just that had been fruitless.

She could confront Stone about what she'd found. But the guy was careful, and had resources. Besides, she doubted he'd confess his sins.

She could wait for Uncle Tom to reply to her. But it might be a long time before hell froze over.

It seemed the only person who'd consistently wanted to work with her, or professed to, was Jared.

When the answer came, she wasn't surprised. Part of her, the primal instincts that lived in her gut, had already known what she was going to do next. After all, if one had to take a gamble, where better than Las Vegas?

Chelsea had made a lot of bad decisions in her life, but none so poor as trusting the smooth-talking actor who'd seen her dance in a burlesque show at the Legacy Lounge, then hired her to dance at his friend's party a couple weeks later. The promise of financial security and the allure of a bad-boy grin were her two greatest weaknesses. Unfortunately, Finn Tucker had turned out to be her worst nightmare, and the past several weeks had taught her there was no waking from it.

Pride goeth before the fall.

Her mother had always said that, referring to her dancing. Chelsea had been twelve the last time she'd heard her mother give any advice, but she'd hung on every word the legendary dancer Phoebe Bennigan had said. Her mother's lifestyle had shaped much of Chelsea's life, but she'd be damned if she'd die the same way her mother had—at the hands of a man.

A whimper and a moan from the corner of the dirt-floor cabin indicated the girl Finn brought in a few days ago was finally coming around. Though it would be better, for the girl's sake, if she stayed unconscious.

Chelsea hurried to her side, bringing a bottle of water from the case Finn had dropped off along with some protein bars and the girl. She cradled the woman's head in one hand as she lifted the mouth of the bottle toward her lips.

"That could be drugged," said Loretta, the other woman in the cabin. When Loretta had been dumped here two weeks ago, she'd been wearing heels and a dress, her face made up as if she were prepared for an interview. Now, like Chelsea's, Loretta's nails were jagged from clawing at the dirt floor around the walls or the caulking around the window, looking for an escape. Her mascara was faded to gray circles around her eyes.

Chelsea was sure she must look the same way. Where it wasn't matted with dirt, her blonde hair hung limply. Her skin was sallow, her lips chapped and sore from dehydration and gnawing them.

Finn had turned them into animals. No, animals at least had a fighting chance. They were caged pets, at his mercy.

"It's better than nothing," Chelsea said as the new woman hesitated to drink, her wild eyes darting between them. "Besides, he wants us strong before we run."

The stranger's eyes widened but she took a sip of water. Whether she was hoping it would bring her renewed strength or more blessed numbness was unclear. Bear—Finn's cohort in a bear mask, who seemed to be their primary keeper—had been drugging her for the past couple days.

"What's your name, honey?" Chelsea asked.

"Erica." Her name was a rasp against her throat. Erica was somewhere around Chelsea's age, closer to twenty-four than Loretta's seventeen. But Loretta had been blessed with Marilyn Monroe curves that made her appear more mature.

"Does anyone know you're missing?" Loretta asked.

"I don't know." Erica choked back a sob. "I ran away to Hollywood a couple months ago, and I still don't know many people. Only my roommate would notice I'm missing, and I'm not sure she'd care until rent comes due." Her head whipped around and she found the strength to sit up. "What is this place? What are we doing here?"

"He—Finn—calls it the Hunting Grounds," Chelsea said. Though he'd drugged her drink the night she'd come to do her solo burlesque performance for him and a couple of his friends, she remembered that much before passing out. They'd been laughing about taking her there.

"Finn." Recognition lit Erica's eyes. "That bastard." The rest of Chelsea's sentence seemed to register. "Hunting Grounds?"

"Fuck Finn Tucker," Loretta muttered. "And fuck Tristan."

Chelsea scowled at Loretta. Loretta had recognized Bear's real identity almost immediately, but Chelsea had convinced her to keep the information to herself. If she ever wanted to get out of here, the less she appeared to know about the perpetrators, the better.

"He promised me a part in a Stone film," Loretta said. "Instead, I get hell. I'll claw his eyes out if he gets close enough."

"And the other guy?" Erica asked.

"We call him Bear," Chelsea said. "He always wears a bear mask, and is in charge of training us." Seeing that Erica seemed fully alert, Chelsea handed her the water bottle and pushed to her feet. "They want us to fight back, or to run. They get a thrill out of it." When she'd woken up here nearly a month ago, there'd been two women already here, but they'd been taken out into the night a few hours later, leaving Chelsea in the cabin alone. The howls of the hunters, the echoes of

laughter and shouted lewd comments that had filled
the night... they had haunted her ever since. She lived
in fear of them coming for her.

"And then what?"

Chelsea met Loretta's gaze before turning back to
Erica. "I don't know. Maybe they're released after the
hunters have had their fun." But she doubted it.
Loretta hadn't been here as many weeks as Chelsea,
and hadn't seen what had happened to the other
women. Hell, Chelsea hadn't seen, either, but she'd
heard screams, and shots, and could fill in the blanks.
Still, it wouldn't do to have Erica or Loretta break
down now. She needed them all strong. They'd only
survive this together.

She'd learned that the hard way, that her need to
be independent of everyone might cost her life. She
could hear her brother's voice in her head, saying that
very thing. She could also remember their last words to
each other, said in the heat of anger. She'd had plenty
of quiet time for reflection over the past few weeks.

She'd just come home from Legacy Lounge, where
she danced three nights a week. The rest of the time,
she took the occasional private dancing gig, when she
wasn't taking day courses in business at the
community college. But the dancing was what paid the
bills. Jared had offered to help her with tuition, but
she'd be damned if she'd become a burden to him, as
their mother had. If she were honest with herself,
dancing was about more than the money. Dancing was
empowering. But Jared had only seen the dangers.

*"Move in with me," Jared said as she removed her
coat and he spied her costume. He couldn't hide his
scowl, or the disappointment that flitted across his
face. "You won't have to dance anymore and you'd have
your own room."*

*"I can take care of myself," Chelsea said. "Besides,
I like dancing and you can't stand that lifestyle."*

"This isn't taking care of yourself."

"I feel alive when I'm up there on stage. I feel in

control."

"I'm sure that's how Mom felt, too. Alive. *Until it led to her death. It only takes one instant for everything to change."*

"Stop trying to be the goddamn hero all the time. I'm not underage anymore and can make my own choices. Besides, you got to go off and join the military while I was stuck here, dealing with Mom's death. I'm smarter than she was. I know who to trust."

Except she hadn't. She'd trusted Finn, and had been cocky enough to think she could handle a private party on her own with only three men in attendance.

Deep down, she realized she was angry that Jared had left her, just as her dad and then their mom had, but it felt good to get the words out, to lash out at someone.

They'd been a mockery of a family, thanks to their mother. Phoebe Bennigan had danced and lived the party lifestyle that so often went with it, slept around, had kids with different men without thinking of the consequences, then gotten herself killed. Jared was gone by then, having joined the military the moment he turned eighteen, where he could feel like he was protecting the entire world from harm. Chelsea could see now the military must have given him a brotherhood he could depend on, as well as the sense of purpose and control that his life had lacked. She would have made the same decision, had she been in his shoes, rather than hang around and watch their mother run her life into the ground again.

Chelsea, on the other hand, had decided dancing wasn't the worst choice her mother had made. It was the men she'd chosen who'd been the death of Phoebe Bennigan. Chelsea had that in common with her mother now, too.

She swiped at her nose and eyes before the tears could fall. Dirt smeared across her cheeks, but it didn't matter. After four weeks in this hellhole, she was ratty, filthy, and beyond recognition. But she wouldn't give up.

Bennigans fought until the end.

His muscles were so tight with frustration that an ache was starting to pound behind his eyes. Jared parked in his garage and walked into his kitchen, tossing his keys onto the counter with one hand as he reached to loosen his tuxedo tie with the other. At least he wouldn't have to wear a suit again for a while. He couldn't say he was going to miss working for Stone, especially since it hadn't produced any leads on where Chelsea had gone.

At one time, it had been a different uniform he'd worn. He still missed the military, and the rules he could count on, a life that made sense, the rituals that made him feel part of a bigger picture, that made him matter. There, he'd felt like the world was at least partly under his control. He realized Chelsea had probably been missing those same things if she'd taken a job as a dancer. She'd told him once that dancing for men was her way of proving her body was her own, and controlling the outcome. If he'd just had the patience to try to understand—

The hairs on the back of his neck rose the second before he felt a gun pressed to his back. *Fuck.* His muscles braced for attack, ready to defend himself.

"Don't turn around." The female voice raised more goosebumps. His body recognized her instantly.

His initial adrenaline rush turned to relief, quickly followed by hot, liquid awareness that *she* was here. She'd come, which meant she was taking a leap of faith. With him. Of course, there was the matter of the gun. Perhaps she wasn't *quite* ready to make the leap.

He ignored her command and turned, drinking in the sight of her. She was still wearing the dress from the party and... sneakers. He grinned. "I see you found your duffel bag." It was slung over her shoulder.

She retreated a couple of steps, moving out of

arm's reach. Her cheeks were flushed and her eyes were the brightest blue he'd ever seen, sparking with anger.

She kept the gun pointed at him. "I said *don't* turn around."

"I don't take orders from others. Not anymore."

"I can see that." A line of consternation dented her brow. "Then we have a problem."

"Only if you shoot me. I'm guessing you won't."

"You really want to make that bet? We don't know each other."

"I know you want answers. I've got some. Can't get more if I'm unconscious or dead." He saw the flicker of doubt. She'd expected him to cower before her—rather big—gun. But it was her eyes that had the power to tear down a man's defenses. "How'd you get in here? I'd like to know, in case someone else tries to break in."

"I doubt they'd come in the way I did."

His eyes widened. It had to be the bathroom window above the shower. He hadn't gotten around to fixing the broken lock. She'd squeezed through there? His eyes went to her slender hips and he swallowed hard at the image of her wriggling through the tight space in her little black dress. "You never know. Stone seems awfully anxious to get his hands on you."

"So do you."

Jared's gaze drifted over her again, lingering on the curves he'd briefly held. The memory of the way her backside had been pressed against his crotch at the Roadhouse still filled his dreams. There was no denying he wanted his hands on her again. "True. But the difference is I want to help." Would she finally stop running and discuss this? That would require a measure of trust he wasn't sure she had to give, unless he laid all his cards on the line. "I need your help, too. You cost me my one lead to find out what happened to my sister."

"Chelsea? She's your sister?"

"Yes." He slowly backed to a picture on the mantel

and pointed to his smiling sisters. "That's her on the left. She went missing a month ago. I think Stone's somehow connected."

She lowered her gun. "How do I know this isn't a trick to turn me over to your boss?"

"I don't work for Stone anymore. And you've got your duffel bag. That should give you plenty of ways to maim or kill me if I'm lying."

She eyed him cautiously. "My rifle's in there. And my heels. Can't believe you kept them."

He grinned. "Figured you might want them back."

"Not on your life." At his laugh, she grimaced. "They hurt like hell."

"Truce?"

"Truce," she agreed, but didn't offer her hand. And didn't holster her gun.

Baby steps.

"You go first," she said. "What do you know?"

That she had the ability to rock his world in a cat-burglar suit or a simple black dress. That her fears and dreams and everything she felt or thought was reflected in her eyes. That he couldn't get her out of his head, and didn't want her to leave his side. Not, at least, until he'd gotten the chance to explore her just a bit more—or a lot more. As she stood in front of him, waiting for information, his gaze went to her mouth, tracing the perimeter like a man obsessed. His new favorite shape was the sweet curve of her bottom lip.

"What do I know?" He grinned. "That your feet smell like flowers."

CHAPTER TEN

Flowers?

Skye snorted. She couldn't control it, nor could she control a shiver of desire as Jared's gaze remained locked onto her mouth. Whatever thoughts were flying through his head, they brought out ripples of warm honey in the depths of his brown eyes. She found herself entranced and jerked her gaze away, but it landed on the hard edge of his jaw, where the skin was so smooth he must have shaved before the party. It made her think of tactile things like physical contact. Desire did a slow roll through her body like a shot of tequila, warming her from the inside, turning her muscles to liquid heat.

"You really think we can work together when we don't trust each other?" she asked.

His gaze was serious. "I do. Walk with me. I need to get changed and then we'll talk."

As if she'd let him out of her sight. She told herself it was only because she needed to make sure he wasn't going to retrieve a hidden weapon or call Stone, that she followed him past the kitchen, through a sparsely decorated living room with a brown leather couch, and down a hallway. She hated to admit she appreciated the clean, masculine lines of his home, but she'd had a few minutes to explore his setup and find her weapons before she'd heard his car. She'd even borrowed some antibacterial ointment and bandages for her scraped hands, knees, and feet. She'd pay him back.

As for the man himself, he seemed unconcerned with her suspicious nature. When he spoke, his tone was friendly and solicitous. "Have you eaten? I planned to cook a late dinner."

She stopped in the doorway to his bedroom, hesitant to enter his personal domain. Oh, she'd checked it all out earlier, but with him here it was different. He disappeared into the walk-in closet beyond. Her hand still held her gun, ready in case he emerged with his own weapon drawn. She'd just have to be ready for that event, because she'd be damned if she'd follow him into such a personal, closed space.

She raised her voice so he could hear her. "How did you come to work for Stone?"

"I'm co-owner of GSS. After I learned he might be linked to Chelsea, I convinced Stone, as a high-profile man of the world, he could benefit from our services. I learned later that he was being blackmailed, though I don't know what for."

He reappeared in the closet's doorway, his crisp white dress shirt unbuttoned to the waist. Her eyes drank him in for a second, following the trail of golden hair from his chiseled pecs to a glimpse of washboard abs.

When she looked back at his face, he was watching her with heat in his eyes. "Penny for your thoughts," he said.

She swallowed. "There's no way I'm showing my hand for a penny."

"Guess I should up the ante, then." He turned to reach into the closet for something and she tried to ignore the way his tuxedo slacks hugged the curve of his ass and firm lines of his thighs. The grin he shot her over his shoulder told her he knew her thoughts, for free.

She leaned a shoulder against the doorframe, affecting a casual pose when the reactions churning within her were anything but calm. "What have you found out so far about Chelsea's disappearance?"

Jared moved to his dresser and looked at her in the mirror as he tucked the bowtie from his tux into a drawer and undid his cufflinks. "Chelsea was hired to work at a private party at Legacy the night she disappeared. Her planner had the name *Stone* written beside the time. Video surveillance shows her arriving, but not leaving. That was a month ago. I haven't come across anything about her since." He leaned back against the dresser, suddenly looking lost. "That's why I need your help." His gaze was hard now as it met hers. "I've been patient long enough. I could have taken you from the rooftop, or at the cowboy bar, or in Stone's office and forced answers out of you, but I didn't."

It pricked her pride that he thought she was such an easy mark, but even more than that, she wanted to know why he'd held back—not that he could have overtaken her, but she was curious. "Why not?"

He crossed the room, stopping only a couple of feet away. "I sensed you'd only resist, and I can't afford another dead end. I feel like I'm running out of time—if Chelsea's still alive."

Her heart flip-flopped as she caught the pain behind his words.

"I'm sure you feel similarly about Loretta," he added.

"Her father hired me to find her. I'm not sure if he wants me to continue the search, but I can't give up."

He frowned. "You haven't heard the news, then?"

"News?"

"I'm sorry, Skye. Mark Sheldon... His body was found at the ranch. He'd been shot."

"He was the other casualty." She slumped against the doorjamb. He reached for her but dropped his hand when she shook her head. It wasn't that she didn't want comfort. She desperately did. And that scared her. She didn't deserve his comfort, couldn't let herself depend on it, even for a second. Dependence was weakness.

"I'm sorry for your loss." Jared's gentle words

washed over her like a balm. "Was he a friend? Something more?"

"Not much more than a cohabitant on the ranch, and the father of a friend. I knew there'd been another body found besides Darren's, but it hadn't been identified." She squeezed her eyes shut as the full impact hit her. "I can't even tell Loretta. If she's run away, I at least need to find her to give her this news." If Loretta were even alive to be told. She opened her eyes and met Jared's understanding gaze. "I don't know if she left the ranch willingly or was abducted, or if she's alive or dead."

"It's the same with Chelsea."

"All I know is her note indicated she left because Stone promised her a part in his next movie. Do you know if he's capable of harming them?"

"I don't know. The man's secretive, even among his security team, but I've heard things."

"Things that make you think he's dangerous."

He moved into the closet, beyond her view, but his voice called back to her. "In my gut, I'm more sure than ever that Stone is up to no good. The man's ego is as large as his corporation. Are you ready to trust me?" He exited the closet in sweatpants and a T-shirt, and still her mouth watered.

"I'm ready to try," she admitted. Her body was apparently already on board. She just had to convince her brain.

He eyed the gun still in her hand, pointed at the floor. Reluctant to let him touch her, she moved aside as he passed through the doorway. The man had a unique effect on her body, and she liked it entirely too much. She could have sworn he'd grinned at her reaction, but he didn't say anything as she followed him to the kitchen. There, she placed her weapon on the counter.

He opened the refrigerator. "I'll make us dinner while we talk. I suppose you could call it a midnight snack at this hour, but I have a steak thawed."

Her stomach rumbled but she didn't take charity. And she didn't eat food people other than Uncle Tom or herself had prepared. "No, thanks."

"Come on. I won't bite. We're partners now, right? Trust is important to me."

It was the solemnity in his expression that had her moving around the kitchen to Jared's side. "Fine. But only if you let me help."

"You're my guest, but it's obvious that you think I'll poison you, so I'll let you help." He jerked his head toward the refrigerator. "There are salad fixings in there if you want to throw them together." He turned back to the stovetop grill he'd preheated and laid the huge T-bone on it, then sprinkled salt and pepper to season it. "It's only one steak, but it's big enough to share."

Sharing a steak sounded a bit like a date, and too intimate for the talk they'd be having, but she was starving. Besides, if they were sharing, he definitely wouldn't be drugging the food.

She began chopping veggies, relaxing at the familiarity of it all. She used to help Tom cook for a small army. Colorful bell pepper, mushrooms, and chunks of bright red tomato flew beneath her blade as she chopped with practiced ease, and not once did she think about using the knife as a weapon.

Out of the corner of her eye, she watched him pull silverware from a drawer. His hands were beautiful— wide, with long tan fingers and trim nails. She remembered admiring them the first time she'd seen him on the rooftop. The toned muscles of his forearms rippled. His biceps flexed beneath his shirt as he moved with confidence.

She raised her gaze to find him watching her, his head tipped as if he were studying a puzzle. "What?" she asked.

"I'm trying to figure you out."

Her body tingled, but she kept her hands busy sliding the chopped vegetables into a bowl. "I'm not that complicated. Besides, why bother? We only have to work together for a short while."

"But working together requires trust, which comes from knowing each other. Don't you want to get to know me? You sure as hell interest me." The sizzle and pop wasn't from the stove. The air seemed charged with whatever was brewing between them. "I think I liked you even when you were a potential threat to me on that roof, lying through your teeth with the bag full of guns at your feet. And I didn't want to like you, because you're supposed to be a means to an end." He stepped closer. "I think the salad's done."

She tensed and he took the knife from her fingers, setting it on the cutting board. He reached over her shoulder to the cabinet door behind her. The smell of warm male mingled with grilled steak, and she waited a long moment before releasing her breath, as if she could hold his essence within her. She was pitifully close to dropping all her boundaries, stepping into him, and pressing her nose to the underside of his jaw. She'd like a taste of the skin there.

No man had been physically close to her in over a year, unless she counted sparring in the Pit. But sexually? She'd limited those encounters and never let the partner linger. And she'd always—*always*—been in control of her emotions, her body, and the relationship itself. These emotions, and the uncertainty they stirred, were foreign and frightening.

"What are you doing?" she asked.

"Just getting a couple of plates." He set them on the counter but didn't move away. Instead, he seemed to lean a little closer. His breath stirred the hairs at her temple. His mouth was on level with her eyes and she could see the full softness of his lips. Her muscles tightened, ready to both attack and submit to him.

But where would an affair between them get her? After they found the women they were looking for, there was no connection between them, nothing holding them together.

So what, exactly, is the problem? Her libido piped up with the question. Normally, brief and satisfying was her thing. But some innate warning system told her Jared was different, that once she crossed that line with him, there would be no going back to her old life.

He scanned her face and must have read her confusion because he backed away, regret dousing the heat in his eyes, and went back to the grill to transfer the steak onto a plate.

They worked in surprisingly companionable silence for a few minutes, as if agreeing not to address their issues with each other until the meal was prepared and other needs satisfied, but her eyes were always on him, covertly watching his every move. He *liked* her? Why did that have such a powerful effect on her?

"There are beers in the fridge," he said as he carried the food to the table. "Or there's soda or water. All of them sealed." So he'd noticed her idiosyncrasy. Most people thought her preference was odd. He addressed it as if it was no big deal and she felt a twinge of gratitude.

"Beer's fine. Bottle opener?"

"Second drawer on the left."

They sat in the small dining area just off the kitchen. It seemed more close and intimate than the one at the ranch, but that was quite possibly due to the man sitting across from her.

Jared sliced the steak into equal halves and dished hers onto her plate. He held her gaze as he took a bite, proving he hadn't drugged the meat. He must think she was slightly crazy, but it was a survival thing for her. She'd never let anyone pull anything over on her again. She'd learned the hard way.

She sighed with pleasure after the first bite.

"Impressed?" He grinned as he watched her dig in to her meal.

Feeling the need to tease and distract from her consternation that he'd broken through her defenses, she managed a nonchalant shrug. "I'm used to men cooking for me."

"Really?" A spark lit his eyes. Jealousy? Interest? Something predatory, certainly. Her belly tightened and heat flooded her. It was the same primal reaction that had stunned her on the rooftop, at the Roadhouse, and in Stone's den. As if her body knew his was meant for her pleasure, and craved it.

"You saw the ranch where I grew up," she said. "Lots of guys around." And a few had even known how to cook. Mostly they grilled while she created the side dishes, but still, she wasn't totally fibbing. And she'd cooked her own food, but technically, they'd *tried* to grill for her.

Heat and something akin to possessiveness definitely lit his eyes now, which was absurd. They barely knew each other.

And yet their chemistry was undeniable.

"And you were the only female?" He took a long pull on his beer bottle as he waited for her response.

She lifted her own bottle and let the sudsy brew cool the heat building within. "Most of the time." She didn't explain that it had been a lonely existence. Most people kept to themselves at Three Fortunes, their suspicions or desire for solitude preventing personal attachments.

"Well, you haven't tasted anything until you've had mine."

She blinked and tried to remember what they'd been talking about. "Your what?"

"Steak."

Her belly tightened in a foreign but pleasant sensation. Her mouth was watering, and it wasn't just the food stimulating it. She had the urge to slip his fingers, one by one, into her mouth and suck on them. Where the hell had that come from? She cut another piece of steak instead. "Tell me more about Chelsea."

He set his knife and fork down and picked up his beer, sitting back in his seat as he took another long sip. "We had a fight just a few nights before she disappeared."

"I'm guessing, since you went to all this trouble, you don't think she just ran away."

"That wouldn't be like her, going quietly into the night." A smile tugged at the corner of his mouth. "She's a fighter, much like you."

Pleasure at the compliment filled her. "We do what we have to do to survive."

He searched her face for a long moment. "I figured as much, after studying you."

"How have you been *studying* me?"

"It wasn't easy. After I found out who you were from your rifle registration, I found your name. The truck registration led me to your ranch, which led to your uncle's identity, but little else on either of you. Just that Tom brought you to the ranch when you were six."

Tom had made sure there was little record of her existence, before or after age six, keeping her name out of the news reports back when the incident that had changed her life had occurred. Had Jared found anything?

He seemed to be waiting for her to fill in the blanks. Her thoughts and feelings tumbled together as she struggled for what would be an appropriate explanation for why she was a ghost. In the end, she suspected he'd know if she were lying, so she went for the truth. *Another boundary crossed.* She'd never let anyone in this far, never told them the truth. Only Tom knew the whole story. But trust required honesty.

"My parents died in a house fire when I was six," she said. As his mouth opened to express condolences, she held up her hand to stop him. "Their deaths were probably the best thing that could have happened to me." She saw his shock and pushed out of her chair. "Maybe we should talk about this another time." When she'd shored up her defenses.

"Don't run." His words were a soft command.

"I'm not running."

"You always run when you're feeling vulnerable."

"I'm not vulnerable," she said with force. But uncertainty seemed to fill her skull like a constant cloud. "It's just that it's late, and my childhood is a long, pathetic story." She didn't want Jared's sympathy. She didn't deserve it. "Let's figure out a plan for tomorrow and get some sleep."

Jared stood, too, and shifted as if he would block her escape. "Where are you staying tonight?"

"I have a motel room."

"Stay here tonight." His eyes were warm with compassion. "It'll give us more time to talk."

She didn't want to talk. Didn't want to stay here—unless it was in his bed, forgetting everything but the attraction between them. And that desire to lose herself in him was even more dangerous than spilling the secrets of her past.

"Did I say something wrong?" he asked when she went still.

"No, I..." She sighed, and because she needed something to do, she scooped up their empty plates from the table and took them into the kitchen. Jared followed with their empty beer bottles. "It's just hard to talk about."

"And part of a soldier's training is to leave emotion out of it." His arched brow indicated it was a question, an opening to a deeper discussion.

"That was Viper's philosophy."

"Who's Viper?"

"He's in charge of training programs."

"I'd like to understand why Stone might see you as a threat." He leaned against a counter, watching her as if he had all the time in the world to listen.

She began washing plates so she wouldn't have to react to any judgment she might see in his expression. "My uncle took me in." She felt a twinge of pain at the thought of Uncle Tom, and again hoped he was safe and didn't hate her. "I learned early on that he didn't want to talk about the past. Which was fine, because I didn't either. Still don't." She shot him a meaningful look.

"Sounds like you didn't have the ideal family life when your parents were alive. That must have been difficult."

And lonely. But she'd been lonely even before they died. She supposed she'd always been lonely, she just hadn't noticed until lately. "I was a mistake."

"Pardon?" He moved closer, then took her shoulders and turned her, reaching behind her to shut off the water faucet. He tipped her chin up until she met his gaze. "How could you think you were a mistake?"

She inhaled deeply through her nose to clear it of the remembered stench of smoke when she thought about that night. The air was filled with Jared. The tang of his skin and a hint of his aftershave filled her nostrils, and then her lungs, becoming part of her.

And scaring the shit out of her.

She was familiar with emotional distance and earned respect. That was the way things were done at the ranch. Empathy and compassion were there, but the expression of any tender feelings was quietly discouraged. A soldier was tough, ready for anything. But Skye wasn't ready for *this*, for Jared. He knocked all of her hard-learned lessons aside as if shooing away a fly. With him, she found she wanted to talk, to be understood and comforted.

He made her weak.

"I was a mistake," she repeated. "My parents didn't have time for me. Rather, they had no interest in being parents. They were drug dealers with a history of drug abuse and trafficking." She'd seen the police records once, in her late teens. That had been the first time she'd traded favors with someone. Her parents had apparently been in and out of jail before they'd had her.

"Then they probably weren't capable of caring

about anything but making money or getting their next high," Jared said.

Or she hadn't been interesting or lovable enough. Shame filled her and she roughly shoved it away. "The official report says cooking meth is likely what started the fire that night they died, though I didn't understand that at such a young age. I'd thrown a tantrum earlier that evening and they'd told me to leave. I went to one of my special places nearby, before they could deal with me in other ways."

"Other ways?"

She avoided his probing gaze. Other ways could be anything from drugging her food or drink, to hurting her physically. "When the house exploded a little later, I thought I'd caused it." The memories of their harsh words still echoed in her ears, her mother's slap still stung against her cheek. She blew out a breath to expel the negative energy. "Happy now?"

"It's not quite enough."

"What more could you want from me?" She'd nearly shouted the words and gritted her teeth to hold everything else in.

Jared's hand lifted and her eyes tracked it as if it would lash out at her. Memories of how her parents, both of them, had used physical *discipline* to keep her out of their way were too close to the surface.

He froze, then slowly resumed the movement, tucking her hair behind her ear. She exhaled in relief, and shuddered at the contact.

"You're going to have to get used to being close to me," he said. His fingers lightly touched her shoulder, and he drifted his knuckles down her arm. "I can't have you scared of me, now that we're partners."

She felt frozen except where his fingers scorched her skin. "I never said I'd be your partner. Besides, partners don't have to touch."

"They might. And I can't risk you freezing up on me—physically or mentally—if something comes up where we have to have each other's backs. You'll learn to trust me, learn that I would never drug you or hurt you in any way."

"I won't freeze up." But he was right. While they'd occasionally practiced team exercises at the ranch, the emphasis in training had been on survival of the fittest, the survival of one person. Herself. She'd never worked with a partner. Never had to, never wanted to.

"You don't know for sure, though." One eyebrow rose as she opened her mouth to protest. Apparently, he could see how she was frozen with fear right now. "Just an hour ago, you were ready to starve to death rather than eat my cooking."

"I ate," she pointed out.

"Only because I ate first." His hand had moved down to her wrist. He loosely encircled it with a finger and thumb, then brought his other hand up and placed his palm against hers. She'd never thought of holding hands as a particularly sensual, intimate experience, but her breath caught and dizziness swamped her. She locked her legs against the sway of the dual waves of anticipation and panic that threatened to crash over her.

I won't faint. She chastised herself. She wasn't weak. Not anymore. His words, his hands, couldn't sway her. Steeling herself, she met his gaze. *Do your worst.*

But she didn't trust herself to speak the challenge.

Jared saw the war she waged with herself. All evening he'd resisted the compulsion to touch her, but he couldn't keep from reaching for her now, especially when she'd seemed to turn a corner.

She hadn't run.

She'd trusted him enough to stay. And she'd gone beyond that, sharing pieces of herself. Just little bits, but important ones, enough to tell him he'd broken through some kind of barrier. And he was beginning to understand the influences that had shaped Skye, and why she ran from people. If Jared was reading things correctly, her uncle hadn't exactly been a source of great love and support. At least, not the touchy-feely kind.

If anyone deserved consolation and craved contact, it was the woman before him. He couldn't—wouldn't—back away from Skye now. But he had to start slow and easy.

His hands enveloped one of hers. Her fingers were soft, but small rough spots attested to her great strength and purpose. She was a survivor, no matter what the world threw at her. He admired the hell out of that.

With a hand on top of hers, he stroked her as if petting an uncertain animal. Her eyelids drifted shut and her nostrils flared as if she were tolerating his touch, not wanting to want it. Every muscle in his body tensed to resist the desire to pull her against him and cradle her in his arms. He focused on the pads of his fingers brushing the smooth plane of her hand. From wrist to fingertips, his open palm memorized hers. As his fingers reached the end of their journey, her lips parted on a soft sigh. Her long lashes fluttered as her eyes opened to meet his gaze.

His groin tightened, but he ignored his body's demands. This was about Skye, and her needs. If he pushed too far, she'd never trust him. But, even with his restraint, she pulled her hand away.

She cleared her throat. "See? I didn't freeze up."

He smiled. "We'll see."

"We just did."

"Because you knew I was going to touch you and you wanted to prove something to me."

She pressed the delicate pillow of her bottom lip against her bow-shaped top one until they formed a flat line. Then she shocked him by grabbing his hand and pressing it against her. His palm lay flat against her sternum, his fingertips splayed across the soft swells of her breasts. "Do you feel that?"

Jesus. The pressure of his erection bordered on pain. "Your chest?"

"My heart." The light thump was steady against his palm. "It's a normal rhythm. I know how to control it. I *learned* how to control it. Even if everything in me is screaming to run away, my body will do what needs to be done."

When you're using your head to control your reactions. For some reason, it made him want to push her past control. Maybe because she was testing his limits, as well. His own heart revved like a race engine the moment he breathed her in. His gaze flicked to her lips, imagining what it would be like to taste them, to feel their softness.

As if sensing the predatory turn of his thoughts, she released his hand and stepped back, then turned to the counter where she'd laid her gun. She picked it up, along with her duffel, and moved toward the front door.

"Where are you going?" he asked.

"To my motel room."

"We need a plan."

"I have one."

He arched a brow, amused at her insistence on doing this on her own. He'd wear her down—because he needed her, he told himself. Not because he liked being around her, as prickly as she could be. "Care to share with your partner?"

"I'm going to try again to reach my uncle."

"How? Didn't he scatter with the others?"

"He and I designed a way to exchange messages, but he hasn't responded to my attempts." Worry creased her brow. "I'm also going to track down Tristan Floyd. He's part of this, too. He worked at the ranch. Somehow, Stone got to him. I'll also retrace Loretta's credit card purchases and sweet-talk somebody into letting me see the video surveillance."

"Stone will be looking for you. Ryan, his son, reported you'd broken into his study. He's probably filed a police report," he added, almost certain Stone wouldn't involve the police, even if his life depended on it, but willing to lie to keep Skye here. "He's probably got his own people out searching the motels."

She stopped, and her shoulders slumped almost imperceptibly. "Should be easy to hide in plain sight if I stick close to the Strip."

"Stay here. He won't expect you to be with me." He tried not to be frustrated when she looked around like a caged animal. "I won't touch you again, if that's what you're worried about."

That made her stiffen her spine. Apparently, challenging her fears or her pride was the way to get a reaction out of her. "You give yourself too much credit. I already showed you the lack of impact you make on me."

"Then it won't be a hardship to stay here." He shrugged as if he didn't care either way, but she wouldn't be the only one facing an endurance challenge if they were under the same roof. He hadn't been imagining the chemistry he felt when he was with her. "If I come too close, you can shoot me. But give me fair warning first."

CHAPTER ELEVEN

Finn didn't need a mask. These girls were his. Besides, they'd never be able to tell anyone about this, and he preferred his prey knowing he was coming for them. It elevated the excitement.

He undid the last of the locks on the cabin door and entered. The three women were huddled together in a corner, blinking into the early morning light pouring through the front door.

"Get up. It's time to train." He waved a gun to get them to move faster.

"Where's the other guy?" the dancer asked. Chelsea, he remembered. His gaze swept over her lithe form, noting that she'd lost weight. He'd make sure they ate well before the hunt. Lethargic game would never satisfy the hunters. The girls would need a store of energy to burn.

"He's taking care of something else right now." He stepped closer to her. "You missing male company? I'm right here, baby." Maybe they could have a little fun before he killed her.

She scowled and looked away.

He walked over to his newest recruit, who'd been staring glassy-eyed at the wall. Erica flinched as he nudged her with his foot. "Get up. You're first to train. You need the most work."

Erica didn't move and he pulled back his leg to kick her. Before he could release it, Chelsea pushed at him. It was a weak effort, given her long confinement, but the fact that she'd tried surprised him. He turned to her, his hand raised, but she only lifted her chin.

He grunted his approval. "Well, well, there's a little fire in the hearth. I like it." The spark would bring more money. He kept his gun pointed at Chelsea as he stepped over to Loretta. "And you? Would you like a turn?"

Loretta spat at him and he backhanded her. Chelsea leapt between them. "Don't touch her," Chelsea said.

He growled, then forced himself to restrain his temper. "I won't—for now." He glared over Chelsea's shoulder at Loretta. "But that's the least you deserve for the trouble you've caused me. I told you not to tell anyone you were leaving. You could have ruined everything."

Loretta squared her shoulders. "Someone's coming for us, aren't they?"

He sneered. "They were, but I'm taking care of it. It all worked out quite nicely, actually. Your debt has been paid. Not only did you lead me to Skye Hamilton—a very fine specimen who will make a superb addition to your pathetic group," he added, his smile growing as Loretta's face paled with fear and surprise, "but your father already paid for your mistakes."

Her eyes widened and she glanced toward the door as if she'd see her father walking right through it to take her home. "H-how?"

"With his life."

As Loretta crumpled to the ground, Chelsea lunged at him and shoved at his shoulders. "You bastard!"

Finn knocked her away and she fell on her ass in the dirt in front of Loretta.

Loretta's howl of grief echoed in the small room. "No! You didn't. You couldn't have…"

He crouched next to her. "Very good, baby. You could have made it in Hollywood after all. Everyone says you need a well of painful experience to draw from if you're going to get the big parts. Too bad only a handful of people will get to see the show. But they'll pay a hell of a lot of money for a ticket."

Jared showered as he contemplated his options for finding Chelsea, and for handling the new partnership with Skye. Thankful for a day he wouldn't have to wear a suit and tie, he pulled on a pair of jeans, soft with wear, and a plain T-shirt and headed for the kitchen. There, he spied the most beautiful sight he'd ever woken to, even as the woman in his field of vision shot a hateful glare at his coffeemaker.

She'd pulled her hair back into a messy bun, securing it with a rubber band. A few strands hung down around her face. They caught the light coming in through the kitchen window and glinted like threads of honey nestled in warm chocolate. She'd politely refused to borrow his sisters' clothes without their permission, and the T-shirt he'd found for her to sleep in hung to mid-thigh. Her long legs were bare, as were her feet.

He stopped and swallowed hard.

She caught him staring and turned her glare on him. "Could you get a more complicated brewer?" At least this time the sparks of blue fire in her eyes were directed at the situation and not at him—or so he hoped.

Stepping closer, he reached past her to press a couple of buttons. He hid a grin when she scooted a few inches away. His little rabbit wanted to flee again, but he wouldn't let her undo the progress they'd made last night. "I take it you're not a morning person."

"What, did you discover that during your research into my background?"

"No." He leaned back against the counter, weighing the anger in her voice with the fear in her eyes. Was she worried what he'd think about her now that he had more information? "But I do know that your library history shows you're an avid reader. I'm guessing you were self-taught in almost every subject. That takes dedication, and intelligence."

The emotion in her eyes turned to wariness. She seemed uncomfortable with the compliment. "Uncle Tom liked living off the grid as much as possible."

"He must not have liked you choosing a job that would take you away from the ranch, then, let alone one that puts your life at risk." He turned to reach into the cupboard behind him for a mug. She'd have to reach past him to get her own mug, and he took some perverse pleasure in testing her.

She frowned. "He didn't like it, but he doesn't know the details, either. He's always warning me not to draw attention to myself."

"Is he paranoid, or a conspiracy theorist or something?"

"My father was the same way. Cautious. Suspicious. I figure it's a hereditary trait."

The coffeepot was nearly full, the aroma of the fresh brew awakening all the senses, and she looked past him longingly toward the cupboard. Then she caught the smile that was tugging at his mouth and rolled her eyes. With a determined set of her shoulders, she began to step around him.

"Chicken," he said softly. He instantly regretted his taunt when the gleam in her eyes turned calculating. She shifted closer to him and his entire body tightened with anticipation. Would she dare?

She would. She leaned her length against him and reached up past his shoulder to the cupboard handle. "Excuse me."

But he couldn't go anywhere. He didn't want to. Holy hell, he could feel her nipples pressing through both her shirt and his. One hand still held his coffee mug, but his empty hand went to her hip and held her in place. She had to feel how aroused he was. The evidence was pressing urgently against the zipper of his jeans. His fingers twitched with the desire to slide just a few inches lower, to the edge of the shirt she wore—*his* shirt—and stroke the skin beneath.

Keep it light, his brain warned. *Don't scare her off now.*

"You're excused." He shot her a cocky grin and slapped her ass lightly.

Her eyes widened and her lips parted, but whatever retort she'd been about to sling at him died on her tongue. Her nostrils flared as she took in a sudden breath, and the blue of her eyes deepened to indigo. A savvy soldier like Skye might think she could use her body as a weapon, but any kind of weapon could backfire, could be turned against the person wielding it. She was just as aroused as he was.

But she pushed away and retreated a couple steps.

He took mercy on her, and himself, and handed her the mug he'd already taken down, then turned to get a new one. She poured her coffee and replaced the pot, stepping around the kitchen island without offering him any, as if she needed the distance between them as much as she needed the caffeine.

He enjoyed flustering her—even if it was killing him slowly and painfully.

She eyed him warily over the rim of her cup. "I plan to spend the morning retracing Loretta's steps again. When she left the ranch, she took one of Mark's credit cards with her. It was used in a Hollywood convenience store about a week after her disappearance. The night you found me in Malibu, she used it in Vegas."

"Logical to follow that trail, then."

Skye frowned into her coffee cup. "Yeah, except it hasn't led anywhere. Nobody has let me see the surveillance recordings. And nobody anywhere seems to have seen her."

"Why didn't you approach Stone directly?"

"I tried. Couldn't get past his assistant. And the more I asked questions about the man, the quieter people got. It was eerie. It's almost as if people don't just respect him, they're—"

"Afraid of him?" Jared nodded. "I got the same feeling."

"That's why you took a job with the man, to get close to him."

"Yes. He's very private. And I didn't find anything that made me believe he would have kidnapped a woman, or two women, and done them harm. I mean, the guy can get female companionship any time he wants, with little effort."

Skye sighed and set down her cup. "It doesn't make sense, does it? It's like the Latin phrase Loretta put in her note."

"Latin?"

"Yeah. Mark said Loretta never took Latin in school. She wasn't exactly the studious type, so I assumed she picked it up somewhere recently." Skye quoted the phrase. "It means something like *live fearlessly and play ferociously.*"

Jared grunted. "Sounds like the motto for a rich playboy."

"But you've never heard it before? Maybe Stone said it, or wrote it somewhere?"

He shook his head. "Sorry, haven't heard it."

Jared's phone rang and he moved to answer it as Skye went to refill her mug.

"I've got news for you," Dev said after Jared's greeting.

"About Chelsea?" In Jared's periphery, Skye's body turned toward him as she overheard.

"Sorry, no. About the attack on the ranch. Two bits of news, actually."

"Hit me."

"You asked me to look up the deed on the ranch and it's actually owned by three men. Well, two men, seeing as one's deceased."

"That makes the ranch name make more sense."

"Yeah. What's more interesting is who Tom Hamilton co-owned the ranch with. David Wilson is dead, and I haven't tracked down the new owner of his share yet."

"And the other?" Jared asked, losing patience.

"Robert Stone."

"And the other bit of news?"

"An unconscious man was admitted to the Flagstaff Medical Center early this morning in critical condition. His last known residence was Three Fortunes Ranch."

His eyes flicked to Skye and held. She shifted her weight, eager to hear what he was learning. "Who was it?"

Dev gave him all the information he had, and when Jared turned to Skye, she must have read the concern in his expression.

She set her cup down and straightened as if bracing herself for bad news. "What?"

"That was Dev. I had him look into a couple things for me."

"And?"

"First, the deed to the ranch. When you said Stone went to talk to your uncle, something about that seemed odd. I decided to research the deed. Apparently, your uncle was only co-owner at Three Fortunes. There really were three fortunes that came together to purchase the land."

A furrow creased her forehead. "That's news to me. Who else?"

"Tom Hamilton, David Wilson—who is now deceased—and Robert Stone."

Her lips pressed together for a long moment as she digested the information. "Stone and my uncle have known each other for decades, then." She sank onto a barstool. "I don't understand." Her uncle had obviously never mentioned a link to Robert Stone. "But maybe that's why he didn't want me bringing up the past?" She cursed. "And Tom won't call me back to discuss any of this."

"There's more. One of the men from the ranch

turned up this morning at Flagstaff Medical Center. It's not your uncle," he quickly added. "We've kept in touch with authorities there and they informed us—"

"Who was hurt?"

"His name is Leonard St. Vincent."

"Viper." The name was an exhalation of breath. Concern flashed across her features. "What happened? How is he?"

"He'd been stabbed and beaten pretty bad. A neighboring rancher apparently found him on his land, unconscious and nearly dead."

Skye's hand went to her forehead. "We have to go to him."

"It would put you out in the open again."

"Shit."

Jared watched the play of emotions across her expressive face as she considered the ramifications and consequences of each possible course of action. The woman hid a lot, but when someone she cared about was in danger, she threw away all caution.

A need rose up inside, the need to have her think of him that way, as if he were someone she cared about.

"Stone, or whoever wants me for their damn redemption, might follow," she conceded. "Or it might be a trap."

Those had been his thoughts, exactly, but he could see how important this was to her, and it would give them the chance to look for more clues at Three Fortunes.

"We'll go together," Jared said. "Consider me your new bodyguard, courtesy of Global Security Solutions."

"You'd do that for me?" Gratitude shone in her eyes.

To cover his sudden yearning to fulfill her every dream, he forced himself to turn away and grab his phone. "Of course. We're partners now, remember?"

She frowned. "Anyone close to me tends to end up dead, missing, or seriously injured."

"Give me some credit." He winked to lighten her

mood, but her scowl deepened.

"When can we leave?"

"A few minutes, just long enough to pack an overnight bag." He rinsed their cups in the sink.

"I need to change anyway. Can't exactly go road-tripping in this, or in my cocktail dress. We need to stop by my motel and grab my things."

He set the coffee mugs in the dishwasher, surprised when he sensed Skye come up behind him. She lifted a hand to his shoulder and brushed it lightly, her touch gone almost before it registered. "Thank you." Her bare feet padded softly across the tile floor as she hastily retreated.

His skin still burned from the contact. The yearning was back, threefold.

"Dev was okay with you taking off like this?" Skye asked as they turned onto US 93, heading south into Arizona. They'd left her clunker in Jared's garage in favor of using his car for the four-hour drive to Flagstaff.

Jared's lips twisted in a wry smile. "He's had to put up with it for weeks. But he agrees finding Chelsea is a priority. And I'd do the same for him if the tables were turned."

"Must be nice to work with a friend who understands." She turned in the passenger seat to examine him. He inspired loyalty from others where she couldn't even get her uncle to be honest with her. How could he have been so close to a man like Robert Stone that they'd purchased a ranch together? And how had he kept such a thing a secret for over twenty years? But it did explain, maybe, why Stone had leverage over her uncle—enough that Stone could demand Tom kick her off the ranch. She hoped Uncle Tom called her back soon because she had a million questions for him.

Jared grunted. "He's certainly taken on more than

his fair share of work this past month."

"How'd you come to form GSS with him?"

"We met in Afghanistan, while I was in the Army."

She smiled. "I had a feeling you were military. Dev was a soldier, too?"

"No." Something undefined flitted across his expression, but he didn't elaborate. "I worked as an MP—a military policeman. I got out because it was time to come home. My sisters were growing up, the younger one, Haley, getting into more mischief than her aunt can handle."

"*Her* aunt?"

"Chelsea, Haley and I have three different fathers. Aunt Jane is Haley's father's sister. Haley's father never wanted anything to do with her, but his sister was willing to step up when our mother died. Anyway, Jane took in Haley and Chelsea, until Chelsea was old enough to move into an apartment with friends. Jane was threatening to put Haley out on the street if I didn't come back."

Skye gasped. "Would she have?" She couldn't imagine what would have happened to her if her uncle hadn't taken her in. She'd have become a ward of the state, she supposed. She felt pain when Tom had told her to leave, but to be a young girl like Haley, dependent on an adult who didn't want you, would be a lot more frightening.

He shrugged. "Jane was at the end of her rope. I received at least an email a day from her, begging me to come get Haley. She needed a handler."

And someone she could depend on, Skye suspected. A man like Jared who wouldn't drug his kids just to keep them out of his way while he conducted business.

"I missed my sisters," Jared continued. "So, I applied for a discharge from the Army and moved back to Vegas."

"And bought a house big enough for all of you." The room she'd slept in last night had a bed with clean sheets and a nearly empty dresser, as well as a few personal touches that were clearly feminine. Across the way, there'd been a similar room. Jared had occupied the master suite down the hall. "What happened to them living with you?"

"Chelsea was already renting an apartment with a couple other girls and refused to move in with me. I was worried about her exotic dancing and probably gave her too much hell for it. It pushed her away." He scowled at the road ahead. "Then, Jane caught wind of Chelsea's job and changed her mind. Said she wouldn't let Haley move in with me permanently until I proved I was settled and stable. I'd started to make progress there when Chelsea went missing."

Wanting a reprieve from thinking about Chelsea, Jared changed the subject. "Tell me about Viper."

Skye smiled softly. "He's always been there for me. He's a black belt and knows more about defense techniques than anyone I've ever known. For someone to take him down like this..."

"This Tristan guy who may have led the attack on your ranch must be a mean bastard to do this to him." Before bed, he and Skye had done some searching online but had yet to find anything on a Tristan Floyd that matched Skye's description.

Out of the corner of his eye, he caught her nibbling her bottom lip. He took a chance and reached over to lightly squeeze her jean-clad thigh. Before leaving Vegas, they'd stopped by her motel room so she could change and check out. He removed his hand before she could become uncomfortable with the gesture of support. "But Viper is obviously tough. He survived."

"You and Viper would have a lot in common, actually. He was an Army Ranger."

"I think I like him already."

She snorted. "He won't like what you've done to me. Consider this fair warning."

He slid his sunglasses down his nose to meet her eyes. "And what exactly have I done to you?"

"You stalked me and ended up leading the enemy to our home." There was no heat in her accusation, and Jared sensed she blamed herself more than him.

"I gave you space—"

"When you weren't trying to corner me in a bar, or in a study, or lure me to your home."

"Where I fed you a steak dinner—"

"And tried to keep me from my morning coffee." She tried to glare at him, but her lips twitched.

He laughed. Damn, he liked the way she kept him on his toes. "Anybody ever tell you that you would make one hell of an attorney?"

"Maybe once or twice." She tucked one leg under her on the seat. "I don't let anyone take advantage of me. Anyone," she repeated, in case he hadn't caught the warning in her words.

"Duly noted. And for the record, Counselor, I'm glad you stand up for yourself. But sometimes letting someone stand by your side is more powerful."

CHAPTER TWELVE

The beeping monitors were incessant, but a welcome reminder that, despite the swelling and bruising that marred his face and almost every inch of his body, Viper's heart was still beating. Skye stopped in the middle of his small hospital room, unable to move any closer. She'd never been inside a hospital before. The residents at Three Fortunes had always seen to each other's needs. Everything from broken limbs to concussions to stitches had been treated by Viper. In his time of need, he'd been alone and at the mercy of strangers.

She sucked in a breath and instantly regretted it as her nostrils filled with the alcohol-cleanser smell that permeated the air. It traveled up her nasal passages, down her throat, and seemed to grab her by the gut, gripping and twisting it like a rag.

"I'll get us some coffee," Jared said from behind her.

Without thought, Skye turned and reached out to stop him. His biceps flexed beneath her fingertips as her action surprised him. She was a little surprised herself at the sudden neediness that had come over her.

Jared's hand covered hers. "Hey, it's okay. I'll stay if you want. I just thought you'd like some time alone with him."

She swallowed past the strange lump in her throat. "Thank you. I appreciate you thinking to hire a guard for his door." The six-foot-five wall of muscle outside Viper's room was courtesy of Jared's connections at GSS. If Stone or Tristan had tried to destroy the ranch, and had come after Viper, he might still be in danger, especially if Viper could identify his attacker. Having the backup was a balm to her worried mind. "And pulling some strings to get me in to see Viper."

"You're welcome. I'll get that coffee." With a squeeze of her hand, Jared backed out of the room. Though the coffee would only churn in her sour stomach, she appreciated the gesture, and could use the time alone to regroup.

The door closed with a gentle click, leaving her with the unconscious Viper. Had Uncle Tom gotten away that night, or was he, like Mark, lying dead somewhere? Or, like Viper, critically wounded? As the days went by without a text or a phone call from Tom, deadlier scenarios had played through her mind. Anger filled her at the injustice of this attack on them. It was so senseless. What had been the goal? Why the hell had Darren considered taking *her,* his redemption? She was the reason Viper was fighting for his life.

She forced herself to take a step forward. Then another. The greenish-blue of three-day-old bruises covered Viper's body, disappearing beneath the hospital gown. One side of his face was swollen where he'd been hit, or kicked. Viper had suffered several stab wounds, broken ribs, and a ruptured spleen that had required emergency surgery.

"What did they do to you?" Frustration and fear roughened Skye's voice until she thought it might dry up and crack. She reached for the chair by his bed and sat, staring, uncertain what to say. Her skillset couldn't make this better. She couldn't fight for Viper. He had to do the fighting. "Come back to me, Viper. I need someone around who can kick my ass."

Her mind drifted to Jared. Last night, they'd seemed to turn a corner. She was coming to believe he would help her, if she let him. The idea of partnering with Jared, of trusting him with her life, seemed more and more necessary. But it was still terrifying. What if

Jared ended up like Viper? Or Mark?

She focused on the positives. Viper's color, beneath the bruises, looked good. And beneath his closed eyelids, his eyes flickered with movement as if he would respond to her. That was good, too. But the nurse had warned her not to expect too much. The injuries had been serious, especially left untreated for a few days, and he was lucky to be alive. He was heavily sedated, so at least he was out of pain. Still, it was hard to see such a large, powerful man lying prone and motionless.

She stood again suddenly, unable to sit here and watch, to do *nothing*. "I promise I'll be back soon, but I have to go."

She left Viper, closing the door softly behind her and nodding toward the guard, but her mind was reeling. How could one feel both hopeful and full of rage, both hollow and hard inside? So hard that the rock around her heart solidified, pushing inward. Squeezing. Threatening to crush her.

As she stood in the hallway, trying to grasp the jagged remains of her life and make them fit back together when they seemed like pieces of different puzzles, Jared returned from the cafeteria, two steaming cups in his hands. She watched him approach, saw the lift of one corner of his mouth as he caught sight of her, and felt the rock behind her ribcage knock faster and harder against her sternum.

Could she do this? Could she let herself depend on someone, and let them depend on her?

Even while alive, her parents had never been there for her the way parents should have, and she'd thought she'd been the reason they'd died until she'd grown up and realized that had been a kid's mind tricks. She'd depended on Tom for the basic needs of life, and he'd come through for her. But other things like a steady love and trust... She'd never allowed herself to need that from anyone. Something about Jared was making her want that. *Need* that.

But taking that leap meant making herself vulnerable. Letting another person into her tiny inner circle, and then possibly losing him—or, worse, watching him walk away—was a risk she wasn't sure she could survive.

"Everything okay?" Jared stopped in front of her, holding out a coffee.

"I can't..." She swallowed, trying to get a grip on her words. "I need some time." She hurried past him, down the hall, feeling like a coward, but knowing that if she faced Jared now, she might totally break down. As a partner, she sucked.

Jared shoved the coffee cups into the hands of a surprised nurse and took off after Skye. The wild look in Skye's eyes, the paleness of her face. Shock. Grief. Frustration.

He was familiar with all of these, and he knew how overwhelming they could be, how they could make you want to run to the ends of the earth—even to the hellfire waiting on the battlefield—especially when those emotions hit all at once.

He turned the corner at the end of the hall and felt a moment of alarm. She was gone. The emergency exit stairs were at the far end of the corridor. There was no way she'd have gotten that far without him catching a glimpse of her retreating back or hearing the heavy door close.

He surveyed the rest of the hall. There were several doorways that led to individual patient rooms. A nurse exited one while an orderly went into another. Knowing Skye, she would be looking for a quiet place to escape—or to hide until she could regroup and return, shields in place and guns and blue eyes blazing. He saw a closed door marked Supply Closet and headed toward it.

He stopped just outside, indecisive. How to

proceed with his wounded warrior? She was forged in fire and steel but grew skittish and defensive at the lightest human touch or hint of vulnerability. She'd said she needed time, but after she thought things over, would she be willing to take a risk and trust him fully, or would she run again?

He rapped lightly on the door. "Skye?" No sound came from within. Still, he sensed she was inside. "I'm not going anywhere. I just want you to know that. I'm here for you. That's what partners do." He leaned against the wall beside the door as the seconds stretched into a minute. Finally, the door opened a crack.

Blue eyes narrowed on him through the small opening. "I said I needed some time." Snappish was better than the shock he'd read in her expression minutes ago.

"And that's something I can't afford. You've been known to disappear on me." They stood there, staring at each other. He gestured at the door that remained mostly closed between them. "Can I come in?"

She released her hold and stepped aside. That was all the invitation he was likely to receive.

Careful not to brush against her despite the tight fit, he entered and closed the door, shutting out the world. The closet was just large enough for his broad frame and a few inches of clearance on either side. Opposite him, easily within arm's reach, Skye leaned against the shelves, as if pressing back into them would give her more personal distance from him. Which was why it shocked the hell out of him when she suddenly reached out and grabbed him by the shirt with both hands.

The remnants of pain in her eyes had been burned away by a flare of temper. "Why don't you just leave me alone?"

"You agreed to a partnership. I'm not going to let you abandon me."

She gaped. "Abandon? Look, I just need to

regroup. I can't think. With Loretta missing, and Mark dead, and Tom gone, and Viper..." Her gaze moved to the closed door as if she were thinking about the world beyond, but words failed her.

He softened his tone. "That's why you have me. That's what partners do for each other. They provide stability when the other one's going off the deep end."

She met his gaze with a glare. "I'm not going crazy."

"Good to hear. I needed to see that for myself. Besides, I'm your ride, remember?"

"I can get another ride."

"Why? I'm right here. Lean on me."

Her shoulders sagged. "People who get close to me get hurt. I'm a disease, a curse."

"That's not true."

"Really?" She counted off the people she'd hurt. "My father, my mother, Loretta, Mark Sheldon, who knows who else was hurt during the ranch attack, and now there's Viper. It's karma or fate or whatever."

"Why would you say that?" He wasn't the only one burdened by survivor's guilt.

"I'm not a nice person."

He huffed out a laugh that feathered the hair around her face. More had come loose from the rubber band. "Bullshit." They might not know each other on the deepest of levels, but he had the ability to gauge people's motivations within a few minutes. And he'd seen firsthand the depth of her feelings for Viper and her uncle. "Each of those people made choices that put them in danger. What happened to them wasn't your fault."

"And the ones who were my fault?" Her grip tightened on his shirt and he bit back a wince as she caught some of his chest hair in her grip. "The jobs I took, the money and favors I accepted, all with the delusion I was creating justice?"

In his search for her, he'd heard the stories about her being a gun for hire, but he'd also seen glimpses of the woman she was. "You did what you had to do. You were trying to *help* others, not hurt."

"They were bail-jumpers, perverts, cheaters, and criminals, but still…"

"I refuse to throw stones. I probably would have done the same thing to help someone in need."

She ignored his platitudes, intent on berating herself. "Why are you letting me off easy? So I'll owe you? You helped me find Viper, and now you're protecting him. You didn't turn me over to Stone. So what do you want in payment? What's the trade?"

"I'm not that kind of person. I help people because they need help, not because I expect payment." His own temper heated and he clenched his hands at his sides to keep from ripping her fists from his shirt. Doubtless, she was so lost in her grief and confusion that she didn't realize she was so physically close to him. And moving closer.

"*All* people let their greed, or their baser needs, steer them. See an obstacle? Obliterate it. Someone in your way? Get rid of them, or try. Kid getting in your way, messing up business? Drug them." She was lashing out, grasping for something that would push him away. Except that she had a death grip on his shirt as if begging him not to leave her. He didn't like the pain that made her voice quiver. As if realizing she'd revealed too much, she stopped and blinked. And he replayed what she'd just said.

Fuck. Drugging kids? Was she talking about being drugged herself? He didn't want to believe the world could be so cruel, but could see in her eyes that this was personal. Someone—probably multiple someones— had hurt her deeply. No wonder she didn't want anyone touching her food or drink. No wonder she ran.

He didn't want her to go there. Didn't want to see her break. Some part of him knew she would never want to see him again if she broke in front of him. She might never forgive him for witnessing that.

And so he provoked her. "Fine, you want to pay

me? A kiss."

She blinked. "What?"

"That's what I want."

Her hurt turned to surprise, then wariness. Her eyes narrowed. "Why a kiss?"

"No questions." He put his palms on either side of her face. Her hands were still fisted in his shirt, probably leaving wrinkles that would give the nurses no doubt as to what they'd been up to in this tiny closet, surrounded by sheets and blankets that smelled like industrial fabric softener. He leaned forward slightly and inhaled, filling his nostrils with Skye's light scent instead. She smelled like the outdoors. And flowers, always the hint of jasmine, such a delicate fragrance for such a strong woman. He wanted to taste her, so badly that he could feel the blood pumping through his limbs. But it had to be her decision. She was already confused as hell, tormented by a maelstrom of emotions she'd held at bay for too long. He wouldn't be the one to push her further away.

Cupping her face gently, he dipped toward her, still not touching his lips to hers. The heat of her hands had his nipples tightening beneath his shirt, and the light pain from her grip had become pleasure, spiked with need. When she didn't back away, he pressed his lips to her forehead and skimmed his palms from her cheeks to the sides of her neck.

"Sweet Skye. You don't even know that you have all the power here."

She stiffened but didn't stop him. He moved his lips across her forehead, pressing kisses along the crease of worry there. He continued to her eyelids and the tip of her nose.

But he stopped short of her lips, taking a shuddering breath to rein in his desire as he waited to see if she'd accept his challenge.

On a moan of surrender, she tipped her head back and lifted her mouth to meet his.

Shock. Wonder. Softness. Heat.

A quick inhalation, followed by a moan of desire that might have been him, but could have been her.

And a sudden, consuming hunger.

Skye inhaled to fill her lungs with more of his scent, even as a hundred sensory images slammed into her at once. Her blood roared in her ears as her brain tried to make sense of something that didn't make sense at all. How could this man be her anchor and make her soar at the same time?

She'd kissed men before but this was different. The sensations, and the confusion, permeated her on a whole new level, which made it all the more amazing that she wasn't resisting, or dropping Jared to the floor with a couple of well-placed defensive moves. She'd only rejected her first impulse to defend herself because she sensed his own hesitance. He was holding back in deference to her mood, conscious that she might perceive him as a threat. The soldier was analyzing her weaknesses, using her needs to manipulate her into doing what he wanted, into agreeing to this ill-fated partnership.

And she didn't fucking care, as long as he kept making her feel like this, like a bolt of lightning sizzling through the air. Hell, she kind of admired his skill at shattering her defenses so effectively. It was only his lips and hands touching her, but his heat radiated like a furnace from a hard body that was only inches away. She wanted to press against his hardness and feel all of him—just feel, period. She'd stifled her desires for so long that they roared to the surface and threatened to consume them both.

Her core caught fire as if her walls were simply paper and he was a lit match, though his body remained unengaged in the blitz. If he'd made a move to get closer to her, she might have been able to break the spell, but the very fact that he was holding himself back was enough to encourage her, to let her explore on her own.

Or maybe she was wrong. Maybe he wasn't enjoying this as much as she was.

Curious, she opened her mouth to him, and was rewarded with another rush of heat as his tongue slid against hers. He smelled of warm male and tasted of mint and coffee—he must have indulged in a sip or two before finding her. The light rasp of his beard stubble against her chin was a reminder that he'd rushed out of the house this morning to get her here as fast as possible. *I help people because they need help, not because I expect payment.* His sacrifice was as provocative as the moist heat of his mouth. He slanted his head to capture more of her and her tongue parried with his. Her heart quickened until she worried the organ would push through bone, muscle, and skin to get to him. And she'd be perfectly okay dying such a death.

Which was when the reality overcame the curiosity.

She unfurled her fingers, which had clutched his shirt in an embarrassing display of neediness, and took a quick step in retreat. Her butt hit the shelf behind her, sending a jolt of pain that would become a bruise, but also bringing her back to reality like a drowning woman gulping for that first breath of air after breaking the surface of the water.

He was still so close she could feel his warm breath. Her cheeks flushed as she realized why. Her stubborn hands must have reached out when she bumped the shelf. Again, they'd grabbed onto his shirt. She stared at the offending appendages and through sheer, concentrated willpower, uncurled her fingers and dropped her hands to her sides.

"I'm sorry." Her voice shook. She followed her apology with a curse that negated it. "No, I'm not sorry. I accepted your challenge. And now we're even." With brisk motions, she ran her hands over the wrinkles in his shirt as if she could iron out all evidence of her temporary insanity.

"Skye." Her name was a growl dredged up from deep in his throat. "Unless you want to pay me for the wrinkles in my shirt with another kiss—or *more*—I suggest you stop touching me like that."

She stared at him in shock. Her touch affected him that powerfully? She gripped her hands at her sides, unsure of the solidity of the shaky new ground on which they stood together.

He leaned back as if he, too, suddenly needed space. "I suppose we should check out the ranch, if you're up for it."

"I am."

His gaze filled with concern. "It won't look like you remember it."

No, she didn't suppose it would. "I can handle it."

"If it's safe, we can stay there tonight and make arrangements to visit Viper in the morning. Maybe he'll be awake by visiting hours and be able to tell us who did this to him." He stopped with his hand on the doorknob. "Thanks for the kiss. And don't worry. You'll get better with practice." He winked.

Her jaw dropped. Had he just insulted and dared her again? His mischievous grin told her the answer was yes. He probably thought he was lightening the mood, letting her off the hook for the way she'd almost lost complete control with him, but she couldn't let his comment slide. "Thanks for the tip, but sometimes, if satisfaction wasn't achieved, it's the partner who's to blame." She shrugged as if her heart wasn't pounding to get out of her chest again. The thought of practicing with Jared did wonders for her imagination. "But cheer up. I'm not to everyone's taste."

"Some tastes are acquired over time. And I hope we'll be spending a lot of time together." He reached a hand up as if he might touch her face. At the last second, he paused, then traced her bottom lip with one long finger. His eyes sparkled with heat and the light of battle.

Oh God, what was she doing, playing with fire? She was so out of her depth. And yet, she'd never felt so alive.

"She came with *him*," Tristan said on the other end of their phone conversation.

Finn watched Loretta try to build a fire. He was teaching them basic survival techniques—not in case they survived, since there was no chance in hell he could let that happen, but in case the hunt lasted more than a day. The challenge was always more fun that way. Loretta was a quick learner. He wondered if Skye had helped train her at the ranch.

But Skye and Jared had joined forces? *Damn it.*

"Taking Skye was going to be challenge enough," Tristan said. "Now we have to deal with the bodyguard?"

When had Tristan turned into such a pansy-ass worrier? Finn sighed. "Just stay out of sight. You don't want her to recognize you."

"Why not?"

Because she knows you attacked her ranch. "You're supposed to be long gone, remember? And you don't want Viper to suspect you're the one who put him in the damn hospital."

"I'm keeping my distance."

Finn was betting Skye would want to stay close to Viper until he was out of the woods. They just had to get Jared away from her. Divide and conquer. He'd been saving a certain useful bit of information about Jared Bennigan. It was time to use it.

He wanted Skye in his stable, tonight—without Jared in tow. That guy was a complication he didn't need, but it was all part of the game, if he thought about it.

Patience. Preparation. Anticipation.

Live fearlessly and play ferociously.

It was that last part he liked the best.

CHAPTER THIRTEEN

Skye was lost in thought as she drove west from Flagstaff toward the ranch. She'd convinced Jared that she should drive Phil Barton's truck back to Three Fortunes while he followed in his SUV. A glance at the rearview told her he was still right behind her as she exited the interstate. Ahead, the sun was getting low in the sky.

She was grateful for the time to think, and to rebuild her defenses. The kiss had shaken her, and so did the desire for another one. Or more. Leaving an unconscious, but guarded, Viper at the hospital and wondering if Uncle Tom was in the same predicament somewhere, without help, only put her more on edge. She checked her phone as she pulled onto the ranch property, but there was still no message from Tom. She refused to revisit all the reasons he might not have been able to check in with the message service.

The electricity that normally charged the security fence had been permanently cut, but the main house had suffered only minor external damage from stray bullets. As she got out of the vehicle, Skye was trying not to feel homesick. It seemed ridiculous, considering she was home. But it reminded her what she'd had a short time ago, and what she'd lost. Standing in the kitchen brought a strange mix of nostalgia and tension, since it was the place Jared had asked her to trust him, asked her to call him, and she'd refused, going out on her own instead.

It creeped her out that the house she'd lived in for

so many years was partly owned by Robert Stone, a man who made movies, got rich off the extravagant spending of others, and took advantage of beautiful, vulnerable young women. Stone was everything Tom Hamilton had professed to despise.

Had Mark Sheldon been targeted on purpose, because he'd dared to go after Stone? Had Tristan betrayed his own, shot Mark, and then pursued Viper? And what about Uncle Tom?

"Maybe I should call my uncle again," she said as Jared joined her. "Leave another message. Or hang out in Williams or Ash Fork, see if I can pick up a lead on anyone else from Three Fortunes. Someone had to see something."

Jared cupped her chin and eyed her critically. "I think you need a breather. I'm going to change and go for a run, check out the property."

She nibbled her lip. She could use a bit more alone time to sort things out in her head. The powerful emotions stirred by seeing Viper in the hospital, and by Jared's kiss, had her confused.

After making sure the house was clear, Jared changed, though he kept his gun close at hand in a holster, and went for a jog to check out the premises.

In the kitchen, she unpacked the groceries they'd picked up in town, but she wasn't hungry. Instead, she felt antsy, amped up. There were ghosts here.

Through the kitchen window, her gaze landed on the spot in the yard where Darren had died. Who'd wanted him to take her down? Stone had already convinced her uncle to turn his back on her. Why would he then attack the ranch he owned?

Viper had been wounded somewhere around here, too, possibly at Stone's hands—or, rather, at the hands of hired men such as Darren and Tristan. Men who owed Stone some kind of debt, if that's what the torn cards were all about. Skye had been their redemption, which meant Stone wanted *her*. But for what?

The incessant questions, the memories of that

night of destruction and chaos, made her twitchy. She hadn't had a good workout in days.

After a quick change, she headed outside to stretch her legs. Even in April, the late afternoon could get cool in the high country, and a chill spiked the air and stung her skin. She'd knotted a sweatshirt around her waist but preferred the sleeveless tank top and leggings she wore beneath. The cold was invigorating against her bare arms.

As she crossed the open yard to where the barn had been, she ignored the tightness in her throat, focusing on picking her way across the debris. Viper's Pit was no more. The gym where she'd trained all her life to stand strong and fight for what she believed in had been burned down to the concrete block on which it had stood.

An unexpected jolt of loss hit her like a punch to the gut. She bent over at the waist, her hands braced above her knees as she gasped for air, feeling as if she'd just run a race. Expletives ran through her head as she cursed her enemy. Why had Stone's men done this?

"You okay?" Jared's voice startled her.

She straightened and spun to face him, taking in his sweatpants and damp T-shirt. Sweat formed a V on his chest and he was breathing more heavily than normal. "I will be when we castrate Robert Stone and Tristan Floyd." She'd hang their balls from the ranch's gate.

"I hope you get your chance." He looked over the charred foundation. "At least there were only two casualties, and one of them was his own man."

"Darren Boscoe. I haven't found anything about him yet."

"There are two listed in the Vegas area, but I have yet to look into them further. That was going to be today's plan." Before he'd dropped everything to help her.

"I hope everyone else got away, and I'm grateful someone found Viper in time to get him help." She balled up her fists as anger and frustration swarmed her. They'd been ambushed, and it had been her fault. All of this destruction couldn't be simple retaliation because she'd spied on Stone in Malibu. There had to be something more going on.

Jared took one of her hands between his and pried her fingers open. "I can help you relieve that pent-up stress."

Her breath caught. Her gaze shot to his mouth. Was he suggesting...?

"I saw some sparring gloves in the shed out back," he said before the flush creeping up her neck could give her carnal thoughts away. He grinned. "Along with all the ammo stored there."

"We were always prepared for anything..." Her words drifted off as she realized how utterly unprepared they'd been for Stone. Still, he hadn't won. Not yet, anyway. They'd survived so far, and she'd come back swinging.

"We could spar on that flat patch of land off the back porch." Near where Darren had died. The sympathetic twist of his lips told her Jared was aware of the direction of her thoughts. "We'll replace the bad energy with good."

She swallowed and pulled her hand away, tossing him a casual grin to disguise her deeper turmoil. "As long as this offer isn't out of pity. I won't go easy on you." The thought of punching someone, even Jared's handsome face, had definite appeal.

"Not pity. Foresight. I'm going to learn all your tricks so you can't escape me again." Jared's grin told her he was teasing.

"Probably not all of them."

"Then you're agreeing to a match?" He looked like a little boy who'd just been given a new toy.

"Sure, but I feel compelled to warn you. I know how to fight dirty."

Jared realized his mistake the moment Skye landed a right hook, then followed the move by wrapping her left leg around his knee and throwing her body at him, using the momentum of her own weight to take him to the ground.

Or maybe he'd made the mistake the moment he'd approached her after his run. He should have just gone inside for a shower. But he hadn't been immune to the way she'd hugged herself as she looked forlornly over the ruined buildings. This had been her home, all she had of her family, and he knew how hard it was to lose someone or something one loved.

He enjoyed igniting the spark of challenge in her eyes, and their first couple minutes of light punches and dancing around the makeshift ring in the grass had been almost enjoyable, flooding him with adrenaline. But when she took him to the ground and climbed on top... Holy hell, it was lust that flooded him now.

He dredged up an old martial arts technique and flipped her to her back in the grass, then hastily shifted so she wouldn't feel his arousal. He pushed to a standing position and took several steps back. But she came at him again, tossing off her gloves to fight barehanded, and giving him no time to gather his wits. She was a formidable opponent.

"Skye, maybe we should stop." He pulled off his own gloves.

But she was on him like sugar on candy, and he'd barely blocked a couple of blows before she was again trying to take him down. His training superseded the logical portion of his brain and he maneuvered her until he'd backed her against the house. How had they ended up across the yard? Damn, the woman jumbled his thoughts. And overwhelmed his senses—another tool in her arsenal.

His body pinned hers to the wall. "Just give me a second."

She was merciless and hooked a leg around him,

going for his knee again, but he shifted and stopped her, using his weight to keep her still. Her eyes went wide as his pelvis aligned with hers.

"Um, yeah, I told you to give me a second." He could see that she felt the hard ridge beneath his sweatpants. But he wouldn't let her go now and risk her taking him down again. That would be humiliating. Besides, he liked feeling her pressed up against him.

"Is *that* because of me or the fighting?"

He released a harsh laugh. "That's all you." Did the woman not see what she did to him? For Christ's sake, he'd first kissed her in a hospital supply closet. He obviously lacked willpower where she was concerned.

He sucked in several breaths tinged with the sharp scent of the junipers that dotted the property, light sweat, and the always-present hint of jasmine. It had to be her shampoo, and it made him want to bury his nose in her hair to confirm his theory.

"Really?" She licked her lips.

"Really. So, uh, maybe you could unwrap your leg from mine?" She still had one leg hooked around his. He slid a hand from where it gripped her arm, down to her thigh, stopping at her knee.

But instead of cooperating, she bent her knee further, pulling him even closer against her, fully aligning her body with his. At the same time, she slid her hands around his waist and up his back.

"Show me what you can do, soldier." She touched her mouth to his.

He started slow, unsure if this was a trick, some distraction so that she could take him down to the ground again. Using his lust against him would be a cruel joke—and a magnificent tactical move, especially since she'd confessed she fought dirty. But she seemed content to cling to him. A soft moan reverberated from her chest through his, which was now pressed against her beautiful breasts. Her fingers slid up into his hair and he shivered. His tongue darted out to trace the line of her lips and she opened to him with a sigh of surrender.

His resistance broke. The kiss went from hot to sizzling as her tongue launched a battle with his, tasting and assessing, like some kind of recon mission. It was different from the vulnerability he'd sensed from her yesterday at the hospital. This was the strong, curious, adventurous Skye, and he was happy to let her explore.

She nearly crawled up his body, still anchoring herself with her leg and using her hands to hold onto his head. His blood pumped harder, his need growing as she let him deepen the kiss, then returned his passion with a wildness that spurred him.

Suddenly, she turned her head to the side, breaking contact. With her lips, at least. There was no room for her to retreat, and her head thunked against the wall behind her. Her leg went lax and he released his grip on her knee so she could lower it.

She worked to catch her breath, her eyes searching his face. He had no answers for the chemistry between them. It simply was. But in her wide eyes, he saw the confusion and wariness their hunger generated.

Welcome to the club. He wasn't sure he'd ever felt such an instant physical connection to a woman. Certainly not in recent memory. But because he could see her shields already slamming shut and locking into place, he decided to lighten the mood.

"Guess the training got to you, too? Or was it me?" He winked.

"Definitely the training." Her grin wobbled. She licked her lips and he nearly leaned in for another taste. But he had the feeling she'd taken enough big steps today. It was better to leave her wanting more, and give her time to sort out her feelings.

He could use some time himself.

Skye paced the kitchen, feeling sweaty and grimy but exhilarated after pounding on Jared.

Oh hell, so it was the kiss that had her energized.

But she was also unsatisfied and restless. Nobody made her feel vulnerable like that, especially twice in one day, and got away with it.

A moment later, the creak of floorboards from upstairs ceased, replaced with the sound of pipes running water to the shower. Where Jared was currently naked.

Who was he to take over her life, her house, and her hormones? Who was Jared Bennigan, really? She only had his word, and what information he'd given her, to go on. And lately, everyone she'd thought was trustworthy wasn't. The people she'd counted on in her life had held things back or disappeared, leaving her alone. How could she trust that Jared wouldn't do the same?

You can't trust anyone. Uncle Tom's constant reminder rattled around her brain, feeding off her adrenaline.

Skye paced the kitchen for several long moments. The shower was still running. It was now or never. Making her decision, she hurried to her uncle's bedroom, which she'd lent to Jared for the night.

An orange slice of sunset broke through the part in the heavy drapes and now slanted across the bed, where his change of clothes had been carefully folded and stacked. A reluctant smile tugged at Skye's lips. Definitely a military man.

She shot a glance at the closed bathroom door, and a shot of anticipation rushed through her at the sound of Jared in the shower. Her adrenaline rush wasn't entirely due to her snooping expedition.

Spying his wallet on top of the dresser, she went to it, telling herself it wasn't an invasion of privacy if it led to her trusting him further. Besides, restoring her trust in herself and her instincts was top priority.

The leather trifold lay open, as if inviting her to

take a look. She surveyed his driver's license, which had been issued in Nevada, and a couple credit cards. Looking through the cash compartment, she ignored the money and stopped as her fingers brushed a thicker piece of paper. A photo? God, maybe he had a wife and kid stashed away. Or, at the very least, a fiancée. A man with Jared's attributes didn't stay single for long. Unless by choice.

She pulled out the paper and froze. *No.* It couldn't be.

Bracing her shaky legs as a red haze of anger threatened to suck her under like a riptide, she held the half-card up to the light. The two of hearts stared back at her, and she nearly laughed at the irony of the number and suit.

He wanted her to trust him, to be his partner, and yet he had a card. Rather, half a card, with a jagged edge where someone had ripped it from its mate.

A card like Darren's.

And Tristan's.

And anyone else who owed Stone some kind of warped debt.

You're my redemption, Darren had said. When he'd failed, had she become Jared's problem—*his* redemption?

She ran her thumb over the jagged edge. It was still rough, more freshly torn than Darren's. She turned the card over and her stomach clenched as her suspicions were confirmed. The Legacy logo, or half of it, stared back at her.

He was playing her. Their kisses, their embraces—hell, even the times he'd cheered her up or comforted her—they were part of some grand plan to trap her. He'd used her, used her feelings and her sympathy for his missing sister. Was Chelsea even missing, or some made-up reason for Jared to supposedly link forces with Skye?

"Skye?"

She swung toward the bathroom door. She hadn't

heard him turn off the shower, hadn't heard him open the door. Hadn't heard anything beyond the rush of blood in her head.

He'd stopped in the doorway, a towel slung around his waist and another held against his head as if he'd been rubbing at his wet hair, which stood out in every direction. The sultry smile that had automatically curved his lips faded as his attention shifted to her hand.

His gaze whipped to his dresser and his wallet before swinging back to her. "Making yourself at home?" He walked into the room and crossed his arms as if *she* owed *him* an explanation.

She forced her jaw to unlock and her mouth to move. "It *is* my home, after all. Or maybe you've forgotten that you don't hold all the power in this *partnership.*"

He took a step toward her.

She immediately took a step back, holding a palm up. "No touching! Enough of this *partners need to trust each other* bullshit."

"It's not bullshit." His tone was as hard as his eyes.

"It's *all* bullshit. What's this?" Skye thrust the card toward him, dismayed to see it wavering as her hand shook. *With anger. It shakes with anger, not hurt. Not betrayal.* She didn't know Jared well enough, didn't trust him enough, hadn't fallen far enough, to be betrayed. But the swell of emotion pressing inside as if it could crack her ribcage open sure felt like pain.

"You recognize it?" Jared's tone was more curious than upset. The lack of congruency of emotion gave her momentary pause.

Still, Skye wrapped her anger around her like armor. "Enough to know this is from Stone's casino, and that it signifies some kind of debt."

Jared's brow creased. "Debt?"

"What kind of debt do you owe Stone?" Her skin went cold, her palms clammy as she let her anger build and flow like lava.

"Nothing. I—" He broke off and swore as his phone rang. As she made a move to leave, he picked his phone up off the dresser with one hand and snagged her arm with the other. "We're not done. Just give me a second."

"I think I've given you enough."

But he didn't let go of her as he answered his phone. "Bennigan." His expression hardened as he listened. His eyelids slid closed and his nostrils flared. His grip on her arm gentled and Skye felt a moment of concern that she quickly stifled. "Thank you, Emily. I'm a few hours away, but I'll be there as soon as possible. Keep her there, please. Threaten her if you have to. I owe you."

Threaten her? Who was he after now?

He switched the phone off and went to shove it into his pocket before he remembered he wasn't wearing anything but a towel. Skye saw the moment he realized he'd have to let go of her to get dressed.

She smirked and steel flashed in his eyes. Instead of letting her go, he tossed the phone to the dresser and tugged her to him. Her struggles went unheeded.

"Stop." His command was low and gruff, demanding but not forceful. She stopped struggling, figuring he couldn't hold onto her forever. Better to let him get his excuses over with and then she could walk away. "You're not going to run away from conflict this time."

"I don't—"

"Yes, you do," he interrupted. "And you have no reason to run, not from me."

"What do you care? By the sound of that phone call, you have places you need to be."

He nodded. "I do, actually. That was Emily, the bartender at Legacy Lounge."

"I knew you were still linked to Stone."

"She called because Haley's there, drinking. She's underage." His expression grew sad for a moment. "I'm obviously failing Haley as much as I failed Chelsea."

"So there really is a sister—or two?"

His mouth pressed into a thin line for a long moment. "There are two. I'm not lying to you. About anything. I thought we'd gotten beyond all the distrust. We agreed to be partners." Hurt flared in his eyes.

She looked down to avoid seeing the pain, which meant her gaze connected with his bare chest. "Then what's the card about?"

"I found it tucked into Chelsea's day planner at her apartment. It's one of the reasons I figured Stone is connected to her disappearance." His gaze landed on the card, which had fallen from her fingertips to the floor. "But I didn't think it meant anything." His gaze lifted to hers again. "Obviously, you do. You've been holding out on me."

She felt the fight leave her body. He was right. She had been holding back. "Darren had one on him when he died. That's what he was pulling out of his pocket to show me when he was shot. I think Tristan was trying to keep him from talking to us, since he also had a card."

Jared's grip tightened as if he were trying to hold on to his patience. "Why didn't you tell me?"

"I didn't trust you. I'm still not sure I trust you. That's why I went through your wallet." She waited for his vengeance. When it didn't come, she pulled back to search his face. She found only bafflement.

"Tristan had a card, too?"

"That night you found me in Stone's study, I found the other half of Darren's card, marked with his name, along with another half-card marked with Tristan's name, in Stone's desk drawer. Darren had mentioned that I was his redemption. I have no clue what that means, other than I think these cards could be a symbol of some kind of debt he owed."

He went silent, absorbing this information, but he didn't lash out at her.

She shook her head. "Why aren't you angry?"

He let out a harsh laugh. "I suppose I would have

done the same thing if I were in your shoes, having grown up as you did." She stiffened, but he moved to stroke her back, soothing her. "That wasn't an insult, just empathy. I hope you'll finally believe me. I have nothing to hide." His arms instinctively flexed around her as if he could block out her doubts.

"I guess I don't either, not anymore."

He dipped his face down to hers but didn't kiss her mouth. Instead, he put his lips to her ear and pressed a gentle kiss there. "Good. Stop fighting me. We'll accomplish so much more together." He pulled away. "I have to get back to Vegas and help Haley."

"I'll come with you." Several emotions crossed his face, so rapidly that she wasn't sure what she was seeing. Surprise. Relief. Gratitude.

"I'd like that," he said.

Something inside her shifted. Perhaps she could be a partner, after all.

CHAPTER FOURTEEN

Four hours later, Jared had arranged for the guard to remain outside Viper's hospital room. Hopefully Skye'd be able to talk to Viper soon, but Haley was the priority now, especially since the young woman was on Stone's turf.

"You and Emily are friends?" Skye asked, matching Jared's long strides as he headed for Legacy Lounge.

"Not friends, exactly. I got to know her a bit when I was working security," he said. "Guess she's not as loyal to Stone as some of his employees are, or she might have cut her ties to me when I was fired. Or maybe she hasn't heard that bit of news, though she was still working the party last night when Duffy, Meyer, and I were let go." He slid a glance her way. "How do you know Emily?"

"Mark's credit card was used here, supposedly by Loretta, the day after the Malibu party, though Emily didn't recognize her picture." Only a handful of days had passed, yet Skye felt as if she'd traveled around the world. "She's how I learned about Stone's Henderson house party."

Emily caught sight of them as they wove their way through the tables to the bar. She was mixing a drink for a customer, but tipped her head to indicate a door off to the side. Jared took Skye's hand and pulled her into a large storage room lined with shelves of supplies, a desk, and a cot set up in the corner.

Jared let go of her to hurry to the girl asleep on

the cot, her face flushed and blonde hair mussed.

"There was a guy here, buying her drinks during Happy Hour," Emily said as she entered the storage room. "I would have stopped him earlier if I'd seen them, but it was busy and they were in the back corner. She looked so much older in those clothes and that makeup, but up close you can tell she's still a baby. Apparently, my waitress finally figured it out, too, and she's the one who told me."

Skye moved closer to Haley and saw the smudges of makeup on her pale face. "Is she okay?"

"Just sleeping it off," Emily said. "I woke her a little while ago to drink some water and take a couple aspirin."

"Thanks," Jared said, getting to his feet. "I owe you."

"Yeah, well, I'm pretty pissed, but at the waitress who didn't card her. When I finally did, Haley said she knew people who worked here. She started telling everyone her brother was—and I quote—'the great Jared Bennigan,' and then she told me you could kick my ass six ways from Sunday. And then she broke down in tears. The guy hightailed it out of there during the commotion, probably figuring the police would be here soon to arrest him." Emily's amusement turned to concern as she looked at Haley. "She looked ready to bolt if I suggested contacting anybody but you. She said something about you being hurt, and how she had to know you were okay. She was willing to lie down as long as I promised to only call you."

"I'm glad you did." Jared brushed strands of hair away from his sister's flushed face.

Skye couldn't believe she'd doubted this man's agenda. Actions spoke louder than words, and Jared's actions were of a committed, loving brother. He had every right to be angry and frustrated with Haley, and yet the emotion she sensed from him was concern. And maybe a bit of self-flagellation, judging by the guilt she read on his face.

"Haley's condition isn't the only reason I called." Emily glanced at the closed door, as if worried someone might barge in. "Before she passed out, Haley mentioned something about Chelsea. You still haven't found her then?"

Jared shook his head and turned to Skye. "Chelsea danced here in the lounge twice a week, for the past couple months."

Emily frowned. "Here, we set up shadowbox-like screens where the audience only sees silhouettes. It's a classier kind of striptease. Some of these women can be divas, but Chelsea was one of the professional ones, and always polite. Definitely too sweet for a job that tends to suck the soul right out some girls. I didn't know she was hiring out for private parties until you came to question me."

"Chelsea's disappearance, and my preoccupation with it, is probably why Haley's chosen to act out like this."

Behind him, Haley moaned and her eyelids flickered. "Jared?"

"Right here, Bossy Pants," he said.

"Don't feel well." Haley didn't look like she'd be bossing anyone around anytime soon.

"I have to get back out there." Emily jerked a thumb over her shoulder.

"Thank you, Emily," he said. "I owe you."

"Just take care of her. She said something about a birthday?" Emily arched her brows, and then excused herself to return to the bar.

"Shit." Jared shoved a hand through his hair. "She sent me the email but I haven't had time—"

"Don't need you," Haley said, pushing his hand away. But as she tried to sit up, he gently pressed her shoulders back to the cot.

"Take it easy. There's no rush."

"So you'll be eighteen soon?" Skye asked Haley, returning to Jared's side.

"Saturday," Haley mumbled, opening her eyes

again. "Who are you?"

"This is a friend of mine," Jared said.

"Thought you were busy with *work*." Haley pushed herself into a sitting position and Skye grabbed a water bottle from a nearby shelf, and put it in the young woman's hand.

"She's helping me find Chelsea," Jared explained. "So don't be rude. She's looking for someone, too."

Jared smoothed the sweat-damp hair from Haley's cheek, drawing her gaze to his. He smelled the alcohol on his baby sister's breath and his gut clenched. "Why would you do this? Not only is it illegal, it's extremely dangerous."

Haley's defenses went up immediately. "I was careful. I wasn't even going to drink. I was waiting for you."

"Why were you waiting for me here, on a school night?"

"Do we have to talk about this now?" Haley cast a glance toward Skye, but he wasn't going to let her dodge his questions.

"Don't worry about her. She won't judge you." And he couldn't send Skye away because he was afraid she was in danger, especially here, within the enemy camp. At the moment, he was trusting Emily not to say anything about their presence, but the need to get them somewhere safer pressed on him. "Let's get you home."

"Home?" Haley laughed humorlessly. "Not sure where that would be." She was lashing out from inner pain, and she had a right to that emotion.

"I am."

He talked to Jane, explaining he would take Haley for the night. He drove them to his house and settled Haley on the couch with another bottle of water and a deli sandwich they'd picked up at an all-night grocery store. "Eat. Hydrate."

Haley wrinkled her nose, but at least she didn't

look green at the thought of food. "I'm not hungry." But she unwrapped the sandwich.

"I can make a run to the store or something," Skye said. She was offering them privacy, for which he was grateful, but he couldn't let her leave the house without him. Too much was at stake, and he didn't know if someone was out to harm her. With Tristan on the loose, it was a real and constant threat, especially with the crazy theory about redemption. Besides, she was a part of this now.

"I'd like you to stay," Jared said. Watching them with interest, Haley didn't object. "Tell me what happened," he said to his sister.

"I got a call from someone who said he works with you. He said you'd been hurt." Her eyes flicked over him.

"I'm fine," he said. Skye perched on a side table, seemingly reluctant to get too close. He could see she felt like an outsider but didn't know how to draw her in. "What else did the man say? Did he give you a name?"

"Floyd," Haley said. "And he asked me to meet him at Legacy, said that he'd send a cab for me and that you'd be calling him soon and we could both wait for your call."

Jared gritted his jaw. *Tristan Floyd.* It had to be him. He could see Skye was thinking the same thing.

Jared saw the misery on Haley's face. "Did he hurt you?"

"No." But Haley wrapped her arms around her waist. "Just wanted to talk. He bought me a drink. Or two."

"I'll kill him," Skye said, surprising both of them into looking at her. She waved a hand. "Sorry. Continue."

Haley sighed. "He said it would steady my nerves while we waited."

Jared shuddered, thinking about what could have happened to his baby sister if Emily hadn't stepped in.

"I'm sorry I drank," Haley said. "I thought maybe he was right, maybe it would numb things until you returned. I didn't want *you* to leave me, too."

Guilt stabbed at Jared. Haley's father had left. Jared had left. "You could have been drugged by him, or taken advantage of..." As the images swirled through his head, he felt Skye's hand at his shoulder, halting his words.

Haley had gone pale again and her teeth were beginning to chatter. Skye picked up a throw Chelsea had given him as a housewarming gift and draped it across Haley's shoulders.

He pushed off the couch and paced until he could get his anger under control. He'd almost lost another sister, and for what? Why would they go after an innocent girl? Because they knew it would get to him, and to Skye.

Skye cleared her throat. "Maybe we should let her get some sleep, and you and I can discuss things."

She was right. Haley didn't need any more stress, and he and Skye had plans to make.

He helped Haley to her bedroom and made sure she was comfortable. "You can have Chelsea's room again," he told Skye as they moved out into the hallway.

Skye stroked a hand down his arm. "She'll be back soon, sleeping there."

"I don't care if she wants to live in India, as long as I know she's safe." And happy. Happy would be nice. The Bennigans deserved a stable, secure, content life, without complications and drama. Skye was the very antithesis of calm and drama-free. And yet when he was with her, he felt more alive than he had in months, maybe years.

He watched her turn down the sheets on the queen-size bed, and wondered if he should suggest she sleep with him on his king bed. Or not sleep. But she looked exhausted, and Haley was just across the hall, so he battled down his lust and focused on tomorrow.

"Tomorrow, we'll see if we can find out more about Tristan Floyd and Darren Boscoe and how they might be connected to Stone."

Skye hid a yawn. "Sounds like a plan."

As she straightened, he stopped in front of her and leaned down to press a kiss to her forehead. Unable to resist tasting a bit more, he claimed her mouth in a hot, but brief, kiss. He pulled away before he could lose himself in her. "Good night, partner."

He turned and walked out before she could respond, because the heat that had flared in her eyes, and the way her body had briefly melted into his, was almost too much temptation to resist. She'd be walking out of his life soon, back to Arizona and her world there, and he didn't need another complication in his life. He needed to find Chelsea, get his sisters settled and happy, get his own life on track, and then, months from now, he could consider his own life plan.

For now, though, indulging himself in Skye Hamilton was a luxury he couldn't afford.

CHAPTER FIFTEEN

Finn stalked to his kitchen to add a shot of Bailey's to his morning coffee.

"I swear I don't know where the fuck your head is at lately," Ryan muttered. "You're obsessed with the Hunting Grounds when we have so many other things going on that require our attention."

Finn sneered. "I thought you were handling everything else just fine on your own."

He'd arrived home late last night, after expecting to encounter Skye at the ranch—and take her to the Grounds. And then Tristan had called with the news that both Jared and Skye had shown up at Legacy. Together. Fuck.

Finn hadn't anticipated Ryan showing up at his condo at the butt crack of dawn, hadn't expected to learn late last night that Skye had shown up with Jared Bennigan to pick up his inebriated sister at Legacy when it was supposed to be Jared, solo, and he certainly hadn't expected to be blindsided with bullshit criticism.

Ryan shook his head in disgust. "Fine. Pout if it makes you feel better. Then grow the hell up."

"Maybe I'm tired of you taking all the credit for shit we've built together. We discovered your father's ledger together. We invented the Redemption Club."

"Reinvented," Ryan reminded him.

"Whatever, man. It's ours now. And the hunts were my idea."

"I agreed to *let them* be yours, but you can't

neglect the rest of our plans. And I refuse to let you put the rest of us at risk because of your personal agendas. My dad's been asking questions, trying to figure out if Skye was the one who was blackmailing him and to determine who attacked the ranch. He's looking for her now, too."

"Let him dig. I've set things up so that all roads lead away from us. He won't suspect."

"He's smarter than you give him credit for. You're risking everything. You keep on the path you're on and you'll be kicked out of the Club."

Finn looked up sharply. "You wouldn't do that."

"Try me." His best friend turned his back on him and walked out.

Finn immediately phoned Tristan. "We need a new plan." He'd underestimated the bond that had developed between Jared and Skye, but soon he'd have her to himself. Despite his workout, there was another kind of release he needed. The kind only Skye Hamilton could provide.

"Last night, I followed them to Bennigan's place," Tristan said. "Want me to arrange a little home invasion?" He sounded eager for action.

"Too risky, especially with three of them." He only wanted Skye, anyway. "Luring Jared back here didn't separate them, so we'll have to make a bigger statement."

"What do you have in mind?"

Finn looked out the window of his condo. Far off in the distance, the rising sun hit the mirrored windows of the Vegas strip, a hunting ground of a different type. Skye was out there, somewhere, at this very moment. His blood heated at the thought.

Finn grinned as he made his decision. "A message, of sorts. And it'll have the added bonus of putting our target on edge. Skye will have the lead she's looking for, and we'll lure her right into our hands. In the meantime, we get to have our fun, too. You up for it?"

Tristan chuckled. "Aren't I always?"

"Good. Because today, we hunt."

Skye was unprepared for the impact of finding Jared, clad in cotton pajama bottoms and a plain white tee, toasting bagels while Haley sat on a barstool, chatting with him and looking decidedly less pale. It was like having a real family, or at least the imaginary family she'd envisioned in her head since she was a child.

She slid into the barstool next to Haley. "How are you feeling?"

"Better." Haley grimaced as she met Skye's gaze. "I'm sorry I wasn't very nice yesterday."

"You weren't feeling yourself."

"Still working on that." Haley pressed two fingers to a temple and closed her eyes.

Skye moved to a side cabinet where, on her first thorough exploration of Jared's home, she'd spied medicine. She removed a bottle of pills and shook out two for Haley's headache, then poured a glass of orange juice to boost her blood sugar.

As she moved about, she felt Jared's eyes on her, but she didn't meet his gaze. Skye had been shocked by her desire to slip into his bed last night, just to feel his arms around her. But those desires weren't right. They couldn't be. He was meant for a woman who could give him a stable, loving family. What the hell did she know about love and family? Besides, he hadn't invited her into his bed.

"Are you going to call and check on Viper?" he asked as he spread cream cheese on a bagel.

"Already did. He was still asleep, but he's out of the woods and the doctor thinks he'll be awake by this afternoon. I'll call back then." She was certain Jared was too busy with family matters to accompany her back to Flagstaff today, nor would he be happy if she offered to go by herself. Besides, they had avenues to explore here in town.

"Viper?" Haley asked as Jared slid a bagel in front of her. "Is he a wrestler or something?"

Skye laughed. "He's a friend. Kind of like a father figure, actually."

"Never had one of those."

Over Haley's head, Skye met Jared's gaze. He'd never had a father, either, and he and his sisters had different fathers. And their mother hadn't exactly been maternal. Yet they'd created a family unit.

"He got the nickname in the military. It kind of stuck after he came to the ranch and he taught us how to strike fast and hard." Skye smiled her gratitude as Jared handed her a plate with a bagel. He'd even applied cream cheese for her. She lifted her head to thank him and found him watching her.

"I didn't drug it," he said, handing her a cup of coffee, too.

"Hadn't crossed my mind," she said, hiding her surprise at that fact. Sure, she'd just watched him serve Haley an equivalent breakfast, so maybe that's why her guard had dropped. Then again, maybe he was just adept at getting past all of her walls.

Something warm passed between them and she looked away, only to find Haley watching them with undisguised interest.

Skye cleared her throat and ignored the energy flowing between her and Jared. "Plus, he didn't like his first name, Leonard."

Haley laughed, then sobered. "Why's he in the hospital? Is he sick?"

"Some men attacked the ranch where she lives," Jared said, joining them with his own plate. "That's why I smelled like smoke last time I saw you."

"That's why you're here now?" Over a bite of bagel, Haley met Skye's gaze. "Are you going to stay?"

"Your brother's helping me," Skye said. After that, she had no clue what would happen. The ranch was her home, but it was also partly owned by a megalomaniac who might kick her out.

"He's good at that. At helping."

Jared seemed uncomfortable with the compliment.

"I'm going to help others, too," Haley said with the force and optimism of a teenager confident she could change the world. "I'm going to be a doctor or a lawyer. Or maybe a therapist."

Skye envied her, both for having the strength to voice her desires and, apparently, the guts to make them happen.

Jared grunted. "Staying away from illegal activities like underage drinking might be a good start."

Haley winced, but didn't refute his opinion.

Skye cleared her throat. "I suppose we need a plan of attack for today."

"First, we drop Haley at Jane's so she can get ready for school."

"Can't I stick with you guys today?" Haley asked, her gaze full of longing that made Skye's heart hurt.

"No." He ruffled a hand over his sister's head as if she were five years old, but Haley didn't seem to mind. "You're grounded for the weekend."

Haley's shoulders slumped. "For my birthday? This sucks." But she didn't argue. "I've learned my lesson."

Over the rim of his coffee cup, Jared arched a brow. "Which lesson would that be? Never to meet up with a stranger in a strange place? Never to believe a message from someone you don't know? Or never to drink alcohol?"

"Maybe I should stick with you this weekend to make sure I've learned my lesson?" She slid Jared a glance from beneath a thick fringe of lashes. "You can keep your eye on me and make sure I study."

He snorted. "Nice try." He sighed and took his cup to the sink. "I'd love to have you here, but it's not time yet, kiddo. Just another few days at Jane's." He held up a hand as Haley began to protest. "Consider your punishment a community service. She needs some things done around the house."

"I thought now that I'm here, I could stay," Haley said in a small voice. "Don't you want me?"

Jared reached out and squeezed Haley's hand. "Skye and I have business to settle first. The sooner we find a lead on Chelsea and get her back here, safe, the sooner we can all get on with life."

And wasn't that the truth. His statement turned the bite of bagel in her mouth to a tasteless mass of glue. She only had a few more days here and, hopefully, things would be back to ordinary.

Except *ordinary* didn't sound so good to Skye anymore. She wanted extraordinary. She wanted Jared—in her bed, not in her heart. The latter would be way too complicated. He didn't need another dependent female in his life. Not that she was at all dependent, but he'd see her as one more woman to handle. And she didn't like the vulnerability that went with a relationship. Emotions made things messy.

After dropping Haley at Aunt Jane's to get ready for school, Skye and Jared headed toward their first lead. Jared had tracked down a local Darren Boscoe who was listed on the utility bills for a trailer home, not far from Jared's house.

Several minutes later, they pulled into a trailer park and had to lean forward to squint at the numbers. *Park* was a rather grandiose term, considering the rusting roofs, cracked foundations and dented siding of most of the homes. A few were simply campers that had been set up long term, if the flat tires and discarded parts underneath the vehicles were any indication.

But Boscoe's trailer had matching fabric curtains and even a planter with flowers by the front door. A doll lay in the red dirt, a pink ball with a cartoon character on it not far away. Boscoe had children? Skye tried to reconcile that with the man who'd come on to her at the Roadhouse, and the one who'd attacked the ranch.

"Home, sweet home," Skye remarked. But she'd

seen worse. She'd once taken a job to flush out squatters who'd trespassed on a ranch, carving out a little plot for themselves to make their own. Sometimes they made themselves at home long enough to plant pot and harvest a crop. People did what they had to do to survive.

They got out of the car and approached the door. A child's cries came from within. The woman who answered Skye's knock was younger than her and would have been pretty if she hadn't seemed so tired and rundown. She had a baby boy on one hip and a young girl who looked to be about three attached to the opposite leg. The little girl's eyes were filled with tears, her nose runny from crying.

"If you're my fairy godmother, you're just in time." The woman had a sense of humor, but her eyes swept over them with distrust.

"We're here about a man named Darren Boscoe," Skye said. "Do you know him?"

She glanced from one kid to another. "Yeah, you could say I know him." Her eyes filled with tears and she quickly blinked them back. "I *knew* him. If you're here to collect a payment, you're too late. He's d— gone." She'd quickly changed her wording after a glance down at her daughter. The bitterness in the woman's tone could have been anger at the man for dying, or for leaving her with debts to pay and a family to raise.

"I'm sorry for your loss. I met him briefly before…" Skye couldn't think of a more tactful way to put things in front of the kids, so she let her words trail off. The guy had basically come on to her, though that had probably been a ploy to get close to her, and then when that hadn't worked, he'd gone on the attack.

"May we come in?" Jared asked. "Just for a moment."

The mother sighed and stepped aside to let them in. "Be my guest. If you can distract her from her tears, I'll do anything."

"I'm Jared, and this is Skye." He followed the woman over the threshold. His large frame seemed to fill the cramped space. The inside of the trailer was neat and tidy, the sign of a woman who was trying to keep her life together when everything around her must have felt like it was falling apart. Skye admired her grit.

"I'm Carly." She pulled away from the little girl's grasp to put the baby in the high chair. "This is Eddie and the sweetheart whose meltdown you interrupted is Macy. She's missing her daddy this morning. He used to wake her with a special song each morning. Apparently, Mommy doesn't sing it right." She put a weary hand to her forehead. They were all still absorbing the magnitude of their family's loss.

While Darren had made poor choices, Skye cursed whoever had pushed him into a situation where he'd lost his life. Had he owed Stone a debt? If so, why, and how? And why would Skye be the repayment? None of this made any sense.

Jared squatted beside the tearful girl, who was now wide-eyed with curiosity. Her crying had turned to hiccups. "I'm no singer, but I'm pretty good at pony rides." The girl's eyes grew even wider, filled with hope now.

At Skye's and Carly's incredulous looks, he grinned sheepishly. "I have two younger sisters." He winked at Skye and she felt herself go warm all over. And parts of her that had never tightened with pleasure did so as he picked up the girl and held her with expert hands on his knee, bouncing her gently as he made horse noises. The girl grinned, and then let out a squeal of laughter.

Another squeeze in Skye's abdomen had her nearly gasping. God, was that her ovaries talking? Freaking ridiculous. A woman like her couldn't have a family. She couldn't imagine being a mother, caring about anyone so much that she'd ache if she lost them. Seeing Carly's pained expression reminded her how much loving someone could cost a person.

The little girl's attention was locked on Jared as he spoke to Carly. "We have some questions about Darren."

"Are you cops?"

"No. We're looking for a couple of missing women—women we know personally," Skye said.

"At least you have a better story than the last guy. You going to offer to buy me off, too?"

"What do you mean?"

"Another man was here right after I learned about Darren. Offered me a few thousand bucks to keep my mouth shut, and encourage the police not to investigate the shooting too closely. But I figured he's probably the one who got Darren into this mess. Something about him rubbed me the wrong way." She sighed. "Would have been nice to have the money, though."

"You refused?"

Carly's chin shot up. "I have principles. I wasn't about to promise I wouldn't talk about Darren, or look for the guy who shot him. Besides, I have other options. Just got my beautician's license and was looking to get a job." Her face fell. "But that was before, when Darren could watch the kids part of the time. Childcare's expensive." The fight went out of her. She turned away to shake more Cheerios out of a box and onto the tray in front of Eddie. "I should have taken his money, but there was something about him. Something too cocky, like he was so certain I was beneath him, you know? Grated on me."

"Did you get a name?"

"No, but he was young. Handsome. Seemed kind of familiar, like that guy in the latest fitness drink commercial." She hummed the jingle and her daughter giggled.

Skye pulled out her phone and searched the Internet using keywords from the product and jingle. She found a link to the commercial and chills rolled over her skin. She knew that face.

Jared took the phone from her outstretched hand. "That's Finn Tucker, a friend of Ryan Stone." He searched for the actor's credentials and held the screen out to Carly.

Carly barely had to look through the various screenshots featured on Finn's page to decide. "That's him. Smooth talker, you know? Did he take the girls you're looking for?"

"We're not sure, but he is connected to them," Jared said. Through Stone. "Could Darren have known Finn, maybe through Legacy Hotel and Casino?" He pulled a fat crayon out of the box on the coffee table and opened up a coloring book with one hand while balancing Macy on his knee. The girl was enthralled with his movements.

"He had a gambling problem," Carly said. "I used to find a few spare chips here and there, in the pockets of his pants when I was doing laundry, or in the car. Stashed them away to cash later, when I needed grocery money."

"Did he owe a lot of people?" Jared asked.

She shot him a sharp glance. "Is that why you're really here, to squeeze us for money?" She threw an arm wide. "Look around. Not going to find much here."

The baby was starting to get agitated, so Skye stood and moved over to him, lifting a spoonful of some orange substance that was, maybe, apricots. "We aren't here for that." Skye smiled for the baby's sake. Little Eddie seemed to calm and accepted the spoon. "We're trying to help, to find justice for Darren. For you."

Carly settled on the spot on the small couch that Skye had vacated and watched Jared color for Macy. "All I know is he was afraid of something."

"Why?" Jared asked, with a glance at the girl who'd moved out of his lap and to the table to color. She was preoccupied with her task and not listening.

"I think he owed a lot of money." Carly picked up a crayon, coloring alongside her daughter. The movement seemed to soothe the woman. "When he got drunk, which he'd been doing more and more over the past year, he used to pull out this thing and stare at it. It was just a stupid torn card, but he'd sit and stare for a long time. Said one day he'd have to do something... It was like he was dreading that *one day*."

Skye recalled the date on the card she'd found in Stone's desk drawer. "Did the drinking get worse about eighteen months ago?"

Carly looked up. "Yes, as a matter of fact." She glanced at Eddie. "I'd just found out I was pregnant again. Macy was just over a year old. We were about to be evicted from our tiny apartment. Darren and I were stressed. He took off for a couple months. Walked back in as if nothing had happened, but he was different. Changed. When I tried to ask him about where he'd been, he had this crazy look in his eyes. He had a deed to this trailer, so we finally had a place that was ours. I stopped pestering him. But one time he said something about how he got this place..." She stopped coloring and seemed to stare off into space for a long moment.

"What did he say?" Skye prompted.

"That he'd played the best game of his life and it had paid off. But that he still had a debt to pay. He mentioned something about paying to become a member of the Redemption Club. And that he wasn't sure it was worth the price."

CHAPTER SIXTEEN

Finn unlocked and opened the gate to the property only a privileged few—those Redemption Club members who were lucky enough, and rich enough, to participate—knew as the Hunting Grounds. A little farther down the drive, he parked in front of the single-room cabin and turned to his passenger.

"Did you bring your mask?" He reached into the backseat and tossed the bag to Tristan. "There are extra in there if you need one."

Tristan nudged the duffel at his feet. "I have mine. I've been using it when I come here, in case Loretta might recognize me. Only one girl for the both of us?"

"That's all we can spare at the moment. I've promised a big hunt to Club members as soon as we have Skye. The other two in the stable are reserved for that hunt. Or I might decide to have a special event just for her." Hunting and taking down such a prize would be worth it. "Today is just fun for the two of us, so it's just the one woman. Unless you want to pay me fifty grand for better game?"

Tristan shook his head. "This'll do."

Finn led the way to the shed that served as a small armory. Tristan selected a crossbow and Finn went with a handgun—easier to carry, and just as effective, but he made a mental note to have Tristan teach him how to hunt with a crossbow sometime. Besides, an actor never knew what skills could come in handy when auditioning for parts. It helped to expand one's repertoire. Thanks to the few months the

Grounds had been active, he had a well full of experience and emotions from which to draw inspiration.

He pulled on his animal mask, the fox he always wore on a hunt. The masks were lightweight and fit to the hunter's face in such a way as to not obstruct his vision or mobility. They were a precaution to protect identities, not that anyone would be left at the end of a hunt who would talk about the event, but the disguising of humanity had the side benefit of heightening the prey's level of fear.

"I'll release the girl. Remember, when one of us takes her down, I have plans for the body, so don't mutilate it."

Tristan slid his bear mask into place. "I'll try to restrain myself." But they both knew, when the bloodlust was allowed free rein, anything could happen. One time, when drugs had been chosen to enhance the event and tensions were running high, three hunters had turned on each other and one man's throat had been slit. In the madness, the real target had nearly gotten away.

"You want something to heighten the experience?" Finn gestured to the drawers of drugs. Some of the herbs he'd taken from Stone's conservatory were in one drawer. Some, he'd given to a chemist, a Redemption Club member, who'd enhanced their effects and turned them into pill form. Those drugs could be found in another drawer. The great thing about the Club was there was always an expert who could fill any need. And they couldn't say no if they wanted to earn their redemption.

Tristan shook his head. "Not for me. What about the girl?"

"She's not well-trained for survival in the wilderness. I haven't had the time to properly prepare her."

"She should keep her wits about her, then?"

"Unless we select a hallucinogen to make her more

courageous. I was thinking something to boost the adrenaline might be called for." Finn reached for the pill that would amp up his game.

As Skye and Jared walked into Legacy, intent on questioning Robert Stone about the Redemption Club after Carly's revelation, two very large men wearing badges that identified them as security stopped them.

"Stone wants to talk to you," Thing One said.

Skye's hairs stood on end in anticipation. So, the man had been expecting them.

"Good, because we want to talk to him, too," Skye said. They followed Thing One across the casino floor. "You know these guys?" she whispered to Jared, who marched right beside her.

Jared shook his head. "Never seen them before. Must be my replacements."

"Should we make a break for it?"

From behind them, Thing Two nudged her in the shoulder blade. "No talking."

She resisted the urge to send a roundhouse kick into his knee. Or slip the knife from her boot into his gut. That would be satisfying. At least they hadn't searched them and taken her weapons.

Jared shot her a lopsided grin that said he knew what she was thinking.

Toward the back of the casino, they checked in with a third minion, who apparently guarded the hallway beyond. A few of the dozen doorways that sprouted off the hall were open, and as they passed, she could see card tables within, constructed of dark wood and lined with cobalt blue felt. The doorway at the end was closed and marked Private. The minion in front knocked and Stone called out to them to enter.

Inside, the furnishings were just as posh as the rest of the casino, and a private bar was set up in the corner. Stone was fixing a drink there as they came to a stop near the poker table. The guards stood near the closed door, making Skye's hair stand on end because she knew the threat was there, but couldn't face it without taking her eyes off Stone.

"Welcome to Legacy Hotel and Casino." Stone's gaze was trained on Skye, but his expression was void of all emotion. "I take it you're the woman who tried to disrupt not one, but two of my parties, and broke into my home office."

"That would be me," she said. "I believe you had something to do with the disappearance of a friend." She saw no need to sugarcoat what Stone probably already knew.

"You're talking about Loretta Sheldon. I can promise you I'd never heard of her until my staff told me you'd been asking around."

"Gee, I feel so much better having your promise." The sarcasm hung thick in the air. She sensed Jared go stiff beside her, probably readying for Stone or one of the guards to go on the attack after her remark. "And I suppose you've never heard of Three Fortunes, either?"

Stone laughed, surprising all of them. "You're forthright. I like that." He stepped closer and peered into her eyes. She struggled not to back away. "Your eyes are just as remarkable as they were when you were a child."

She hid her surprise. Was he claiming he'd met her? He had known Tom from the beginning, so it was possible. "They're beyond my control."

Stone's expression hardened. "So is this situation."

"Did you destroy Three Fortunes?" Jared asked. "You said you were going to handle things when you learned Skye was investigating you. Did you attack the ranch?"

His gaze didn't waver. "No."

"How do you and Tom Hamilton know each other?" Skye asked.

"That's a complicated question. And the answer carries consequences. What do you know about the past?"

"About how you're connected to it?" Skye snorted. "Nothing. But it's the present I'm interested in. I know you visited my uncle at the ranch the same evening we were attacked. I know you wanted me gone. Why?"

He sent her a humorless grin. "So many questions. I'm guessing your uncle hasn't been in touch. He's really the one you should be talking to about this."

"I'm asking you. It's your name that continually comes up." She reached into her pocket and pulled out Chelsea's and Darren's half-cards, and set them on the desk. "And don't try to tell me these aren't from your casino."

Stone cocked an eyebrow. "And if I say they aren't?"

Skye bit back a curse. She was tired of this man's games. "I know you sent the men to attack the ranch. That somehow, I'm considered their redemption. What's the Redemption Club?"

He laughed. "Well, well. And here I thought your uncle would open his big mouth and tell you everything. Guess you aren't behind the blackmail and death threats, after all." Beside Jared, Skye went still. "That's all I wanted to know." He turned away as if dismissing them.

"I'm not done," Skye shouted, stopping the man in his tracks.

Stone turned back to them, his face red with anger. "You don't want to cross me."

She already had. So why was she still alive? "What kind of questions do you suppose the police would have for me regarding you, and the Redemption Club? We believe your son, along with Tristan Floyd and Finn Tucker, may be involved in the disappearance of at least two young women." She searched his expression for any flicker of recognition, but saw only a flash of surprise.

"That's a serious accusation."

"So is blackmail," Skye shot back at him. "Or running a group that trades in dirty deeds." She scooped up the torn cards. "These may not prove anything, but they're enough to raise some questions with the local authorities."

Stone's eyes turned hard. "Threatening me won't work."

"And your son?"

"Stay away from him, and from all of my properties, or I'll have you arrested. I hear that runs in the family."

Shock ran through Skye. Of course Stone knew about her family history, but to throw it in her face like that...

Stone gestured to the door. "You can show yourselves out now. If I were you, I'd drop your investigations and go back to your lives. Forget you ever heard my name."

"You're not me," she said, standing her ground. "And we'll do everything in our power to find these missing girls."

Stone studied her a moment, then nodded. "I'd expect nothing less after what I've heard about you two. But know that I'll do everything in my power to protect myself, my family and my interests."

CHAPTER SEVENTEEN

Jared's long strides ate up the hallway. Frustration churned inside. He couldn't wait to get Skye far away from Stone, far away from this damned hotel. But he also felt there were answers here. Stone hadn't blinked when the Redemption Club had come up. He recognized the name, which wasn't shocking because it was tied to Legacy somehow, but how did it involve Chelsea?

"What do you think I'm supposed to know that I don't know?" Skye asked beside him.

His head swiveled to her as they dodged casino patrons. "What?"

"The blackmail. What did he think I know about him that I could hold over him? It's got to be something from the past, but he said himself that he hasn't seen me since I was a child."

"I don't know. He never revealed the details about the blackmail, only that he was hiring GSS services to protect him from threats. But your uncle must have known him if they're on the deed together. Could Tom have been blackmailing him?"

"That wasn't my uncle's style. Besides, he seemed to want nothing to do with Stone or the past."

His phone buzzed with an incoming text from Dev. *Just received a package with a thumb drive. Note says, "Hope this helps," and is signed E.*

The glass doors at the exit swished open and a blast of hot air hit them as they moved beyond the air conditioning and into the heat of midday. Jared slid his hand around hers and tugged her into a jog to his SUV. "Come on. We're going to my office."

She shot him a surprised look. "Global Security Solutions?"

"Looks like Emily sent us a thumb drive." The bartender probably hadn't wanted to risk being seen with them again at Legacy.

The building that housed GSS was nothing special. Just an ordinary office building. But Dev enjoyed comfort, with a bit of flash, as well as all the best electronic gadgets money could buy, so Jared wasn't surprised when they walked through the GSS doors and Skye stopped and gaped.

"Wow," she said. "If we weren't in a hurry to see what's on that thumb drive, I'd ask you about two million questions."

He grinned. "There'll be time, later." *Maybe.* If she didn't run off to her life when this was over. And wasn't that selfish of him to want her to stick around? A huge city like Vegas was worlds apart from her quiet ranch. Asking her to stay was too much like something his mother would have done, manipulating her lover to trap him. Eventually, though, the man always left, and the break was always bad for all of them. Jared refused to put either Skye or himself through that.

"He lives," Dev said, stopping in the doorway to Jared's office.

Jared rolled an extra chair behind his computer. He pulled out his laptop and laid it in front of Skye. Beneath dark brows, blue eyes much lighter than Skye's flicked over her with unconcealed interest. Jared felt a surge of possessiveness that he fought to reel in.

This was Dev, his best friend.

And Skye, his... he had no clue. Which made the possessiveness all the more confusing.

Jared introduced the pair. "I believe you two spoke on the phone?"

"Looks like you two connected despite what I had to say," Dev said, grinning.

"Because of what you had to say." Skye shook Dev's hand, but quickly turned to the computer.

Satisfied that she didn't flock to Dev like all the other women who seemed entranced by the man's dark good looks and dangerous vibe, Jared grinned at his friend. "You have the package?"

"The thumb drive." Dev handed it to him with a last, curious look at Skye. She didn't even look up as he left.

"It's surveillance footage from Legacy Lounge," Jared said when the files had loaded. "Two different dates."

Skye touched a finger to the date. "The night of the Malibu party. The other is—"

"The night we picked up Haley."

A few minutes later, Jared found the footage of his sister arriving at the bar. And the man who had sat in the corner nursing a beer stood to greet her. "Skye, take a look at this." She moved closer and her hair tickled his nose. He wanted to turn his mouth to her neck and press his lips to her pulse point.

She gasped. "That's Tristan."

She clicked on the other file, then fast-forwarded through the footage another few minutes until she found what she was looking for. "The timestamp says 3:00 a.m., which is when the charge on Mark's credit card was made. There's no sign of Loretta, though."

"Wait, that guy." A man was approaching the bar, removing his wallet from his pocket. "Isn't that Tristan?"

He turned his face to the camera and she nodded. "That's him. Which means Tristan used Mark's card, alone?"

Jared met Skye's gaze and could see they shared the same thought. If Tristan had Sheldon's credit card, he had probably met up with Loretta at some point after she'd left the ranch. Or he'd stolen it. Unless Finn or Ryan had given him the card to make a money trail for Skye to follow.

Skye sat back in her chair and stared at the screen. "That's why nobody recognized Loretta's picture when I showed it around. It was probably Tristan using it the entire time." She shoved her hands through her hair and released a strangled groan. "These guys have been playing games with us this whole time. And if Loretta doesn't have that card, I shudder to think how she's been living day by day. If she's even alive." She owed it to Mark to keep searching.

Jared shook his head. "I have to believe she is, because if Finn did something to her, that means Chelsea..." Chelsea could be dead, too. "We'll find them. Alive."

"I think it's time to call the hospital again and see if Viper can add to what we've found." The heat from the pavement licked at her ankles like flames as they crossed to his vehicle. "I want to thank you again for taking care of him. He's like family."

"I know, which is why I was happy to do it." He shut them inside the car and cranked up the AC. He tipped his head toward her cell phone. "Want to wait until you have some privacy?"

"No, it's fine. Besides, he might have something to say that could help our investigation."

Skye's throat tightened as Viper answered on the other end of the phone.

"Was wondering when you'd be in touch," the older man said.

"You're the one who was unconscious." All teasing fled as she recalled the last time she'd seen him. "How are you doing?"

"A few bumps and bruises aren't going to keep me down."

"And the stab wounds and surgery?"

"That either."

"Good to hear. They're taking care of you then?"

"Yes, including the gorilla at the door. What's that

about? He says he works for some place called Global Security Solutions."

"A friend of mine arranged for him. Jared Bennigan. He owns a security company."

"Thank him for me."

Skye met Jared's gaze and smiled. "I will."

"And tell him to keep an eye on you, too."

"Viper." Skye's tone held a note of warning.

He chuckled. "Don't get your panties in a knot. I know you're perfectly capable of taking care of yourself. Blah, blah, blah. But Tom was wrong about some things—sometimes it's okay to count on your team and not take the whole load on yourself. Jared's the guy you met up with at the Roadhouse?"

"Yes," Skye said. "He followed me from California. It's a long story." In the passenger seat, Skye shifted uncomfortably, knowing Viper and Tom shared their negative opinion of her going so far from the ranch, even for her job. "I was working with Mark Sheldon to find his daughter. Loretta had run away a couple weeks before and nobody had heard from her. The credit card trail led to Hollywood, which matched the note she'd left for Mark. We weren't expecting trouble, but it sure found us." She swallowed hard. "And now Mark's dead."

"I heard. The sheriff came around to ask questions this morning. Mark was a good man. Didn't know his daughter had run away, though."

"Do you remember anything about who attacked you?"

Viper's words were bitter. "Asshole ambushed me from behind. I was already injured. Almost made it to the road before the guy tracked me. I think he kept me in some kind of kennel, but I was pretty out of it."

"Did you see his face?"

"Weirdest thing. He wore a mask. Looked like a bear or something."

"Could it have been Tristan?"

"Tristan Floyd?" Surprise filled his voice. "He was

the right height. I suppose it could have been him. But why would he attack me?"

Skye's stomach squeezed with guilt. "I think he's part of whatever happened to Loretta. At least, that's our theory at this time. I'm so sorry you had to go through this."

"Not your fault, darlin'. But if Tristan's involved in this, you should have a twenty-four-hour guard, too."

Her glance cut to Jared, who had overheard and was grinning. She rolled her eyes. "I'm fine, and Jared and I have become partners."

"He must be something special."

Jared was, but there was no way she'd admit that in front of him. Especially when she had no idea what to do about just how special Jared was becoming to her. "All signs indicate someone from Stone Studios made a promise to Loretta. They followed Jared, as he was sort of working for Stone at the time—"

Viper interrupted. "Stone Studios? As in, Robert Stone?"

"Yes. Did you know Stone is part owner of the ranch?"

"You need to talk to your uncle."

She rolled her eyes, not that he could see it. "So I've been told. Just today, by Stone himself, actually. But Uncle Tom hasn't responded to my messages. I was wondering if you could try. Maybe he's afraid talking to me would put me in danger?"

"I'll call him, but if Tom's gone deep underground, I wouldn't hold my breath waiting for a reply."

She gave him the emergency cell number she had for Tom and hoped Viper could get through to the man. Assured he would follow doctor's orders and stay under guard at the hospital until she could come check him out in a few days, she hung up.

They tried driving by Finn's condo, but nobody answered the door. There was no sign of him, and no return phone call from Ryan, which wasn't exactly a surprise. And they couldn't walk into the hotel and demand to speak to the guy. His father would throw them out on their asses.

The frustration, combined with waiting to hear from Tom and making sure he was alive and well, was driving Skye crazy, so as they left Finn's condominium and the sun was getting low in the sky, she came up with a new plan. "What did Haley want to do for her birthday?"

Jared glanced over at her, surprised by the question. A slow grin spread across his face, making her pulse race. "Miniature golf."

She straightened, intrigued at the thought of a new challenge. "Really? I've never done that."

"It used to be a family tradition for birthdays. Miniature golf, pizza, cake." He shook his head. "I was surprised that's what she wanted for her eighteenth. When I told her to send me her wish list, I was expecting something more complicated."

"Do it."

"Do what?" He steered onto the freeway before sparing her another glance. "Her birthday wish list?"

"Yeah. Tomorrow's her birthday. Why not surprise her now?"

"Kind of defeats the purpose of being grounded." But she could see he was intrigued by the idea. "I was going to surprise her this weekend."

"She's a good kid. Even I can see that. She needs time with you." Skye had spent many lonely days and nights on the ranch, with nobody to talk to. She sympathized with Haley. "Drop me off at your place and head over there. I can just hang out for the evening. I'll try to find out more about Tristan Floyd on the Internet, check if there were new charges on Mark's credit card." Though she doubted it.

Jared sent her a considering glance. "Come with us."

"You think Haley would be okay with that?" Longing pierced her before she could stuff it away again. "This should be special time between the two of you."

"She likes you, and she usually takes a while to warm up to people, so that's saying something. Besides, it'll help keep her mind off the fact that Chelsea's not here." He frowned, and Skye would suddenly do anything to put a smile back on his face.

"If you think it's okay, I think I'd enjoy it. But I've never really been on a family outing. Or a birthday celebration." There were things she'd resigned herself to never having.

"You didn't celebrate birthdays at the ranch?"

On occasion, but it had never been like on television or in the movies. "It was probably different than you'd imagine."

"Try me."

"The guys who came and went typically didn't share personal information. Actually, it was discouraged. So birthdays were rarely celebrated unless someone had been at the ranch for a year. The anniversary of their arrival was considered a kind of birthday. But Uncle Tom always made sure to celebrate my actual birthday. There was usually a barbecue, and s'mores." She grinned at him. "That was my favorite part. Oh, and there were some competitive games, and a shooting competition."

"Shooting?" Jared shot a speculative glance her way. "You must be pretty good."

"One of the best," she said with pride. Her smile faltered. "But I don't know much about *normal* family life. I feel like an odd duck any time I'm off the ranch."

He covered her hand with his. Beneath their joined hands, her thigh warmed. "It's not like Haley, Chelsea, and I had the ideal family life, either. We make some of it up as we go. The important thing is being there for each other." His gaze met hers briefly. "It sounds like a difficult life, especially for a young girl. I admire the woman who grew from that."

The warmth of his compliment permeated Skye's body. He accepted her. He understood her. She hadn't realized how much she needed that from another human being.

"Where the hell are you?" Ryan's anger vibrated through the phone. "I've been trying to reach you all day."

Finn felt his own temper rise. "What do you care? I tried to come by this morning, but you were occupied." He'd had the Do Not Disturb sign on his suite at Legacy and wouldn't answer Finn's knock.

"Cut the jealousy. Green's not your color." But the amusement in Ryan's voice told Finn that his friend loved being on top. *Enjoy it while it lasts.*

"I wanted to celebrate with you, but you were indisposed."

"Celebrate what? Did you get a part?"

"No." Something much better, something that had provided much-needed stress relief. The rush of a fresh kill, better than any drug's high, still vibrated throughout his body. "I hunted."

"Without me?" All trace of pleasure was gone. "You went alone?"

Finn grinned, though Ryan couldn't see his expression. If he could have, it would have mirrored the smug expression Ryan had worn in Malibu when he'd had that half-naked woman in his bed and Finn had been left out in the cold. "I went with Tristan."

"Which means you earned absolutely no money for last night."

"Got something much more important. Respect. And a way to catch an even bigger fish."

"That Skye woman? You need to get over that. She seems like the type to fight hard. She'll be more trouble than she's worth." Ryan didn't have a fucking clue what Skye's value was.

Finn's grin widened. He was dead on his feet, and yet, exhilarated. Last night had reminded him why he was after Skye. No way would he give up now. "And that's why she'll bring the big bucks. I've already got three hunters lined up, just from posting her description on the Redemption Club loop. It'll be magnificent, and we'll be a couple hundred thousand dollars richer."

Ryan was quiet for a long moment. "It might be too little, too late. I've called a meeting of the Club founders."

"Shit. No. This is going to be big. I can't take time away from it now."

"Then don't come." The quiet tone of Ryan's voice tipped Finn off.

"Is this meeting about me?"

"I'm going to propose that someone else take over the Hunting Grounds. You're abusing your privileges."

"Fuck, no. The hunts were my idea. It's my baby."

"And you're ruining it, putting it at risk like this. You never should have taken Loretta so close to there. The meeting's tonight, ten o'clock. The usual place."

"I'll be there." And he'd defend his interests. Maybe he'd even take over the whole thing. "*Intrepidus vive ferociter ludeque.*"

Ryan hung up without returning the salutation. Fuck him. Finn didn't need him anymore. He had bigger game to hunt.

CHAPTER EIGHTEEN

Skye had expected to feel curious and a bit overwhelmed, but she hadn't thought she'd enjoy herself so much, especially at a game where she only had to swing a stick at a tiny neon ball. Haley's squeal of delight when they'd shown up at Aunt Jane's to surprise her with the outing had been a marvelous way to kick things off. The teen's excitement was contagious.

"You sure you never played? I think you're a ringer." Jared winked at Skye. The butterflies in her stomach were new, and yet she enjoyed the feeling. She forced herself to embrace and explore the novelty rather than stifle her response. She was determined to revel in every aspect of her first family outing.

"I never hit a ball with a stick, though I have played other games of accuracy," Skye admitted. "I've thrown horseshoes and darts."

"And fired guns," Haley added. She tossed her long blonde ponytail back over her shoulder as she lined up a putt—and sank it right through the center of the windmill that was the eighteenth hole. She promptly celebrated with a victory dance worthy of a pro football touchdown.

"I have discharged a gun a time or two," Skye conceded, amused at the twinkle of bloodlust in Haley's eyes. The girl had fired question after question Skye's way during the course of the evening.

"Have you ever killed someone?"

Her entire body went numb and her smile slipped. Her palms went cold and clammy on the putter's rubber handle.

"Skye?" Jared stepped to her side and placed a hand at the small of her back. "Hey? You okay?"

"I was just kidding," Haley said. Eyes the same shade of caramel as her brother's, but tilted up slightly at the edges, went wide. "Really? You killed someone?"

"I don't think this is a conversation I'm ready to have." Skye cleared her tight throat and licked her dry lips.

Uncle Tom had told her time and again that she hadn't been responsible for what happened to her parents, but her six-year-old brain had taken on the blame, and it was hard for her twenty-six-year-old brain to shake off decades of survivor's guilt. And the people she'd killed since... well, that fell under the heading of justice. Why else would God give her these skills and bring people into her path who needed her? But it never felt good to take a life.

Jared was watching her with concern, so she forced a smile and responded to Haley. "Let's just say I didn't kill anyone who wouldn't have killed me, or someone else, first."

Haley nodded with the wisdom of a young adult. "Makes sense. Kind of like Darwin's theory."

"Survival of the fittest?" Could it really be that easy for this girl to accept her past transgressions?

"We've been studying it in biology class. Maybe we could try those shooting lessons next weekend? Not that I'd use them to hurt anyone," she hastily added.

Skye shot Jared a glance before looking away. Neither of them knew what would happen by next weekend—or, hell, by tomorrow. He could be back on the job at GSS and she could be back at the ranch, picking up the pieces. By herself. It wouldn't be the same. But if Viper could find Tom, maybe they could begin again and rebuild Three Fortunes.

Except ranch life didn't hold quite the same appeal it had before, especially after spreading her wings these past few months, working with people outside of their tiny group. And after learning part of that community belonged to Stone.

No, the ranch definitely didn't seem like home anymore.

"I'd love that, if I'm in town." Skye added the qualification, not wanting to get Haley's hopes up. "We're hoping to find your sister by then."

"And then what?" Haley asked, leaning on her putter as she watched Skye intently. "You'll just leave?"

"Well, I do have a life in Arizona." *Maybe.*

"Right. I understand." Haley grabbed their three putters and headed toward the window where they returned the equipment.

Skye watched helplessly as the birthday girl's shoulders slumped. Skye's words must have seemed like a rejection to a girl who'd been essentially abandoned by one person after another. Her father, her mother, even her sister and brother had moved on in one way or another.

"Haley, Skye would help if she could," Jared said as they caught up to her at the exit. He sent an apologetic look to Skye when Haley wasn't looking.

"Tell you what," Skye said. "How about you come to the ranch for a week this summer and learn to shoot where I did. We have a shooting range, and nobody around for miles."

Haley's face lit up. "You mean it?"

"Absolutely. Consider it my birthday gift to you. That is, if it's okay with your brother." Shit, should she have asked his permission first? What if he didn't want Haley learning how to shoot? What if he wasn't planning to see Skye again after the investigation ended?

Jared's expression was shuttered, but he nodded. "I think that would be a great idea."

An hour later, Jared dropped Haley off at Aunt

Jane's. He was glad to see the GSS guard he'd arranged to sit in a car and watch the house, just in case, was in position across the street.

After miniature golf, a pizza, and an ice cream cake—and a rain check for shooting lessons—Haley had practically bounced into her aunt's house rather than putting up the usual argument. Her expression hadn't deflated even when Aunt Jane reminded her she wouldn't be going anywhere for the rest of the weekend.

Jared had Skye to thank for his sister's happiness.

"You don't really have to come," he said as he pulled into the garage at his house. He turned off the car and glanced at Skye in the passenger seat. The garage door slid down behind them, but the light from above cast a faint glow around them. Still, Skye's expression was hidden.

"To graduation?" she asked.

Haley had surprised them both on the way home by inviting Skye, who'd handled it with grace and promised she'd think about it and reply soon.

But he'd caught the split-second when Skye's eyes had gone wide with the idea of participating in another family ritual—one she admitted she'd never gone through herself, since she'd been homeschooled on the ranch. There had been fear and interest in those bright eyes.

Jared wanted to show her all the parts of the world that she'd missed by being shut away on the ranch, and replace the portion of fear with excitement and hope.

Skye gripped her hands together in her lap. "If you don't want me to come..."

"I'd love for you to be there. I just don't want you making promises you can't, or don't want to, keep. It's entirely your choice."

"I want to come. But I don't know where things will stand."

"Between us?" He knew where he'd like them to

stand. His body leapt to attention the moment she walked into a room or he heard her voice. His need for her had grown steadily over the past week, and it was getting harder to shut out the voices of reason in his conscience. And hell, the raw hunger he sometimes caught in her eyes made him think she was ready to push past reason, too. "I'll take as much as you'll give me, Skye. So stop me when it's too much."

"Who's stopping you?" She leaned forward at the same time he did, as it seemed they'd both met the limits of their restraint. The hunger in him rose to meet hers halfway.

He cupped the back of her head and pulled her close until his lips met hers in a soft kiss, a reawakening of the senses. But his senses were already alive with her, eager for more. He slanted his mouth over hers, nearly whimpering when she immediately opened to him, welcoming him home.

Part of him imagined having this every day and night, having Skye in his home. The other part of him warned him to take it slow. His rabbit was still skittish. So he kept it simple, kept it about passion and shallow needs. There would be time for deeper consideration later.

After several long moments making out in the car, during which he felt like a randy teenager again, she pulled back. Her breath came in tiny pants against his lips. "Can we go inside now?"

His cock swelled at the sexy rasp in her voice. Was she suggesting taking this further? "Of course."

But as he led her inside and flipped on a soft light, then tugged her down next to him on the couch, his conscience warred with him. Skye, for all of her physical strength, didn't let people past her emotional walls casually. If this was leading where he thought it might be leading—God, where he *hoped* it was leading—he wanted to know she was okay with this just being a physical release. Because neither of them were ready for more complications in their lives.

His hands landed on her shoulders to stop her before she leaned in for another kiss. "You're sure? This isn't some kind of avoidance technique?" She'd gone silent for a while after Haley's question about killing. Something about it was troubling her.

"Absolutely." She climbed into his lap and he caught her against him with a noise that was half laugh, half groan as her hips wriggled. "Besides, I wouldn't mind a little avoidance." She leaned forward to suck his bottom lip into her mouth.

He grinned and returned the light nip to her bottom lip. "Sometimes avoidance is healthy."

"Especially if it involves exercise." She pushed him back into the sofa and slid her palms up his torso and around his neck, then up into his hair, her nails gently scraping his scalp. His hands stroked down her back, locking around her waist. She had to feel how aroused he was. All that separated them was two layers of clothing.

She leaned forward and pressed her mouth to his, just a nibble at first, a taste that had every muscle in his body tensing. But a smart soldier waited for the right time to attack. So he let her sample, his desire building to the brink of pain as she wriggled in his lap. She kissed the corners of his mouth, then the middle, then darted that mischievous tongue of hers out to swipe at the seam of his lips.

He had his limits. He tipped sideways, pulling her down with him until he was lying on his back with her lithe body sprawled on top of him. He shifted one hand up into her hair as the other drifted downward to her tight ass, holding her soft curves flush against his hardness.

She nibbled her way up his neck until her mouth was next to his ear. "Jared?"

A strangled growl sounded low in his throat. "Mmm?"

"I'm tired of fighting you. Show me what I've been resisting."

CHAPTER NINETEEN

His body froze but still blasted her with furnace-like heat. Though the cushions below prevented him from pulling back, he ducked his head away enough to look into her eyes. Several long moments went by and then he shifted away. Skye stifled a stab of disappointment as he lifted her off of him and rose.

Her heart's steady beat sped up as he held out a hand and tugged her to her feet, then led her down the hall to his room. His bed was the predominant feature, and again, it was sparsely decorated. Still, she appreciated the clean lines.

Seeing her curious gaze, he grimaced. "Sorry. I've been too busy to decorate. And I think I'm waiting until the people who are meant to share this house with me are here to make some decisions." As he spoke, he gently walked her backward to the bed.

Was she one of those people, or did he mean his sisters? Or some future woman he hadn't met yet? She didn't dare ask. *Nor should you care.* She didn't want forever, she wanted tonight. And tonight was about feeling, about letting passion rule. She didn't want to overthink it. She didn't want to think at all. Trained to focus on surviving the moment, she'd never lived for the future.

He nudged her back on the bed and began a slow prowl up her body, skimming her clothed curves with his large hands. She nearly yelped when his fingers made contact with a strip of exposed flesh above her waistline. But he seemed content to torture her, returning to the outside of her clothes as his hands continued their journey over her breasts, her collarbone, and up into her hair. He settled his length against her. His erection pressed against her belly, sending more tingling sensations outward.

She wrapped her legs around his waist and lifted her pelvis to meet his, the barriers of clothing merely adding to the relentless tease. "As your partner, I insist you share everything. Right. Now." She rocked her hips into him.

"So demanding." He gave a wicked grin and she leaned up to press her lips to it.

She fisted her hands in the back of his shirt and held him in place, trailing her kisses along his jawbone, blazing a trail across his skin to the hollow just below his ear before following the path of his cheekbone back to his lips. Using her teeth, she captured his bottom lip. And felt his surrender as he returned her kiss with urgency.

She gasped as he slipped a hand between them to touch her. Just like that, the advantage shifted. He pressed her back against the bed and devoured her. There was no better word for the way he filled her senses and fed off her at the same time. Hot. Wet. Slick with need. Those were the sensations that hit her all at once. He was in constant motion, his hands, his lips, his tongue. All touching her in some way, all seeking more contact. And still more.

When he gripped her wrists with one hand and pulled them over her head, trapping them there, she moaned and surrendered her body to pleasure. She tightened her legs around his waist and used her heels to command his pace. He laughed against her breast, the air cooling and pebbling her nipple tighter beneath her shirt.

"Relax. Let me enjoy you." His words were spoken against her abdomen as he slid downward. When she forced her body to relax, he released her hands and she slid her palms over his shoulder blades, anchoring him to her. She wasn't letting him leave until she was ready.

Somewhere in the back of her mind, she realized she'd read about this in some romance books, but she'd never had this with a man in the past. *This...* She sighed. This was oh·so·much better.

Because her body, her soul, had been waiting for *him.*

The thought caused a niggling of alarm, which she buried. Instead of listening to the cautionary voices, she threw herself into the glorious moment, opening to him in every way. Leaving no doubt as to what she wanted from him.

He responded with a renewed onslaught. One hand moved along her side, down to her waist where his fingers found the edge of her tank top and dipped beneath, then traveled upward again to cup her breast over the cotton of her bra. As if there were a string attached to her nipple, the brush of his thumb, even through the soft material, caused her to arch her back and press the mound into his palm. A moment later, he'd removed her shirt and bra. As he tugged off her pants, his mouth slid in a searing path along her inner thigh.

Oh, God, yes! She wanted his heat on every part of her. In her.

Skye was like a firecracker in his hands, burning fast and dangerous.

He didn't know what he'd done to deserve this beautiful woman, but he'd do it again and again and again if it meant the same result.

When he brought her close to climax, he rolled over to his back, pulling her on top of him, then reached down and pulled her knees up on either side so she was straddling him. "You want to be in control?" He smiled up at her. "Show me." He wanted her to run the show, to control the speed and how far they went. At least, this time.

She quickly accepted her new position of power, and chose to torture him slowly and thoroughly. Her fingers tugged his shirt up and off. He lay there, letting her drink him in as she traced his muscles with her fingers. The slow grin that spread across her face made his entire body tighten with need.

He did his share of drinking as well, getting downright drunk on her as his gaze caressed her curves—every curve. The proud tilt of her chin, the gently rounded shoulders that looked delicate but could carry the weight of the world, the two precious round globes hanging like ripe fruit, and a slight nip at the waist before flaring at the hips. As his gaze lowered, those hips rocked against him. His hands gripped them to hold them still.

Too fast. He wanted to slow things down. He wanted to savor this night. Who knew how many more they'd have together?

Her heated gaze traced the contours of his chest and moved lower. She licked her lips and he felt his erection reach for her. He muttered his thanks to the gods that he'd tucked condoms away close by, just in case. In case his dreams about Skye came true.

"There's a condom in the drawer. Just let me—" The rest of his words came out in a hiss as she leaned across him to the drawer, putting a pert, rosy nipple right at the level of his mouth. There was a God. He pulled a nipple into his mouth and she cried out—a half laugh, half moan.

"I thought I was in charge," she said. He thought he might go off like a rocket as her questing fingers brushed his erection through his jeans. "These pants need to go. Like, *now*. Forever. You should be naked, always."

"Likewise, sugar." He lifted her off him a moment and made swift work of removing the remainder of his clothing. She watched as he opened the package and rolled the condom into place. Her eyes widened. "Can I try next time?"

Next time? He wanted to shout his approval. "Anything you want. I'm yours to experiment on."

"I think I'm going to like this partnership." She climbed back on top of him, but he resisted sliding into her. He wanted her wet and writhing for him, but resisted the urge to take charge again. Besides, watching her have her fun was more sensual than anything he'd ever seen before.

"You'll like it even more if you'll let me try something."

She looked down at him, her eyes sparking with curiosity. "What?"

"Put your hands on the top of the headboard to brace yourself."

"Brace myself for wha—"

He put his hands under her arms and lifted her until her hot center was over his mouth, then he feasted on her. His tongue delved into her, then lingered on the bundle of nerves that would send ripples of pleasure through her. He blew against her moist clit and she shuddered, her thighs quivering around his head.

"*Oh.*"

She was so damn sweet. Like nectar. All for him. The thought had possessiveness streaking through him. He suckled the nub and licked until her breathing was irregular. She was panting now. Begging. For him. One of her hands reached down and gripped his hair as if she were holding on for the ride. With a last lick, he sent her over the edge. He slid her back down over his body, then tugged her hips into place and found her center. He drove in deep.

She cried out with pleasure at the contact against her sensitive nub and collapsed against him. Her lips curved against his as he filled her. She wiggled her hips, clenching against him and he hissed out a breath. Christ, she was so tight. So hot. He wanted to make this last, but couldn't wait anymore.

"Ride me." He issued the order through gritted teeth, trying to hold back the desire to push into her and let himself go. He wanted this to be good for both of them.

Her eyes locked with his, unashamed and unwavering—the confident, sassy Skye he'd seen on the Malibu rooftop.

The one he'd fallen for in that first moment he'd seen her.

Fuck, he was a goner.

But then she began to move and all thoughts fled as his nerve endings zeroed in on pleasure. His hands locked onto her hips for dear life. Her breasts bounced softly, her eyes slid closed, her mouth opened on a moan, and her head fell back as she came apart again. His last thought before he followed her into the void was that he'd never see anything more beautiful than Skye Hamilton, in all her naked glory, letting down every last defense. For him.

When the phone rang early the next morning, Jared ignored it. When the second volley began, he nuzzled the warm, sweet-smelling neck his nose was pressed into, muttered a soft curse and rolled to his back.

Beside him, Skye shifted and moaned but didn't open her eyes when she spoke. "Your caller is most definitely not the good, so he or she must be the bad."

"And he'll be the ugly if I get my hands on him," Jared said, pushing into a sitting position as he saw that it was Dev calling. He answered, but as Skye tried to slip out of bed, he wrapped his free arm around her to anchor her to his side. He was gratified she didn't put up even a token struggle. She simply snuggled up, her head on his chest as if it belonged there. *Christ*, he was such a sap.

"This had better be good," he said into the phone, growling because he hadn't had time yet to get his feelings sorted out. Last night had been incredible. And he already wanted more.

Dev grunted. "Someone didn't get his beauty sleep. Guess I don't have to ask if Skye's with you?"

"She is." At that, Skye looked up at him, propping her head on the back of her hand, her palm right over his heart. The idea of waking up to this every day was tempting, especially now that the fantasy of her in his bed, naked, was replaced with the real thing. But that wasn't realistic. He had a stable life to create, for both his sisters' and his own sake.

"That'll save you some time, then. The police are looking for her."

"What?" His entire body must have tensed because Skye frowned and pushed into a sitting position.

"They found a dead woman at the ranch, with a message pinned to her."

Jared felt his insides go cold. "Was it...?"

"No, it wasn't Chelsea. Jesus, I'm sorry, Jared. I didn't mean to scare you. I certainly would have shown up in person and handled things more delicately if it had come to something like that. And it *won't*. We'll find your sister. But this mess is growing more complicated and more dangerous."

"Who was it?"

"The girl was identified as Erica Dubois. I just emailed you the coroner's report. She was twenty-two years old. Moved to Los Angeles a couple months ago."

"But found dead on an Arizona ranch? *Skye's* ranch?"

Skye's face was pale as she mouthed the question. *Who?*

"Dev, I'm going to put you on speaker so Skye can hear." He pressed the button as he told Skye about the police finding Erica's body. "What was the message pinned to the woman?" he asked Dev.

"Erica found her redemption. Yours awaits at the Hunting Grounds. I'm coming for you, Skye."

"What the hell are the Hunting Grounds?"

"I was hoping you knew."

"Not yet." But they'd sure as hell find out, as well as how it linked to this so-called Redemption Club and Robert Stone. And Ryan Stone and Finn Tucker. And Chelsea and Loretta. He sighed. This puzzle just got more and more complicated. "And, yeah, I know. Keep you posted." He hung up.

He wanted to pull Skye against him again and hold her, but he could see she was already mentally pulling on her battle armor. And probably blaming herself for someone else getting hurt, as she'd blamed herself for her parents' deaths.

Her brow scrunched in thought. "I don't know anybody named Erica. Why would someone kill her to get to me? Why do they want me?"

Screw it. She wanted to be tough and independent, but someone was out to get her, and he needed to feel her, feel that she was safe and healthy. He reached for her and tugged until she toppled against him. His arms wrapped around her.

"Shh," he soothed. "Just give me a moment." She stiffened, but as he stroked her back, her body melted into his. "I need to hold you. It could so easily have been you or Chelsea or Loretta lying dead at Three Fortunes."

She sighed, her warm breath heating his skin. "We have to find Finn. And castrate him."

"Agreed." Not letting go of her, Jared reached with one hand for his phone, scrolled through his emails and brought up the coroner's report Dev had emailed. But it was the picture of the woman that had his skin turning clammy. "Shit. I know her."

She pulled out of his arms to sit against the headboard beside him. She took the phone and examined the picture. "She looks vaguely familiar. How do you know her?"

"She's the young inebriated woman I escorted from the Malibu party. I put her in a cab and that was the last time I saw her. That's also when I saw your ranch truck parked on the side of the road with Mark in it."

"That's why she looked familiar to me. I saw her near the pool with Finn Tucker before she started raising a ruckus and caught your attention."

"It has to be Finn who's at the root of this. Why would a powerful man like Stone stoop to direct threats?" Stone struck him as the type to have others do his dirty work and avoid any ties to it. Openly challenging Skye didn't ring true of Stone's *modus operandi* with women.

He scrolled through the pictures in the file until he came to a photo of the message that had been left with Erica's body. "We've heard the redemption theme several times, but the Hunting Grounds is new. Any idea what it is?"

"I haven't heard of it. Unless... God, you don't think Finn is *hunting* girls, do you?"

"If so, and if Chelsea and Loretta are part of this, they're in more danger than we thought." But at least there was hope they were still alive.

As Skye handed back his phone, it chirped with an incoming text.

"It's Emily," he told Skye. He scanned her message. "She served Ryan drinks at Legacy Lounge last night, and overheard him talking about Redemption Club."

"So he is hiding out there, he's just refusing to talk to us." Skye pushed off the bed. "Let's go ask him about the Hunting Grounds."

CHAPTER TWENTY

Skye spotted Ryan lounging poolside, next to a stacked redhead in a barely-there bikini who couldn't be much more than eighteen.

"Guess these guys can get any woman they want." Skye muttered the statement under her breath as she and Jared walked around the Olympic-sized pool to get to the man with jet-black hair. Ryan Stone. The thirty-year-old kept in shape, but his face and trunk were soft around the edges, evidence of someone who lived a life of luxury and indulgence. And too much time on his hands to both work out and party.

"These women aren't what they truly want," Jared said. "They're ornamental. Or maybe it's just Finn's tastes that run to the deviant. Hopefully, we'll get something from Ryan if we push a little." If Ryan's father hadn't already warned his son to be on guard.

They stopped beside his chair. A moment later, Ryan whipped his expensive sunglasses off his face and sent them a glare. "What the hell, man? You're blocking my rays."

Skye didn't move. "The great Ryan Stone, I presume."

Jared made himself comfortable on the empty chair beside him.

Ryan sneered. "Who are you two, the new cabana boys? We don't need any towels, but you could fetch us some drinks." He shoved his glasses back in place but didn't sit up.

"I have some questions for you about the Hunting

Grounds."

Ryan's body tightened for a split second, before he could control his reaction. Skye circled his chair to talk to the redhead on his other side. "You might want to take a break from the sun. You've been baking your brain a bit too much if you're hanging out with this guy." The redhead scooped up her towel and, after a huff of irritation, hurried away.

"Hey!" This time, Ryan sat up. "Stop scaring my girls away."

"You do remember me." Jared grinned a humorless smile. "I'm touched. Frustrating when someone messes up your plans, isn't it? Is that what happened with Erica Dubois? I scared her away, so you got mad. You and your friend hunted her down and killed her?"

"What the hell are you talking about?"

Skye took a deep breath to rein in her anger. These guys tossed women aside as if they were yesterday's trash. "The girl from the Malibu party. Erica. She was found dead. And there was a little note for me about how the killer was coming for me, that my redemption awaits at the Hunting Grounds. Blah, blah, blah. *Intrepidus vive ferociter ludeque* and all that nonsense." She caught the way he stiffened again when she spoke the Latin phrase.

"I don't know what you're talking about."

"It's Latin," Skye said, stepping closer. "And I know you know what it means. As for the threat..." She held her arms out to her sides. "You and Finn want me, take me. Take me to Chelsea and Loretta and whatever other girls you're hurting." They had to be so fucking scared. Forget hanging this guy's balls from the ranch gate, she'd shove them down his throat.

"Who are you talking about?"

"Chelsea Wright," Jared said, eyeing him with cold anger. "She's my sister. She danced regularly in Legacy Lounge, and, more recently, for a little private party here a few weeks ago. She hasn't been seen since."

"Maybe she just took off, man. Or maybe she doesn't want to talk to you. You seem the overbearing sort."

"And my friend, Loretta?" Skye smiled sweetly but shot daggers with her eyes. "She was promised a part in a Stone Studios movie. Are you going to try to tell me you had nothing to do with that?"

Ryan glared at her. "Hell, no, I had nothing to do with that."

"With what?" Stone asked, stepping up behind Jared and frowning down at him. "I thought I made it clear yesterday never to come back."

Inside, Skye seethed. "Daddy to the rescue."

"When it's necessary," Stone returned. His frown turned to Ryan. "Don't say a word to these people. We'll contact a lawyer if we need to."

"Good idea," Skye said. "And we'll talk to the police. They haven't had a lead to suggest Chelsea's disappearance was due to foul play, but maybe a nudge in your direction would rejuvenate their efforts. Unless you want to explain to us what the Hunting Grounds are." Stone's intense gaze wavered, but he didn't look away. "I'm guessing it's some kind of game, but the price is human sacrifice? Somewhere not too far away from here. Maybe if we search your other properties, we'll find your son's gruesome theme park?" Judging by the way Ryan was growing more and more rigid with anxiety, Skye figured she was on the right track. "Either your son or his friend Finn killed a woman, left her body for us to find, with a message for me about my redemption."

"Shouldn't you be looking for Finn?" Stone's words could cut glass. "My son has been here for days. He has nothing to do with your missing girls."

"Oh, we are looking for Finn. He's been hiding out. Probably wise, considering the kind of trouble he's going to be in. We were hoping Ryan would be willing to help find him." Ryan simply glared back at her. "Right. Well, it was a long shot, but soon you'll have to choose. Your friendship or your freedom. Because I have a feeling Erica's murder is going to come back on you, buddy. Let's see your father pull you out of that mess."

A moment later, a sneer crept across Ryan's handsome face. "Go fuck yourself."

They were drawing attention from sunbathers around the pool. Good. Let everyone know the filth that lurked beneath the glamorous facade of this hotel.

Stone laid a hand on Ryan's arm and spoke in a low voice to Jared. "Get a leash on her and get out before I call security."

Skye stepped closer to Stone. "Your son is a liability. I suggest you *get a leash* on that."

Jared's eyes met hers and she nodded. Time to go.

"Enjoy the beautiful day while you're still free to do so," she called back over her shoulder. "And if you talk to Finn, tell him I'm coming after him, too. If either of you harms another person, I'll make sure you die a slow and painful death."

Let Ryan Stone and Finn Tucker feel like the hunted for a change.

Chelsea bit back a startled scream as the cabin door flew open. She'd been dozing in the afternoon sun that streamed through the single barred window, dreaming about the life she'd had, the life she'd taken for granted.

The man in the doorway had on his usual bear mask. As an intimidation tactic, it was effective—or it had been the first few times. After weeks of seeing him like this, it seemed ridiculous. Still, it turned his eyes into beads of black and disguised the humanness in his features. If he was human at all. He had the soul of a demon, but at least he'd been training them in the art of survival for the past couple weeks. Even as her brain worked out why he'd do such a thing, she'd soaked up all the information he shared.

He turned his head from her to Loretta. Recently, she'd been more reluctant to partake in the training. In fact, she'd shut down in many ways over the past few days. Chelsea was worried, especially since Erica had done something similar, and she'd been taken into the wild yesterday and hadn't returned.

"What did you do to Erica?" Chelsea scrambled to her feet. If fight was what these men admired, fight was what they'd get.

She eyed the door behind Bear, gauging their different sizes and strengths. She nearly slumped with defeat as she realized her chance of getting by him, especially with that gun in his hand, was nil. If it had been a knife, she might have risked it. But that would leave Loretta here, alone, young and scared.

"We each hold our own fates, and the power to redeem ourselves, but she was a poor keeper of hers." Bear sounded disappointed.

Erica hadn't survived, then. Despair filled Chelsea, squashing out the tiny light of hope she'd nurtured for weeks. "I'm hoping the two of you will provide better sport."

Sport. Her stomach twisted with nausea, but she lifted her chin into the air. "I'm sure we will. Just give us a shot." It was better than waiting here to die.

A flash of white indicated Bear was grinning beneath his mask. "It won't be much longer now, and we'll see how strong you are."

We. There would be more than just him hunting them, then. Would Finn join him or were there others? She'd like to know her odds of survival.

She cursed the night she'd walked into that private suite at Legacy and chosen to dance to pay off a debt incurred when Finn had lent her several months' worth of rent. With college tuition, a prior credit card debt and moving into an apartment with friends, she'd taken on too many financial obligations too fast. Rather than give her brother more fuel with which to argue his point that she wasn't as independent as she believed, she'd gone elsewhere for a loan. But Finn and his friends didn't fight fair. They'd drugged the soda they'd offered her when she'd told them she didn't drink on the job. She'd woken up here.

"I'll go first." Loretta shocked them with her brave words. She limped forward, having strained her ankle during yesterday's training exercise, before they'd taken Erica. Finn, wearing a fox mask, had chased them in the yard, keeping a rope around them as if he were breaking wild horses.

Bear smiled. "Let's get on with it, then."

Chained to an anchor in the wall, Chelsea watched from the shade of the cabin as Bear taunted and chased Loretta, always letting her go, but preparing her for something. For whatever came next.

"When's the hunt?" Chelsea dared to ask when they took a water break.

"Eager for us to chase you?" He leered at her from behind his mask.

"Eager to see you all die," she shot back. She only hoped they didn't force drugs on her as they had Erica before they'd dragged her out of the cabin. The girl had been out of her mind with fear. Chelsea wanted her wits about her. "Just give me a fair shot."

"I can't promise that. That's not for me to decide." His teeth flashed. "But I can promise you it'll all be over soon."

From the corner of his eye, Jared watched Skye pace his living room as he spoke on the phone with Sheriff Anderson, his liaison in Coconino County, Arizona, where Skye's ranch was located. With the way Skye had been brought up, she was nervous when it came to involving outsiders, but she'd agreed that it was important to have the authorities on their side if they wanted to find the missing women. Jared was just glad she now considered *him* an insider.

"I appreciate you telling me what you know,"

Anderson said. "I take these threats personally, especially when they fall within my jurisdiction."

"And I appreciate you contacting me when you found Erica's body." It had been an anonymous tip that had led the authorities to the ranch. "We're almost certain my sister and Skye's friend are somewhere in your area. I'll be driving down tomorrow to start a thorough search of the area." Since Tristan Floyd was a part of this, and had connections to the ranch, it seemed a good place to start. In the meantime, he and Skye were reviewing the list of properties that were in Robert Stone's personal possession, as well as any beneath the Stone Corporation umbrella.

"I can begin organizing the search," Anderson offered.

"I'd appreciate it. And I'll email you what I have."

After discussing a few more details, Jared hung up and forwarded the picture of Finn and information he had on Tristan to the sheriff. He turned to Skye, who seemed jittery with unspent adrenaline.

"Dev sent a file that could be helpful," he said. "Want to look it over with me?"

"Sure." She sat next to him on the couch and he took the opportunity to take her hand in his and lift it to his lips. He watched the heat and surprise flare in her gaze. "What was that for?"

"Just a reminder that we're in this together. You don't have to keep all those thoughts and concerns in your head."

She sank against him, leaning her head on his shoulder. "How do you know what's in my head?"

Because it was in his, too. They were getting closer to finding Chelsea and Loretta. He could feel it, but the answers were still painfully far away. As were the answers to whatever was developing between him and Skye. He hadn't been looking for another complicated relationship, but somehow he'd found one. He'd never wanted another woman to look after—not after what he'd been through with his mother and sisters—but neither did he want a woman who would leave him again, as his mother had, in her own way.

He was surprised to find he wanted to understand what made Skye tick, what had made her strong. "I think part of you has been distracted ever since Haley asked whether you'd killed anyone."

Skye stiffened. "I have. Killed. And it started with my parents."

He went still. "You didn't kill your parents. You couldn't have. You were six."

"I know I didn't *actually* kill my parents, but to a young child, it all gets mixed up, you know?"

"Tell me about it," he prodded gently. "I want to understand."

Could she recount that night her parents had died? Did she have the guts to explain the jobs she'd done? She supposed she'd know exactly where she stood with him when the dust settled.

He draped an arm over the back of the couch. His fingertips were inches from her neck, and the skin there prickled with awareness. His quiet gaze encouraged her.

"The night of the fire, I was misbehaving," she said. "Again. I was something of a wild child." With twenty years of distance from the event, Skye could see how she'd just been a rambunctious kid, but her mother had called her selfish, her father had called her uncontrollable—when they'd paid any attention to her at all. They'd tried to control her with their fists, or with drugs. While it went against her current nature, Skye had once been their rag doll, malleable and often tossed aside.

"It was my birthday." She felt his attention on her but couldn't meet his gaze, instead staring at the flat-screen television adorning the wall opposite them. She swallowed. "At the ranch, the occasion was noted, but in my childhood home they were grudgingly celebrated, if at all. My birthdays were never love and laughter like what you shared with Haley."

"What *we* shared," he reminded her.

She nodded. "But they had promised me pizza and I had a special cupcake my teacher had given me at school that day. I think Miss Abernathy knew I wouldn't get cake at home. I was mad that the pizza we ordered for my special dinner wasn't my favorite." She grimaced. "To this day, I can't eat olives on pizza. My father accused me of being spoiled and sent me out of the house. Said he had company coming over anyway. *Company* meant a customer, but I was too young to understand what that meant at the time, only that it was business. As I walked by, I stuck out my tongue. He saw. With one sweep of his arm, he knocked my beautiful cupcake from the counter into the trash can."

In her head, she could still hear the soft splat, followed by a profound silence. The smell of chocolate icing had tickled her nose and made her mouth water. The beautiful little pink candy rose that had decorated the center now clung to the liner of the trashcan.

"I started crying," she continued. "My father roared at me to get out. My mother told me it was my fault for making him angry. I ran. I hid in my normal spot, in the tree near the end of the dirt driveway." That tree still held the best memories of her youth. "That was my happy place. I must have been out there about a half hour. It felt like forever. I remember it had gotten dark, and I was getting cold. My legs and arms were stiff. But I didn't want to climb down and go back inside."

"And nobody came for you?" Jared finally spoke, his outrage evident in the V of his eyebrows.

"They preferred it when I was gone. I often was off, playing by myself for hours."

"You were six and it was after dark."

"Disappearing while they cooled off and conducted business was the smarter choice. Otherwise, they dealt with me in other ways. I'd learned to avoid eating or drinking if they talked about a customer coming by. If they drugged me, I'd wake up so groggy the next morning. And angry. A little kid shouldn't be that angry, right?"

He stiffened and she looked at him, worried she'd see judgment in his eyes, and relieved when she saw only anger. Anger, she could deal with. "I'm sorry, but I'd like to kill them with my bare hands."

His outrage soothed her hardened soul, smoothing out the tough skin she'd cultivated. She squeezed his hand, surprised to realize he'd interlaced his fingers with hers while she'd been talking. "They had company a little while later. From my perch above them, I saw the two men drive up, go inside and leave again a little while later. Customers, I guess. Anyway, by then I'd decided to stay in the tree. I didn't want to get yelled at again, especially on my birthday, and I guess I thought I was teaching them a lesson, too. I was pretty stubborn back then. Not a good quality."

"It saved your life," Jared pointed out.

"I spent a lot of time up in that tree, hating them, wishing I belonged to a different family. The explosion came just after I had a thought like that. I'd actually envisioned them, gone from my life forever and... Boom." She picked up her water glass and took a swallow, trying to wash the bitter taste of regret from her tongue. As if it were that easy.

"That's why you blamed yourself. But you must realize now it wouldn't have ended any differently if you hadn't been stubborn."

"Or if I had just apologized and picked the olives off the damn pizza, I might have retreated to my room with the cupcake before the guys showed up."

"You would have died, too."

"Maybe I should have." She scrubbed her hands over her eyes.

"Skye."

The concern in his voice nearly undid her, and she kept her eyes tightly closed. "I take on dangerous jobs because I can't do any better. Who would want to hire me for a legit career? I barely have a high school education. I figured I didn't deserve any better unless I was working to rebalance the scales of justice."

"You deserve a future as much as any person does. Guilt has a way of messing with our minds."

She huffed out a laugh. "It wasn't just guilt. Uncle Tom hammered it into me for years to avoid the outside world, that I couldn't trust anyone. Hell, I no longer existed in the real world's eyes. I had no identity. Whenever I questioned him about why I had to hide, he shut me down."

"But you eventually decided to go against his wishes, to find your own path."

"When one of the men—a real nasty sort—who came to train at the ranch bragged about how he liked to set fires, especially if it created chaos and death, I did some research next time I went to the Flagstaff Public Library. Found out he was an arsonist who'd killed a firefighter and the child the firefighter was trying to save. According to the article I found, the police didn't have enough evidence to make an arrest and the parents were left homeless and grief-stricken."

"And the guy survived to brag about his escapades." Anger made his words come out like bullets. "Unless..." He arched a brow at her.

"I didn't kill him, if that's what you're asking. But he's not bragging anymore, either. Nobody else, certainly nobody in the justice system, was making it right for that child's family, or the family of the firefighter. I'd gotten a second chance with Uncle Tom but that kid, that fireman, they'll never get another chance. The least they deserved was justice. I used force to get the arsonist to confess, delivered him to the police, promising I'd hunt him down and kill him if he didn't make a proper confession."

He reached out to take her hand. "Hey. I understand why you did what you did. Just as I understand the police might never have caught him without you."

"I felt useful for the first time. Like I had a purpose. I hadn't felt worthy since that night..." Her gut clenched with remembered fear and guilt. "The night my parents died, the fire trucks came and firefighters put out the blaze, but there was little left of the house. They found me in the tree when I started to cough, but I screamed if any of them tried to touch me. One of them climbed up and sat with me, said some soothing things. It wasn't until Uncle Tom showed up and pried my fingers from the bark that I felt safe." She took a deep breath and dared to meet Jared's gaze. "When I take a job, it's because I want others to feel safe, too."

CHAPTER TWENTY-ONE

"I hope you see the truth now," Jared said. "You aren't to blame for what happened to your parents. Any more than I'm to blame for not being there when my mother was murdered by one of her boyfriends." He and Skye both knew the burden of guilt, and how fighting for others, protecting others, provided some relief.

Skye's sigh was heavy but seemed to diffuse the last of her tension. "Yeah, I know."

"I once thought I was a superhero. Still do, sometimes." He grinned when Skye released a quick, surprised laugh. He wanted to see that sparkle in her eyes, always. He lifted his other hand to her chin and traced her smile with his thumb.

She went still. "Did I pass your test?"

"Test?"

"You were making sure I'm not a cold-blooded killer, I believe?" There was humor in her eyes.

"I thought talking about it might help. Haley's question seemed to be on your mind. You're no saint, but neither am I. Your past shaped who you are now, but I hope you see that you shouldn't have to punish yourself. You don't have to be a vigilante to find justice for people." Growing up among conspiracy theorists and vigilante types couldn't have been easy. He cupped her face so that her eyes met his. "I'm sorry I brought up bad memories."

"I suppose it was good for both of us—strengthens the partnership and all that."

For her to share her story illustrated the trust she placed in him, and he didn't take that lightly. But before he could form the words to thank her for that gift, she gestured to the computer.

"What did Dev send?"

Swallowing down feelings that were too confusing to put into words, he pulled over the laptop and opened the file.

Skye looked at him in surprise. "A topographical map of the ranch."

"All roads seem to converge there."

"Do you think Finn is there now? Hard to imagine an actor-type like him roughing it." From what they'd found on Finn Tucker, he'd been destined to pursue acting. His parents were both in the field, though not so famous that someone outside the entertainment industry would know them without a little help. They'd divorced when Finn was very young. Based on tabloid reports and the years Finn had spent in boarding school making friends with Ryan Stone, they'd been too busy with their own careers to bother with Finn. After that, it seemed Finn had spent more school holidays with the Stone family than his own. Nothing in the files indicated a young man with violent tendencies.

Jared considered what they knew of Finn, and the note left on Erica's body. Jared wasn't going to let Skye walk into something and offer herself up like a sacrifice. "I think Finn wants you at Three Fortunes and knows you won't resist a fight, especially when he's hurting women. Leaving Erica's body for you is him trying to get you to the ranch again. Which is why I'd like you to stay far away."

"But you just told Anderson we'd be there tomorrow, to search for the girls."

"No, I said *I'd* be there tomorrow."

She stood. "You can't keep me out of this."

He'd known this wouldn't be easy, but he wanted to keep her safe. "I know I can't. But I'm asking, for my own sanity, that you stay here, where I can have a GSS guard protect you. I promise to keep you posted. Besides, we don't know that Finn is there. He could just as easily be here in town, and you can keep the search going here. But if you do that, let GSS back you up."

"I don't need backup. I need my partner." She took several deep breaths, struggling to control her temper. "You don't get to play the hero here. I'm part of this, too." She spun on her heel and hurried toward the kitchen.

Yes, she was part of this. She was at the core. And that's what he was afraid of.

She heard Jared enter the kitchen behind her and steeled herself for an argument, which is why she jumped when two arms came around her in a warm embrace.

"I'm sorry," he said in her ear. "I don't want to fight."

"Then don't. I'm coming with you."

"Finn wants you too bad, and Tristan is still out there, gunning for you, too. I can't protect you on all sides *and* look for Chelsea and Loretta. This is about finding them, while keeping you safe."

She sagged against him, loving the feel of him against her back, supporting her. She straightened again and pulled out of his arms as she realized she was being weak. She whirled to look him in the eyes. "I know that. And I can protect myself."

He stroked a finger across her forehead, brushing the tension there. "I'm well aware of that. Do it for my sake. I can't have my attention divided."

"That's why I prefer to work alone."

"So you understand." He scanned her eyes. "You'll stay here?"

She read trust and compassion in his expression, but also fear. Did he think she would botch things? Then again, her track record with people wasn't so good. But no way would she sit here and let him ride off toward danger alone. Still, he wouldn't let this go until she acquiesced, so she gave him a neutral answer. "I'll consider it."

At ten that night, Finn rolled his shoulders to relieve the tension before he opened the side door to the old Las Vegas theater. It was unlocked. Another one of Ryan Stone's playgrounds, it was an abandoned property owned by Robert Stone. That family had more than it could ever need, while the peons who served them, who entertained them like court jesters, had little. Finn supposed he should feel lucky to bask in the glow of the Stone success, and for a long time he had. No longer.

He'd channeled his anger at Ryan's betrayal—calling this meeting and not believing in Finn—into planning the biggest hunt they'd ever hosted. Skye would bring in a record amount of money from people desiring the privilege of hunting a huntress. Tonight, Finn planned to lay out a proposal to appease the Club members who would sit in judgment.

But if that wasn't enough, fuck them. He'd enjoy hunting her himself, as he'd wanted to all along, and rub it in their faces later when they realized he was a genius, infinitely smarter and more creative than Ryan-Fucking-Stone.

As he strode onto stage with determined, confident strides, two bright spotlights switched on, one focusing on him and the other on a podium. Clearly, he was supposed to stand there and argue his case. The Club had only held two of these trials over the past five years, which made this betrayal by his supposed best friend all the more insulting. He couldn't see faces in the audience, but that was the way these things worked—as anonymously as possible. Every member wanted something, something shady and dangerous and usually illegal. They owed debts, or paid them in advance as credit toward something bigger. It was a phenomenal dark deeds bartering system, especially when transactions, and the members who carried through with them, were kept secret.

There were only a dozen charter members, people he and Ryan had recruited over the years, and they were the ones who'd be in attendance today. He knew some of them from previous meetings, but didn't know how many might be on his side today. Probably none, since they were all afraid of Ryan. They'd be firmly in the golden boy's camp. Hell, Finn had happily camped there, too, until recently. A man could only take so much humiliation.

And Ryan was about to heap a bit more on—this time, publicly.

"State your name," Ryan called out as Finn stepped up to the podium.

"Finn Tucker, also known as Joker." Their code names were for more clandestine jobs, and for the records in the ledger. "What are the formal charges against me? I have a right to know."

"Endangering the Club, and its members, for personal gain."

"I've only ever acted in the best interests of the Club. I created the Hunting Grounds for the pleasurable pursuit and financial gain of all of its members. It's become a successful endeavor."

"But you've started committing rogue acts outside of Hunting Grounds activities. You killed Erica Dubois and left her to be found by authorities."

"As a way to lure even bigger and better prey." He smirked. "Hell, Erica wasn't any challenge at all. Any hunter who'd paid to participate would have demanded a refund. On the other hand, her death will lead Skye Hamilton to one of our gatherers, who is waiting at this very moment for her to show up. Skye will make us hundreds of thousands of dollars if we host a big hunt. I just need a day or two to pull it all together. I've already been contacted by three Club members who want to be in the hunting party, and after seeing Skye's picture and portfolio, they're each offering half a million for the privilege to hunt her."

There was a long silence, followed by a wave of approving murmurs. He was swaying the vote in his favor. He could feel it. Everyone here was in this either for the thrills or the money. He was promising both.

Besides, nobody could defeat him when he was on stage. He'd always been good at persuasive arguments. Ryan had made a colossal mistake, taking him on.

"Skye is from a ranch near the Grounds," Ryan's voice rang out. "And you already took Loretta from there. That's too many connections that could lead back to us, or to my father, whose name is on the deed. Ever heard the saying, 'Don't shit where you eat'?" A chorus of soft laughs followed Ryan's remark and Finn stiffened with anger. "Your actions will bring the authorities down on us and put the whole club at risk. Skye already came after me and she's not going to let this go."

"I don't want her to. Her desire to find us is what will bring her to us. There will be no risk once she's been gathered. She's the only one who cares about Loretta, and Skye Hamilton is like a ghost. Nobody knows she exists. All connections will be broken once she and Loretta are gone."

"And Chelsea?"

"Who?"

"Chelsea Wright. Another girl you took in recent weeks. Guess you didn't research her family tree before you took her."

Some of Finn's confidence slipped, but he shored it up. "She was a dancer. She already owed the Club money. Besides, you were there that night we took her."

"*You* took her. If I'd known who her brother was, if you'd done a fucking background check, you would have realized she wasn't a viable candidate for a hunt, that someone would miss her when she was gone."

"Who?"

"Her brother, Jared Bennigan. They have different fathers, and thus different last names, but it would have required only a few questions to connect those dots."

Fuck. Finn's brain scrambled to find a new tactic to convince them of his path. This didn't change anything. "Things are already in motion. We can remedy this. Jared can be dealt with." He and Tristan had already taken care of Mark for similar reasons. Jared was just one of those loose ends that would be tied up.

"I've received a motion that we evict you from the group." Ryan's words rang with the sound of a gavel against a judge's desk.

"From whom?"

"You know I don't have to reveal that."

"Fuck that, Ryan. You know me. You and I are brothers in every way that matters. You know I wouldn't do anything to endanger the Club."

There was a long moment of silence and Finn felt hope spurt through him. Maybe he'd gotten through. He heard a few whispers in the dark arena and assumed the members were consulting with Ryan.

"The motion to evict you came from me," a deep voice rang out. Robert Stone's voice.

Finn's knees wobbled and his gut turned to hot liquid. He'd heard this voice for the majority of his life, but never with such quiet anger as it held now. "Sir, I can explain."

"Ryan's told me about reviving the Club, and I've found out through various unpleasant means how you've managed to fuck things up for yourselves. You're done. The Club is over. It was over years ago, when I ended it the first time. I'm taking charge and ending it again. You're finished, both in the Club and with my family."

"Let me redeem myself." The long pause that followed his plea gave Finn hope. "I can do it. Like I said, I already have plans in place. I'm going to use Skye's uncle to lure her. Tom Hamilton's the only family Skye has left. Besides, he's in the Redemption Club ledger. He's one of us."

"Everyone out," Stone ordered suddenly. Several gasps erupted in the audience, followed by the sound of a muffled argument, and several sets of footsteps retreating. Finn could see shadows of shapes moving among the rows of seats and silhouettes as some people moved through the door at the end of the aisle. A moment later, the lights flipped on and Finn blinked as the darkness cleared. The only people remaining in the audience were Ryan and Mr. Stone.

"Tell me more about using Tom Hamilton," Stone said.

Finn felt exhilaration flood his loose limbs as he jumped off the stage and walked forward. "He's the one who's been blackmailing you." His gaze met Ryan's, but his friend's emotions were, for once, unreadable. "I can get rid of him for you, and save you millions of dollars in blackmail payments."

CHAPTER TWENTY-TWO

Skye brooded over her morning coffee, regretting the promise she'd made to consider not following Jared for twenty-four hours. She had to go with him, had to be there to take Finn down. But before Jared emerged from the room with an overnight bag so that she could argue her position, the chime of her phone sounded.

She scooped up her phone from the table, a spike of hope piercing her as she spied the incoming text. *Tom.* And an address—one that she recognized—along with instructions not to tell anyone he'd contacted her.

"I'm all set," Jared said from the doorway.

She set her phone down and went to accept his embrace, wrapping her arms tight around him. "Be safe."

He tipped her chin up and looked into her eyes. "Thank you. I know you want to come, but—"

She stopped his words with a kiss. "I know you're only trying to protect me. But be warned, I will be right behind you."

He arched a brow. "Twenty-four hours."

She shrugged. "Unless I have a reason to come sooner."

It was his turn to silence her with a kiss. "A GSS guard should be pulling up outside any minute. He'll be here if you need anything."

After another kiss, this one slower and seemingly full of emotions they hadn't spoken aloud, Jared grabbed his bag and left. She went into motion the minute his car disappeared down the road, knowing she had to move her car to the street behind Jared's and return to the house before the GSS guard showed up. She'd greet the guard, let him see she was okay, and then sneak out the back.

She slowed her little used car to a stop in the dirt driveway and got out. She glanced up at the tree she'd loved and then at the trailer that had replaced the ramshackle house she'd hated. Tom had been hiding here? She'd just driven by it a few days ago. But that seemed decades away, from a time before she trusted Jared. Strange how the ghosts of her parents didn't seem to linger here now, as they had the other night. Over the past week, she'd done more to dispel the power of the past than she had in the previous twenty years. She had Jared to thank for a lot of that.

She stepped up to the door, blinking as the midmorning light glinted off the aluminum foil in the windows. The practice was meant to deflect light and heat, a poor man's substitute for air conditioning.

"Uncle Tom?" Her voice rang out along the empty lot, carried away by the hot wind that blew dust around her. She blinked it away and tried the knob. It turned easily beneath her hand. Prickles of warning rose up along her spine and she reached for the gun she'd tucked into the back of her waistband, under her tank top. Her knife and cell phone were in the pockets of the khaki cargo pants, but the gun would look more intimidating if she encountered anyone who shouldn't be here.

Nudging the door open, her gaze slowly adjusted to the lack of light before she took a step inside. There was no movement, no reaction at all to her presence. She took another step and crossed the threshold.

There were signs somebody had been here recently. A couple of cigarette butts stuck out of the ashtray on the table that served as an eating area. Tom's brand. He must have been feeling stressed if he was back to chain smoking.

"Skye?" Tom's voice called out.

She moved to the closed door that likely led to the bedroom. "Uncle Tom?"

"Come in. We need to talk." His voice was raspy. Was he hurt? Had she woken him? Wasn't he expecting her?

She opened the door and froze. She began to lift her gun, but Finn already had his aimed at her from the other side of the cramped room. Tom was sitting on the bed, with Finn standing beside him.

"Uh-uh-uh," Finn said, his eyes glittering. "Don't move."

"Run, Skye," Tom pleaded with her.

Finn pressed the barrel of his gun to her uncle's head. "I suggest you stay."

"Just turn and run," Tom said. "I'm not worth it."

Skye stood, rooted to the spot. She couldn't watch another family member die, not here at the scene of so much death. Not because of anything she did. Not ever. Slowly, she laid her gun on the dresser and put her hands in the air.

Tom's face crumpled.

Finn grinned. "Good girl. And because you're being so cooperative, I'm going to give you a choice. You're going to have a little something to eat or drink. Either way, the result will be the same."

"Drugged?" she guessed.

"If you'd prefer, I could inject you with something, or force it down your throat."

She swallowed hard. No way did she want him anywhere near her, though it might give her uncle a chance to run for safety.

As if sensing the direction of her thoughts, Finn snarled and jabbed the gun into Tom's temple. "Eat, drink. Be merry. Or I'll shoot dear old Uncle Tom."

Dust motes danced in the air as the late morning

sun slanted through the lace curtains in the ranch house's kitchen. Jared doubted the décor was to Tom Hamilton's taste, which meant they'd been Skye's addition. The juxtaposition of her softer side and the tough side he'd experienced in the yard beyond, when she'd taken him to the ground during their sparring match, was an intoxicating blend.

He'd known how much being part of this search meant to her, and yet he'd asked her to sacrifice her own desires. And she had.

He tried dialing her phone and reached her voicemail again. He'd been trying for hours, to no avail, but the guard watching the house had said he'd seen her with his own eyes, and that she hadn't left the house.

Still, worry had a grip on Jared's gut. Was she angry with him and not answering? He sent her another text. *Checking in. Let me know you're okay.*

He was still staring at the screen, willing a reply to appear, when Sheriff Anderson came in through the back door. The ranch house had become a central hub of activity as search parties looking for signs of Chelsea, Loretta, or Finn fanned out in every direction. It was an enormous endeavor, but thoroughness was key. He didn't want to take the chance he'd miss a clue.

He'd also spent a few minutes in Skye's bedroom. He was surprised by how much he missed her after only a few hours away. Or maybe he was feeling guilty he'd made her stay behind. Evidence of the clash within the woman, between bold and soft, was evident everywhere, from her paisley-print bedspread in soft apricot and turquoise to the dried flowers in a vase on the dresser whose top drawer was stuffed full of extra ammo.

He frowned down at his phone, but it refused to be intimidated and stubbornly remained quiet. His internal police radar twitched, sensing something was off. He tried to ignore it for several minutes, then gave up and dialed Dev.

"Do me a favor," he said. "Contact the guard in front of my house and have him walk to the door again and make sure Skye's okay. She's not responding to my texts."

"Trouble in paradise?" Dev asked.

"She wasn't exactly happy about me asking her to stay behind."

"Can't say I blame her. Besides, from what you told me earlier, it doesn't sound like you asked so much as guilted her. Very smooth, using her feelings for you."

He snorted. "Skye doesn't let her feelings get in the way of a job." But something in his chest fluttered. Did she have feelings for him? He doubted she'd have cooperated so easily unless she cared. Skye Hamilton cared about him. He grinned, but it promptly faded. Had he manipulated her? God, he was no better than his mother had been.

"Just send someone around," Jared barked, irritated with himself, and with Dev for pointing out the facts Jared obviously wanted to ignore.

"I will."

"And text me when you hear she's okay."

Dev grumbled. "Remind me never to fall in love."

Love? Was that what this was? He'd always imagined romantic love was manipulative and controlling, as his mother's boyfriends had been. It abandoned you when you needed it most.

But this... This wasn't some clawing need, but more of a wanting. Wanting to be with a woman when she wasn't around, wanting to touch her when she was. Wanting to keep her safe.

Damn. Skye had snuck up on him again, this time finding her way into his heart.

"Skye? Wake up, damn it. Skye!"

She mumbled a nonsense response to her uncle's repeated requests. It seemed all she was capable of. She couldn't even lift her head. Damn, she could barely flutter her eyelids, which sent a sudden jolt of anxiety through her. She fought harder against the seduction of the black void.

"Come on, honey," Tom persisted, the urgency in his tone breaking a little more through the haze. "You can do it."

She tried to rub her sleepy face but couldn't move her hands. Finally, she dragged her eyelids open and reality seeped in as she surveyed her surroundings— her lopsided surroundings. She was lying on her side on a thin mat that smelled of the dirt floor beneath it, her hands tied behind her back.

Zip ties, she thought, feeling the way they restrained her wrists but didn't abrade her skin.

Slowly, she pushed into a sitting position and blinked away the dizziness as she focused on the room. A one-room shack with a bucket in the corner. She didn't want to think about what that was for. Uncle Tom sat at the only furniture, a table and two chairs. His hands were also behind his back. Blood trickled from his temple. The sight of it shocked her brain further into focus.

"What's going on?" She remembered the trailer where her parents' house had once stood. Remembered drinking the bottle of water that had to have been drugged, to keep Finn from shooting her uncle. "Where's Finn?"

Through the barred window she saw the tall trunks and green fringe of pine trees. Was she back in Arizona?

The tiny kitchenette and living area were one space, and the entire cabin couldn't be more than a couple hundred square feet. A hunting cabin, she'd guess, probably used during elk hunting season. Was it used during the human hunts, too? She subdued a shudder as her uncle spoke again.

"We're alone. For the moment."

She glanced around but didn't see anything that could be used as a weapon. There were only a couple of thin sleeping mats on the floor. She was on one of them. Had this been where Finn took Chelsea and Loretta? If so, where were they now? There were no cupboards to hide anything in.

"There are no weapons," Tom said, catching her surveying their surroundings. "And nothing to cut us loose. I already spent the past couple hours looking." *Couple hours?* "The bastard drugged you." His eyes squeezed shut.

She jerked her chin toward his temple. "Does it hurt?"

"Not much. Just a headache." Finn had probably used force, and likely threatened their lives, to get Tom to cooperate. He hung his head. "This is all my fault."

"What? No, it's mine. I'm the one who was looking for Finn. I'm the reason he attacked the ranch. I should have known he'd use you. He and Tristan... Didn't you get my messages?"

He grimaced. "Yeah. Didn't want to drag you further into my mess."

"*Your* mess?" His self-blame didn't make sense. She was able to scoot over to him across the dirt floor and pull herself up to the chair across from him. On the table lay a card. Her heartbeat thudded in her ears as she examined it. Clear tape ran across the center, reconnecting two halves of the king of diamonds. The top half had her uncle's name and a date on it.

Her stomach clenched, threatening to rebel. "What's this?"

He couldn't seem to look at her. His face was so pale it was almost gray. *Ashen.* She now knew what the term meant, and all the fear that went with it.

But she already knew the answer. Somewhere, deep down, she'd known for the past few days. She was his redemption.

He drew in a shaky breath and looked at her as if finally seeing her. "I'm sorry, Skye. So sorry."

"First, tell me where we are, if you know." If Finn came back, she wanted as much pertinent information as possible to escape.

"We're about fifteen minutes east of Three Fortunes. It used to be a part of the ranch. Sold it years ago." He grimaced and looked around. "Never thought I'd see it again."

"Did you sell it to Robert Stone?"

He sighed. "I needed the cash at the time. It basically paid for the barn renovation and Viper's Pit." He looked up at her sheepishly. "So, you know about the ranch?"

"About you two co-owning the ranch, along with some other guy, about a Redemption Club where cards symbolize debts, about nearly everything, I think." Her gaze landed on the card that lay between them. The date scrawled on it was burned on her brain forever. "I know that card means something very bad." Her brain did the math even as her heart didn't want to go there. What did the Redemption Club have to do with the day her parents had died, and why was Tom's name on the half-card? Finn and Ryan had to have been in grade school at that time, and probably hadn't even met yet. "The king of diamonds says you know about the Redemption Club, too. Did you know Finn Tucker before today?"

"No. I thought it was all over when we disbanded the Club."

The breath whooshed out of her. "*We?*"

"Redemption Club began over twenty years ago, before I had you in my life—at least full time, anyway. My brother—your father—wasn't the only bad apple in the Hamilton barrel. I was into some nasty stuff back then, thought I was invincible. We all did."

"Who?"

"Me, Stone, Wilson. We'd been friends in school. We were making money hand over fist doing not-so-legal things. That's how we bought this ranch. But it was getting too dangerous, and we were nearly caught a couple times. By then, some of us had families who could be hurt by our activities, and Stone wanted to use most of his funds to start a legitimate business, so we agreed to shut the Club down. Now, this Finn guy comes along and has apparently discovered everything."

"How could you have kept all of this from me? Did you think I wouldn't understand?"

"You *don't* understand," he snapped. "How could you? I'm capable of horrible things. The Club was about trading services. People would come to us with all kinds of desires, everything from needing gambling money to wanting someone dead. They'd pay in money or in a promissory note to be repaid later." He jerked his chin toward the table. "These cards. They signify debts. Promises to repay. Stone came up with the idea, came up with a system where we tore them in half. The person asking for the favor would keep the bottom half, signifying a debt to be repaid later. The top half had the debtor's name and the date of the debt was incurred. Stone kept those. When the debt was repaid, the two halves were reunited. Redemption was achieved."

"And the denominations? Do they have meaning?"

His lips twisted in a wry grin. "Numbers indicated lesser debts like borrowed money or harassment."

"And face cards?"

"More serious debts. Murder, kidnapping, and the like."

Darren's card had been an eight, so most likely he'd owed a financial debt—the one that had purchased his trailer. Tristan's had been a face card. He'd been more brutal, then, asking for something... worse. It made sense that he'd been the one to kill Mark Sheldon.

Her uncle's card was a king.

"We had a ledger that lists everything, too," Tom continued. "What services they'd requested, as well as who fulfilled it." His gaze, filled with regret, met hers. "Finn probably read about how your parents drugged you, and decided to use it against you. I'm sure he must have the ledger. Stone had it last, had promised to destroy it."

"Why would that have been recorded there?" But she already knew. Her stomach flopped like a dying fish.

"The person petitioning for a service has to provide justification." He swallowed. "I listed why your parents deserved to be dead."

Anger and disbelief warred with the blessed numbness that wanted to take over. He'd contracted her parents' deaths, left her an orphan, and then brushed it under the rug as if nothing had ever happened. She suddenly felt nauseous, thinking about how she'd blamed herself during her childhood years, and how her savior had killed his own brother and sister-in-law. It was twisted. Sick. Even if it had saved her from a life of misery.

Seeing the moment she realized the truth, Tom scowled. "I told you I wasn't worth the trouble. I'm not a good person."

"The old you, maybe. The Tom I know has been hard on me at times, and taught me difficult lessons, but it was always out of love." At least, she'd thought it was. "Wasn't it?"

"And necessity. But after what I've done, I could never let myself get fully close to you, to really love you. You deserve better."

"*You* gave me better. Even when you were holding back, you were better than what I had." But she'd always blamed herself for what happened, believed herself unworthy of love. They'd both held back, afraid to love fully. "Stone was the invisible enemy you were constantly preparing me to battle, the reason you never wanted me to stray far from the ranch."

"Yes."

Anger and fear amped up the adrenaline, simulating a workout in Viper's Pit. She embraced it, coaxed it to its full force, because it made her feel alive. "You always said that a soldier's best weapon was knowing his enemy. How could you leave this out of my education? You always thought Stone would come for me. Why? What do you owe them?" Her gaze fell on the reunited halves of the card. "How did you achieve your redemption?"

"I killed someone Robert Stone wanted dead."

"Then you should have been even, right? You'd already earned redemption?"

"It wasn't that easy. He thinks you saw him, that night at your parents' house, before it went up in flames."

Her jaw dropped. "*Stone* was one of the men that night?" She searched her memory, but the men had become faceless in her mind.

"He found out you were in the tree. I convinced him you didn't remember anything, and that I could keep you on Three Fortunes with me, out of the way."

"So when I popped up recently, he got worried."

"Especially since someone was blackmailing him. He thought it might be you."

"So he tried to have you kick me off the ranch." A humorless smile tugged at her lips.

"But you kept investigating, so he demanded more."

"What did he want?"

Waves of worry buckled his forehead and his eyes filled with tears. She'd never seen him cry. "I gave them you."

"Me?"

"Stone must have suspected I might hide out at the trailer. Finn tracked me down, took my phone and texted you. But I won't let him harm you. They may have used me to get you here, but I've protected you all these years and I won't stop now."

She glanced at the card again before scanning his face. He definitely wasn't the Tom she'd seen a couple days ago, before the ranch had been attacked. But he was the only person who loved her unconditionally. He was her family. Or so she'd thought.

Tom's pain-filled eyes met hers. "I did what was necessary to keep us alive."

She'd suspected living under the radar had something to do with that night. His reluctance to talk about the past had only reinforced it. The six-year-old Skye had blamed herself for what happened that night. Hiding in the tree, wishing the worst upon her parents. And then the worst had happened.

But the twenty-six-year-old Skye knew better. She didn't have that kind of control over the world or the people in it. She only had control over her own actions. Still, the survivor's guilt she'd lived with for years lurked like a blemish on her conscience, a scar that could never be fully erased. A taint on all of her relationships, shaping how she interacted with others, with Jared. God, she'd been afraid for nothing. It hadn't been her. The bars of the cage around her heart loosened.

Tom sighed. "Stone promised to leave you alone, to let us live in peace on the ranch that the three of us had bought, as long as you didn't dig into the past. He made me promise to keep you on the ranch, to make sure you never talked about that night."

"I don't remember their faces. I was up in a tree." She only recalled two men coming to see her parents about *business.*

"Which is the only reason they let you live."

"Who are *they*? Both Stone and Wilson had something to do with this?"

Tom's tortured gaze met hers. "That's how Redemption Club works, the beauty of it. You don't have to do your own dirty work, so you have an alibi."

She was breathing heavily now, trying to absorb the shocks that were coming at her like fists. The blows hit her one after the other, relentlessly.

Tom stopped beside her chair. "They may have used us against each other to get us here, but they don't have a weapon to hold against you anymore. I'm not worth the bullet they'd use to shoot me, so when

Finn comes back, you run and don't look back."

Her insides felt battered and bruised, but he was still her uncle, her only flesh and blood. They'd figure this out. He'd make recompense to the people he'd hurt, he'd redeem himself—without doing anything else that skirted the law. "We'll get out of this together. And then we'll get Stone."

But Tom seemed lost in the past. "I had your parents—" His voice broke and he swallowed before continuing. "I had them killed. My own brother and his wife. I had to make it stop. You were in danger."

"I still am. We both are. We have to get out of here." And find the girls. She wasn't leaving without them.

Misery brimmed in his eyes as he looked back at her. "Skye, can you ever forgive me? I always knew my time with you was short, and I enjoyed more years of peace than I deserved."

"And I always had the sense that someone, some unseen evil, was coming for me. Probably because you and Viper trained me to believe that."

"I wanted you prepared, because I love you."

"This isn't love," she shouted.

"Love is sacrifice. I'll do anything to save you."

"It's too late." She heard the crunch of gravel and the engine of an approaching car. "They want a hunt. They want me."

Chelsea had a bad feeling. It started when Bear didn't drive away. She'd listened for his car after he'd come to check on them, but he hadn't left the property. Unless he'd gone on foot, but that seemed unlikely.

Then a couple of cars had driven up and she'd heard voices. From that, she discerned five men, including Finn and Bear. They'd spent some time talking and laughing, but she couldn't make out their conversation. And then it had gotten quiet again. That had been over an hour ago.

Had they been doing something at one of the other cabins? There were two others nearby, though not so close that she could see or hear what was going on. She hadn't thought they were occupied before. Maybe she'd been wrong. Or maybe they'd brought a new girl.

"You think it'll be soon, don't you?" Loretta asked, her face pale as she lifted off the sleeping mat. The fight had left her since the moment she'd learned her father was dead.

"Tonight," Chelsea said with conviction. She hurried over to their stash of food and water. There was little left, but it was nourishment, fuel for what was to come. "Eat," she commanded, thrusting a protein bar at Loretta and following it with a bottle of water. "We'll need our strength."

"It's all we have left." Loretta accepted the bar but didn't rip it open as Chelsea had with her own. "What if they don't bring supplies for a few days?"

"It'll be tonight," Chelsea said around a dry mouthful. "We won't need anymore." She stuffed an extra bar in Loretta's pocket. She'd need it if the final showdown was finally here.

At least Bear had brought them the occasional change of clothing and let them wash with a bucket of water. Long gone was the seductive dress Chelsea had worn to dance for Finn and his friends. Her pants were fitting looser, but she was also lean from the training. More muscular. She could do this. She was strong. She had a family to get back to. A life.

"Think of what you want most in this world," she said to Loretta, injecting harshness into her tone so the girl would listen. "Make it something worth fighting for."

"I wanted to be an actress." Loretta stared at the window. "Now I just don't care."

"Care about something, or you might as well let them kill you now. If they catch you, they won't be gentle."

"I don't want them to win." Loretta sobbed, then

choked it back.

"Then that's what you care about. If nothing else, we won't let them win. We'll make sure they pay for your dad's murder."

Loretta tore open her protein bar and devoured it.

Jared answered before Dev's ring tone completed the first few notes. "Say you have some news for me."

"Skye wasn't at your house. The guard had been sitting outside, as you requested, but didn't see her come or go. Good thing you put that tracking device on her vehicle."

Jared winced, knowing he'd gone behind her back that first night she'd shown up. He'd intended to make sure she didn't get away from him again. He couldn't take the risk she'd disappear from his life forever. "Where'd she go? Do you have an address?" He was already moving toward the front door, ready to get into his car and drive back to Vegas.

"I swung by there already myself and nobody's there. Just an old, empty trailer. Her car was there, though."

"Where?"

Dev gave a familiar address. After Skye had told him the story of her past, he'd looked up the official report on that night. A chill of foreboding danced along Jared's skin.

"No sign of her?" Jared asked.

"No. I'm sorry. Keep trying to reach her and I'll keep looking for her here, and for Finn."

Jared suspected that was a lost cause. "Do me a favor and forward me that listing of all of Stone's properties again, but add Tom Hamilton's and David Wilson's as well. For a proper hunt, Finn would need room, away from public eyes, so he's got to have a private lot around here somewhere." And if Finn had Skye, that's where he'd take her.

CHAPTER TWENTY-THREE

Inside the third cabin at the Hunting Grounds, Finn grinned at the circle of expectant faces. They were shrouded in masks, but that didn't diminish their expressions of pure, carnal pleasure. The bear was Tristan. And Ryan, though he hadn't been on a hunt in recent weeks, had donned his wolf mask for this occasion. Finn had his fox on. Around the circle, he met the hungry eyes of a cougar, tiger, and coyote.

"Two of the girls were released an hour ago," he told the men. "The head start will make it more of a challenge." He'd made sure they didn't go toward the other cabins so they hadn't seen Skye or Tom.

"Any drugs?" Ryan asked.

"Skye was drugged during transport, but it should be out of her system by now. We agreed that she should be at her full capacity for the maximum bang for your hard-earned bucks." There were several approving nods around the circle. "But if any of you would like to partake, we can visit the shed."

"I'm already high," the tiger said with a chuckle.

"The adrenaline's enough for me," Tristan said. Behind his bear mask, his eyes glittered. "And it'll make the moment that much sweeter when I take the main prize down."

Finn would be the one to take Skye down, but he didn't disabuse any of these hunters of the same notion. After all, they were paying for the dream.

He stepped toward Tristan and handed him the other half of his card. "You've done well. Your loyalty to the Club is appreciated, and you are now absolved of your debt. You've achieved your redemption." Without Tristan, Finn couldn't have covered all his bases. When Jared had left Vegas this morning for Three Fortunes, without Skye, Finn had known it was time to put Plan B into effect, using Tom. Tracing Viper's phone records at the hospital and using the information Mr. Stone had provided about Tom's history, Finn had been able to identify Tom's cell phone and track it. Meanwhile, Tristan had prepared the Hunting Grounds.

Tristan grinned as he accepted the card and tucked it into his pocket. "It was my great pleasure. And my privilege to participate in this event."

Ryan grunted. Finn knew he wasn't happy about Tristan's bonus, but they were making one and a half million dollars off the other three hunters. In fact, Ryan had been unusually quiet all day, and frowning a lot. It was almost as if he *wanted* to see Finn fail.

"Speaking of the main event, I'll release Skye in a few minutes. Give her a fifteen-minute head start and then you may leave this cabin. You all had an hour to survey the immediate surroundings, but she hasn't had the same advantage."

"Will she be armed?" the cougar asked.

"I suppose it's only fair to allow her some form of defense. As for what kind of weapons,"—he grinned—"that'll be part of the surprise."

"How will we know when to start the timer?" Ryan asked. Finally, his friend was coming around. Finn could see the cold, calculating gleam in his eyes.

"When you hear the gunshot, you'll know Skye's time has started. Fifteen minutes later, she's fair game."

Having watched Finn's approach from the window, Skye was prepared as the cabin door opened. He was wearing the face of a fox, which was both ridiculous and reminded her of his conceited madness at the same time.

As he stepped inside, he grinned, flashing his perfect white teeth as he shoved the mask to the top of his head. "Good to see you up and about."

"Stay away from her." Tom moved to get in front of her, but with their hands tied, there was little they could do unless Finn moved closer.

Come closer.

"It's me Stone wants," Tom said. "I'm the one who owes him."

Finn's grin disappeared, replaced with a sneer. "This isn't about Stone, and this isn't your club anymore." He pulled out his gun. "Step aside." Keeping his eyes on Skye and Tom, he drew a hunting knife from his boot with his free hand.

Cold fear sliced through Skye. She was familiar with the weapons, had been trained to use and defend against them, but facing a threat from someone who was gleeful at the anticipation of her death was a different story. And having a loved one in range of the weapons made it all the more difficult.

"Get over here," Finn said to Skye. He jabbed the knife's point toward the ground in front of him in emphasis.

"You won't touch her." Intending to use his body as a weapon, or maybe a shield, Tom went barreling toward Finn. Finn ducked to the side at the last second, ramming the end of his knife's hilt between Tom's shoulder blades and sending him to the ground.

Finn kept the gun trained on Tom and arched a brow at Skye. "Come closer, with your back to me, so I can slice through your ties. Trust me, you'll want your hands free for what's to come."

"What are you hoping to gain by doing this?" She backed to him and he sawed through her ties. She itched to land a backward kick to the man's shins, followed by spinning around to thrust the heel of her hand into his nose, but he had a gun aimed at Tom.

Unaware of the vicious images running through

her mind, Finn grinned as she turned to face him. "Some fun and a whole lot of money. Step back now. I can't shoot you yet, since several men have paid for that privilege, but I will shoot your uncle if you don't comply."

Several men? So, it was to be a group hunt. She tipped her head toward Tom, who was still sitting on the floor. "Aren't you going to cut him free?"

"He's not part of this."

"Like hell," Tom said, struggling into a standing position. But he didn't charge at Finn again. "Stone thinks I'm behind his blackmail, but I'm not."

"I know." Finn's eyes glittered. "But we need a scapegoat. Don't worry, you won't be the only one making a sacrifice today."

Tom met Skye's gaze with apology and a resignation that nearly made her cry out. "I'm sorry, Skye. I tried to be a good role model, to prepare you for the evils of the world. Don't make the same mistakes I did, shutting yourself off to the good things in life, to love."

Finn snorted. "Who better to give you advice than a man who once embraced those evils? Don't get me wrong. I for one, applaud you, but your time has passed, old man." The gunshot was so sudden, so loud in the tiny cabin that Skye's shock was paralyzing. In the next instant, Tom was on the ground, a hole in his chest. She gasped and took a step toward her uncle.

Finn was grinning as he aimed the gun at her. "Stop right there."

"What have you done?" she shouted, her body straining to check on Tom but fighting the threat of Finn's next bullet. "I won't participate."

"Suit yourself, but that shot was the signal to the other hunters that they can come looking for you in fifteen minutes. That's assuming they stick to the rules, of course."

She fought to control her respiratory rate and pulse, struggled to control the emotions twisting through her like a tornado, seeking to destroy Finn. She couldn't look at Tom's motionless body, couldn't think about his death, or she might fall apart.

She forced herself to meet Finn's gaze. "How many? At least tell me that much."

"There are six of us, including me. And three of you, if you care at all about the other girls."

Other girls. "Chelsea and Loretta? They're still alive?"

He shrugged. "Maybe. They've been out there, probably wandering in circles, for almost an hour now. Thought it was only fair to give them a bigger head start. Or, if you choose not to save them, that means fewer hunters looking for you, and better odds of survival if you go in the opposite direction."

"You're going to leave me without any weapons?" She glanced at his gun, wondering if she could take him down and strip him of all weapons. Her cargo pockets were empty. He'd taken her phone and knife while she'd been unconscious. Her gun might still be at Tom's trailer in Vegas. But her hands were free now, and they were lethal. She could kill Finn and check on Tom, maybe get him help before... God, before the other hunters came? She wouldn't have much time.

"There's a shed out there with a variety of guns and other fun stuff," Finn said. "Too bad it's locked. Breaking in will eat up precious time, but you might decide it's worth it." He tossed his hunting knife into the dirt just outside the cabin's open door. "That'll give you something, when you're ready to leave. See? I'm not a total monster." His smile was chilling. "That will change, of course, when your time is up. I'll be waiting for you, Skye. And, fourteen minutes from now, I'll be hunting you." He slid his mask back into place. "See you soon."

"Was that a gunshot?" Chelsea looked down from the tall oak she'd climbed to where Loretta was keeping watch twenty feet below.

"Yes," Loretta called up to her. "Hurry. Or maybe I should just run in a different direction. We'll have better chances if we split up."

Again, she ignored Loretta's plea to split up. They'd already had this argument and Chelsea had insisted they'd be safer if they stayed together. She still believed that. Plus, she'd go insane if she was out here by herself, especially when night fell. The sun was so low in the sky that dusk wasn't far off. And dark... She shuddered to think what the night would bring.

If her guess was correct, the gunshot had come from the direction of the cabins, which should be a couple of miles behind them at the pace they'd been going. At least her daily workouts to stay in shape for dancing, and the dancing itself, had given her stamina, though her month-long captivity had hindered it. She'd been using the sun as a guide, when she could. Though the forest was dense, the sun was low enough that she could tell which way was west. To the south, she spied what she was looking for.

She scrambled back down the tree and tugged Loretta's hand. "This way. I saw a road. It's dirt, but it has to lead somewhere." Despite the training Bear and Finn had tried to hammer into them, her plan was to find civilization as quickly as possible. And if they came across one of the animal-faced hunters along the way, they'd fight it tooth and nail, which was pretty much all they had.

With a bit of research, Jared finally identified the parcel of land he believed hosted the Hunting Grounds. It had once been bundled with Three Fortunes but had been sold off by Tom Hamilton several years ago. The deed was in Ryan Stone's name, which was why it hadn't come up in the first search Jared had done, days ago, before Ryan and Finn had been his primary targets.

He searched for old satellite images that showed a cluster of small cabins and a shed in the center of the property, with only one access road leading to and from the area. The parcel was miles from any populated ranches and thirty miles from the interstate.

Perfectly isolated for Finn's twisted purposes. That had to be the Hunting Grounds.

Before leaving the ranch, Jared took a few precious seconds to tell Sheriff Anderson what he'd found. But while the sheriff was busy rounding up and redirecting the search party from Three Fortunes to the Grounds, Jared took off. He didn't believe the women had that kind of time, nor did he want to turn the situation at the Grounds into a massive firefight, with Chelsea, Loretta, and Skye in the middle of it all.

He, on the other hand, was armed with a map, his car, and a gun. He was one man, and one man could slip in unnoticed.

CHAPTER TWENTY-FOUR

The moment Finn was out of sight, Skye ran to Tom's side, but there was no pulse. The sound of a strangled moan shocked her, until she realized it had come from her own throat. She cupped Tom's face, stroked his brow, seeming to soothe her own irregular breathing by touching him. She channeled her grief into anger, using it to hone her focus. "I'll get him for this. For everything."

Pressing her fingertips to her eyes, she took several deep breaths. *Think, damn it. You can outsmart these assholes.*

In the back of her mind, her instincts were screaming at her to get going. Besides, the hunt was about her. If Tom were still alive, he'd tell her to move her ass. So would Viper.

With a last glance at her uncle's prone body, she grabbed the knife and ran for her life.

Skye purposely made her trail easy to follow, though not so easy as to tip the hunters off that *she* was the one hunting *them*. She'd briefly glanced at the other two cabins and the shed that probably held everything she could ever want to use in this fight, but also had a lock that would cost too much precious time. On the other hand, it could be a trick. She could exert energy breaking in, only to find nothing inside. Besides, she could circle back around and gather supplies later if her current plan failed. If she was still alive.

She silently thanked providence that she was wearing lightweight cargo pants in a neutral color. The tan provided some camouflage, but her white tank top was as bright as a flag of surrender. She ducked behind a clump of juniper bushes and stripped off the shirt, then rolled it in the dirt before slipping it back on. Now she could blend more easily into the wilderness.

She took a few precious minutes to scout the periphery for the trail Chelsea and Loretta had made when they'd presumably left one of the other two cabins. Evidence of their path wasn't hard to find. It appeared they'd gone off together, in the same direction. Maybe they were betting on strength in numbers. It would make it easier for Skye to find them, but also easier for the hunters to pick them off.

So she made her trail in the opposite direction, bending branches, kicking up dirt, and making light boot impressions where the pine needles weren't so thick, so that even the most amateur hunter should be able to track her. Hopefully, that someone was armed. She could use another weapon.

Then she circled back around and selected a ten-foot-high rock outcropping on which to hide and wait. Waiting was the hardest part. But it would be worth it if she could take down a hunter and gain a weapon, preferably something with some firepower. Not only would it improve her odds of survival, but she could then help Loretta and Chelsea with more than just guidance. It was a risk, but she was betting the six men would split up, since they weren't of the pack mentality. She already knew Finn would be out for himself. And if the others had paid handsomely to hunt her, well, these men would likely be reluctant to share the prize.

Right now, her biggest enemy was time. The light was waning. Luckily, the days were longer this time of year and she had another half hour or so before twilight hit. But then, the hunters wouldn't be able to fall into her trap. Unless they were stupid enough to tote flashlights. One could hope.

Her gamble paid off a few minutes later.

She gripped the knife Finn had left her as a man in a coyote mask made his way forward slowly, stealthily. He was a pretty good hunter, stopping every so often to listen and even sniff the air, but she was better. And she had more to fight for. When he was beneath her ledge, she pounced.

She landed on his back, and gravity and momentum did the rest, taking them both down. Unfortunately, he had quick reflexes and landed on a knee, shifting his body weight and throwing her over his head. She landed on her back and he was on top of her in an instant, but his pistol had flown out of reach in the initial attack.

They wrestled, his hands wrapping around her throat as he gained the high ground. She landed a couple elbow jabs and kicks, and one hit his nose. Blood poured down his face and into his mouth, lining it in gruesome red.

"You bitch!" he said. He bared his teeth, stained with the crimson of his blood. "You're all mine. You aren't so tough after all. I may even have to ask for my money back, unless you make this worth my while." One of his hands left her neck to squeeze her breast. She ignored the pain. His other hand continued to push down on her neck, against her windpipe. From beneath him, it appeared it was a coyote trying to maul her face.

She gritted her teeth against the insult and the pain and inched her fingertips down her side. The knife had fallen nearby. She'd seen the glint of metal from the corner of her eye. He didn't notice as her fingers searched the pine needle floor and located the weapon, grasped the bone handle, and jammed it into the side of his neck. His jaw dropped in shock, but she didn't let go. Blood spurted from the wound and he fell to the opposite side, his hands letting go of her as he grabbed for his neck. She used his sideways momentum to roll him off her, pulling the knife out as gravity took him the rest of the way.

She scrambled to her feet and ran for his pistol. The chamber was fully loaded. *Thank you, God.* She aimed it at the hunter as he tried to roll to his side, but he gasped and lay back again. A twinge of mercy tightened her throat, a feeling she might have experienced for any wounded animal, but she didn't finish him off. If she shot him, the other hunters would come running. And he wasn't worth the bullet, or any more of her time.

He took his last, gurgling breath a second later, as she retrieved the small pack he'd dropped when she'd pounced. It contained a full canteen and another hunting knife but no cell phone. She snatched up the whole thing and ran, feeling more confident with a gun in her hand and a knife in her pocket. She traveled as fast as she could, knowing her life, and possibly Chelsea's and Loretta's, depended on it.

"I told you she was magnificent," Finn said with pride. He and Ryan had been close on Coyote's heels as they tracked Skye, but Finn had suspected she was planning to trick them somehow. He'd let the other man spring the trap, then stayed back to watch the fun. "Aren't you glad you didn't take her down with a shot in the back? Wouldn't have been very sporting." Finn had held Ryan's arm to keep him from taking a shot during the scuffle. They'd let her go, content to hunt her later. He didn't want the fun to be over that quickly.

Crouched beside him, Ryan shot him a knowing look. "And one less man in the hunt. I suppose that makes you happy."

"It should make you happy, too. His payment already cleared."

"Maybe taking her down isn't my goal."

"Then why are you here?" Finn knew the answer, had known since Ryan had called him after the failed trial in the theater. Ryan was here to hunt him. The

Stones wouldn't stand for what they'd seen as a betrayal by one of their own, no matter what Finn could promise them. It was kill or be killed, which made this hunt all the more exhilarating.

"I'm guessing it's time to split up, friend," Ryan said, adding a wry twist of his lips at the endearment.

"*Intrepidus vive ferociter ludeque.*"

This time, Ryan repeated the salutation. "And may the best man win."

More careful to disguise her path, Skye moved in wide, concentric circles as she returned to the cabins. If this was to be a fair fight, she could use more supplies, and she was certain most of the hunters would have fanned out by now, eager for the chase. But she was equally certain that someone might have been left behind to guard the campsite.

About twenty yards from camp, in a cluster of aspens and scrubby bushes, she hit pay dirt. The guy was wearing a ridiculous cougar mask and hadn't bothered to disguise the spicy smell of his aftershave. Idiot. And a rookie mistake for someone who claimed to be a hunter. But it was Skye's win, and she'd take whatever advantage she could get.

One down, five to go.

And each man she took down meant better odds for Chelsea and Loretta, too.

Cougar was smart in that he'd chosen to stake out the supply shed and the sole vehicle on the campgrounds. Definite lures. In his hands was a knife. It was a big knife, but size didn't matter. Her pistol would be the most effective way to dispense with the threat, but it would also be the noisiest. And she wanted answers, if Cougar had them.

As she shifted closer, she tossed a rock into the distance to attract his attention as she used the bedding of old pine needles to disguise her footfalls. His attention diverted, she crept close, her knife in her hands as she slid up behind and placed him in a headlock, pressing the blade to his throat just under the edge of his mask. He dropped his own knife in surprise.

"Don't move, asshole," she hissed in his ear. The only movement was in his throat as he swallowed. "Where are the other girls?"

"Fuck you."

She jerked back on his head so that he was straining to breathe. A drop of blood dripped from a small wound where her knife had pricked him. "Wrong answer. Let's try another question. Where are the keys to the shed?" She lightened the pressure on his windpipe so that he could reply.

"Finn has them."

She figured as much. "You don't have a copy?"

"No. And even if I did, I wouldn't tell you, bitch." He began to struggle, his arms whipping out and his legs kicking, trying to get to her.

"Then you're no good to me." She finished him with the knife, rather than having to hold him while he struggled to breathe. She had no way of restraining him, no way to know he wouldn't come after her the moment she turned her back. It was kill or be killed, and he'd made his choice simply by choosing to be part of this hunt. Did this guy have friends, family, kids? Did any of them know what he did for a hobby?

Skye wondered how Jared would react to knowing she'd killed two men today. She was dismayed to realize how much she cared. Until today, she'd been able to count on one hand the men she'd killed. If tonight went as planned, she'd triple the body count, and something like that should leave a scar on her soul that nobody could erase.

Shoving the cougar aside, she pocketed his knife and eyed the car. She could hotwire it, but she had no idea where Chelsea and Loretta were. If she wanted to help them, she'd have to remain on foot. Besides, for all she knew, Finn could have set the car to blow the moment she started the engine.

Instead, she crept to the shed. The lock was sturdy, but basic. Still, without the key, it would take too much time to pick it and she didn't have her lock pick kit. She eyed it a moment, considered her options, and opted for speed.

Firing the gun, she blasted the lock open and hurried to shove what she needed into Coyote's backpack. The sound would alert others to her location, but had allowed her access to water bottles—unlike the canteen, they were sealed, thank you, God—guns, ammo, and... She whistled softly. Her heart beat faster as she spied a lightweight compound bow and a quiver of carbon arrows. She slung both across her shoulder. She began to leave but stopped to eye the drugs in the drawers and, in a moment of impetuousness, picked up a nearby gas can and doused everything in sight, then lit a match.

Grinning, she walked away from the fiery shed and into the woods beyond, in the direction the other women had gone. The evening sun was low in the sky, and their trail would be hidden by darkness soon. She hoped to find them before then, and maybe rid them of more hunters along the way.

Two down, four to go.

Jared's lungs refused to work for several long seconds as the report of the gun echoed through the woods. It was as if the bullet pierced a dam in his head and allowed a flood of images to burst forth and suck him downstream—pictures of what could be going on at that very moment across the forest. Chelsea, Skye, Loretta. Any one of them could have been wounded—or worse, killed—by that shot. Or there could be other vulnerable innocents out there, for all he knew. Other women, or even men or children may have been taken.

Damn Finn Tucker. Damn Ryan Stone. They wouldn't get away with this.

Or maybe Skye or one of the others had shot someone in self-defense. He clung to that hope as his feet began to carry him forward again.

He'd parked half an hour ago on the main road and planned to hike toward where the cabins were located, according to the map on his phone. A billow of smoke and the sound of ammo going off in the distance had him hurrying his steps, especially when an explosion followed. By his estimate, the position of the campground was nearly two miles away.

When he arrived in the wide circle of cabins twenty minutes later, the area was abandoned. A man in a cougar mask was dead, his throat cut. Skye's work or a fellow, greedy hunter who'd offed the competition? Either way, it was one less enemy to worry about.

But when he came across the smoldering remains of what must have been another smaller cabin or shed, he smiled. Based on the damage done, he'd guess it had been Skye's work, which meant she was alive and kicking ass. Or maybe it was wishful thinking. Still, he doubted any of the hunters would have blown up their own campsite. The load on his shoulders lessened, but there was still work to do.

He searched the rest of the area quickly but carefully, looking into each of the cabins, which contained thin mats and buckets that had evidently served as beds and latrines. He could only imagine Chelsea living in this manner. Finn had treated these girls like animals, and now he was hunting them as such. How many masked hunters were out there besides Finn?

In the last cabin, he found the body of a man he identified as Tom Hamilton. The body was cool, but rigor hadn't set in. This was a recent killing. He checked to see that he still, in fact, had cell reception and made a quick call to Sheriff Anderson to bring him up to speed. Anderson promised a search and rescue helicopter was on its way. Jared sent up a prayer that Skye and the others had the strength they needed to outwit and outrun the hunters a little longer.

Did she know her uncle had been killed, unable to defend himself as he'd been gunned down with his hands still tied behind his back? Had she been left to fend for herself, as helpless as Tom?

But she had a secret weapon that nobody, not even Skye, knew about. She had Jared as a partner.

CHAPTER TWENTY-FIVE

"Shh." Chelsea tried to soothe Loretta, though she thought she might throw up at the sight of the wound. "I know it must hurt. Oh God, oh God, oh God." She pressed her fingertips to her eyelids and tried to get a grip, to gather her thoughts and come up with a plan.

Tears streaming down her face, Loretta bit her own hand to keep from screaming. The steel trap had been covered in pine needles, in a shadowed area of a tree near the creek bed. It had looked like the perfect place to get some water and take a quick rest. Apparently, a hunter had assumed the same thing and left the snap-type trap to catch the unwary.

"I think it's broken," Loretta bit out between clenched teeth. Since her first scream, she'd been trying to keep the pain inside, but she had to be in agony, her ankle trapped in the steel grip. Her lower leg was at an awkward angle. Worse, Chelsea didn't know how to release the trap, or if it could hurt Loretta worse to do so. Couldn't opening it cause extreme blood loss or something? She thought she'd seen that on a cable show once.

Chelsea sank down onto the ground next to Loretta and held her hand tight. "It probably is." But a broken ankle would be the least of their worries once night fell. She leaned over to wet a scrap she'd torn from the edge of her shirt and pressed it to Loretta's forehead. The sky had darkened to a soft indigo lined with deep orange, and the first stars were beginning to twinkle. It would be full night soon.

"Go," Loretta said, her voice weak and trembling. "You can get farther without me, anyway. And you have no choice now."

"I have a choice," Chelsea said stubbornly. "I can stay and defend us."

"Without a weapon? We'll both be sitting ducks. Please."

Chelsea didn't even have to think about what was the right course for her. She shook her head. "We're in this together, and we have been since those assholes took us. We're not going down without a fight." She'd rip out throats with her ragged fingernails if she had to.

A few minutes later, Loretta passed out and received some blessed relief. Chelsea was thankful her friend wasn't awake to note the sudden quieting of the birds. It was as if the entire forest had gone still. There was only the sound of Chelsea and Loretta breathing, Loretta's inhalations raspy with pain, when Chelsea picked up another faint sound. She let go of Loretta's hand and stood over her as Bear came out of the trees.

He approached with caution, a freaking bow in his hands, with an arrow notched. He grinned as he spied Chelsea and an unconscious Loretta. "Well, well, look who I caught in my trap. Not one, but two animals. I see Loretta's had enough fun," he said as he shoved his mask to the top of his head. "She barely gave me the time of day at the ranch, but she'll sure pay attention to me now."

"Only because you've got a captive audience," Chelsea shot back.

"Maybe if she'd paid a little more attention to her lessons at the ranch, and here, and less time dreaming of a life that was never possible, she would have seen the makings of a perfect trap and avoided it." He took a step forward.

Chelsea shifted to keep herself between him and Loretta. "You're not going to touch her."

Bear smirked. "Relax, honey. You'll get your turn. And there'll be enough of me left for Skye, too, when she comes along. I figure she'll be following your trail.

Since the others went after her, I came this way. Now you get to be bait."

Loretta had spoken of a woman she knew, a friend. Her name had been Skye. Bear and Finn had taken her, too? Instead of feeling helpless, she felt hope surge through her. According to Loretta, Skye was a kick-ass kind of woman who'd been trained in survival techniques. Surely, she could help. "Another woman's out here?"

"Aw, cheer up. I would have killed her whether you were bait or not. And after she's dead, maybe I'll let you go again, just for kicks. Got to prolong the fun after all the time I invested in you, don't I? As for Loretta, I don't suppose she's much good to either of us anymore." He aimed the bow and arrow at Loretta and pulled the string taut.

The girls had stayed together, as far as Skye could tell from the various tracks that had led from the cabin that had likely been theirs. She'd found a broken twig here, a long strand of Chelsea's golden hair there. As long as she didn't find them dead, she still had hope. At any cost, even her own life, she had to save them. For Mark, for Jared. For herself.

She'd been moving cautiously, aware that at any moment, one of the remaining four hunters might decide to take a shot, but when she heard a woman's scream, she kicked her pace into a run and didn't see the hunter waiting behind a tree to jump out at her.

With a roar, the guy in a tiger mask was on her in an instant. He also seemed high as a kite. Unfortunately, it was more of the PCP variety than marijuana. He fought like a jungle cat, clawing at her clothes and scratching, punching, trying to bite her as if he were a frenzied animal.

Skye channeled her adrenaline rush, using it to focus, like she had on that Malibu rooftop, on the senses that mattered. But the man was truly all over her, attacking from all angles as she struggled beneath him, barely avoiding his teeth. She managed to jab him in the eye through the slit in the mask and he howled with pain but came back at her, slicing with his knife now. But before he could land more than a shallow cut, his weight was gone and another's roar of anger filled the twilight.

Jared. He'd lifted Tiger from her and tossed him aside. He aimed a gun at Tiger's head as the man glared up at him through his mask.

"I dare you to move," Jared growled. "You okay?" he asked Skye over his shoulder.

"Look out!" Skye shouted as the man lunged, his eyes crazy with bloodlust. Jared fired as Tiger leapt on him. The struggle continued until a moment later, the fight suddenly went out of the hunter and he crumpled to the ground.

Jared felt for a pulse. "He's gone."

"Three down. Three to go." She stood on shaky legs, grateful when they held her. "That guy was on something. Nothing could have stopped him but a bullet," she assured Jared.

His gaze swept over her, checking for injuries as he closed the gap between them. He pulled her against him, pressed his nose to her neck and inhaled deeply. After a brief moment to regain their composures, he pulled away. "God, when I saw him on top of you—"

She put a hand on his mouth to stop him. There would be time for processing and comparing notes later. She was just glad he was here, on her team. "Did you hear the scream?"

"I thought that was you."

She sent him a look. "Really?"

He shot her a wry grin. "Sorry. What was I thinking?"

She bent to scoop up her bow, quiver, and backpack, which had scattered when Tiger pounced. "It had to be Chelsea or Loretta. They're out here, too, and there are three hunters left. Let's go." Without waiting for him to reply, she led the way in the direction from which she thought the scream had originated.

It was almost too easy. Ryan hadn't had enough time hunting in the wild to know how to cover his tracks, or to have the intense focus necessary in a game with these high stakes. But Finn had. So when he took a page from Skye's book and backtracked, and found Ryan following his trail, he knew. As he'd known all along.

And when a woman's scream sounded from the distance, Finn took advantage of Ryan's distraction.

Finn stepped out from behind a boulder, gun drawn. "Thought you'd sneak up on me, huh?"

Ryan froze and raised his own gun. His cocky grin slid into place, but there was wariness in his eyes. "This is a hunt, after all."

"The question is what game are you after?"

A flicker of doubt crossed Ryan's features, but he didn't lower his weapon. "I don't want to do this, man. My father—"

The sound of the gunshot ricocheted off the trees, but the bullet's path was true. It ripped into Ryan's chest before he could finish his sentence.

Finn walked over to his friend and kicked the gun from his hands before crouching over him, his hand cupped to his ear. "Your father what? I didn't catch that."

Ryan's mouth opened and closed a few times as he tried to form words.

Finn grinned. "Guess it doesn't matter. I'm in charge now. You were never as fearless or ferocious as me."

With bigger game to hunt, Finn rose and left Ryan to die.

Skye and Jared followed the women's trail as fast

as they could in the waning light. A helicopter hovered overhead, but she couldn't see the details through the tree cover.

"It would be just like those rich playboys to have a chopper to hunt us with," she whispered to Jared. But it kept going to the east and she dismissed the threat from her mind.

"I think it belongs to the sheriff's department," Jared whispered back. Suddenly, he raced forward and positioned himself behind a tree several yards ahead.

"Jared!" she hissed. Her gaze swept their surroundings, looking for a threat, but she saw why he'd thrown caution to the wind. There were two women about fifty yards ahead. And Tristan. He had an arrow notched and aimed at two women.

"Back away from them," Jared shouted. His voice was firm, commanding, and Skye could hear the military policeman he once was, as well as the confident bodyguard who'd found her on that rooftop and tried to intimidate her with a look. He was using the trunk of a pine for cover, his gun aimed at Tristan, who was fifteen yards from him, armed with a sleek, modern bow and arrow like the one on Skye's back. For efficiency, she stuck with the gun as her primary weapon.

"You're interrupting our conversation," Tristan called back, his aim still on Chelsea as he shifted so he could see Jared, but he couldn't see Skye in her hiding place. "Your sister was just going to do a special little dance for me, to see if I'd spare her life. Weren't you, sugar?" He sneered at Chelsea.

"Shoot him!" Chelsea shouted to Jared.

Tristan laughed. "If he does that, you'll die too. I'll have time to release this arrow."

As Jared kept Tristan talking, she searched for a position where she could defend the girls and support Jared. Loretta was on the ground and Chelsea was standing in front of her. Behind them, the shallow creek ran slowly. The soft sound covered Skye's footfalls as she darted from tree to tree, circling around and flanking the group.

But time was of the essence. Tristan's muscles would fatigue over time and he'd release the arrow whether he meant to or not. Her entire body shuddered with the need to act. She took position behind a tree, raised her gun and aimed. "Tristan! Put your weapon down."

Tristan darted his gaze toward her to assess the threat, but kept his weapon pointed at Chelsea.

Jared cast her a quick sideways glance as well. "Skye, look out!"

The chill of someone else's presence behind her crept up her spine before she could react.

"Sorry to spoil your plans." Finn pressed his knife to her throat. "Drop the gun."

Skye swallowed as she felt the blade skim the side of her neck. "I didn't take you for the type to wield a knife, Finn. Too messy for a pretty boy like you."

She felt the length of his body stiffen against her back. "Funny, but I thought you'd be tougher to trap. Though I do appreciate how you handled Coyote and Cougar."

"And don't forget Tiger. Looks like you're out one menagerie."

Finn's laughter rumbled against her back. He leaned close. "You still haven't dropped the gun." The knife pricked her throat and she felt warm blood seep down her neck. "Now, Skye."

She dropped her gun. Jared was watching them, but was caught in a standoff with Tristan.

"You, too," Tristan ordered Jared. "Drop it."

"I can handle this guy," she shouted to Jared, wanting to keep everyone's attention off of Chelsea's subtle progress. Jared's sister was creeping closer to Tristan, almost close enough to reach out and grab the bow. Loretta was still on the ground, unmoving.

"I know you can," Jared said. She heard the pride in his voice and wanted to end Finn and Tristan right now so she could run to him and kiss him senseless.

"Now!" she yelled. She reached up to grab Finn's wrist, hissing as the tip of his knife scraped her neck. She twisted the weapon away as she sent a backward kick into his knee, followed by an elbow to his ribs. He howled in pain as she whirled to face him and kneed him in the groin. He went to the ground as her hand went to one of her pockets and pulled out the large hunting knife.

Forty feet away, in her peripheral vision, she saw Chelsea grab the bow and jerk it to the side as he released an arrow. It shot into the ground a few yards away. Jared hurried toward them and wrestled with Tristan until he got the upper hand. He forced Tristan to the ground and jammed his knee into his back as he pulled some zip ties out of his pocket and secured Tristan's wrists. The moment Jared regained his feet, Chelsea launched herself into his arms. He held her close, stroking her hair. She was shaking as she wound her arms tightly around him as if she'd never let go again. He pulled back enough to press a kiss to her forehead and pushed her hair back from her wet cheeks.

"You're okay," he said.

"Can we go home now?" Chelsea released a half-sob, half-laugh.

Skye watched the reunion with bittersweet emotions, but turned to face Finn again as, in her peripheral vision, he regained his feet. "I was hoping you'd come at me again," she said. "Give me an excuse to do to you what I did to your friends. If you know what's good for you, you'll stay down. The authorities will be here soon. You can't win this time." She could hear the chopper close by.

"Taking you down would be good for me." He limped a little as he stepped toward her, trying to close the four-foot gap.

She backed away and held up her knife. The gleam in his eyes shifted to maniacal and he roared and leapt toward her. She flipped the knife so that she gripped it by the blade and threw it at his throat as he lunged. He landed on her, pinning her beneath him and pushing the knife deeper. Finn's eyes lost focus, the crazy vaporizing as he slumped against her. His warm blood soaked her arms and shirt.

She was heaving for breath as Jared ran to her side, pulled Finn off her and tossed his body to the dirt. He reached for her and she gripped his hand so he could haul her to her feet. But instead of steadying her, he yanked her against him and held her close.

"I'm all bloody," she said.

"I don't care." His body was shaking, which was a normal reaction, she supposed, since so was hers. "As long as it's not yours." He pulled away enough to search her eyes.

"Just the scratches on my neck."

His concerned gaze went there, but she didn't want sympathy. She'd survive those wounds.

"It'll be fine," she assured him. "Chelsea?"

"Remarkably uninjured, but Loretta's leg is pretty bad." He slid his hands to the sides of her face and planted a hard and fast kiss on her mouth. "Sorry. That couldn't wait."

The sound of someone tearing down the slope, through the brush from the ridge to the east, had Jared's muscles bunching, bracing for a fight. He raised his gun.

"Stop right there!" Jared shouted. "You're in my sights, and this will be your only warning to drop your weapon and lay down on the ground."

"Bennigan?" a voice shouted in return. "It's Sheriff Anderson."

Jared leaned his forehead against hers. "The cavalry is here." He turned to shout back. "All clear here." The sheriff approached quickly but cautiously.

Skye continued to tremble against him, the aftermath of her adrenaline. But they weren't free and clear yet. "What about the sixth hunter?" she asked

Sheriff Anderson as he approached.

"We found a guy in the woods. He's still alive, but barely. Says his name is Ryan Stone and Finn Tucker shot him."

"Finn shot Ryan?" Skye asked. "Do you think Ryan was the sixth?"

"Makes sense," Jared said, holstering his gun and pulling her against his side. After a quick kiss on her hair, during which she could have sworn she'd felt him inhale deeply, he pulled her toward his sister.

Chelsea ran for Jared. Skye stepped away as he released her to scoop up his sister and hold her again while she cried into his shoulder, clutching him like a lifeline.

This was family. This was what Skye had always wanted. People who fought for each other, through thick and thin. Through life's crazy times, and the sane ones. But all of her family was dead. Her throat tightened and her vision of the trees grew suspiciously blurry as she remembered how she'd left Tom at the cabin. He hadn't been the model father figure, but he'd been enough. And now he was gone.

Sheriff Anderson started directing his men to take over the scene.

"These girls need medical attention," Skye told him, pointing to Loretta and Chelsea. "And Tristan needs a prison cell," she said, nudging the dirtbag on the ground with her boot.

"There's a chopper on the way from Flagstaff Medical Center," Anderson said. "Search and Rescue medics will release the trap and splint her leg. As for Tristan Floyd, he'll be in our custody."

Jared released his sister to look into her eyes. "We'll be home soon. This will all be some nightmare and you can move on. And I won't bug you anymore about dancing, if only you'll come home, at least while you recuperate."

"Home," Chelsea said and sighed. "Your house is perfect."

"Our house," Jared said. "For as long as you want to be there." His gaze met Skye's over Chelsea's head and he frowned. In that moment, Skye's heart stopped and cracked open. As much as she wanted to be with him, she wasn't sure it was the right thing for either of them. He had doubts, too. She could see it.

These words, this family... It wasn't for her. She was the outsider. But Jared, with his protective streak and loving ways, would never tell her that. It was up to her to leave. So, even though the image of home that fluttered through her mind was not, surprisingly, the ranch, but Jared's house in Vegas, she turned away. Jared hadn't offered her anything to cling to other than his passion and his affection, and he shouldn't have to stick around for her sake. He had enough obligations to manage. She'd once hoped he could see her in his life, but hope was just as powerful a weapon in this twisted game as her knife or gun.

"They think they'll be able to release Chelsea in the morning," Jared said as he stepped out of his sister's room and found Skye waiting in the hall. Chelsea was dehydrated and slightly malnourished, but she was safe.

He rubbed at his tired eyes, and saw the same lines of fatigue on Skye's face. Her hair was damp, tied back from her face. A nurse must have helped her locate a shower and a set of fresh scrubs. He'd managed a moment to change his blood-soaked shirt, at least. And someone had bandaged the wound at her neck. He wanted to pull her into his arms, into his bed, and give her peace.

They hadn't had a moment to talk since he'd left her at his house in Vegas that morning, before everything went down. Now, it was after midnight, but the Flagstaff Medical Center, where they'd headed the moment Sheriff Anderson was done with his questions, was infinitely more welcoming than the Hunting

Grounds had been.

"That's wonderful," Skye said. "I'm so happy you have her back." Yet there was a sadness in her eyes, the same sadness he'd seen when he'd been comforting Chelsea at the Hunting Grounds. "Family is important. Family that will be there for you, that is." A shadow fell over her face, and he knew she must be thinking about her uncle.

He wanted Skye to be a part of his family, too, but her expression was so guarded that he wasn't sure how to approach her, other than to remind her of what she'd be missing if she returned to her old life. "When I called to tell Haley the news, she wanted to come see Chelsea right away, but I made her wait until morning when Jane could drive her. Haley mentioned wanting to see you, too, and the ranch."

Skye looked away and didn't respond. Definitely not a good sign.

"How's Loretta?" he asked.

"She's having emergency surgery on her ankle and leg, but the prognosis is good. It'll take some time to heal, for both women. Your sister—both your sisters—will need you more than ever."

"I suppose so. How's Viper?"

"He was awake, so the nurse let me talk to him for a few minutes. I told him about Uncle Tom's death." She squeezed her eyes shut for a moment and he almost reached for her. But her eyes snapped open again and she squared her shoulders, emitting a clear *back-off* vibe. "We'll both be digesting that tomorrow, when it sinks in." Her expression was lost, and a little lonely. So much loss—her uncle, her ranch, her entire lifestyle. Or maybe she was hoping to rebuild, without him. Maybe this was her way of distancing herself.

"I'm sorry about your uncle." He'd heard what she'd learned from Tom about the original Redemption Club, and Tom's part in it, as well as Stone's alleged involvement, from Sheriff Anderson.

"It was a shock, but deep down, I knew there was

a dark secret in his past. What about Stone, and his son?"

"Ryan's being treated here, too, for a gunshot wound to the chest. His condition is touch and go. Robert Stone arrived by private helicopter not long ago. Apparently, he had their family lawyer and a new bodyguard in tow."

"And what about Robert Stone's involvement in the Redemption Club?"

"Now that you've told your story to the authorities, that'll be for them to sort out. If he hasn't been involved in twenty years, it may be hard to find proof, but we'll keep after him. If he was co-founder of the original Redemption Club, he has some serious crimes to answer for. It would help if we could find the ledger."

She snorted. "I doubt it still exists. If Stone's smart, he burned it. It's awfully convenient that my uncle and the other man responsible, Wilson, are dead."

He'd thought so, too. "And the hunters you killed? How are you feeling about that?" He was worried she'd blame herself for killing men who'd been out to kill her. It was self-defense, and so far there'd been no words about filing charges against her, but it was her mental wellbeing he worried about.

She still wouldn't meet his gaze. "I'll deal with it. It's not your problem anymore. *I'm* not your problem."

He read the good-bye in her expression. "Don't run away from me again. I thought we were past that."

Her chin lifted. "I'm not running away. I'm going home."

"I want you with me, in my home." He reached for her and she stepped back. When she only shook her head again, he dropped his hand. This had to be her choice. He'd put himself out there, and she was still tossing up roadblocks. "You know where to find me when you stop lying to me, and to yourself. When you're ready to stop running, come find me."

Then he did the hardest thing he'd ever done. He turned and walked away.

CHAPTER TWENTY-SIX

Four weeks later, Skye was throwing punches at a bag strung up in the yard behind the house at Three Fortunes, the sun beating down on her bare shoulders as her sweat-drenched tank top clung to her body.

From the porch, Viper hollered to her. "Take a break. Replenish and refuel before you run yourself into the ground."

Running herself into the ground was exactly what she'd been trying to do. That was the only way she could keep her doubts at bay, and exhausting herself was the only way she could grab a few hours of sleep at night, especially as today approached.

Today was Haley's graduation day. The girl had been emailing her invitations and updates on their family life, including pictures of Jared's house as she and Chelsea moved in and put their personal stamp on things. At Jared's suggestion, Haley had even been babysitting for Eddie and Macy, Carly Boscoe's kids, on weekends at a reduced rate, and was planning to make it a part-time summer job. In one excellent move, Jared had found a way for Haley to cultivate her desire to help in her community and solved one of Carly's problems. That was the kind of man he was, always giving to others, solving their problems.

Skye didn't want to be a puzzle he had to solve. And yet, a huge piece of her had been missing since they'd walked away from each other.

Jared had said she'd been lying to him, and to herself. She probably had. She'd gotten so good at it over the years. Just another reason why she was no good for him.

She took another swing at the bag she'd hung from a tree limb. Just because the barn wouldn't be rebuilt until next month didn't mean she'd let her workout routine suffer.

Viper started down the porch stairs, his limp the only reminder of what he'd suffered, and the healing he had yet to do. But his temperament was back to normal. "Goddamn it, Skye, if I have to rip that bag down myself, I'll do it."

She landed one more jab and took off her gloves as she walked over to the curmudgeon. It had been just the two of them living in the house since he was released from the hospital three weeks ago. They'd scattered Tom's ashes together. A couple of the men had heard about the rebuilding project through the grapevine and returned, camping out in tents as they helped rebuild the bunkhouse and barn.

"What'd you make for lunch, toots?" she asked as she met Viper at the base of the stairs.

He grunted. "You wish. Get your own damn lunch if you have so much energy." But he handed her a chilled water bottle.

She looked at the cap and pain came flooding back. She hadn't needed a capped drink since trusting Jared. He'd broken through her walls and she hadn't rebuilt them. Hadn't seen the need. She was so perfectly capable of hurting herself that she didn't fear what others could do to her.

Viper stopped her before she could mount the stairs. "Chat with me a moment."

Chat? She narrowed her eyes. Viper never wasted a word in his life.

They sat in the shade of the porch, admiring the late-May sunshine. "Sheriff Anderson was here earlier," he said.

Skye had seen his car come and go. "Yeah?" She stiffened, bracing herself for more bad news. Last she'd heard, the authorities had found the remains of seven bodies in shallow, unmarked graves at the Hunting Grounds. Prior victims, they theorized. People she hadn't been able to save, although Finn would never hurt anyone again. "Did they find more gravesites?"

"No, no, nothing like that. But he did have an update. Ryan's out of the hospital."

"I hope he's in prison, then."

Viper's grimace told her she wouldn't like the news. "He's saying Finn was the one blackmailing his father, and that he discovered the evidence to support that after you and Jared paid a poolside visit to him. That he went to the Hunting Grounds that day because he suspected Finn was keeping the women there. He wanted to help you and Jared."

"And they bought that?"

"It'll be up to the judge and jury to sort that out, I suppose, but it looks like Finn and Tristan are taking the heat for the Hunting Grounds. Loretta will be testifying against Tristan. Hopefully, she'll find justice for herself and her father." Viper shifted to get comfortable. His bones still ached if he sat still for too long.

"She called a couple days ago. She's doing well at her grandmother's house in Phoenix."

"Good to hear. There's more. Anderson said Tom's lawyer has been too scared to come out here in person. Guess he heard the rumors about how vicious we are." Viper grinned, but it quickly faded. "You apparently have some things to settle regarding Tom's estate."

"The ranch is yours now." She'd signed her portion over to Viper, not wanting anything to do with something that had been bought with blood money.

"There's another property."

She froze as she realized what he was getting at. "My parents' place? Tell the lawyer he can sell it."

Viper shook his head, disappointment written on his face.

"What?" she demanded.

"I didn't take you for a coward."

She gaped, then snapped her jaw shut. "I'm not a coward." But Jared had accused her of the same thing. Running away.

"We raised you better than that, to face your fears head·on. Go handle this yourself. Bury your past, and make your own damn future."

"But, the ranch. The repairs."

"I can handle it. Got plenty of help around here."

Four hours later, she found herself standing in the dirt drive of what had been her childhood home, staring at the trailer as if daring it to come at her. When it didn't, she marched one foot in front of the other and entered, then turned in a circle. This was the place where Tom had spent his last days. She stalked through the tiny living area, then eyed the bedroom where Finn had held them at gunpoint. Her throat tightened with a sudden wave of grief. She whirled away and ran outside, gasping for breath.

She sucked in the hot air and looked up to the sky, seeing the branches of her special tree. She stroked a hand down the bark—and stopped as she spied the plastic baggie nailed to the trunk. Inside was a folded paper with her name in Tom's handwriting. She leaned back against the tree and sank to the dirt as she read.

Dear Skye,

I saw you stop outside here a few nights ago. You're probably shocked I still own the property, but it's special to me. It was where we came together. The deed is yours now. Burn the place to the ground if you want to. Or save it as a reminder of what you came from. What you survived.

Thought you might come back sometime and find this note... probably if I'm gone. Or too cowardly to ever contact you again.

That's right. Your big, tough uncle is a coward. I never opened myself up to you fully, never let myself love you. That was my biggest mistake, and my biggest regret.

You're so much better at taking risks. I envy you sometimes. I hope you'll trust your instincts. They've never steered you wrong.

You're a fighter, Skye. You always have been, especially when fighting for others. Don't forget to fight for yourself.

Love, Tom

Surprised to find her cheeks wet, she swiped at them and sat, staring up into her tree, her haven. It had once felt like home, until she'd found a better home at the ranch, with Tom. That no longer felt like home. Home felt like... Jared. It wasn't a place. It was a feeling.

Trust your instincts. Her instincts said it was time to stop running. To run toward something, rather than away. And if she hurried, she could clean up in time for Haley's post-graduation party.

Jared walked in from the backyard with a plate full of grilled hamburgers and set them on the kitchen counter. Flush from graduation, Haley was bouncing between clusters of people, from her friends to Aunt Jane and Chelsea, and back again. He couldn't help the smile that split his face as he saw that both of his sisters were healthy and happy. Chelsea still had shadows in her eyes, but the counseling was helping.

Spying him watching her, Haley bounced his way, beaming from ear to ear. "Thank you, thank you, thank you. This has been the best day."

"There's still cake." Jared winked and handed her a paper plate with a burger. "And you're welcome. Now eat something. You're burning up energy like a hummingbird."

"I have a surprise for you in return."

His brows lifted. "Really?"

She nodded. "It's in your bedroom. Just arrived."

"While I was out back?" He'd only been gone a few minutes.

She pushed him toward the hallway that led to the bedrooms. "Go."

"Don't you want to see me open it?"

She laughed. "Not this time." She shoved him toward the hall again. "I'll save some food for you."

Shaking his head at her odd behavior he entered his bedroom and stopped short as he laid eyes on his surprise. *Skye.*

She stood by the window, her hands clasped in front of her. As if noticing her defensive posture, she dropped her hands to her sides and stepped toward him. She didn't stop until she was close enough for him to reach for her, but he kept himself in check. Still, he could smell the jasmine in her hair and nearly smiled.

She cleared her throat, looking uncharacteristically nervous. "You said to come find you when I was done running."

He arched a brow. "And?"

"I'm still running. I'm running home."

He frowned. "But—"

She lifted a hand to his cheek. "*You're* my home."

He closed the distance and wrapped his arms around her. "I love you."

At his declaration, she leaned back to look him in the face. "What?"

"I love you." He held her gaze, willing her to accept his offering, his heart.

"You... I..." She blew out a breath and tried again. "I'm not used to hearing that, or saying it. In my family, actions spoke louder than words."

He smiled. "Then I'll have to make sure I spend a lot of time—*years*—showing you how I feel." He leaned forward to kiss her again, deeper this time, leaving her trembling.

Before the heat could erupt above a sizzle, he pulled back to look into her eyes. "You don't have to say the words. Just know that I'm not going anywhere. You aren't going to lose me, and I'm sure as hell not going to let you go after I've finally got a hold of you. In fact, I want you here permanently."

Permanently? Skye was in a dream. Or falling down that rabbit hole again. Being in Jared's arms, him telling her he loved her... It was all so surreal.

But she wanted it to be real. Desperately. She only had to have the courage to reach for it and grab on tight. To fight for it.

"You want me to move in?" she asked.

"Hell, yes. I don't think I can wait any longer. I want you with me now. Here, in this house, with the rest of the Bennigans. Stay."

The bubble of joy inside her expanded until it filled her whole body with warm light. Could she make this work? She knew next to nothing about being a girlfriend. But she supposed it was something like being a partner, and she'd handled that okay—most of the time.

He traced a thumb over the crease between her eyes. "You're thinking awfully hard."

Her eyes met his again. "I'm in shock. I thought maybe I'd show up here, we could date a little, see where it goes."

"I bet you never went slowly into anything in your whole life," he said, laughter in his eyes. "You throw your whole being into everything you do. It's one of the things I appreciate about you."

She took a deep breath. "I love you." Saying the words loosened something in her chest, and the past fell away as he grinned and held her close. There was only the future now—a future with Jared. "I think my heart knew it the first time I met you. It just took a while for my head to catch up. I want to love you forever."

"It's a deal. Partners forever." He pulled her mouth to his and sealed their promise to each other.

Uncle Tom had told her to trust her instincts, to fight for what she wanted. Jared had promised her he'd be there for her, always, and he'd never let her down. It was time to let go of the past and move forward.

Love wasn't a weakness, it was a strength. The greatest strength of all.

Coming January 2016!

SLEIGHT OF HAND
(Redemption Club, Book 2)

Some skills never fade...

Raised by con artists, Emily Moore has done her share of manipulating others to make ends meet. She's working hard to go legit and make up for her past, but she still knows how to spot an easy mark. And when to walk away from a bad situation. Emily learned life's lessons the hard way, and now a tough exterior hides her one weakness—her love for the man who left her.

Some hurts never heal...

After a high profile murder, Detective Adam Wilde's brother disappears, becoming both the Las Vegas Police Department's primary suspect and the real killer's target. Tanner has hardly been an upstanding citizen, but Adam believes he's innocent. He suspects an underground group called the Redemption Club, which trades in dark deeds, is behind the murder, and it's essential he finds his brother before the Club does. If anyone can think like his brother, Tanner's childhood friend Emily can. But first, Adam will have to repair their friendship and make up for hurting her—even if his rejection was intended to protect them both.

Some gambles are worth the risk...

Their hearts are telling them to let go of the past, but trust has never been easy for either Emily or Adam. It'll take a common purpose, and an undeniable passion, to reunite them. To find Tanner and defeat the head of Redemption Club, they'll need each other—and they'll need to come up with the con of their lives.

ABOUT THE AUTHOR

Anne Marie has always been fascinated by people—inside and out—which led to degrees in Biology, Chemistry, Psychology, and Counseling. Her passion for understanding the human race is now satisfied by her roles as mother, wife, daughter, sister, and award-winning author of romantic suspense.

She writes to reclaim her sanity.

Find ways to connect with Anne Marie at www.AnneMarieBecker.com. There, sign up for her newsletter to receive the latest information regarding books, appearances, and giveaways.

www.ingramcontent.com/pod-product-compliance
Lightning Source LLC
Chambersburg PA
CBHW032208190626
46810CB00019B/2184